W9-AAM-120

She had power and wealth.
Now she wanted love.

"Am I too brazen, Chris? Do I embarrass you?" When he did not answer, could not answer, Kelly said simply, "I want you, Chris. Of course, we could go through the coyness of the seduction game, but it isn't a game that I like very much."

"When you want something, do you usually get it?" he said through a dry, aching throat.

"Not always." She had reached him now. She placed her hands on his bare chest, stroking gently. So close, he could feel the heat of her body.

He crushed her to him, his kiss rough and demanding. "I want you too, Kelly Cole."

Empire
A Tumultuous Family Saga
Set Against the Wild Panorama
of Today's Alaska.

Empire

by *Patricia & Clayton Matthews*

BANTAM BOOKS
TORONTO · NEW YORK · LONDON · SYDNEY

EMPIRE

A Bantam Book / October 1982

All rights reserved.
Copyright © 1982 by Pyewacket Corporation.
Cover art copyright © 1982 by Bantam Books, Inc.
This book may not be reproduced in whole or in part, by
mimeograph or any other means, without permission.
For information address: Bantam Books, Inc.

ISBN 0-553-22577-4

Published simultaneously in the United States and Canada

Bantam Books are published by Bantam Books, Inc. Its trade-
mark, consisting of the words "Bantam Books" and the por-
trayal of a rooster, is Registered in U.S. Patent and Trademark
Office and in other countries. Marca Registrada. Bantam
Books, Inc., 666 Fifth Avenue, New York, New York 10103.

PRINTED IN THE UNITED STATES OF AMERICA

H   0 9 8 7 6 5 4 3 2 1

Prologue

The executive jet was bound north out of Fairbanks, flying toward Prudhoe Bay. The Brooks Range loomed just ahead—forbidding peaks shouldering up into the pale light of the brief winter's day.

So far it had been a routine flight and, as the aircraft was on autopilot, the pilot and copilot were relaxed, almost somnolent.

The copilot gave his head a sharp shake, and yawned, stretching. "Christ! If O'Keefe keeps flying our butts off, we'll be like zombies up here. Doesn't he know that the FAA says that a pilot can only fly so many hours at a stretch, even on a private jet?"

The pilot, Jim Carson, smiled lazily. "You've been around Alaska long enough to know that the rules don't apply to the Coles."

The other man shrugged. "*He's* not a Cole. He's an O'Keefe."

Jim Carson moved in his seat, trying to get comfortable. "He's married to a Cole, and he runs Cole Enterprises, and that makes him a Cole, in my book."

"Yeah, he's married to a Cole, right enough." The copilot sighed. "Boy, I wonder what it's like being married to Kelly Cole? Not only has she got all the money in the world, she is one luscious hunk of female. O'Keefe really has it made. I suppose he's sacked out back there in his bunk, while we're up here trying to keep awake."

"Wrong again. If I know O'Keefe, and I think I do even though he hasn't been around that long, he's probably up to his armpits in work even on board the plane. I sometimes think he never sleeps. He's told me more than once that when he's flying is about the only time he can catch up on the paperwork."

While they were talking, the copilot leaned forward to scan the dials in front of him. Now he looked ahead and whistled softly. "Jim, look." He gestured.

Jim Carson peered ahead. A bank of clouds had suddenly loomed up, towering impossibly high. "That's the cold front we were warned about. It must be moving faster than they thought it would."

The copilot said dubiously, "We going to try and fly into that?"

"I think we'd better go up a couple of thousand. Disengage the autopilot, will you, Buck? I'll ask Fairbanks for clearance." He spoke into his mike: "Fairbanks, this is Cole One Niner. Come in, Fairbanks."

A voice said laconically, "This is Fairbanks, Cole One Niner."

"We're flying into heavy turbulence, Fairbanks. Request permission to climb to thirty thousand."

"One minute, Cole One Niner."

After a few moments: "Permission granted, Cole One Niner. You may go to thirty thousand."

Jim Carson edged the nose of the jet up. As he leveled off again, they were directly over the Brooks Range.

He activated his mike again. "Fairbanks, this is Cole One Niner."

"This is Fairbanks. Go ahead, Cole One Niner."

"Am now flying at . . ."

In the Fairbanks Tower, the controller spoke urgently into his microphone: "Cole One Niner. This is Fairbanks calling Cole One Niner."

There was no answer.

"Cole One Niner, I can no longer read you. What is the difficulty, Cole One Niner? Come in, Cole One Niner."

Still no answer.

The controller looked back over his shoulder. "Mike, will you come here for a minute? I think we've got a problem. The pilot of the Cole private jet cut out a minute ago, in mid-transmission, and I can't raise him."

*   *   *

The Fairbanks *Daily News-Miner*, January 28:

"At approximately 1:00 P.M., Jan. 27, a Cole Airlines executive jet, carrying Christopher O'Keefe, president of Cole Enterprises, reportedly crashed in the Brooks Range, north of Fairbanks.

"According to airport officials, an air controller at Fairbanks Tower was in communication with the pilot of the Cole aircraft, but contact was lost in mid-transmission. A pipeline worker north of Chandalar Camp reported seeing an explosion in the air at the approximate location of the aircraft. Although search planes have gone over the area, no sign of the Cole jet, or its occupants, has been found.

"The area in which the plane is presumed to have crashed is heavily forested, a rugged area, and at this time of the year, virtually inaccessible. Planes continue their search, but their efforts are hampered by a heavy storm front. Experts say there is a good chance that the wreckage may never be found, or almost certainly not until spring.

"On board the plane, in addition to Mr. O'Keefe, were the pilot, Jim Carson, and the copilot, Buck Roberts, both of Fairbanks.

"Christopher O'Keefe is survived by his wife, Kelly Cole O'Keefe. Jim Carson is survived by his wife, Nella, and a son, Donald. So far as is known, Buck Roberts has no relatives in the Fairbanks area.

"Investigation is being made into the possible cause of the crash."

Follow-up article from the Fairbanks *Daily News-Miner*, February 5:

"At the time this article is being written, Chris O'Keefe, president of Cole Enterprises, has been missing one week, the victim of an airplane crash in the Brooks Range.

"No trace of the private jet or its occupants has been found, despite extensive air searches, and it is generally accepted that O'Keefe, his pilot, Jim Carson, and his copilot, Buck Roberts, are dead, victims of the unexplained tragedy. However, two members of O'Keefe's immediate family have not given up hope that he may still be alive.

"His wife, the former Kelly Cole, has made only one brief

statement to the press: 'I am firmly convinced that my husband is still alive.' Her half-brother, William Cole, vice-president of the oil company, Cole 98, talked to this reporter freely, and stated that he, also, believes that his brother-in-law is still among the living, putting it in his own inimitable way: 'Old Chris might be hurting out there somewhere, but he's alive. I feel it in my bones. Chris is a tough bird, tough as whang leather. He will come back, even if he has to ride a grizzly bareback.'

"When asked if the company misses O'Keefe's hand at the reins, Will Cole replied: 'Sure, Chris is missed. He is the guy who makes things go, but Cole Enterprises ain't about to close its doors. I'm here, ain't I? I may not be Christ, but I'm always willing and able to step in and run Cole.'

"Will Cole is not noted for his modesty, so his statement may be taken as a measure of the loss Cole Enterprises has suffered by the untimely disappearance of Christopher O'Keefe.

"Those readers who know their Alaskan history know that the Cole family has played an important role in the development of our state, beginning with Jeremiah Cole, the patriarch of the clan.

"Jeremiah Cole came over the Chilkoot Pass in 1898, along with a horde of gold seekers, but unlike most of them, Jeremiah made his strike in the Klondike. He was also unlike most gold seekers in another, perhaps more important way. Once he found his gold, he held onto it, and used it to a good advantage. A few years later he found a second rich claim near Fairbanks.

"With the money from his strike, he founded Cole Enterprises in 1908, starting with a dogsled mail delivery service, later adding a fishing fleet and a cannery in Anchorage, followed by a logging and lumber company when the building boom began. Later still, he added a shipping company, with a fleet of boats that provided mail delivery, passenger and freight service to the coastal towns inaccessible by land transportation.

"When the great migration to Alaska began, after World War II, the Cole Steamship Line became a booming business, and Cole Airlines, which started operations in 1939, is today one of Alaska's largest.

"However, the fact that Cole Enterprises is today one of

the largest, if not *the* largest company in Alaska, is due to a more recent development, the discovery of oil at Prudhoe Bay, for which Will Cole, Jeremiah's grandson, was mainly responsible.

"In view of this fact, when Will Cole was demoted back to vice-president of Cole 98, and Christopher O'Keefe was appointed to take his place, there was a great deal of speculation in the business community, and many questions were raised, to which neither Jeremiah Cole, Will Cole, nor O'Keefe has ever supplied answers.

"Jeremiah Cole now resides on the family estates on Cole Island, off the coast north of Juneau, where he has lived since his retirement three years ago. He is still quick of mind and sharp of tongue, although his health has been failing for several years. In his last statement to the press two months ago, Jeremiah Cole stated that he fully intends to live to celebrate his one-hundredth birthday, which falls on February 8, of this year.

"When Jeremiah Cole does pass away, he will leave behind him not only Cole Enterprises, but a fine family, which he can well be proud of.

"His son, Joshua, now serving his second term in the United States Senate, also makes his home on Cole Island, when he is not in Washington.

"Kelly Cole, wife of the missing Christopher O'Keefe, and Senator Cole's daughter by his second wife, Margaret Kenyon Cole, now deceased, makes her home in Anchorage and on Cole Island, and is a lovely and charming addition to the social and civic scene, while Dwight, also Senator Cole's son by his second wife, lives in Fairbanks, and is active in environmental affairs.

"William Cole, Joshua's son by his first wife, Regina Mills Cole, also deceased, has been vice-president of Cole 98 since the oil company was formed in 1969, and served two years as president of the entire company. Will is married to Louise Parker Cole. They have no children.

"Since O'Keefe's tragic disappearance, the family, except for William and Dwight, has been in seclusion on Cole Island. One can only hope that some miracle will occur, and O'Keefe will indeed be found alive, as his wife and brother-in-law believe he will be.

"Perhaps, as Will Cole says, O'Keefe will come down out of

the rocky vastness of the Brooks Range riding a grizzly bear. It is something to hope for, and would certainly be a colorful addition to the many legends about the Cole family."

Book One

*"Alaska made a pact with the Almighty.
The weather he gives us here is a test."*

One

The day they interred Jeremiah Cole, three days following his one-hundredth birthday, was gray and frigid. A light snow had been falling since dawn.

It was the kind of day, Kelly reflected, that Grandfather loved. When asked his opinion of Alaskan weather, he invariably gave the same reply: "If you like sunshine and balmy breezes, you shouldn't be here. Go back to the Lower 48. To survive and prosper here, you have to be hardy. In fact, Alaska made a pact with the Almighty. The weather he gives us here is a test. If you can't stand it, go back to where you came from. Too damned many of you Outsiders coming up here, anyway. Who needs you?"

Never diplomatic, Jeremiah Cole.

Kelly did not have his fondness for foul weather, and if she had an option, year-long balmy weather would be her choice. But she had no option—she was a Cole and Alaska was her home. To many, the name Cole was synonymous with Alaska. Or vice versa. She might go Outside, and often did; she might threaten to live somewhere else—she could easily afford to—but she knew that she never would. She loved this wild, vast, capricious land; and if lousy weather was the price to be paid, it was a small one.

She shed no tears for her grandfather, as she sat under the canopy by the casket, with family on either side, and mourners from all over the state—and a number from the Lower 48 as well.

Grandfather had lived a full life, and he had attained his last goal: the chance to celebrate his one-hundredth birthday with his mind intact. How many people could say that? He had been in constant pain the last two years, confined to a wheelchair. He was relieved of that now, as well as the

attendant problems of Cole Enterprises. And oh, God, Grandfather, she thought, did your dying leave, or create a basket
of those!

No, if she shed any tears today, they would be for Chris....

With a wrench almost physical she ejected the image of
Chris from her mind. She had thought of little else for the
last two weeks. She simply could not believe that he was
dead, though she had learned to keep this conviction to
herself. Her father and Will claimed to share her belief, yet
Kelly suspected that they were merely humoring her. As for
Dwight, her younger brother...who could tell what he
believed these days? Today was the first time he'd set foot on
Cole Island in six years, and that was a surprise to all of
them.

Grandfather Jeremiah had seemed to share her belief that
Chris was still alive. Now Grandfather was gone. Perhaps that
was why she felt so alone.

She looked both ways along the folding chairs under the
canopy. Her father, Josh, sat on her immediate right, his
handsome face sallow with grief, his clothes more rumpled
than usual, his theatrically white hair tousled.

Although Josh had been a disappointment to Jeremiah
Cole, there had been respect and affection between the two
men, and, Kelly suspected, Josh was the only person present,
aside from herself, who really grieved for the man in the
casket.

Jeremiah's death had been the signal for a whole new ball
game, and the contest for power positions within the corporate structure of Cole Enterprises was going to be a bloodlet-
ting that likely would become a legend with time. Of all the
people under the canopy, probably she and Josh were the
only two who did not give a damn.

No, that wasn't quite accurate. Although she did not care
for herself, she had to be vigilant enough to see to it that
Chris did not have his throat cut—in absentia, so to speak.

Her half-brother, Will, for instance, would begin to make
his move to regain the presidency, now that Grandfather was
dead and Chris was missing. To regain the throne, Will was
capable of almost any sort of maneuver. Will had been decent
enough to keep a low profile since Chris's disappearance, but
Kelly knew it wouldn't last. Will had been bitter since his
sudden demotion—his humiliation, really.

She had never taken much interest in the family business, until she'd married Chris. Always before there had been more important things to claim her attention. Grandfather, bless his male chauvinist soul, had never believed that women should concern themselves with business matters, and that had been fine with Kelly, until Chris became a part of her life. Chris was one of those rare men who could devote himself eighteen hours a day to business, and still have time for his woman; but his drive and enthusiasm had, inevitably, spilled over into their personal life. To her astonishment Kelly had found herself fascinated with the things he had told her. It seemed, in some strange way, that he had become the head of a company that she had never heard of before, instead of one that had, at one remove, been a part of her life since birth. Through Chris, secondhand as it were, she had come to see Cole Enterprises through new eyes, and she knew more now about the various facets of the company than she would have dreamed possible.

Dear God, how she missed him!

Tears stung her eyes, and she moved involuntarily. Josh groped for her hand and squeezed it. He put his mouth close to her ear. "Hang in there, honey. It'll soon be over."

She nodded mutely, not trusting herself to speak, and not wishing him to know that it was for her husband, not her dead grandfather, that she was concerned.

Grandfather had told her the night of his birthday party: "It won't be long now, girl. I made it to where I wanted. Don't grieve for me when it's over. I've lived more in one lifetime than most people do in three. Grieve for that man of yours..."

"No, Grandfather! Chris is still alive, I just know he is!"

"Could be, girl, could be. I Godalmighty hope so. Without him, Cole may dissolve like snow in summer when I m gone. Will, I don't know, I just don't know..."

Kelly glanced over at her half-brother, seated on her left; his face looking naked without the ever-present cigar. He was staring at the casket, his prominent nose jutting like the figurehead of a Viking ship. Six-four, with shoulders suitable for a pro football lineman, Will was flamboyant, forceful.... No, he *was* a force. On his other side sat his wife, Louise; cool, poised, perfect features as expressionless as a mask. The Snow Maiden, Kelly had once heard Will call her in anger.

Growing up, all the way into her teens, Kelly had worshiped Will Cole. Fifteen years older than she, he was more like a favorite uncle than a half-brother. And since Josh's political career—first in Alaska, then in Washington—called for him to be away more than he was at home, Will became something of a surrogate father—lusty, energetic, loving life to the hilt; much, she suspected, as Grandfather must have been in his youth.

But then there had been a growing estrangement between her father and half-brother, and on Jeremiah's retirement and Will's elevation to company president, Will began making his home in Fairbanks, to be near the pipeline, and Kelly had seen less of him. After she married Chris and Grandfather had kicked Will downstairs and moved Chris into his place, the rift had been inevitable. . . .

She started at a touch on her arm. Her father was urging her to her feet, and she realized that the minister's interminable eulogy had ended. To keep from looking at the casket, Kelly glanced beyond her father to her brother, Dwight: "A hippie well past his prime," Will had called him with a sneer.

Tall, gaunt, with a full, untrimmed black beard, Dwight had the solemn, fanatical look of the puritanical missionaries of old. Even though he had condescended to attend the funeral, Dwight was attired in worn jeans, a Windbreaker, and scuffed boots. To Will, it was like waving a red flag, and but for Josh's intervention, he would have chased Dwight off the island.

Yet Dwight *could* relax and show a sense of fun on occasion, Kelly knew; she saw more of him than either her father or half-brother.

Now Josh nudged her elbow. "We can go now, honey. No need for us to watch Pap put into the crypt."

He held up his umbrella as he stepped out from under the canopy, and Kelly ducked under its protection. This was taken as a signal, and there was a general exodus as everyone broke for the line of limousines waiting to drive them to the big house a mile away.

As they hurried along, Kelly sent a glance back at the gray mausoleum. Jeremiah had bought Cole Island before she was born, and built the mausoleum at the same time as the mansion. He buried his wife, Mary, Josh's mother, there, and

Enterprises. As for Will . . . you know better, honey. He'll be
leading the pack."

"Damnit, Josh!" she snapped, angry at him for voicing
what she had been thinking only minutes ago. "You are
Jeremiah's son, the closest to him in blood. I should think
just this *once.*"

"No, not this once. Not now, not at any time." His voice
was curt. "I crossed that Rubicon long ago. I went into the
company after college, after I married Will's mother. Your
grandfather kept nagging at me about following in his footsteps, and I knew that if I didn't make a stand, he'd be
whipping me into line like those sled dogs he used in the
early days. At first I thought he'd disown me." He laughed
wryly. "He probably would have if I hadn't been his only
whelp. But I stood up to his rantings, and strangely enough, I
think the old man came to respect me more in the end than
he would have if I'd remained with the company. But with all
that wheeling and dealing," he shuddered, "I would have
gone out of my mind."

"Wheeling and dealing?" she said scornfully. "What is
politics, if not that?"

"Not when I started out, honey, not for me. I was charged
with idealism, do or die for the common man, on the side of
the good guy tromped on by big business, like Cole Enterprises. And it worked for me, worked for a long time. Now,
I've learned a painful lesson. You compromise, grit your
teeth, and compromise. Even then the common man often
ends up sucking hind tit." He sighed. "Poor Dwight. That's
something he has yet to learn. I feel sorry for him when the
day comes that he does. He may never recover. It'll be worse
for him, because he's gone further than I ever dreamed of."

"How many times have I heard you arguing with Will
about that very thing? How many times have I heard you say
that the world needs its Dwights? Without their opposition,
the ones on the other side would have nothing to fear, would
be able to do as they please. With people of Dwight's
courage, no matter how far out, they tread more cautiously.
Now didn't I hear you say that, Daddy?"

"You did and it's true. But that's no help for somebody like
Dwight. The Don Quixotes of this world end up ridiculed
and scorned. Or mad, if they're not mad to begin with."

"Ralph Nader seems to be doing okay."

"They'll probably get him in the end. Besides, Nader's become trendy. Or vice versa, if that makes any sense." His voice trailed off as the limousine stopped before the house. "Kelly..." He leaned toward her, and she winced at his bourbon-scented breath. "Don't worry, I'm not a morning drinker. Not yet. But I felt that I needed something to get me through all this 'pomp and ceremony.' But about Dwight. I know you see him often, almost every time you're in Fairbanks, and God knows I don't see him often enough. But I do love him. Tell him that for me, will you?"

"Why don't you tell him yourself, Daddy?" she said challengingly. "He's right here, not in Fairbanks."

"It's too late for that, I can't."

"It's never too late. And I've never understood about you and Dwight. You're not a cold man, Josh. You're warm, affectionate, and I've never doubted that you love me." Her mouth twisted. "At least not since I got old enough to have any sense."

"I don't know." His shoulders rose and fell. "It's the same with Will and me. Maybe it's something in the Cole genes. As far back as I can remember, Pap never, not once, told me that he loved me. We Cole males have to be so manly, what they call macho nowadays. It's all right to speak your love to a woman, wife, daughter, mistress, but not to another male. Don't ask me to explain it, Kelly, I can't. It's a flaw in me, perhaps a fatal one."

"I'll tell him, Josh, I'll tell Dwight that you love him," she said softly, as the driver opened the car door.

By the time Jeremiah bought the island thirty years ago, he was several times a millionaire, and he had spared no expense in building what he wanted. The house sat on a small knoll, facing south, the water of the inlet visible winter and summer, a pine-shrouded slope rising up behind it, providing some protection against winter blasts.

The house itself was either a monstrosity, or a marvel, depending on how one viewed it. Most men loved it, while most women hated it.

Kelly loved it, certainly not for its architectural beauty,

although she didn't think it as hideous as many people did, but for two reasons: most of her growing up had been here, and it was comfortable, if nothing else.

The house, a low, rambling structure, had been built for comfort, Grandfather's comfort, Kelly was sure, but comfortable nonetheless, unless your idea of comfort included sophistication.

Sophisticated it was not. In 1898, when Jeremiah struck his lode, he had lived in a one-room log cabin for a year, with mud chinking the cracks, one oilcloth-covered window, a dirt floor, and a crude bunk.

The exterior of Cole House was rough-hewn logs, the cracks mortared with mud that had to be replaced almost every year.

"You should be grateful that he stopped there," Josh had said once when Louise, Will's wife, complained. "The inside could have been patterned after that Klondike cabin as well."

Fortunately, it was not. The logs had been bolted to thick stone blocks, brought to the island at great expense, which kept the house cool in summer. The thirty-some rooms were heated by fuel oil and were comfortable even in the severest winters.

The hardwood floors weren't carpeted, but Jeremiah had been lavish with polar bear rugs, so that a person could walk barefoot through the entire house without once touching a toe to wood.

The furniture, mostly built to order, was massive, functional, always with an eye toward comfort. The only pictures were hunting scenes—dark, bloody things, Kelly always thought. The walls were hung with mounted heads of Alaskan animals, none, so far as Kelly knew, bagged by her grandfather. His choice of wall decorations had always puzzled Kelly, since he had never hunted for the sport of it.

Josh offered an explanation once: "The Cole mystique, my darling daughter. We Coles must prove to the world that we are male through and through." This from Josh, who found it distasteful to kill even a marauding rat.

Up until her death ten years ago, Kelly's mother had tried, without any great success, to bring decorative, feminine touches to Cole House; but any time Jeremiah found a lace curtain, or the like, he ripped it down contemptuously.

Louise, Will's wife, had tried harder, but her efforts had been only marginally more successful, and she had been only too happy to move bag and baggage to Fairbanks.

It was only during the past few years, when Jeremiah's health began to fail, that Kelly started brightening up the interior, subtly, a touch at a time. Jeremiah, confined to his own quarters in the west wing most of the time, noticed and grumbled, but did nothing about it.

The one place she had left strictly alone was the big room—the baronial hall, Kelly had dubbed it. It was long, paneled in dark wood, with a huge fireplace at one end, a bar at the other, with couches scattered about, and it was used mainly for entertaining.

In the beginning there had been a long table, seating up to forty people. The table had been a whim of Jeremiah's, patterned after the dining table in Hearst's San Simeon Castle, to which Jeremiah had once been invited back in the thirties. That was the reason Kelly called it the baronial hall.

Those members of the family at home dined there when Kelly was small, but she could never remember seeing more than six people at a time around the table. According to Josh, the few times Grandfather had given parties, they had been total disasters. Jeremiah Cole had not been a social animal, although he tried, to the point of pain. Unlike William Randolph Hearst, he could not host forty people at once, not even if they toadied to him. In a room with a half-dozen friends—"The old tyrant never *had* that many friends"—or an equal number of employees, he was in total command.

When Josh, about fifteen years ago, became a prominent figure in Alaskan politics, Jeremiah gave up his conceit, allowed the table to be removed; and thereafter Josh used the room to entertain. Josh could handle a hundred people, including enemies, with ease and aplomb. After that whichever family members were at Cole House, at any given time, they ate their meals in the smaller dining room off the kitchen.

The wake was held in the baronial hall.

Kelly and her father stood in the entryway welcoming the mourners, receiving condolences, while Will circulated and Dwight stood off in one corner, nursing a Coke. Kelly felt sure his beard hid a sneer of contempt.

At one time or another Kelly had met most of the hundred or so mourners, but she knew very few. Most of them were Alaskans, business or political connections.

One of the exceptions was Bry Tucker, head of Alaska's most powerful union.

Kelly had always thought that Bry Tucker was typecast for the role of union leader—burly, craggy of face, with thick eyebrows that would have made John L. Lewis proud, an aggressive, bullying manner, and as opinionated as any of today's young revolutionaries. Kelly had always found him to be a pussycat.

His huge, calloused hand engulfed hers as he rumbled in his gravelly voice, "I'm sorry, Kelly lass, sorry to see the old boy go. We scratched and spit at each other for something like thirty years, but we had respect for each other. It won't be the same. The Almighty broke the mold with Jeremiah." His glance went to Josh. "Sorry, Senator, but you know what I mean."

"I know what you mean, Bry," Josh said. "No need to apologize."

Something impelled Kelly to say, "If you need someone to fight with, wait until Chris gets back."

"Chris?" A startled look fled across Tucker's battered features, and then his expression went blank. "Yes, lass, Chris gave . . . gives as good as he gets." Then he was gone, almost running.

Kelly gasped, turning to her father. "Why did I say that, Josh? I think I'm cracking up!"

"What do you want from me? A pat on the head and a 'there, there, daughter'?" He patted her on the head. "Platitudes I can give you by the carload. I'm a politician, remember?"

"I remember, Josh. How can I forget?" She laughed shakily.

"It's been a rough day on all of us, honey. Hang in there a little longer. It'll be over eventually."

"Mrs. O'Keefe?"

Kelly turned a controlled face toward the sound of the vibrant voice, to the only woman she had ever felt jealousy toward. The woman was Charlene Baker, Chris's executive secretary. Charlene was about thirty, with lustrous auburn hair, cool blue eyes, and a superb figure she tried unsuccessfully to conceal with tailored suits and subdued colors. She was marvelously efficient, with a quick, incisive mind, and, Chris swore, total recall. If any other attributes were needed, she was unmarried, romantically unattached, and willing to work impossible hours.

Kelly hated her.

"My condolences, Mrs. O'Keefe, Senator Cole," Charlene said solemnly. "I know this is a terrible time, but I must meet with both of you soon. There are some things that absolutely must be resolved. I seem to be in some sort of limbo. I've tried to talk to Mr. Will Cole, but he's so busy it's impossible."

"It seems everybody wants to discuss business today," Kelly said acidly. "Maybe Grandfather would have liked that, but I find it in very bad taste."

"Now, Kelly," Josh said suavely. He gripped her arm hard, his fingers digging in. "You must forgive Kelly, Charlene, she is rather distraught. She thought a great deal of her grandfather."

"I understand and I do apologize," Charlene said. "But this is the first opportunity I've had to speak to either of you. You've been in Washington, sir, and my calls to Mrs. O'Keefe were not returned."

"I have more important things on my mind, Miss Baker," Kelly said curtly. "My husband is missing. Or perhaps even dead." As the word escaped her, Kelly was appalled. It was the first time she had spoken the word aloud and it had been without forethought. Could it be that she was accepting what everyone said was inevitable?

Charlene's eyes sparked blue fire. "You may believe Chris is dead, but I do not accept that."

Kelly felt a sudden wave of kinship toward the woman. She said eagerly, "Do you have any reason to think that he is alive?"

"It's just a feeling I have, but I'm sure I'm right. Chris is . . ."

Josh broke in smoothly, "Charlene, there is a reading of my father's will in the morning, at ten. I think you should be there, not that I'm saying you're a legatee, but you should be present. Afterward, we'll talk about what's troubling you. I'm sure everything can be resolved satisfactorily."

Charlene nodded and moved on before Kelly could collect herself. She started after the woman, but her father tightened his grip on her arm.

She whipped around. "Damnit, Josh, I wanted to ask her about Chris! Why does *she* think he's still alive?"

"Probably for the same reason you do, Kelly. She doesn't want to believe that he isn't. Okay, okay!" He held up his hands. "I'm not saying he isn't either, but you shouldn't tee off on her just because she believes as you do."

"But Chris is my husband, I love him."

He said quietly, "There is such a thing as loyalty, honest affection. She doesn't have to be in love with the man." He cocked an eyebrow. "That is the reason you're angry, isn't it? You're jealous."

"Yes, I'm jealous," she said in a subdued voice.

He shook his head. "You, of all people. You're one of the most attractive women I know, and that's not just fatherly pride speaking. Why should you be jealous of Charlene, or any woman?"

"Aren't wives supposed to be jealous of their husbands' attractive secretaries?"

"Many women are, true, but you've no reason to be."

"You don't know Chris, Josh. He has a strong sex drive. I once called him a satyr . . ." Abruptly realizing what she was saying, Kelly felt herself flush crimson. "Dear God, I *must* be losing my mind! Josh, handle the others, please? I can't take any more today."

Without waiting for a reply she plunged away, pushing her way through the crowd, intent on finding privacy. Then she saw Dwight leaning against the wall, a Coke in his hand. Although many of his followers smoked pot freely, and some, she suspected, used the hard stuff, Dwight never drank alcohol or used drugs. "What's going on in the world is enough to screw up my head, without helping it along with booze or drugs."

She veered toward him. Although the room was packed now, there was a cleared space around Dwight, as though he had a strong odor. Unfortunately that was often true, she reflected wryly; he did not bathe as often as he might.

"Must you stand off by yourself like this?"

He shrugged. "If anybody wants to talk to me, here I am. But I haven't noticed any rush to my side."

"You could help greet the mourners. You are family, you know."

"Am I?"

"Dwight . . ." She sighed. "You know, the way you look, even the way you stand, puts people off. You don't even have to open your mouth."

"If I rasp them, good! That's how I like it, with this bunch."

"You could compromise a little. I haven't even seen you speak to Josh, not once."

"If he wants to talk to me, he can see me. I've been visible all day."

"He doesn't know how to approach you, Dwight. He just told me."

"Bullshit," he said contemptuously. "If I was one of his constituents, he'd have no problem."

"Don't be so righteous, brother! That's what irritates me so about you and your kind. It's all or nothing. If somebody doesn't agree with you, you have no time for them, not even your own father."

"That's the way it has to be, Sis." He raised and lowered the Coke bottle. "Either for us, or against us, no in-between."

"He does love you, Dwight."

"Again, bullshit."

"No, he does. He wanted me to tell you."

"Why doesn't *he* tell me?" Dwight looked across the room at their father. "It's a long walk, you know, about twenty yards."

"He can't, he doesn't know how."

"Doesn't matter, anyway." He shrugged. "There are more important matters than whether Senator Joshua Cole loves his number-two son, the hippie."

"He doesn't get along that well with Will, either."

Dwight grinned. "Now there, Father and I are in full agreement." He stood away from the wall. "I'm about to shove off, anyway. I've paid my respects, such as they are."

"No, you can't go." She placed a restraining hand on his arm. "Brad's going to read Grandfather's will in the morning, at ten. You have to stay for that."

"Why?" He laughed shortly. "Surely you don't think that Jeremiah Cole left me, the black sheep, anything in his will? No way, dear sister, no way."

"I don't know why not. You are his grandson."

"You're dreaming, Kelly." He was openly sneering now. "Jeremiah Cole was a rapist. He got rich by raping this country, and since when does a rapist compensate his victims?"

Kelly was swept by a gust of anger. "If you, Dwight, can be considered a victim, it's because you've made yourself one." Her anger left as quickly as it came, and she said wearily, "But suit yourself. Leave now, or stay." She started off.

"Oh, I'll be there, Sis," he called after her. "It should be a real circus, the reading of Jeremiah's will, and I was always a sucker for a good circus."

Two

The room Jeremiah Cole had called his study was, in reality, a library. It did contain a desk and a number of comfortable chairs, but the walls of the rather large room were lined with bookshelves, from ceiling to floor, and there wasn't any available space without a book. Jeremiah had left school at an early age; but after he became rich he read voraciously, reading anything he could get his hands on. His range of reading material always amazed Kelly—from the classics to the latest best seller, fiction or nonfiction, even several versions of the Bible, which he had always scorned as a fairy tale for losers. "But whoever put the words down could write like a sonofabitch."

At the solemn ten o'clock gathering Brad Connors sat at Jeremiah's desk, the blue folder containing the will open before him. Arranged in a semicircle before him were Kelly and Josh, side by side on the short couch; Will and his wife, Louise, in chairs set somewhat apart from the others; and Dwight, lounging against one wall of books, a half-empty Coke bottle in his hands. Charlene Baker was also present, seated off in one corner.

"Well..." Brad cleared his throat. "All the principals are present, so we can proceed..."

Kelly said, "Chris isn't."

Brad looked distinctly uncomfortable. "I know, Kelly, but we'll touch on that shortly. Bear with me for now, all right?"

Josh grasped Kelly's hand and squeezed. She retired into a rebellious silence.

"As I said, all the principals are present. There are, of course, generous bequests to the staff here, but we needn't touch on those at the moment..."

There were always at least ten employees on the island; a

18

large household staff and a crew to take care of the island itself. Jeremiah had been very demanding of any company employee, but his attitude toward the island staff had been relaxed. So long as they did the minimum amount of work required of them, and did not get too far out of line, they remained, and were paid well. Some of the people had been in his employ since Jeremiah purchased the island.

Brad was going on: "And so I will now read the pertinent sections of the last will and testament of Jeremiah Cole." By the time he had finished with the personal bequests everyone in the room, with the exception of Charlene, had been generously taken care of. Even Dwight was bequeathed fifty thousand dollars, which wrung a grunt of astonishment from him.

Now Brad fell silent, staring down at the document.

Will broke his silence. "There has to be more to it than that, Connors. That's the personal stuff." He waved his smoldering cigar. "The company, what about the company, the stock, the control?"

"Well, that's the reason I pushed for this early reading. I know you're all anxious . . ." Brad paused, took a deep breath, then said in a rush, "Shortly before his birthday, Jeremiah Cole wrote a new will. Wait, I must qualify that. He added a codicil. It pertains to the company, and the stock."

He paused again and Kelly reflected, not for the first time, that all attorneys are natural actors, well aware of the value of the "pregnant pause."

"For hell's sake, man, will you get on with it?" Will said explosively. "Why did he change his will, and what did he change?"

"As to the why, I don't know. Jeremiah was never one to give reasons. I'm sure you're all well aware of that." All of a sudden Brad seemed to relax, and now actually appeared to be enjoying himself. He made a steeple of his fingers and stared directly at Will as he went on, speaking slowly and distinctly. "I can quote the codicil verbatim without even looking at it. In effect, what your grandfather did, was placed all his Cole stock into a trust, and his stock, as you of course know, amounts to seventy percent of the outstanding shares. The other thirty belongs to you, Josh, and Kelly."

"A trust?" Will leaned forward. "Who administers this goddamned trust?"

"Three people. I, for one." Brad held up a hand. "I didn't ask for the chore, Will, I tried to persuade your grandfather otherwise, but he remained adamant. The other two are totally disinterested parties. Judge Oliver Waters of Fairbanks, and Roger Blair, of Blair Supermarkets..."

"I know who he is," Will interrupted rudely. "He retired years ago, put out to pasture by his two sons. This trust, how long is it to run?"

"Until Christopher O'Keefe either returns or is declared legally dead."

"Jesus Christ in a wheelbarrow, is Chris to haunt me into my grave? And he isn't even a Cole!"

Kelly said hotly, "He's my husband, and as much a Cole as you are!"

Will batted a hand at her without looking around. "What does it take to have him declared legally dead?"

"I can't advise you on that, Will," Brad said coldly. "You'll have to consult another attorney."

"You can be goddamned sure that I'll do just that." Will stared at the attorney intently. Finally he said in a soft voice, "That's not all, is it, Mr. Trustee? That's not the bottom line?"

"I'm afraid not, Will."

"Then stop pussyfooting!" Will said in a snarling voice. "Put everything face down on the table."

"All right, Will, as you say... the bottom line. Kelly is to become president of Cole Enterprises and chairman of the board for the duration of the trust. Or until..." He broke off, looking at Kelly, a hint of apology in his eyes.

Kelly was stunned into absolute silence, and Will sat as though turned to stone, the thick cigar poised halfway to his mouth. A gasp came from Charlene Baker.

"And Will, what is to happen to him?" Louise demanded, her usual composure shattered.

"He will return to being vice-president of Cole 98, the position he held before the plane crash."

Will broke his silence, slamming a fist on his thigh. "No! Goddamnit, no! I won't stand for that again!"

"You do have a choice, Will. That is spelled out in the language of the trust. Accept the vice-presidency of Cole 98, or resign from the company altogether."

Will shot to his feet. His fury was almost too much to

contain. "I won't take this! The old fool was senile, and I'll prove it in court, if I have to."

"As we lawyers say, Will, everyone is entitled to his day in court," Brad said with a faint smile. Then he became formal. "But it is my considered opinion that it would be a waste of your time and money. At the time Jeremiah dictated the codicil, he was in full possession of his mental faculties. He was anything but senile."

"We'll see, we'll see," Will muttered. He took Louise's arm. "Come on, Louise. Let's get the hell out of here. I've heard enough."

Brad said quickly, "Wait, there's more. You should hear the rest."

"Why should I?" Will said with a sneer. "It's clear I'm getting a shafting." He plunged from the room in long strides, half dragging the silent Louise along with him.

There was a long silence after the door slammed behind them, which Dwight finally broke with a short laugh. "The old boy did have a talent for stirring things up, you know? Even from beyond the grave. But it is a hoot to see brother Will so rasped. Thanks for talking me into staying, Sis. I'd've been sorry to have missed this." He drank from the bottle in a mocking toast.

His little speech jolted Kelly out of her stunned inertia. She turned an angry look on her brother. "You think I wanted this? I'm more surprised than you are!"

"Oh, I'm not surprised; nothing Jeremiah could do would ever surprise me. No, I'll have to amend that." His bearded face took on a look of awe. "That fifty thousand he left me, now *that* surprised me."

Kelly had already turned away. "You know I can't abide by that stupid trust, Brad. There's no way I'm qualified to run the company, and even if I was, I wouldn't do it." She shook her head so violently that her hair whipped back and forth across her face. "No, nothing can force me to take on that job."

"Now, Kelly." Josh took her hand. "Don't be hasty."

"No!" She flung his hand off. "Don't waste that campaign charm on me, Daddy. I won't do it, and that's final!" She sprang to her feet.

"As I tried to tell Will, Kelly, there's more. You should at least hear me out," Brad said. "In fact, I insist that you hear the rest."

"You didn't insist with Will."

"It more directly concerns you than Will."

"Okay, I'll listen, but don't expect me to change my mind." She sat down again.

"I don't expect you to. The opposite, in fact," he said wryly. "You must understand that I debated heatedly with your grandfather about this part. I consider it damned unfair, discriminatory, unconscionable, but he remained stubborn as ever, so I was left with no choice."

At a sound behind her, Kelly looked around to see Louise slip back into the room. Louise closed the door softly, standing against the wall beside it.

"For God's sake, Brad," Josh said in exasperation. "Will you let the other shoe drop? Even for a lawyer, you do blather on. That's unlike you."

"I know, Senator, and I'm sorry. But it pisses me off, damnit."

Kelly stared in surprise. It was so totally out of character for Brad to use a vulgarism, and without so much as an apology. She said quietly, "All right, Brad, let's hear the rest of it."

"The trust, Kelly, has a morals and competency clause."

"You'll have to explain that."

"If the trustees agree that any of your actions as president of Cole endangers the company, we are empowered to remove you."

Kelly laughed. "Grandfather never did have much respect for women in business."

Brad looked even more uncomfortable. "You don't understand, Kelly. It's not only that. If your competency as president was ever in question, if your actions threatened active harm to the company, I can see myself, however, reluctantly, voting to remove you. But I also said there is a morals clause. And that means that if you, in our combined judgment, commit an immoral act, we are also empowered to remove you. Now, I cannot see myself doing that, but I'm afraid that I can't speak for the other two trustees."

Kelly wasn't sure she had heard aright. "You mean, the trust gives you the right to judge my private life?"

"That's the gist of it," Brad said.

Josh said angrily, "That is incredible! Pap had some weird notions, but this one tops them all."

"I agree, Senator, but your father was a misogynist. He hated women, I'm sure you know that. He felt that women had betrayed him all his life, and that they not only have no business sense, but are weak creatures with no moral spine."

"Grandfather never hated me, Brad!"

"I'm sure he didn't, I'm sure he loved you, Kelly, but the rest applies. People often insert strange clauses in their wills." Brad sighed heavily. "I've seen weirder ones than this. As I said, I argued with Jeremiah, to no avail. He did make one comment, and that didn't make a whole lot of sense. He said that since Will had gone bad, how could he be sure you wouldn't? He said there had to be a safeguard written into the trust document. That's all I could ever get out of him."

"Then why did he want me to head up the company, if he felt that way?"

"I asked him that very question when he dictated the codicil. He said that you were the only choice. The Senator, he knew, would never accept the post. He refused to consider Will, which I must confess baffles me, but Jeremiah would give no reason beyond that one comment. Dwight, of course, he would not consider, either. Sorry, Dwight."

"It's okay, Counselor," Dwight said laconically. "He's already shattered one of my misconceptions, by leaving me something in his will. Two in one day would have been too much."

Brad turned back to Kelly. "You were the only one of his blood left, Kelly. I'm sure you know that he considered Chris one of the family."

Kelly said sharply, "And what provision did he make for when I refused?"

"None. I asked him about that. He said that he knew you would not refuse the responsibility. He mentioned duty, duty to family and company . . ."

"Well, he was wrong, wasn't he?" She stood up again. "Even if I had thought of considering it before, this morals clause would have ended it. I would never think of accepting it under those conditions! He must have been senile, as Will said, to even suggest such a thing. What would you do, Brad, you and your fellow trustees, place a bug in my bedroom? Install hidden cameras?" Her voice became bitter and sarcastic. "Maybe even hire a private eye to follow me around?"

"Of course not, Kelly. Why would you even think such a thing?"

"Why shouldn't I? How else could you keep track of my 'immoral behavior'? Certainly you couldn't expect me to come to you and confess my indiscretions. I couldn't live with such pressure on me. There is no way, Brad, that I will stand in for Chris. You can just wait until he comes back."

Brad was shaking his head. "We can't do that, Kelly. It's been too long already. You have to face it, Kelly, he's not coming back."

"Then let Will continue running Cole, as he has been doing since the plane crash. It seems to me that the company is managing to survive okay."

"Your grandfather was very specific about that. Will was to be replaced at the reading of the will, and the reading was to be done as soon as possible after the services. That's the main reason I pushed so hard."

"There are other people in this room with Cole blood, Josh and Dwight. I know what you've already said but..."

Dwight interrupted, "There is no way that I'd saddle myself with it, Kelly, even if the old man had pointed the finger at me, not even if I thought it was the only way to save the company, which is a hoot right there. I've been fighting Cole since the pipeline started."

She whirled on her father. "Then you, Josh! It's time you shouldered some responsibility, instead of accepting a free ride."

He flinched, and her heart went out to him; the charge was unfair, but she was not about to recant.

He said heavily, "I can't, Kelly, as you are well aware."

"You're forgetting something, Kelly," Brad said. "The codicil is very clear. It's to be you, and only you."

Kelly felt trapped, cornered. She said wildly, "You're all trying to make me feel guilty, but it won't work! I will not do it. As far as I'm concerned, Brad, you can run that will through the company shredder."

Josh stood up beside her. "Kelly, at least think about it; you owe Chris that much."

"Don't try to put that guilt trip on me, too! I owe Chris my love, and my belief that he is still alive. That's all I owe him."

"And if he *is* still alive?" He touched her arm.

She looked away from her father to Brad. "There is something everybody seems to have forgotten here. I have no qualifications for the job. None! Not only have I never held a job, *any* job, but I know absolutely nothing about Cole."

"I think you underestimate yourself, my dear," Josh said.

Charlene Baker said, "I'm quite willing to help in any way I can, Mrs. O'Keefe. In the time I worked for Chris . . . for your husband, I learned a great deal about the company, and I know his thinking on many business matters."

Kelly stared at her. "Another country heard from. This begins to sound like a conspiracy." She shook her head. "No! For the last time, no!"

She started out of the room.

Brad called after her, "Your father is right, Kelly. Think it over. Don't make a hasty decision that you may regret later."

She continued on without responding. As she neared the door, Dwight stood away from the wall to intercept her. In a low voice he said, "Hang in there, Sis. Don't let them con you into doing something you don't want to do."

She stared into his bearded face, searching for sarcasm. She could detect none. "Why should you care? You've always wanted Cole to fail. If I should somehow lose my mind and take over, the chances are likely that it *would* fail."

"I'm thinking of you, Sis. Give me credit for that much. You're the only Cole I have any feeling for." His eyes were grave. "If you take over the top spot, the animals will be at you, the vultures will start to circle. They'll destroy you, believe me, they will. Don't do it, Kelly."

Three

Will was halfway down the hall before he realized that Louise was no longer with him. He shrugged and strode on.

Louise had an unfailing instinct for self-preservation. If she sniffed the scent of a loser about him, she probably wouldn't hesitate to bail out; and it would seem that he was on a losing streak, at the top of a greased slide, with no handholds all the way to the bottom. She had mentioned divorce a couple of times in the past.

Not that he cared all that much about Louise. They had not even shared the same bedroom, much less a bed, for years. And even when they had shared a bed, he would have been better off sleeping with one of those inflatable sex dolls on sale nowadays. At least he could have filled it with warm water, and gotten *some* semblance of warmth!

To hell with Louise!

He pushed open the door to the big room and strode down to the bar. Although it was well short of noon, he splashed a glass half full of Jack Daniel's, dropped in a couple of ice cubes, sloshed the liquor around for a moment, then gulped at it until the glass was empty. He poured another. Maybe it would anesthetize his thrumming nerves. He relit his cigar and consumed the second drink more slowly.

His memory vividly recreated the scene in the study, and he shuddered in anger and humiliation. By nature Will was an optimist; even as a Cole, things had not always gone so easily for him, yet he had always managed to triumph over adversity, by cleverness and sheer force of will. He was not averse to plowing ahead like a bulldozer, if all else failed, but during the last year, since Christopher O'Keefe had come into his life, it seemed that nothing had gone right for him. And to think that it was he, Will Cole, who had been responsible for bringing Chris into the Cole orbit! How many times had he cursed the day that had happened!

Christ in a wheelbarrow, how differently he felt from yesterday, from last week! Since the news of the old man's death had reached him, Will had existed in a state of euphoria, sure that his long run of bad luck had broken. With Chris missing, almost surely dead, and the old man in his coffin, he would soon be riding high again.

Some people might consider it callous, at least in bad taste, to exult in the death of his grandfather. But what the hell, the old man had lived to be a hundred, far beyond the norm. So, why be a hypocrite about it? They had never hit it off, really, not even in the halcyon days, when Will had been on top of the world, gloating about the fact that he'd been one of the few Alaskans, the *only* Cole, to foresee the fabulous oil discovery at Prudhoe Bay.

That had opened the old man's eyes, and forced his hand; he'd had no choice but to turn Cole Enterprises over to Will when failing health forced his own retirement.

Will's memory performed another jump, to that bitter confrontation when Jeremiah had kicked his ass out of the catbird seat without warning, demoting him from head honcho of the whole works to VP of Cole 98; and worse, putting Chris in his place! Will could replay that scene in his mind word for word . . .

"Will?"

His wife's voice shattered his reverie, and he turned on her savagely. "So there you are. Where the hell did you disappear to?"

She said serenely, "I went back to the study to listen to the rest of it."

"Trying to see if you could salvage something for yourself out of the wreckage?"

"Not exactly, and you should have stayed. It may not be as bad as you think."

He grunted and took a drink. "I fail to see how it could be any worse."

"Even if Kelly takes over, and she may not, there's something in the codicil that could mean she won't last very long. And then the whole thing would be up for grabs."

He shook his head to clear it. "I don't follow."

"If Chris doesn't return, which everyone but Kelly is sure

of, and Kelly does take over the company and falls on her face, then the only thing they can do is turn to you to run the company, despite the terms of the trust. It's either that or everybody stands by and watches the company go bankrupt. I can't see them doing that, Will." Her voice had taken on that faintly hectoring tone she adopted when she wanted to lecture him.

As always, he reacted to that tone like a bull with banderillas sticking out of back. "Hell, woman, you don't know what you're prattling on about. If Kelly takes over, they'll prop her up, keep her out in front, all that beauty and charm highly visible, while the lower echelon makes the important decisions. Probably that goddamned Connors!" He splashed more bourbon into his glass and paced, drinking. "No, I've been dumped on enough, I'm getting out. I've given my life to that company and where has it gotten me? I can get a job anywhere, some place where my efforts will be appreciated and where I'll be paid closer to what I'm worth. I'm forty years old, Louise. If I can't make a move now, it'll soon be too late."

As he paused to sip his drink, Louise said, "Are you finished ranting for a moment, and ready to listen?"

"Listen to what?" he snapped.

"To what I heard when I went back to the study."

As she began to tell him about the morals and competency clause in the trust terms, Will listened with growing interest and a mounting excitement. When she was finished, he rapped the bar with his knuckles. "Aside from the fact that she knows zilch about running a company like Cole, that girl will never be able to abide by any such moral strictures. I know my sister too well. She's been spoiled, had everything she ever wanted, including men, and she loves a good time. Once she finally realizes that Chris has bought the farm, she'll break loose." A slow grin spread across his face. "Especially if she has a nudge in the right direction."

"I thought you'd see it that way, Will. Of course, it all depends on her taking over. When she stormed out of the study a minute ago, she swore that she never would."

When Josh and Brad Connors were finally alone in the study, Josh looked at the attorney in speculation. "What do you think, Brad?"

Brad shrugged. "I don't know, Senator. She's your daughter, you know her better than I do."

"I'm not sure how well I know her, daughter or not," Josh said ruefully. "But it is a hell of a situation to throw her into, whatever her final decision. What bothers me is what will happen if she doesn't accept the post. What is going to happen to the company?"

"That bothers me, too, Senator. More than I wanted to admit to the others." Brad leaned back, massaging his eyes. "I tried my damnedest to get your father to take that into consideration, but he just would not listen. He kept repeating over and over his absolute conviction that Kelly would fall in line."

"But if she doesn't, who will run Cole?"

"Again, I don't know." Brad sighed. "Frankly, I haven't examined all the legal aspects. I've had my head in the sand, hoping that she would accede to your father's wishes. I suppose there is legal precedent for the trustees appointing someone for the duration of the trust."

"Not Will, I hope."

"No, not Will. Your father was emphatic about that. And that, as I said, puzzles me. True, I've never gotten along with Will. Still . . ."

"You're not alone. Neither have I, and he's my own son. It seems we've always been on opposite sides as far back as I can remember, even to debating the choice of desserts. Will can charm the birds out of trees, especially if the bird is female. The thing is, he can be charming only if *he* wants to be. Other times he can be a nerd. His talent for charming people, I fear, is equaled by his talent for alienating them, right and left."

"But there seemed to be a deep bitterness toward him in Jeremiah, almost a hatred."

Josh nodded slowly. "I know, there is a mystery there. I tried to talk to both of them about it, but neither would discuss it. Brad, this thing about Chris being declared legally dead . . . and for God's sweet sake, don't breathe a word of this to Kelly, but what would it take? I've heard something about a person being declared legally dead after seven years. Would we have to wait that long in this instance? You know, of course, that two search parties have been sent out, with no sign of the plane being found. But now that spring is coming, the terrain will become easier to search."

Brad was nodding. "If some tangible evidence is found of his demise, that will simplify matters, naturally. If not ... well, it can become a tangle. Under normal circumstances, the seven-year time span does apply, but it's my opinion that the courts might find these circumstances abnormal, since an industrial empire cannot remain rudderless indefinitely. I'll tell you something in confidence, Senator ..." He made a rueful gesture. "That very thing scares me. I was bluffing a little when I told Will that it would be futile to fight the will in court. It may not be futile at all. A court just might find that Jeremiah Cole was incompetent when he inserted that codicil. On the face of it, it does seem an irresponsible action. There is so damned much at risk here. I must confess that I just don't know."

"We'll see how Kelly feels in the morning. I feel guilty as hell, Brad. She's right, you know. I should be the one to take over, but, Jesus, how can I?" He stood up to walk over to the window. "Aside from the fact that the job is beyond me, there are some things in the political arena that could go awry, if I were to resign to take over Cole." He faced about. "I suppose that sounds pompous, making myself out to be the indispensable man, but right now I do stand in the way of a couple of matters that could bring disaster to Alaska if my opponents have their way."

"I'm aware of that, Senator. How goes the battle, anyway? I haven't had much else on my mind but Chris since he disappeared, and haven't kept up-to-date."

Josh ran his fingers into his hair, giving it that tousled look so endearing to those who watched him in debate. "Both good and bad. So far I've been able to block the latest bill to move the state capital from Juneau to Anchorage, but it'll crop up in the next session of the state legislature, you can be sure."

"Senator, would it really be such a disaster if the statehouse was moved to Anchorage?"

"Aside from the fact that it would be moved farther away from Cole Island, as my opponents are prone to say?" Josh smiled slightly. "No, of course it wouldn't be a disaster, Brad. But it would be a totally unnecessary move, an unnecessary expense. And all for what? Just because Juneau is a little more inaccessible, restricted to growth because of a limited land area? Not a good enough reason, in my opinion. Also, the relocation of a state capital is always traumatic to the public for a time. There's also a certain flouting of tradition. The advantages, in my honest opinion, do not outweigh the disadvantages."

"And the movement for secession from the Lower 48, the drive for separate nation status? How does that look?"

"It's gaining followers every day, worse luck," Josh said grimly. "So far, we've been able to block it easily enough, but that issue worries me, Brad. It truly could be a disaster for Alaska. All the advocates can talk about is how the federal tax system is draining money out of the state since the oil boom. If we seceded from the United States, all that money would stay here, et cetera, et cetera. That, of course, is true enough, but it is sorely shortsighted. The oil will not last forever, then where would we be? Among the many advantages to being a part of the United States is the defense umbrella provided. We're vulnerable up here, Brad. Alone, we would have to build our own defense system, Army, Navy, and Air Force. That would bankrupt us in short order."

Brad was nodding. "I fully agree with you there, Senator. We would be left adrift like a crippled boat drifting in a sea of threatening icebergs if we cut all ties with the States."

"Fortunately, enough people still see it that way, but there are some formidable guys lining up behind secession, and they're growing in number every day. Even Will, who should know better. He claims that Cole Enterprises would be far better off if Alaska went it alone. I sometimes think that he's taken the other side just because I'm leading the fight against secession."

"It's clear to me, Senator, that you're badly needed where you are, not merely because of the vital issues you've mentioned. Your resignation from the Senate to take over the company, even assuming that the trustees would approve your appointment, would be a grave mistake."

"Which brings us back to Kelly."

"Which brings us back to Kelly, yes."

Both men fell silent for a few moments, busy with their own thoughts.

Finally Brad said wistfully, "Damn, but I miss Chris! Not only because of the company, but because he was my best friend. And that's funny, come to think about it. I'm sure you know, Josh, that I was in love with your daughter, before Chris entered the picture."

"Yes, I knew," Josh said soberly. "Chris was my friend, too, although I must confess that I was turned off him at first, when Kelly brought him home. Here was this construction stiff, a bulldozer operator, courting my daughter. I was sure that he was a fortune hunter. But he does grow on you. The way he got into Pap's good graces so quickly also put me off. Nobody was more amazed than I was when Pap appointed him president of Cole. I figured not only had he conned Kelly into marrying him, but he had conned Pap into giving him the job, a construction worker one day, president of Cole the next. Again, Chis proved me wrong. He ran Cole like he was born to it."

"Do you believe he's alive, Senator? You just said 'does grow on you.'"

Josh gave a startled grunt. "I did, didn't I? Sometimes, listening to Kelly, I almost believe. God knows, I want him to be alive, but I don't know how that's possible."

"About the will, Senator . . . perhaps if you had a word with Kelly in private, she might agree to follow your father's wishes."

"No." Josh shook his head forcibly. "That would be the worst thing I could ever do. She has to make up her own mind. Anything I might say at this stage would only get her back up."

After the scene in the study Kelly fled the house, hurrying through the gentle snow to the cabin.

She built a roaring fire and stood with her back to the flames, staring across the room at the canvas on the easel—a portrait of Chris, about two-thirds completed. She had started it after their honeymoon. She hadn't worked on it in the apartment in Anchorage, only here in the cabin, in secrecy. Chris didn't know about it, she wanted it to be a surprise for him. She knew he would have balked if asked to sit for it, but it wasn't necessary; she knew every line of his face as a blind person knows Braille.

She moved the easel over to where most light fell on it,

then stood back, chin propped on one hand, studying it intently.

The broad chest and wide shoulders, enclosed within the old mackinaw, were completed, as well as the shock of dark blond hair, tousled from the blowing wind, as she had so often seen it when Chris was at the tiller of the sailboat. The other features were only sketched in—a faint suggestion of the strong jaw and flaring nostrils. The rest of his face remained to be done, especially the eyes. She hadn't yet decided whether to try for that penetrating look he got when he was concentrating on some particular problem, or that gentle look that came when he made tender love to her.

She had lied to Chris that day when he found the paintings here. She *had* tried a portrait once; it had never been finished.

She crossed the room again and dug through the stack of old canvases until she found it, then carried it back to the fireplace and propped it against the couch so that the firelight fell full on it. She sat down cross-legged on the hearthrug and studied it intently. . . .

Gene Morgan had been her own age, seventeen when they met during her junior year in high school in Juneau. He had been a slim, athletic youth, with a puckish charm. He shared her love of sailing and was like a seal in the water. Yet for all of his love of strenuous activity, there was a surprising sensitivity under the surface.

They fell in love and spent almost every day of that summer's school vacation together. Kelly was just becoming proficient enough at sailing so that Josh and her grandfather finally consented to her handling the sailboat alone. She and Gene sailed almost every day, and played tennis often. As competitive and athletic as she was, Gene beat her badly. "Just because you're a female, babe, don't expect me to let you win. In fact, if you ever do beat me, I'll probably break my racket over your head. I hate to lose at anything, you might as well know that now."

Kelly really didn't mind; in fact, she attributed the fierceness of his play, his demand that she do her damnedest against him, to her later proficiency at the game.

When the weather was too rough for sailing, swimming, or playing tennis, they often sought the privacy of the cabin. It was there that Kelly lost her virginity, on a chill, gray day, the rain lashing at the window, on the hearthrug before a roaring fire.

It was a hasty fumbling episode, a snatch-and-grab encounter, and neither were fully unclothed when Gene entered her. Yet he was a considerate lover, gentle within his limits. Kelly did not attain a climax; it was only after several tries that she finally experienced the tension and full release of orgasm. During these interludes of passion, Gene improved only slightly as a lover, but it didn't matter all that much to Kelly. He wanted her, and their closeness, the sharing of their bodies, was enough for her at that time in her life.

The year before she had taken an art course in high school, and had fooled around with brushes and canvases intermittently since, but she had found no subject that really interested her, and she had the good sense to realize that she was horribly inept as yet. However, the process of struggling to make some vision come alive on canvas fascinated her.

Late one afternoon, after they had made love before the fire, she fondled his face, her fingers tracing each beloved feature, and she was seized by an inspiration.

"Gene," she said hesitantly, "I've been trying to paint, you know."

He raised his head to stare at her. "No, babe, I didn't know. You mean, pictures?"

She nodded. "And you know what I'd like to do? I'd like to paint you."

"Me?" He jabbed a finger against his chest, then fell back laughing. "Babe, you're off your skateboard, a goofy idea like that!"

"It's not all that funny." She struck him on the shoulder with her fist. "But if that's the way you're going to look at it, just forget the whole thing."

"Hey!" Sobering, he caught her hand. "You really are serious, aren't you?" At her nod he said, "Okay. It might be neat, at that. Me, Gene Morgan, you know, immortalized on canvas! How about that?"

And so it began. During their afternoons in the cabin, usually after making love before the fireplace, she painted. There were many false starts, as she worked timidly at times, and at other times feverishly. She had to scrape away four efforts before something began to take shape that she liked.

"Man, you do throw paint around," Gene said once. "You're paint from your ass to the tip of your nose."

What surprised Kelly most was his patience, sitting perfectly still for long periods of time. Later, in retrospect, she realized that Gene was vain about his looks—after all, last year he had been voted the handsomest boy in his class—and this was probably the high point of his young life, those good looks being put on canvas for all time.

Kelly was utterly absorbed in the portrait. She didn't know if it was good, bad, or indifferent, and didn't really care; the doing was what was important. In time the painting became more important to her than their lovemaking.

One afternoon, when the painting was, Kelly judged, about half completed, Gene announced, "We're going to have to skip a couple of sessions, babe. My dad promised to take me on a hunting trip before school starts. We're flying to Canada on Saturday. We'll be gone ten days."

Kelly never saw Gene again. The small plane carrying Gene and his father crashed in the wilds of Canada and their bodies were never found.

Now, in the cabin, Kelly stared at the painting. She had made up her mind several times to destroy the half-finished portrait, but could never bring herself to do so. She turned with it now, placing it gently on the flames, and watched bemusedly as it was quickly consumed.

She had never finished the portrait of Gene Morgan and he had died in a plane crash. She had never finished the painting of Chris and he had . . .

"No!" she exclaimed.

There was no connection between the unfinished paintings and the plane crashes. To believe that would be to believe in black magic, primitive superstitions!

Determinedly she crossed the room to her paintbox. Back before the easel, she took out and prepared her brushes, and then feverishly mixed paints.

Within a short time she was absorbed in finishing the portrait of Chris. Her concentration was so total that she was aware of nothing else. Once, she thought she heard a knock on the cabin door and a voice calling her name. She ignored it and painted on.

Another time, she straightened up to ease the ache in her back and was astounded to see that it was the middle of the afternoon and she realized that she was famished. She sneaked up to the main house and into the kitchen through the side door. Relieved to find the kitchen empty, she quickly made two thick sandwiches, found a half-full bottle of white wine, and hurried back to the cabin.

She gobbled the food too fast, washing it down with gulps of the chilled wine, and plunged back into painting again.

It was long after the early Alaskan darkness fell before she was finally satisfied. Standing back, she looked at the portrait. It was Chris, so real that it brought an ache to her throat. She had painted him with a slight, musing smile on his lips, and the special look he got in his eyes when he made love to her.

Now, now it was finished, and he would come back to her. . . .

She shook her head sharply. Damnit, she was hung up on that to the point of obsession.

Quickly she cleaned her brushes and put them away, then cleaned the paint from her hands and clothes as best she could. She left the painting where it was. She didn't want anyone to see it, not yet, but there was little danger of that. Everyone had long ago accepted this as her particular sanctuary, safe from invasion.

With a last, lingering look at the painting, she left the cabin and returned to Cole House.

Sneaking past the dining room where the others were at dinner, Kelly went down the hall to her room, and took a long, hot bath. Exhausted, she went to sleep at once, but awoke soon after, feeling hot and feverish, still on a high from the painting. She threw back the covers, removed her pajamas, and tried to get back to sleep lying nude atop the covers. It didn't work. In the end she got up and took two strong sleeping pills, something she rarely did.

Now she dreamed, dreamed of Chris beside her, his hands on her familiarly, those long-fingered, incredibly sensitive hands stroking her intimately, searching out those secret places no longer a secret to him.

In the dream she writhed, moaning, reaching her arms out to him; and then he was gone, as insubstantial as smoke, and an echo of his voice seemed to sound in her mind.

It was one of those dreams where the dreamer knows she is dreaming, and Kelly strove to awaken. The dream was painful; to awaken and find that it was indeed a dream would be preferable.

Then he was back, his mouth on hers, his kiss a sweet fire that swept through her, that consumed her. She felt his heated breath in her ear, and heard the familiar murmur of words, their private love song. An ecstasy began in the center of her being, like a new sun being born and then burst from her in a blinding explosion of rapture. She heard, dimly, her cry of completion.

Then he was gone again, leaving her arms and heart empty. Feeling bereft, she struggled to sit up, struggled to shatter the cocoon of the dream. She finally succeeded in raising her head.

In the French windows opening to the outside, she saw the shadowy figure, framed by the blowing curtains—Chris, dressed in the old mackinaw and scuffed boots, the way he usually dressed when out in the field.

His whisper came to her, carried on the breeze: "Take the job, my sweet. Don't let them destroy what your grandfather worked so hard to build. Do it for me, Kelly. Hold it together for me. Do it for me, for our love."

Fully awake now, and knowing that she was awake, Kelly blinked hard. There was nothing there—no Chris, no shadows, only the curtains billowing in the wind.

She was out of bed in an instant and to the window, and outside, bare feet cringing on the cold flagstones. The snow had stopped, the clouds had blown away, and the patio was washed by pale moonlight.

"Chris?"

There wasn't a soul in sight. She stood for a few moments, shivering in her nakedness. Finally she trudged back into the house, closing the French doors.

Had she left them open when she went to bed the second time? In midwinter? Try as she might, she couldn't remember. Her mind had been in such a turmoil over the will that nothing else had stuck in her memory.

Getting back into bed, she pulled the blankets up to her chin, trying to get warm again.

Usually when she dreamed, Kelly could not remember the details afterward, yet she knew that the details of this one would remain in her memory forever. But *had* it been a dream? Everything had seemed so real, even down to the orgasm. She felt herself blush in the dark. Was that all it had been, an erotic dream? What, in a man, would be called a wet dream? She was certain that a medical opinion would declare it as such. "You have been without a man for weeks, Mrs. O'Keefe, without sexual intercourse. The body, in sleep, has its own way of dealing with deprivation."

Yet the words Chris had spoken to her before he vanished had nothing to do with sex. Could she have dreamed those words because of the scene in the study, and the feelings of guilt she had experienced for flatly refusing to follow the wishes of her grandfather?

Or could the dream be a subconscious reaction to having spent the day finishing his portrait?

If it hadn't been a dream, there was only one other possible explanation, and that she did not want to believe.

Kelly had never believed in psychic phenomena. But if what had just happened was not a dream, or if Chris had not been here in the flesh, his ghost had spoken to her.

And if it had been a ghost, Chris was dead, truly dead.

"No!" she said aloud. "He is *not* dead, I will not have him dead!"

The words sounded so selfish that she felt a hot flush of shame. Tears came and she turned her face into the pillow to muffle the sobs.

When Kelly went into the dining room the next morning, they were all there, except for Dwight, whose absence did not surprise her; but she did experience a small start of astonishment at the presence of Will and Louise. She had expected them to be gone. Then she understood. Will had changed his mind—he intended to remain with Cole Enterprises and fight.

Before anyone saw her, Kelly said in a firm voice, "I have an announcement to make."

Five pairs of eyes swung in her direction—Will and Louise, her father, Brad Connors, and Charlene Baker.

Josh pushed his chair back, getting to his feet. He took a step toward her. "Kelly, are you all right? You missed dinner last night and I . . ."

"I'm fine, Daddy." She held up a hand to stay him. "I had

some thinking to do. Brad..." She looked directly at the attorney. "I have decided to do what Grandfather wished." She switched her glance to Will, and was faintly surprised to see a wide grin spreading across his face. "God only knows how it'll come out, but I have made up my mind to accept the presidency of Cole Enterprises."

Book Two

"If we cut Alaska in two,
then Texas would be the third largest
state in the Union."

Four

After taking off from the Fairbanks airport, Will Cole turned the Bellanca north, angling slightly east, maintaining a low altitude. His gaze was searching for the broad slash of scarred tundra left by the construction machines clearing the way for the Trans-Alaska pipeline. One he had located it, he would follow it to his destination.

"There it is, Mr. Cole," said Red Patterson, his cabin companion, pointing a finger.

"I see it, Red. Thanks."

He aligned the Bellanca with the pipeline and flew steadily north.

In 1957 a geologist for an oil company had kicked a tree in moose country on the Kenai peninsula south of Anchorage and said, "Drill here."

They drilled on the spot, and that was the start of the first oil field and the discovery of oil in Alaska. It was only one of the wells brought in during the next few years in and around Cook Inlet, but it was the first, and the Anchorage Chamber of Commerce appropriated the geologist's boot and had it plated with gold.

In Will Cole's opinion, they would be ass-deep in goldplated boots if one of *his* was plated every time he brought in a producing well in a new location, and he had only a smattering of geology. When he was attending the University of Alaska, the idea of oil ever being discovered up here was as farfetched as a man ever setting foot on the moon, so why waste time studying geology?

Also, he had been one of the first with the foresight to envision the possibility of vast oil reserves on the North Slope, and he had gotten Cole 98 into the oil lease business early. He let somebody else do the drilling. It was never decided exactly how much money was spent over a span of years drilling one dry well after another on the North Slope until oil was finally discovered in 1967, but it mounted up into the millions, some said more than a billion.

Will had been fortunate enough to have leased several tracts of land not too distant from the first producing well on the North Slope, Prudhoe No. 1, and Cole 98 commenced drilling operations within a short time. Cole 98 was considerably smaller than the other companies in the consortium, but a percentage of the oil that would be flowing through the Trans-Alaska pipeline when completed would belong to Cole 98.

Cole Airlines had many modern aircraft, including several jets, along with pilots, at Will's disposal, but he preferred the Bellanca. He had flown her into and out of every nook and cranny of Alaska without harm. He was fond of the plane, and as familiar with her as with an old friend. He kept the aircraft in excellent condition, having it serviced by Cole Airlines mechanics after every flight. Will often boasted that he could land it in a truck bed.

Plane crashes were common in this harsh climate, especially private planes. Roads were few, and most people who could afford one, owned a small plane. Will rarely flew the Bellanca on out-of-state flights, since there was an executive jet at his disposal. He could boast, and often did, that he had never made a landing in the Bellanca that he couldn't walk away from.

Except for Red Patterson, he was alone in the plane. Privately Will thought of Red as his "gofer," in the sense that the term had been coined by the movie industry. Red was his fetch-and-carry man; one of his more difficult chores was nagging Will to be on time for appointments. However, he never thought of Red in a contemptuous way. Red served a valuable function, although he rarely spoke a dozen words a day. Yet he was his own man, no yes-man, no sycophant; he didn't hesitate to speak his mind. Will happened to know that the man was terrified of flying, which said a great deal for his guts, considering the air time they logged together.

All along the tundra below were men and scattered equipment. They were into March now, and winter had slowed construction considerably. Will's destination was about twenty miles north of Livengood Camp, beyond the Yukon River.

That, he had learned, was where Bry Tucker, the president of the union representing most of the pipeline construction workers, would be this morning. Apparently the welders doing repairs on the already completed pipeline section had some sort of beef and were threatening to strike, and Bry Tucker, like a latter-day Jesus venturing among the wicked, was going to bring labor peace to the tundra.

At a cost, Will thought dourly, probably at a high cost; another number of bucks added to the already staggering cost of the pipeline.

He had butted heads with Tucker once before, at a union-management session. There Tucker had come on suave and soft-spoken—as soft-spoken as that gut-bucket voice of his would allow—but getting what he wanted. Will fancied that he could size up a man, any man, pretty quick, and he knew that the place for a confrontation with the Irisher was on his own turf, on a construction site. Not only had Tucker been a construction worker before becoming a union official, he'd been a professional boxer in his youth, and a good one, Will understood.

But it was high time somebody stood up to the arrogant bastard. Not long ago Tucker had boasted that he could "close down the pipeline with a snap of my fingers any time I wish," a boast receiving wide circulation in the press.

Will flew over Livengood Camp, a large cluster of buildings, as comfortable, he knew, as any motel back in Fairbanks. He admitted that it might get lonely and boring as hell, nothing to do after a long day's labor but eat and sleep, play cards or pool, read, or watch movies. Although if the rumors he'd heard were correct, booze and hookers, even drugs, were being smuggled into the camps.

The Bellanca droned on, its shadow skimming along the tundra like an enormous bird of prey in close pursuit of the plane. Far up ahead loomed the forbidding Brooks Range, a huge hump of brown rock and snow.

My country, Will Cole thought; still my own country, even if it is being overrun by Outsiders.

A big man, Will Cole, six-four, with a big voice, a booming laugh, a lusty appetite for life, and an explosive temper.

Will began to lose some altitude. He paid little attention to the instrument panel. Except for the fuel gauges, most instruments this close to the North Pole were not much use anyway. He flew by sight and the seat of his pants; in this instance mostly by sight, since all he had to do was follow the pipeline.

Now he saw two red bulldozers, several trucks, and pickups parked in a cluster. To one side was a helicopter. Nothing was moving, except for the lazily rotating chopper blades, and Will knew that Bry Tucker was here, undoubtedly transported by the whirlybird.

He peered about for the best place to land; since the Bellanca had skis instead of wheels, all he needed was a hundred yards or so of even, frozen tundra.

"Oh, my God, look!" Red Patterson exclaimed from the other seat.

Will took his gaze from the ground and looked up ahead. "Jesus Christ in a wheelbarrow!"

About the worst Arctic hazard to flying, except for an actual blizzard, was a "blowing snow condition." The sky may be clear, not a snowflake falling, when a sudden, and strong, wind can sweep across the tundra, picking up loose snow as it comes, until the ground is, in effect, experiencing a blizzard. It can last from a few minutes to several hours, but while it exists ground visibility is practically zero.

And there was one on its way, a wall of snow at least fifty feet high, and it would almost certainly hit before they could touch down.

Will took a last look at the spot he'd picked out to land, fixed it firmly in his mind, and took dead aim at it, both hands gripping the wheel strongly.

"Hang on, Red, here we go!"

"Mr. Cole, you're not going to land in *that*?"

"What would you have me do?"

"Well . . ." Red drew a deep breath. "Sometimes they don't last very long. Maybe we could circle a bit . . ."

"And sometimes they last for hours. I have that meeting back in Fairbanks at two, remember? You were careful to remind me of it when we left the airport."

"I know, Mr. Cole, but nobody can land in that!"

"I can. Just watch me." Will's teeth flashed white in a grin. "What the hell, when you went to work for me, I didn't promise to see to it you'd live forever, now did I?"

They were into it now, flying blind. The force of the wind

was fierce, and there was a great deal of buffeting. Will's big hands fought the wheel. He let the air speed drop just short of stalling.

He was literally flying by the seat of his pants, feeling for the ground with his ass.

If he cut the speed too low, too soon, the Bellanca would plummet like a stone. If he hit the ground at too high a speed, the plane would bounce, possible with enough force to disintegrate.

He waited until all his instincts told him that the ground was there.

Now!

He hauled back on the yoke, and the plane touched down with only a slight bounce and glided smoothly along on the skis.

Will gently braked the aircraft to a stop, cut the motors, and leaned back. The only sound was the wind screaming at them. He extracted a Monte Cristo from his pocket and lit it before glancing over at Red with a solemn face. "Well?"

"Mr. Cole, if I may say so, that was a damned fool thing to do!"

"Granpap Jeremiah says it's only a damn fool thing if you don't get away with it."

"Mr. Cole . . ." Red sighed, gesturing. "Look."

Will looked. The wind had died as suddenly as it had started up, the snow settling. He glanced toward the cluster of machines and saw men running toward the plane.

"Looks like a few people might have been a touch concerned. Let's go reassure them."

They reached behind the seats for their parkas and shrugged into them, put on mittens of mouton fur. Will wore a black corduroy jumpsuit and mukluks. His parka hood was lined with white wolf fur.

Red pushed open the door and jumped down, with Will right behind him. The men running toward the plane, on seeing that the passengers were all right, slowed to a walk, then stopped altogether at a gesture from the big man in the lead. All the men wore thick clothing. Some wore face protectors, with breathing holes, and snow goggles.

Will and Red Patterson advanced to meet them.

The big man, about Will's height, with rust-colored hair

and a nose that had been broken several times and reset crookedly, was in his fifties. He said sourly, "I might have known. Will Cole, showing off as usual."

"Mr. Tucker, I presume," Will said with a grin. Then he scowled. Privately he was willing to grant the truth of the charge. He had been showing off, a little; he had found, in the past, that showing off, if he got away with it, often gave him an edge in any confrontation, with one man or a group.

He made his voice harsh. "I hardly think you know me well enough, Tucker, to make a remark like that."

"Not personally, no, but your reputation precedes you, Cole."

"And so does yours." Will gestured. "Now suppose we get to the bottom of the trouble here."

"I don't know as it's any of your damned business, but come along and I'll show you."

They started toward the pipeline. Will pretty much knew what the trouble was. It was another of many, and expensive, foul-ups that had plagued the pipeline from the beginning.

When two sections of pipe were welded together, X-rays were taken of the welds to ascertain how strong they were, and only recently it had been discovered that one of the firms doing the work had submitted X-rays showing good welds, when in reality the welds hadn't been X-rayed at all. The welders had worked so fast that the X-ray teams couldn't keep up and had covered up their inefficiency by submitting false X-rays. Now several hundred welds had to be uncovered and X-rayed again. A number had been found faulty and had to be rewelded.

As they neared the work area, all the men headed for their trucks or pickups and climbed into the heated cabs to await the outcome of the discussion. Will noted that the two bulldozer operators hadn't even bothered to leave their cabs.

Will, Bry Tucker, and Red Patterson stood together around one faulty weld.

"So," Will said, "what's the beef here?"

"It's the weather, that's the beef," Tucker replied. "It's ten below today, not counting the wind chill factor."

"So what are you giving me, a weather report? Winter's still here and this is Alaska."

"And these welders are freezing their tails off!" Tucker snapped. "They want the tents put up."

In extremely cold weather, tents were erected around the welds, with portable heaters, so the welders wouldn't freeze. Also, if the wind was as strong as it was today, it made the welding difficult.

"At only ten below? Come on, Tucker, nobody freezes at only ten below," Will said. "Up here, we consider that just a little chilly."

"These men are not used to working in this kind of weather. All the welders in this bunch are from Oklahoma and this is their first year up here."

"Tucker, we don't start using the tents until it gets much colder than this."

"I want the tents up now or the workers walk."

"*You* want? You're not working out here. You've just been flown in from a nice, cozy office, right?"

"Listen, I spend far more time in the field than I do in my office. Look, I don't know why I'm wasting my time talking to you, anyway. Of all the members of the consortium, Cole 98 must be down somewhere near the bottom of the totem pole. What authority do you have out here, bucko?"

"Totem pole, huh? That's down-to-earth jargon. You're a real old-timer, aren't you?" Will jeered. He rapped mittened knuckles on a stand of pipe. "And never mind where Cole 98 stands. The others are all afraid to dirty their hands, to do anything about a million things going sour with the pipeline. So if they won't do it, it's up to me. And you seem to forget something... I'm not just head of Cole 98, but head honcho of Cole Enterprises, the whole shooting match."

"You've elected yourself spokesman for all the oil companies, eh?" Tucker looked at him with skeptical eyes. "Now that's what I call democracy and they say *I'm* a dictator..." He gestured abruptly. "Never mind, *I* represent the men, the union, make no mistake about that, bucko. And I say they get tents. Now."

Will shrugged negligently. "Oh, I'll see to it that the tents are erected tomorrow. It is pretty cold out here, colder than I realized, and I have no wish to see anyone suffer unnecessary hardship."

Tucker stared at him, taken aback. "Just like that?"

"Just like that. If a man's right, I never give him a hard time. But if he's wrong, that's an entirely different matter." Will faced the union boss squarely, face hard as flint. "Like three weeks ago, the men up at Chandalar Camp wanted a special barbecue sauce flown in from Texas for a weekend barbecue. When it wasn't flown in on demand, they went on a strike for two whole days. Now, that's completely and utterly unreasonable."

"I had nothing to do with that," Tucker said quickly. "That was a wildcat strike, unauthorized by me. Disciplinary action is being taken."

"I don't believe you," Will said flatly. "I think you gave the unofficial word to call that *wildcat* strike."

"Can you prove that?"

"Of course I can't prove it. But I don't need to prove it. That's really why I'm out here today. To tell you not to pull a stunt like that again or it's your ass that will be held responsible, never mind this wildcat business."

"You'll hold my ass responsible?" Tucker's stare was incredulous. "Who the hell do you think you are to threaten me like that? Oh, I know you're a Cole and the Coles are big, big men in Alaska. I've battled your grandfather for years. You're all good at flinging threats around. But let me tell you what I can do, and I'm not just talking about the pipeline now. I've got more clout than you know. For instance, your old man is soon up for reelection in the U.S. Senate. If I want to make the effort, I can see to it that he isn't elected."

"You're full of it up to your Adam's apple," Will said calmly. "But I'm not worried about Josh, he can take care of himself. And if he can't, it's still his problem. I've never voted for him, anyway. But when I was talking about your ass, I mean I'll whip it from here to the North Slope if there's any more Mickey Mouse labor troubles."

"You're threatening me physically? Jesus!" Tucker threw back his head and laughed. "I've got a few years on you, true, bucko, but I not only worked construction for years, I was a pro fighter for five years. And what have you done? Sat on your duff raking in all that dough in a cushy office!"

"I know about your pro record, Irisher. But no championship belts. Why is that, you suppose? Second-raters, that's all you ever fought, second-raters. And up here we don't go by Marquis of Queensberry rules, we fight with everything available. As for my sitting in a cushy office, you know better."

Tucker cocked his head, studying Will in speculation. "You want to try me now? I'm feeling pretty chipper this morning."

Will hesitated, tempted, temper running strong in him.

At his side Red Patterson cleared his throat. "Mr. Cole, you have to be back in Fairbanks..."

"All right, Red, stop nagging!" he snapped, gaze never leaving Tucker's face. "That would be a pretty sight, wouldn't it? The union president and the president of Cole going at it like two sled dogs, in front of these men?"

"It's all the same to me. They've seen me fight before." Bry Tucker shrugged. "Anyway, it was your suggestion, bucko. Show you what an agreeable guy I am, I'll let you pick the time and place."

"Like I said, if you get out of line, I will. I'm going to be around much more from now on, in your hair constantly. You'll be seeing much more of me."

"Oh, goody gumdrops! Of course—" Tucker's smile was enigmatic—"I'll be seeing you much sooner than you think."

As he started off with Red, Will wondered what Tucker meant by his last remark. At a sound to his right he glanced up at the cab of the nearest bulldozer, and saw the operator looking out the open door.

Will shrugged, striding on. So one of the workers had eavesdropped on the conversation. That could be to his benefit. Let the subject of his talk with the union boss get around, and the workers would know that Will Cole was going to keep a closer watch on them.

He was satisfied. That had been his real purpose in coming here today.

He quickened his step. Good humor restored, he said, "Hurry it up, Red. Don't want me to be late for that meeting, do you?"

A voice spoke behind them. "Mr. Cole? Could I have a few minutes of your time?"

Five

Christopher O'Keefe, leaning out the half-open door of his bulldozer, had listened with great interest to the exchange between Bry Tucker and Will Cole.

Chris was one of those rare birds, a native Californian. After graduating from Cal State Los Angeles six years ago, he had determined to see some of the world before settling down. His goals in life were largely undefined, and he was hoping to find himself by knocking around the globe for a spell.

And the funny thing was, he was enjoying himself more now, here in this ball-breaking cold, than he had at any one place on his odyssey. That was what he had named it six years ago—Chris's Odyssey, the search for the golden fleece.

Oh, there had been other times when he had enjoyed himself, times when he had marveled with open-mouthed awe at the many wonders of the world—many more than seven. He had sweated in tropic heat, loved women of every size, description, and color; he had roistered and drunk and fornicated and fought, and worked at every job imaginable. It had been a ball, it had been an adventure he would never regret, but ironically his golden fleece was here, in the land of searing cold and the midnight sun—ironic because he had come from the land of eternal sunshine. He loved it here. It was, strangely, as if he had come home.

And yet, despite his liking for the country, and the job, there were several things that he was unhappy about; and that was why he had the bulldozer door open, letting in an Arctic blast, staring after Will Cole in an agony of indecision.

Chris was tall, rangy, with even features, with wavy blond hair long and rather shaggy at the moment, and intense brown eyes.

Abruptly he muttered, "Ah, to hell with it!"

He jumped down to the ground and loped after Will Cole and his red-haired companion. "Mr. Cole! Could I have a few minutes of your time?"

The big man broke stride, turning about. The man with him moved to intercept Chris. "Look here, fellow, Mr. Cole is a busy man."

"Never mind, Red." Will Cole clamped a hand on the redhead's shoulder. "What is it, young man? Didn't I just see you in the cab of that bulldozer back there?"

"You did, Mr. Cole. I'm Christopher O'Keefe. I've been working on the pipeline six months and I've seen some things..." Chris broke off, still reluctant to play the role of squealer, as juvenile as the reluctance might be.

Will's gaze sharpened. "Six months, huh? Then I expect you *have* seen a few things."

"I have."

"But why tell me? You have some ax to grind, a hard-on for somebody?"

"No ax to grind. It's just that I've seen some things that boil me."

Will exhaled softly. "All right, Christopher, I'm listening."

"Union featherbedding for one. I've always thought that a man should give a day's work for his pay, and God knows we're paid well. But I expect you know about that."

"Some." Will took a long cigar from his pocket and stuck it into his mouth, unlit.

"But that's not the worst part. It's the liquor trucked out here and sold at outrageous prices, the hookers brought out in campers, charging fifty, a hundred a pop. Even drugs are sold, the hard stuff."

"You know this for a fact?" Will's voice was harsh. "Can you prove it, and prove who's behind it?"

"I've seen it with my own eyes, but I don't know for sure who's behind it, only a rumor. And there's more... workers drive equipment off the job, dump trucks, cats, even bulldozers. They sell them somewhere, probably in Fairbanks."

"You say you've heard rumors of who's behind it. Is there a name attached to the rumors?"

"Yes. Milo Fanti. The same rumors say that he was a Mafia big shot, who was sent up here into exile."

"Milo Fanti? I've heard the name." Will turned his back to

the wind, skillfully lit a kitchen match, and cupped his hands around the cigar until it was burning evenly. Then he looked at Chris appraisingly for a full minute. "Christopher O'Keefe? Chris?"

"Right."

"Like your job?"

"Well enough."

"You're about what . . . twenty-six, seven?" At Chris's nod, Will said thoughtfully, "You have ambitions, or you want to remain a dozer operator for the rest of your natural life?"

Chris felt a stir of temper. "I have ambitions, sure."

Will grinned. "But it's none of my business, right? Well, maybe, maybe not. But I'm in a position to do you some good."

"In exchange for what?"

"In exchange for doing a little undercover work for me."

Chris frowned.

"You said all these things boiled you. Here's your chance to do something about it. I'd like to put a stop to all this. But I need some proof, some names, not just rumors."

"Other people have said they would like to stop it. Nobody has so far, or even tried very hard, as far as I can see."

"When I tell you I'll do something, you can take it to the bank. I'm not just blowing smoke here."

Chris was silent for a few moments, studying Will Cole. "Okay, I'll see what I can find out, but I want your word on something."

"What's in it for you?"

Chris batted a hand at him. "No, not that. I'm not asking to be paid. If I help you and you act on it, that will be pay enough. What I want from you is your word that you'll take action if I come up with anything."

"I just gave it. We'll shake on it." Will held out his hand.

Chris didn't take it. "Shaking hands is not a good idea, there're too many eyes on us. I'll tell them that I braced you for a better job and got turned down. But if they see us shaking hands, they'll know I'm lying."

Will nodded approvingly. "Good thinking. You're fast on your feet."

"I want you to know one more thing. If I turn some hard facts over to you and you *don't* move on it, that'll be the last you hear from me."

Will's stare turned flinty. "I just gave you my word and my word is good. Ask anybody."

"Oh, I'm sure you mean it now. But if you stir things up, you're going to be tromping on some important toes, and that may influence your thinking."

Will said coolly, "When you find out anything, Mr. O'Keefe, call my office in Fairbanks. Give the girl your name. She'll have instructions to patch you through no matter where I may be. Come along, Red, we're running late."

He turned on his heel and strode toward the plane. Chris stood where he was, watching as the two men boarded the plane. In a few minutes the plane began to taxi. Then Will Cole poured the power to it, and the aircraft lifted off, trailing a cloud of snow behind it.

At a shout from Cody Brant, the job foreman, Chris glanced behind him. The men were piling out of the warm truck cabs and going back to work. Chris headed for his machine and climbed into the cab.

There were two bulldozers on the job; they were being used to unearth and rebury the sections of pipeline completed and buried months ago. It's a damned good thing part of the pipeline is aboveground, Chris mused, or we'd be at this the rest of the year.

He fired a cigarette, watching the sparks from the welding torches fly into the face of the stiff wind still sweeping across the tundra.

At a clanking sound, Chris glanced to his right. The other dozer operator was climbing down out of his cab. Reaching the ground, he looked up, saw Chris watching him, and turned his back. The man's name was Ben Slocum, a big hulk of a man from Oklahoma. He had only been working the pipeline for two months, his first time in Alaska, and already he was cursing the cold with foul-mouthed vigor. Many of the workers were from the South, or the near South, and they hated the vicious cold.

Chris watched Slocum, smiling to himself in anticipation of what was about to happen. Then he heard the man curse and he laughed aloud as Slocum turned.

His penis was out, and he had urinated all over the front of his trousers, the droplets freezing as they splattered.

Chris cracked his side window and called down, "You dumb bastard, haven't you learned yet not to piss into the wind?"

Slocum gawked up at him, face flushing scarlet. "What are you laughing at?"

"Why, at you, turkey. At the size of your pecker," Chris said casually. "I've seen bigger ones on toy poodles. And you'd better put it back into your pants before what little you've got freezes off."

Slocum hastily stuffed himself in and zipped up. He glared up at Chris. "Where I come from a man never talks about another man's peter!"

"In your case, that could be because there's so little to talk about." Chris realized that he was feeling belligerent, and knew that it sprang from vague feelings of guilt over agreeing to spy on his fellow workers. Even allowing that somebody should do it, it was a demeaning endeavor.

"You sonofabitch, you can't talk to me like that!" Slocum yelled. "You and your snotty ways! Whyn't you come down here where I can whomp the shit out of you?"

"Thought you'd never ask," Chris said cheerfully. "I'll be happy to oblige. Don't go away now."

He opened the door and climbed down. There was nothing like a little sparring match in this weather to warm up the blood. Boredom was as much the enemy along the pipeline as the cold, and a fistfight always livened things up. Besides, he didn't particularly like Ben Slocum, a foul-mouthed, ignorant redneck.

Chris stepped gingerly to the ground; it was slick as glass, and the wind pricked at any exposed areas of the skin like needles of ice.

At least he had on Sorel boots with neoprene soles, soles that didn't slip easily on oil or ice. Slocum wore square-toed work boots, with leather soles. Still, that wasn't as bad as when he'd arrived. The first week the silly bastard had tried to get around in cowboy boots and tumbled ass-over-teakettle a number of times before he'd finally gotten the message.

Of course, with all the thick, heavy clothing they wore, neither could inflict much damage on the other.

Chris danced in and out, flicking light jabs at the other's exposed face, while Slocum lumbered like a bear, swinging sledgehammer blows that missed almost every time. Once, he swung so hard that his momentum carried him around and around like a top on the slick ground. Finally, his feet flew out from under him, and he landed on his tailbone with a yelp of pain.

It was slapstick, pure slapstick, and Chris doubled over with laughter. And then agony exploded in his thigh. From the ground Slocum had aimed a boot at him, barely missing his genitals. Chris was slammed back against the bulldozer. By the time he could straighten up, Slocum was on his feet and coming at him. It was no longer a game; it was in deadly earnest now. Adrenaline pumped through Chris, charging him up, but not beyond the point of caution. He ducked down and away from Slocum's charge; and as he did so, he swung a fist into the man's midsection, getting all his weight into it. His first sank through layers of clothing, burrowing into the soft beer belly. Air whooshed out of Slocum. He stumbled on past, bent over with his hands across his belly, and rammed headfirst into the side of the bulldozer.

Chris turned, guard up, as Slocum ricocheted off the side of the machine and sprawled on his back. Chris approached him warily.

It wasn't necessary. The fight had gone out of Slocum. He was half stunned by the collison with the bulldozer and lay moaning. He had scraped skin from a goodly portion of his forehead, from which blood oozed.

A voice bellowed from behind Chris: "All right, playtime is over, you guys! The weld is done. Cover the pipe, so we can head back to camp. This is the last one today." It was Cody Brant. Hands on hips, he stood glowering down at the prone Slocum. "Is he able to navigate?"

"Oh, sure," Chris said. "He's just a little groggy."

Brant jerked a thumb. "Then we get him into the cab, so we can finish up here and get our butts back to camp."

Chris managed to scrape a handful of loose snow from where it had blown against the huge bulldozer tire. He dumped it onto Slocum's face and scrubbed vigorously.

Slocum came out of it, shouting, "What the hell!"

"Time to get back to work, so we can knock off for the day. Come on, on your feet."

Chris helped the man up and steered him toward his machine. Awareness seeped back into Slocum's eyes, and he jerked his arm out of Chris's grip. He thrust his face close, his breath foul. "I'll even things with you, peckerwood, first chance I get!"

"It's your option, turkey," Chris said.

Going back to his own bulldozer, Chris realized that he was limping. He touched the spot on his thigh were Slocum's boot had connected. It was sore as a boil. He was going to have one hell of a bruise for a few days.

He pulled himself up into the cab and shut the door. Before him was an array of levers and pedals. He pulled the two clutch levers, one for each track, and the bulldozer lurched into grinding motion, black smoke pouring from the exhaust stack, making the hinged lid dance. At the exposed pipe he braked the heavy machine, and manipulated the lever that controlled the hydraulic dozer blade.

Six

Will Cole was late, after all, twenty minutes late, and the half-dozen men waiting in the Cole boardroom scowled at him in varying degrees of displeasure when the door finally swung open and he loped in, Red Patterson trailing in his wake.

Of course Will was always in a hurry and he was always late. This cut little ice with the men awaiting him. Each man represented a powerful oil company. Operating at the top executive level as they did, they were not accustomed to being kept waiting.

To make matters worse, Will was still wearing his black corduroy jumpsuit, under a fur-lined parka, and mukluks, smeared with dried mud. He shed the parka. slinging it over the back of the chair at the head of the table.

All six of the men in the room, immaculately turned out in suits and ties, faced him like a group of disapproving bankers.

Ignoring the frigid reception, Will said breezily, "Sorry to be tardy, gents. I was up the pipeline a ways. Had to wait fifteen minutes to get clearance to land at the airport." He paused for a breath and to fish a cigar out of his pocket. "So, what's your pleasure, gents?"

"Pleasure?" asked one.

"Drink! What would you like to drink?"

"But it's only the middle of the afternoon. I don't want a drink at this time of the day."

"Rest of you feel the same?" Will's gray eyes raked over the stony faces. He shrugged. "Different strokes for different folks. Granpap Jeremiah always says a man should act kind of skittish around anyone who doesn't drink, especially up here in Alaska. Must be coldblooded as a snake, he says. Otherwise, he'd freeze his gonads. Alcohol's the best antifreeze

ever invented. As for the time . . . who watches clocks in the
land of the midnight sun?"

Terence Blanchard, the only one of the six Will knew
personally, said, "We *are* here on business, Will. At least I
assume so. You asked us here."

"Damn right it's business. Serious business." Will jerked
his head. "Bring in the briefcase, Red. You know the one."

The redheaded man went into the adjoining office, which
was Will's own, and Will turned his back on the others. In
the far wall he pressed a button, and the doors to a large
liquor cabinet slid silently open. Will splashed a glass half full
of Jack Daniel's and strode to the window, looking out on
downtown Fairbanks and sipping bourbon. The building he
was in was located on Cushman Street; Cole Enterprises
occupied the whole top floor. Will could barely make out the
serpentine twist of the Chena River which ran through the
town. Now the river was frozen solid, the banks piled high
with snow.

The six men in the boardroom gazed at his back, all
wondering exactly what this was all about and what kind of a
man they were dealing with. For instance, it was said of Will
that he had once wrestled a grizzly bear to a draw. They
didn't know whether this story was apocryphal or not. Except
for Blanchard, they were relatively new to Alaska and had
learned that it was the land of the tall tale: Paul Bunyan
country, with the bone-cracking cold an additional mythic
fuel.

There were many tales about Will Cole, and it was difficult
to sift fact from myth. Until recently, it hadn't mattered so
much. As VP of Cole 98, Will had had some clout, but had
not been in the same league with these men. Now, since
Jeremiah's retirement and Will's elevation to the top spot, he,
Will, was playing first string, and it was a whole new ball
game. Waiting, they exchanged uneasy, furtive glances.

Will, back still to the room, was thinking about them, and
his thoughts were not particularly flattering. They were all
soft, office types. He wondered if any one of them had ever
gotten oil and mud smeared on him around a drilling rig. He
wouldn't have been at all surprised to learn that not a single
goddamned one of them had ever *seen* a rig.

Their kind took no risks, never got their hands dirty. They
were indoor men who never placed themselves in physical

danger. They didn't do things for the pure joy of doing them, but only for the power and money it gained them. Their twin gods were profit and greed. Will knew that he was just as hungry for power and money, but they had no other reason for being.

Red Patterson returned with a bulging briefcase. He said, "Mr. Cole?"

Will faced around, finished his drink with a toss of his head, and took the briefcase. He turned it upside down and dumped the contents onto the table, a mass of newspaper clippings cascading down. Will combed through them with his fingers, letting several trickle down separately from the larger pile. "*This* is what I wanted to meet about. Did any of you know about this? Here...from a Los Angeles newspaper: 'Trans-Alaska Pipeline Thievery Estimated at $1 Billion!'" He glared around. "A billion, gents!"

Blanchard said, "I think they're exaggerating the amount, Will."

"Exaggerating, hell! Here..." He scrabbled through the stack for another clipping, then waved it at them. "Twenty-some odd dump trucks disappear, then it's learned that they've been sold down in Mexico. Jesus Christ in a wheelbarrow! Some sonofabitch steals twenty trucks, gets down to Mexico some way, and sells them!" He rapped the table with his knuckles. "That is absolutely unbelievable!"

"Mr. Cole, you must have known there was thievery going on," one of the men said. "We've known it for some time."

"I knew, sure I knew, at least I'd heard rumors. But I didn't know it was on this scale. The news had to get to me from out-of-town newspapers. I know that Outside newspapers like to badmouth us, but today, less than two hours ago, I had some of this confirmed by a pipeline worker. Now, I'd like to know what's being done about it."

"We have a security force, Mr. Cole, but we don't have enough men to patrol eight hundred miles of pipeline."

Will was silent for a moment, gaze jumping from face to face. "I'm getting a feeling here. You guys don't really give a damn, do you?"

"Well, Will..." Blanchard cleared his throat with a slight air of embarrassment. "The whole thing is cost plus, after all."

Will dropped down into a chair. "And that's it right there,

ain't it, gents? Whatever the cost of the thievery, we just add it to the cost of the construction. In fact, it's even better that way. The more the pipeline costs, the more we all come out ahead, since our percentage is much higher that way."

"Cole 98 is a member of the consortium, Mr. Cole," one man said coldly. "You profit as much as we do."

"You know what cost plus is, gents? It's a goddamned license to steal, no more, no less. I wasn't for it in the beginning. I felt sure that bills would be padded, that there'd be featherbedding, pilferage, that kind of shit, but this..." He slammed a fist into the pile of clippings. "This is too much!"

"Perhaps you have a solution to offer, Mr. Cole? We would be most happy to hear it."

"Not at the moment, no, but I'm sure as hell going to look into it. In fact, I've already started something going."

"Good luck, Will," Blanchard said dryly. "You know, one thing I don't quite understand here. I've known you for a long time and I've heard stories. Don't get angry now, but some of the business dealings Cole 98 has been involved in in the past haven't been... well, all that ethical." He added hastily, "Business-wise, I mean."

"If I'm locked into business competition with someone, I'll bust the other guy's head to win, if necessary, but this is different. You know who's going to pay for all this? The taxpayers. And the guy at the gas pump. I know, that's to laugh, people like us worrying about the poor taxpayers. But damnit, there has to be a limit. Worst of all, these newspaper stories—" waving a hand at the clippings—"are giving us a black eye up here. The Lower 48 must be thinking we're all becoming criminals in Alaska! There's even talk of a congressional investigation into the whole mess."

One man who had yet to say anything spoke up. "The exigencies of the situation demand that we overlook certain things. The energy crisis, the demand for oil. The pipeline is desperately needed, Mr. Cole. With it in operation the United States will no longer be so dependent for oil on those Arabian bandits."

"So anything goes, huh?" Will sneered. "Like this bastard, this union guy, Bry Tucker. Where does he get off saying he can close the pipeline down with a snap of his fingers? That's why all those strikes have been settled so quickly, isn't it? Give 'im anything he wants so long as he doesn't make waves? What the hell, if the toilet paper is a little rough for the workers, Tucker threatens to close down the pipeline until his men get softer TP!"

"The only alternative, Will," Blanchard said quietly, "is to see the pipeline closed down. Costly delays, that much longer getting it finished."

"But this man is a dictator. There has to be a better way to deal with him than just to give in to all his demands."

"If there is, we haven't found one."

"Well, let me tell you something. That's where I was today, up where they're repairing some welds. I learned that Tucker was to be there, all ready to have the welders walk. If I hadn't gone up there, we would have had a strike on our hands." He wisely didn't add that *he* had given in to Tucker's demand. Since it had been a reasonable request, Will didn't believe that he had made a wrong decision. "And I warned him that he wouldn't be getting everything his way from now on."

"I notice there's one thing in those articles you haven't mentioned, Mr. Cole." This came from yet another quarter, accompanied by a smug smile. "The crime wave here in Fairbanks, in Anchorage, and Valdez. Gambling, illegal liquor, drugs, and prostitutes making a thousand dollars a night. *That* has been covered in your local papers. Surely you're aware of that, so why haven't you gotten around to that, Mr. Cole?"

"I'll tell you one reason." Will gave the table an angry rap with his knuckles. "Those guys work their tails off out there ten, eleven hours a day, seven days a week, then get one, maybe two weeks' R&R leave. Most of them come to Fairbanks, Anchorage, or Valdez. They've got a pocketful of cash, they haven't been laid in weeks. What are they supposed to do when they get here? Play with themselves? What the hell, they can do that out there!"

The man who had asked the question reared back, sharp nose elevated as though he'd suddenly received a whiff of ordure.

Will leaned toward him. "And don't give me that superior look! Where do *you* go after a day's work, if you ever do a day's work? Home to the wife and kiddies in a nice pad in Anchorage? Maybe a twice-weekly stop-off for a quickie with the mistress and/or secretary?"

"I didn't come here to be insulted!"

"Then don't insult my intelligence!" Will snapped. "A man has appetites and by God he's going to satisfy them one way or another."

"Gentlemen, gentlemen," Blanchard interposed. "This will get us nowhere."

Will batted the air with one hand. "You're right, it won't. We're not getting anywhere, anyway, so we might as well break this up. Oh, there is one thing we do seem to agree on. Although I can't prove yet who's behind it, I've learned that liquor, drugs, and hookers are being trucked out to the work camps. That, I intend to put a stop to. Now, good day, gents, and thank you all for coming. If anything's to be done, I see that it's up to me to do it." He made a gesture of dismissal, got up, and turned his back on them to pour himself another drink. He stood at the window as they left in a group, all except Blanchard, who approached him tentatively.

"Will, are you going to play the bull in the china shop bit? If you do, if you start making waves, you may get pretty wet yourself."

Will turned, glowering. "Don't spout clichés at me, Terry! One thing . . . if I get wet, you can bet your socks a few other people will get drowned."

"You Coles." Blanchard shook his head. "You always go your own way, regardless."

"Seems to me you're forgetting a few things about us Coles, Terry. Alaska owes a hell of a lot to Granpap and Josh, never mind me. It's quite possible that Alaska wouldn't even be a state but for Josh, not that I'm sure that's such a good thing. And Granpap sure as hell contributed his part to the development of Alaska."

"I'm not denigrating what Alaska owes to the Cole family, Will, but times change."

"Not all that much." Will swept a hand across the window. "Except for the automobiles and electricity, maybe a thing or two else, Fairbanks is not much different from the boomtown it was when Granpap came here in 1903. Aw, hell, Terry! Let's not hassle each other." He clapped Blanchard on the shoulder. "We've known each other too long for that."

He walked with Blanchard to the door, arm still around his shoulders. "You'll be at the house tonight?"

"Sure thing, Will, and take it easy, okay?"

Will laughed. "Now you should know better than to say that to me."

Smiling to himself, Will went into his office. He was hardly inside the door when the intercom buzzed. He thumbed the button. "Yes, Cora?"

"Your father is here to see you, Mr. Cole."

Will drew a startled breath, frowned briefly in annoyance, then said, "Okay, Cora, send him in."

He sat down behind his desk, took the humidor from the drawer, and removed a Monte Cristo. He had it going, his head wreathed in smoke, by the time Joshua Cole entered the office.

All of the Coles were big men, but easy living and sixty-four years had put a layer of fat on Josh, contributing to the beginning of a small pot. Expensively tailored, meticulously groomed and manicured, except for the rumpled hair, he stood in the doorway flashing his wry smile. His hair was snow-white, had been for a long time, but aside from that he could easily pass for a man of fifty.

They had never hit it off well. Most of the time Will thought of his father as a soft man, an office type who had never dirtied his hands with hard work—in a bag with the men Will had just met. Yet, when he was not angry with him, Will knew this was an unfair assessment. Josh was tough-minded, enormously intelligent, if devious on occasion, possessing all the attributes that went toward molding a consummate politician. And when he raised his voice, he usually got his way. In Will's opinion he didn't always have the best interests of Cole Enterprises in mind, yet he usually disqualified himself from voting when a bill opposed to Cole interests was on the floor of the Senate.

Besides, Will thought, if he hadn't decided on politics as a career instead of business, where would I be? Sucking hind tit, where else?

He said, "Hi, Josh."

"Hello, Will."

Will motioned. "Sit and take a load off. What brings you to

Fairbanks, Josh? I thought you were in Washington. I wasn't expecting you. Nothing urgent, I hope. I'm up to my armpits in problems now."

"Depends on what you call urgent. I had to make a quick trip to Juneau and I thought I'd fly on up here and see you. I suppose you've read, or heard about, all the newspaper articles? Crime wave in Fairbanks, and all the rest?"

"Have I heard!"

"It seems to be causing quite a flap all over the state. Decent citizens are forming committees, signing petitions, putting together reform groups, things like that. All demanding a clean-up of the state. There's one here in town, and they want to meet with us in the morning."

"Reform movement! Jesus!" Will snorted. "So what does that have to do with me, Josh?"

"You're a Cole, Will. In Alaska, with Pap retired, you are *the* Cole. Reform movement starts, you're going to be expected to lend your name."

"Josh, you know as well as I do that it'll come to nothing in the end. What are the construction workers to do when they're off work and ready to raise a little hell? They have to do it somewhere. Man has to be a hypocrite to claim otherwise." He jerked his head toward the boardroom. "That's just what I tried to tell those jackasses in there."

Josh sat up. "Just what jackasses are those?"

Will told him. For a long moment his father regarded Will out of thoughtful gray eyes. As well as being big, all the Coles had gray eyes, from Jeremiah down to Kelly.

Finally Josh said quietly, "There is one difference, Will. You have to live in Fairbanks after the boomers are long gone, and those oilmen will be back in their own particular bailiwicks on the Outside when the pipeline's finished."

Will grunted. "Always the politician, huh, Josh?"

"Politics are my business," his father said, unoffended. "Besides, somebody in this family should be concerned about the Cole image, don't you think? Certainly my father never has, nor you. About as diplomatic as a bear in a honey tree, both of you."

"That was a low shot, Josh, I shouldn't have said that. You don't deserve it, I'm sorry. But the crime wave hitting the pipeline is a hell of a lot more important than what happens when it's playtime for the workers in town. The pipeline has priority over everything else, to my way of thinking. And that reminds me." Will rapped the desk with his knuckles. "I promised to call Granpap today."

Before he could reach the intercom, it buzzed. He thumbed the button. "Yes, Cora?"

"Mr. Cole, your wife is on the line."

"Now what does Louise want? Never mind, Cora, I know what she wants. She's calling to remind me to be on time for her party tonight. I can't talk to her now. Tell her I'm on another line and will call her back, okay? Then get me Jeremiah, Cora."

Waiting, he said, "Can you come to the house tonight, Josh? The minute Louise heard that all those oil company biggies were going to be in town today, nothing would do but that she give a dinner party. She invited all of them. Don't know how many will show, after our little get-together awhile ago. But come if you can. It might be interesting. We didn't know you'd be in town."

"Since I'm staying over, I'll be there." Josh got to his feet. "Maybe we'll have a chance to continue our talk."

Will nodded absently as his father left. His secretary said, "It's ringing, Mr. Cole." Will picked up the receiver and put it to his ear. He drummed on the desk as the line to Cole Island gave off that idiotic long-distance hum. Since his retirement last year, Jeremiah spent all his time on the island, but he still demanded that Will call him at least once a week.

Like a hound on a leash, Will thought bitterly, he'll only let me range so far. But some day, some day!

Will brought his attention back as that thin reed of a voice said in his ear, "Hello? That you, Will boy?"

"Yep, Granpap, it's Will."

Jeremiah had a male nurse in constant attendance, yet he usually managed to answer the phone himself. "If *he* answers it, caller'll have to ask if I'm still alive. If I answer, caller'll know I'm still alive, if not kicking."

Now just ninety-nine, Jeremiah was grimly, stubbornly, determined to live to one hundred. Most organs were badly deteriorated with age, barely functioning, heart not much stronger than a whisper; but his mind, when he rallied himself out of the memory mists of the past, was still keen as a honed hunting knife.

"How'd the meeting go, boy?"

Will was startled into momentary silence. It was spooky how the old boy kept his finger in; he had to have a spy or two in the company.

Covering his surprise, Will related the essence of the meeting.

"So, how did those oil slicks react?"

"About as expected. They're not about to move off dead center, disturb the status quo. Anything to be done, I'll have to do it myself."

"Anybody can do it, you can."

At the unexpected praise, Will's face split in a grin. "You sure I can do something, Granpap?"

"Sure you can do'er, boy. Giving Alaska a bad name, all this. Can't have that, so get in there with both feet, boy, a-kicking and a-clawing."

"I'll do my damnedest, Granpap." Still grinning, always stimulated by the old man's lust for action even at age ninety-nine, Will rapped his knuckles. "By Jesus, I'll sure try."

He hung up slowly, drawing on the cigar. He had never gotten along with the old man—in fact, he'd never really liked him very much—but by Jesus, he had to admire him. Jeremiah Cole had built an empire in the Alaskan wilderness, doing it with brains, guts, and brawn, ruthless when necessary, as single-minded as a feeding shark.

Cora had stacked some letters on the desk for his signature, along with some reports to be gone over. Will quickly scrawled his signature on the letters, then picked up the reports. He scanned through a couple, tossed the rest aside with a grunt, and swiveled around to stare out the window. It was only late afternoon, yet it was already dark. The days were short at this time of the year.

Still exhilarated by the events of the day, he decided that it was recreation time, time for a little R&R for a hardworking executive.

He thumbed the intercom. "Cora? I'm going out. I have some things to tend to, and if anybody wants me, you don't know where to reach me. And you don't. And no, I don't need Red."

From a clothes closet in the bathroom off his office, he got out an old, hooded mackinaw. The hood on the mackinaw could be pulled down to almost hide his face. Where he was going, he didn't wish to be recognized as Will Cole.

He took a private elevator down to the basement garage. Instead of the Cadillac, he drove out in the three-year-old Ford—muddy, rusting, standing high on snow tires. Will was always careful to make sure that the license plates were mud-splattered enough as to be unreadable.

He drove to downtown Fairbanks, to Second Avenue, usually called Two Street. Some people called it The Strip nowadays, after Las Vegas. There was little resemblance, except perhaps for the fact that pleasure was for sale in both places.

Two Street was lined with bars, liquor stores, hock shops, massage parlors, and sex shops. The neon-lighted store fronts tried with indifferent success to light up the street. Hookers, both Eskimo and white, weaved in and out of the throng of rough-clothes construction workers, who filled the street.

Will had never been a patronizer of brothels, fancy or otherwise. Not that he had any particular moral scruples against prostitutes. It was just that he'd never had any trouble getting women, so why pay for it?

He'd never paid Penelope Hardesty a dime. Will knew that he was, generally speaking, insensitive to the mystery of the female sex. This had never bothered him. If he stepped on their feelings, too damned bad. But with Penelope something had warned him early on that if he ever once offered her money, he'd never be welcome in her bed again.

Except sexually, Penelope made no demands on him. She had a fine mind and was an excellent businesswoman; but at the same time she possessed a warm, affectionate nature, and she met Will's every demand in bed. Never once had she asked him to declare his love for her.

Strangely enough, Will felt more affection for Penelope than for any woman he'd ever known, even Louise.

He had known Penelope for some time now. The pipeline boom had been on the verge of exploding, all the legal barriers finally out of the way, and Will had been waiting for the official word from Josh, in Washington, that the last legal obstacle had been cleared. Waiting with him were a number of important Fairbanks businessmen, all in the Cole boardroom,

working on Will's liquor. Will wasn't running the whole
company then, but he was head of Cole 98, and had taken
over the boardroom for the day, with Jeremiah's grumpy
consent. "I know there's money in oil, boy, but it's such filthy
stuff. Just don't get me personally involved in this pipeline
business."

When the call came from Josh and Will passed on the good
word, the room exploded with shouts of jubilation. Legal
obstacles had held up the pipeline for an interminable time.
Construction had started a number of times, only to be
stopped by court order. Men and equipment were standing
by, the expenses mounting daily. Now that the waiting time
was over, the relief was enormous.

By evening only a half-dozen men were left, all well on
their way to getting smashed.

"I have a thought, gents," Will said. "There's a new
whorehouse in town, a real fancy place, and I understand that
the girls are great. I move that we adjourn and pay it a visit.
For those of you interested, the treat's on me."

They were all interested.

A quarter of an hour later they piled out of Will's Cadillac
before a plain, two-story house just off Second Avenue. In
those preboom days the area was relatively tame, yet Will
knew that the ingredients were being put together—the
sharks knew a boom was coming.

"You're sure this is the place, Will?" one of the men asked.
"Looks more like a rooming house to me."

"I'm sure. Come along, gents."

Will led them up the steps, across the veranda, and gave
the special knock, the signal he'd been told to use—one short
rap, a wait, then two more.

The door was opened by a monster of a man, with the
battered features and cauliflower ears of an ex-pug. Will
identified himself, and they were let in. The foyer was as
drab as the outside had been, but once they were ushered
into the next room, the contrast was striking.

Almost all the entire lower floor had been hollowed out and
transformed into one huge, beautifully decorated room. The
lighting was dim, but *not* red. Neither was the decor. Everything was done tastefully in yellows and blues. Except for the
numerous couches scattered about, it could have been a

salon. Most of the couches held either a woman alone, or a woman and a man. But for the extremely scanty clothing, displaying the merchandise to advantage, the girls did not resemble hookers in the least.

And the woman coming toward them could have been a fashion model fresh from New York. She had the figure for it—tall, *very* tall, and slender, with a small butt and proportionately small breasts.

Not to Will's liking at all. His tastes ran more to the Rubens mold, voluptuous, ample breasts and ass, something a man could grab a handful of and hold on.

"Welcome, gentlemen," she said in a low, husky voice. "I am Penelope Hardesty." Her brown eyes sought out Will's and she smiled slightly. With a shake of her head, causing long, coppery hair to ripple, she said, "We've never met, but I know you. You're Will Cole."

Will made no pretense of surprise. It was his assumption that every person in Fairbanks knew Will Cole.

"Happy to make your acquaintance, Miss Hardesty." He grinned. "Or is it Ms.?"

"I'm hardly an ardent feminist, the business I'm in." She glanced around. The men accompanying Will had already drifted away, pairing off with the girls, and they were alone. "My friends call me Penelope, Mr. Cole."

"And mine call me Will. Even my enemies." He cocked his head. "Do you have many? Friends, I mean?"

"Very few. And before you ask..." The brown eyes hardened briefly. "I work here, I am the..." She grimaced. "I am the madam. But I do not *work* here."

Will said gravely, "I understand."

"Do you? I hope you do." Again she looked around the room. "We're quite busy tonight. I see that only a few of the girls are still available."

"Oh, I didn't come here for that." Will gestured negligently. "My friends, they're my guests. I'll foot the bill. But I don't patronize whorehouses."

"Oh? And why is that?"

"Two reasons. First, I don't take other men's leavings," he said bluntly. "And second, I don't find it necessary."

For just a moment she looked angry, then she threw back her head with a burst of laughter, a rich outpouring of bawdy mirth. "I think I'm going to like you, Will Cole." She touched his hand briefly. "Would you care for a drink? I assume you are going to wait for your friends?"

"I hadn't given much thought to it. They're old enough to make it home by themselves. But I think I would like that drink, Penelope."

That was the way it began.

Will's friends did have to make it home by themselves. Will waited until they were all safely on their way, spacing his drinks so he wouldn't get too smashed. Then Penelope came to him, as he had known she would. Something had passed between them in those first few minutes. It had been a long while since Will felt that instant current passing between a woman and him.

When he saw her coming in his direction with that gliding walk, he fancied he could hear the silken sound of her long legs rubbing together, and he got an instant erection.

She stopped at the couch where he sat, held out her hand, and said simply, "Come with me, Will Cole."

He uncoiled his long length and stood up. Her glance dropped for just an instant to the bulge in his trousers. A twist of amusement touched her full lips, but when she looked at him again, her eyes were hot. Her hand, already slippery with perspiration tightened around his. She was only a few inches shorter than he.

Her apartment in the rear was small but reasonably comfortable. Beyond that Will didn't notice, not then. She could have been leading him through a king's palace for all the notice he took.

Her bedroom was feminine enough, but without many of the frills Will associated with bedrooms inhabited solely by females. But the bed . . . the bed was large, dominating the room.

There was no dallying, no preliminary coyness, on her part. She peeled the hostess gown down like the skin of a grape. Her slender body was alabaster white, except for the copper bush of pubic hair, and she was all angles and meager curves. Her breasts were small, not much larger than apples, the nipples brown and tumescent.

Despite her skinniness, some of her bones seemingly prominent enough to poke a man's eye out, Will's lust was all-consuming.

On the bed, they came together like a pair of antagonists. Later, he couldn't remember if she had guided him into her or if his member entered her like a key drawn in by a magnetic lock, a key that turned her into a wild thing under him. She rose, driving against him, muttering words he could not understand, her eyes without focus.

Underneath that cool model's exterior dwelt a wanton.

The fierceness of her passion was so totally unexpected that for a moment Will almost lost control of the situation, his male dominance challenged. But he took the challenge, probing her with stallion thrusts.

Almost immediately she arched against him, clutching, mouth open in a silent scream, pelvis shuddering.

Will didn't let up, his own orgasm fast approaching. And when it broke, she had a second climax, with him this time, her body rising, supporting all his weight.

When he rolled off her, Will had another moment of doubt. Had he been the dominant one after all? Or was it the other way around?

Penelope exhaled with a gusty sigh. "God, I needed that!" She looked at him quickly, already laughing. "I know, a cliché, right? But true, how true! I haven't been to bed with a man since I came to this town. Seem strange to you?"

He raised up, resting on one elbow. He placed his other hand on her flat, still heaving stomach. "A little, yeah."

"Oh, it wasn't for lack of opportunity. But I'm picky, too damned picky, I suppose." She gazed into his eyes, face solemn. "That comes from too many years as a working hooker. It makes a woman particular, when she has a choice. I *was* a whore, for many years. Call girl, to put a fancier name to it. That disgust you, Will Cole? That I peddled my ass, I mean? I recall your remark earlier about other men's leavings."

It did disgust him. A little. He said, "What's past is past. But one thing . . . am I right in thinking that this is the start of something?"

"Well, I should hope so! I'm not strong for one-night stands." Her gaze held steady on his. "Of course, it's more or less up to you."

He nodded. "If it's up to me, then it's on. But so long as it *is* on, one condition. No peddling your ass, as you so delicately put it."

She bobbed her head. "Agreed." She placed her hand on his limp organ, cupping it. "Of course, I may have agreed too quickly. Is this going to be any good to me again tonight?"

"Jesus Christ in a wheelbarrow, woman!" he growled. "Give a man a minute, will you?"

But even as he spoke his member began to grow in her hand.

Two years now, Will mused, as he maneuvered the muddy Ford down the alley behind Penelope's place, and the passion between them still blazed unabated. His interest in a woman seldom lasted this long. He was reasonably confident that Penelope had kept her end of the bargain; he certainly had. He hadn't slept with another woman since that first night with her.

There was a garage attached to the rear of the house, a two-car garage where Penelope kept her Porsche. She had given him a battery-operated door opener. Will pressed the button, the garage door swung up, and he drove inside. He pressed the button again, closing the door, and got out of the Ford, mounting the steps to the door off the garage, the only rear entrance to the building.

He keyed the door open and entered the short hall. On the left was Penelope's office, on the right her apartment. At the far end of the hall was the door leading into the other part of the house.

Will turned right into her apartment. Penelope wasn't there, but he knew she would be before long. When the back door opened, red lights flashed on in strategic locations in the house. At the bar in the small living room, he poured himself a strong bourbon on the rocks, sprawled in the easy chair, then pulled the hassock over, and propped his feet up. He lit a cigar and went to work on the drink. He hadn't warned Penelope of his coming, he rarely did. But she'd know as soon as she saw the lights flashing.

He was halfway through the drink when the door swung open.

"Well!" she said tartly. "Comfy?"

He grinned lazily. "Like a bull with a salt lick and a pasture of heifers all to himself."

"That's probably more apt than you know, lover." But she

was smiling as she crossed to him. She touched his cheek, and he placed a hand on her Venus mound. Penelope sucked in her breath, eyes closing. He could feel the heat of her through the thin material of the dress.

"Oh, no!" She stepped back. "You're going to have to wait, lover. I'm busy right now." She started toward the door. "Enjoy yourself."

"Hardesty?"

Will had told her early on: "I can't keep calling you Penelope. It makes me think I'm going to bed with my maiden aunt."

She had turned back. "Yes?"

"I heard today that reform groups are forming in Fairbanks, swearing to eliminate vice and crime in our fair city."

"I've heard rumors to that effect."

"Aren't you running a little scared then?"

"Why should I be?"

"They might come after you," he said slyly. "This ain't exactly a church social you're running here. Also, I had a meeting today with several oil company executives. They expressed horror and shock at the terrible things that are going on."

"What are the names of these executives?"

He told her the names.

She nodded. "All patrons here, at one time or another."

Will sat up straighter. "Well, I'll be goddamned! But then, I don't suppose I should be all that surprised."

"No, I don't believe you should. So, why should I be worried?"

Will was roaring with laughter as Penelope left the room, closing the door softly after her.

Seven

When Brad Connors told Kelly that he was flying from Juneau to Fairbanks on business, and that he had been invited to Louise's party, Kelly decided to go with him, although she had previously turned down Louise's invitation. She changed her mind because she was bored. Winter on the island was a dull time despite the many hours she spent in the cabin painting. At least in summer she could take the sailboat out onto the sound, or ride horseback; or even go into Juneau for a game or two of tennis, visit friends, take in a movie, whatever.

Kelly was terrified of flying. She had managed to keep her fear a secret from most people. There was no reason for her fear, it was just there. Still, born with the innate Cole stubbornness, she flew quite a bit. The big jets didn't terrify her quite so much, but the smaller the plane, the more acute her terror. And Brad's plane was an old Piper Cub, a two-seater, propeller relic. Every time she flew with him she was ice-cold with terror, but she would be damned if she would give into it. Sometimes she woke up in the small hours of the night, the thought in her mind, like the aftermath of a nightmare, that she, or someone close to her, would again some day perish in a plane crash, which only drove her to fly again and again. She would never forget the horrors of Gene's death.

Although they had been having an affair for almost a year, Brad did not know of her fear of flying, and Kelly was determined that he never would. He'd asked her once why she didn't have a pilot's license. "Will and your father do. Even Jeremiah, although he hasn't flown in years."

She had passed it off with a laugh. "Flying is man's work, Brad."

"It just strikes me as a little odd. Flying a plane up here is like driving an automobile in Los Angeles. You can't get along without one, especially if you live in Juneau."

"I can always find someone to fly me," she had said, and left it at that.

On the way to Fairbanks, the little Piper Cub buzzing along over the cloud-covered landscape, Kelly breathed a little easier, now that they were over the Wrangell Mountains, which was always a hazard to flying out of Juneau.

Brad said, "Are you going straight to Will's when we get to Fairbanks? Or will you wait and let me escort you to the party? My business will be done by four, or five at the latest."

"I'm not going straight there, no," she said. "A little of Louise goes a long way."

"Then you'll wait and go with me?"

"Of course. You're my fellow, aren't you?" She smiled and touched his hand.

"I sure hope so." He risked a quick glance at her, returning her smile, then switched his attention back to piloting the plane. "But there'll be a couple of hours to kill. What will you do all that time?"

"Oh, wander around, shop a little, maybe drop in on Dwight for a little while. We won't be expected at the party until seven."

"You mean I won't see you before then?" he said with a touch of dismay.

"What did you have in mind, Counselor?" she said artlessly, knowing full well what he had in mind.

Brad, she was sure, was deeply in love with her, although he had never said so, in so many words; and she very much doubted that he ever would. Brad was a very sensitive man, with a pride as rigid as a ramrod. His beginnings had been very poor; and although he was now fairly well off and quite successful, he would never propose marriage to her. She was a Cole, there was all that Cole money, and Brad would be fearful that people would think that he had married her for that very reason. Kelly was just as content to leave it that way. She liked Brad, he was fun to be with, he rode well, could manage a sailboat acceptably, he played a decent game of tennis, and he was more than adequate in bed.

Kelly had a great affection for Brad Connors, but she was far from being in love with him; and it would be an embarrassment to them both if he ever did ask her to marry him. By unspoken, mutual agreement, they kept their infrequent rendezvous as discreet as possible, since their affair would be a political embarrassment to Josh, and her grandfather had yet to accept the new sexual morality. He would be outraged to learn that his granddaughter was having sexual relations outside of the marriage bed.

To their left now the snow-shrouded heights of Mount McKinley jutted up above the cloud cover. They were approaching Fairbanks.

Brad broke into her thoughts. "I thought perhaps you might like to use my apartment to freshen up before the party." Brad kept an apartment in Juneau and also in Fairbanks.

"That's nice of you to offer, Brad," she said sweetly. "And I do have a key, don't I?" Then she relented and reached over to squeeze his thigh. "You're a sweet man, darling, and I'm being my usual bitchy self. I'll meet you at your apartment around four, okay?"

Brad nodded happily, and reached for the mike to radio Fairbanks for landing instructions. Kelly thought about Brad Connors as she watched the buildings of Fairbanks start to emerge as the plane dipped below the clouds. Like all the Coles, except Jeremiah, she had attended the university at Fairbanks—a better than average student—and during those college years she had slept with several different men.

Most of them had been indifferent lovers, providing relief for awakened sexual needs but little beyond that; and it never took her long to become bored with them. As a matter of fact, this was something that depressed her a little: almost all men bored her, with the exception of Grandfather and Josh. Capable of having a certain objectivity about herself, Kelly wondered if there was some lack in her. Or maybe she had been so spoiled by being a Cole that no man could interest her for long? She finally reached the rather shaky conclusion that the fault lay with the men, or boys, she knew. The Alaskan male was afflicted with an infuriating machismo. Women were secondary in their lives. Their jobs, drinking, sports, hunting, flying, backpacking—all these activities came first. It seemed to be all they talked about, and they were turned off by any woman who might wish to talk about anything else.

Brad was from Outside, although he had lived in Alaska for some years. More important, he was sophisticated, his range of interests wide. He respected her opinions, he listened, and he was a witty, interesting conversationalist. When he did talk about his work, it was usually an anecdote either amusing or intriguing.

And he was an accomplished lover, as concerned with her pleasure as his.

In the early stages Kelly had been certain that she had found a man who would treat her as an equal, both sexually and intellectually, and might even be the man she could marry. He did treat her as an equal, yet it wasn't enough. The affection she felt for Brad never became more than just that, and after every sexual encounter she was left vaguely discontented, longing for something more. What was maddening was the fact that she couldn't put a name to the discontent. Whatever else she was, Kelly was realistic, and she had doubts about the great sexual ecstasy the heroines of popular novels experienced.

It simply could be that she *was* spoiled, that she was sated, that no thrill she could ever experience would live up to her expectations.

Yet she knew that she had to keep searching for something else, whether it was out there or not, and it would be grossly unfair to Brad to marry him, because she knew in her heart that it could only end in disaster.

At Fairbanks International they found the rental car Brad had reserved and made the short drive into Fairbanks. As they drove along Airport Road, Brad said, "You know, Kelly, it would be so damned much more convenient, if Will would use the Cole building in Anchorage as headquarters to run the company. Except for Cole 98 and Cole Airlines, everything else could be run more easily from there."

"I suppose you're right, Brad." She smiled. "But you know Grandfather's attachment to Fairbanks. It all began for him here."

"Not true, he made his strike at Dawson City."

"The first one, yes. But he also made another here, his big strike, in 1903. He formed Cole Enterprises here, in 1908. He started the first mail and passenger sled service out of Fairbanks the same year."

"But when he started the fishing fleet, the canneries, and the steamship runs down to Seattle, it was all done from Anchorage. It had to be from there."

"Yet his heart always remained here, Brad, and you'll notice that he also started Cole Airlines here. As for Will, well, he was raised in Fairbanks, went to the university. The place has sentimental value to him."

"Some sentimental value." Brad made a face. "A boomtown, burgeoning from twenty-some thousand population to sixty-five. It smells, it's smoggy, and it's altogether an unsightly mess. When the pipeline is finished, so is Fairbanks."

"Will doesn't seem to think so. He says when the gas pipeline is built, it'll boom again."

"*If* it's ever built. I notice that you have sense enough not to spend much time here."

Kelly shrugged. "And I never will, so long as I have a choice. But then I have nothing to do with the company."

"Jeremiah doesn't live here, either."

"You know why that is, Brad. The doctors told him that the winters would kill him if he didn't get out. But even after he built Cole House, he still spent the better part of every year in Fairbanks, until his retirement."

"Well, I hate the damned place. Before the boom started a Californian once described it as Barstow of the north. I subscribe to that."

"You get paid well," she said dryly. "And you love to fly, you know you do. How long does it take to buzz up here?"

"Oh, I'm not complaining for myself, not really. But it's just not good business practice. Most of the company personnel are in Anchorage, but the president's office is on one floor here, leased at that. The family home is on Cole Island, and the law firm representing Cole Enterprises is located in Juneau. Now just think about that, Kelly. Isn't that a little disorganized, not to mention messy?"

Kelly laughed. "We Coles are noted for making money, deals, and enemies, not for being organized. Messy, I won't argue. Messy applies to our private lives as well, I think you will agree."

The word messy could be applied literally to her brother Dwight's private life, Kelly thought a short while later, as

Dwight admitted her to the old house on the north side of the Chena River. There was always an odor about the place— mold, stale food, human effluvium, and other smells she couldn't quite identify. And she doubted that the place had been thoroughly cleaned since Dwight and his buddies had taken over the house.

"Sis! Hey, cool! I wasn't expecting you."

His rough clothes felt as scratchy as a bear pelt as he embraced her, leading her into the house, and to the parlor where his girl friend, June, sat before the fire on two cushions. Kelly didn't much care for the girl, but she tolerated her, for Dwight's sake, as she did his other weird friends.

This time Kelly was surprised at what she saw. Often June was in the lotus position, limbs impossibly twined. This time she was knitting, clumsily, inexpertly, and God only knew what the item was, but she was knitting!

"You didn't know, did you, Sis? Of course you didn't, she only told me last night." Dwight was beaming. "Junebug is pregnant. I'm going to be a papa!"

Kelly's first thought was: Dear God, now we'll have a bastard in the family! And a hippie one at that, as Will would say.

She tried to shield off her shock, but something must have given her away, for Dwight's eyes went cold.

"I know what you're thinking, Kelly. I've found another way to blacken the Cole name, having a bastard child, right?"

Kelly sighed. "Dwight, you know I'm seldom critical of your life-style. I think you have the right to live any way you choose. But what's wrong with getting married? Think of the child, growing up a bastard."

"A *Cole* bastard, is what you mean, isn't it, Sis?"

"Marriage is for the squares, you know," June said serenely. "Marriage is a trap. As far as we're concerned, we're as married as any church or legal document could ever make us. Right, lover?"

"Right, babe," Dwight said, his hard gaze never leaving Kelly's face.

"My God, Dwight, the trouble you go to to *cause* trouble," Kelly said in resignation. "But if that's the way you want it . . ."

He snapped, "That's the way I want it!"

"That's the way our Great Leader wants it, Sister Cole," a

giggly voice said behind Kelly. "And we do what O Great Leader commands."

"For Christ's sake, Gordie," Dwight said in disgust. "Bug off, will you?"

Kelly swung about to see one of Dwight's followers, a slight fellow with eyes that seemed to bubble with mischief.

Gordie's look turned malevolent. "Don't you know why your sibling is here, Dwight? She's here for the big bash Brother Cole is giving tonight." His eyes glittered. "Or maybe you haven't received your invitation yet, Dwight? Anyway, she just dropped in because she happened to be in the neighborhood. Right, Sister Cole?"

Dwight said tightly, "You're beginning to annoy me, Gordie. Now bug off!"

Gordie made a mocking half-bow. "As you command, O Great Leader." He turned and shuffled out of sight.

Kelly said, "He's one of your weirder ones, isn't he, Dwight? He's on something, I can tell. I thought you were against drug use?"

"Never mind Gordie, I can handle him." Dwight made a dismissing gesture. "But he is right, isn't he? This party is the reason you're here, isn't it?"

"It's the reason I'm in Fairbanks, yes, but there's hardly any connection between Louise's party and my being here, with you."

He remained unforgiving. "The only times you visit me are when you're in town for some other reason. Dropping in on your way through, a sort of afterthought, if you have nothing else to do for a half-hour." He sneered. "That rasps me, Kelly."

"This from a guy who claims he needs no one, especially a Cole? I live in Juneau, Dwight, and you live here. You expect me to fly over here every day or so? I do stop by to see you when I'm in town. When is the last time *you* were at Cole House to see me?"

"The last time *was* the last time. I'm not welcome there."

"That's not true and you know it! Josh and I are always glad to see you."

"But not the old man."

June had gotten to her feet to cross to stand beside Dwight. Staring at Kelly, she said placidly, "Dwight and me, we don't need anyone, you know."

"The day may come when that's no longer true," Kelly said angrily.

Dwight put his arm around June. "If that day ever does arrive, I won't come to a Cole. Bet on that, dear sister."

Kelly said, "I think I'd better be on my way before this goes any further."

"Perhaps you'd better, Sis," he said stolidly.

A couple of hours later, lying sated in Brad's bed, Kelly's thoughts returned to Dwight and his situation. Brad lay stretched out beside her, a sheet drawn up to his waist. His eyes were closed, a beatific smile on his face, and his hands were crossed over his hairy chest. Brad was the hairiest man she had ever known—hair as thick and soft as monkey fur on his broad chest.

"Brad?"

"Yes, Kelly?" he said without opening his eyes.

"I told you I was stopping by to see Dwight this afternoon?"

"You told me, but then you usually do stop in to see him."

"It was worse today."

He finally opened his eyes, rolling his head toward her. "In what way?"

"That girl he's living with, June something..." She drew a deep breath. "She's pregnant."

"Oh, my." He whistled softly. "Now that's going to stir up a few people, like Will and your grandfather, to name two. If it's really Dwight's." His lips twisted with amusement. "I don't know how they can really be sure, in that rabbit hutch they live in. The way most communes work, it's share and share alike, and that includes sex."

"I never thought about that..." But she was already shaking her head. "No, I'm sure that's not the case. Despite the way he talks and acts, in many ways Dwight is square, and that includes sex. Especially sex. No, I'm almost positive that he doesn't share June with the others."

"You're probably right and I shouldn't scoff at Dwight and his buddies," Brad said soberly. "Besides, the child's real father doesn't matter, if Dwight claims it. The flap will be the same, in any case."

"You know something, Brad? Today may have been the last straw for me. I've been tolerant and understanding, or tried

to be, with his rebelliousness. In a way, I suppose I sort of
rooted for him. But now he's the cause of Grandfather's first
great-grandchild being born a bastard." She laughed abruptly,
a startled sound. "And I can just hear Dwight! All I'm worried
about is the Cole name."

Brad found her hand and squeezed reassuringly.

"But it's not only that," she went on. "There was something
to be said for their fight against the pipeline. It was a cause
with merit and I had some sympathy for them. But it's all
over. They've lost. The pipeline, while not finished, is a fact
of life, and I doubt that it's going to do nearly as much
damage to the environment as they screamed about. Most of
those of Dwight's persuasion have deserted him, gone on to
other causes, whatever. The thing is, there's only a handful
left, yet he's still out there, attacking the windmills with a
broken lance."

"Give him another year or two, Kelly. I was mixed up in
the rebellion of the sixties," he said reminiscently. "I was at
Stanford Law School. Oh, we weren't as committed as the
kids at Berkeley, but we were against the Vietnam mess.
'Hell, no, we won't go!' All the rest of the hippie slogans. Of
course, we were a little more subdued about it, just on the
fringe of it, yet we, most of us anyway, got our vicarious kicks
out of all the student-cop scrimmages. But I read a survey
just the other day." He chuckled. "Most of those kids are now
settled down, with a job, a family, all the rest of what they
used to call the 'middle-class trap.'"

"I've seen those figures, too. But those protesters did some
good. The Selma marches, the Vietnam protests."

"Don't underestimate the environmentalists here, Kelly.
Their protests resulted in many safeguards being incorporat-
ed into the pipeline that otherwise would not have been."

"I'll grant all that, Brad." She stirred. "But those figures
you quoted also mentioned that a minority of the protesters
are still at it, while the others grew out of it, like you did.
Dwight is twenty-seven years old. It's time he grew up a
little!"

"Easy now, darling. Don't get so upset." He put an arm
around her shoulders and cradled her in his arms. "I predict
that your brother will come over some day soon, perhaps
even come into the company."

"As a soothsayer, Brad, you're lousy," she said glumly. "The

Coles never forgive or forget. I would welcome him back into the family, and I'm sure Josh would. But Will and Grandfather? Never! And they're the ones who count when it comes to Cole Enterprises."

He began to caress her with loving, cunning hands, murmuring soothing, nonsensical words into her ear; and her passion reignited, as had been his intention. Kelly forgot everything else as he teased her to a demanding pitch of desire, then gave her surcease.

Eight

After Kelly slammed out of the house, Dwight said brusquely, "I'm going for a walk, June, clear my head."

Shrugging into a jacket, he left the house and walked the short distance to the Chena. In the small, bleak park, he leaned against a tree and stared across the frozen river. From here he could see the building where his half-brother had his offices.

Every time he saw that building his blood boiled. It seemed to him that Will Cole, *all* the Coles, with the possible exception of Kelly, were giving him the finger with that building. And now, if the scene with Kelly was any indication, even she was turning her back on him.

Dwight did not resent being an outcast from the tribe. If anything, he flaunted it at every opportunity. In addition to the full beard, he wore what the rest of the "longhairs" wore—in summer about as little as possible, usually tie-dyed shirts and pants.

Many of the young people into ecology in and around Fairbanks had migrated from California a couple of years ago, finding the pipeline issue fertile ground for their fervor. But now that the pipeline fight was pretty much a lost cause, many of them had drifted away; although a few still lingered, fighting a holding action against the Trans-Alaska pipeline, and gearing up for the fight against the other proposed pipeline—the one to carry natural gas instead of oil down to the Lower 48. They wrote letters, distributed pamphlets, made impassioned speeches at every opportunity and organized frequent protest marches.

"With what we learned fighting this one," Dwight had said more than once, "we just might win the next one."

Eight of them lived together in the old house across the Chena River. Six of the eight were men, the other two women. They had no elected leader, that wasn't their action, but when an important decision was to be made, they usually turned to Dwight. And naturally the fighters to Save Alaska from the Spoilers (SAS) were delighted to have a Cole in the forefront of any demonstration.

Dwight had turned his back on the Coles three years ago, turned his back on all that money, all the raping of the land, the exploitation of Alaska's natural resources, and deliberately set about doing everything he could to annoy the Coles. He had only one regret. While growing up he had adored Grandfather Jeremiah; even now his affection remained strong, even after he had full knowledge of how Jeremiah had raped the land to start and build the Cole fortune.

Jeremiah had taken gold out of the ground, then invested the proceeds in timber operations, fishing fleets and canneries, steamships and airplanes, and finally into oil. Actually the latter had been mostly Will Cole's doing, but it all came down to the same thing—the Cole empire had been built from the ruthless rape of the land the sea. Even Cole Airlines polluted the atmosphere.

Yet Dwight would never forget those many afternoons of his youth spent crouched at the old man's feet, listening with rapt attention to the yarns about the early days, the sourdough days of the Gold Rush; and he knew that the old pirate was bitter and disappointed by his, Dwight's, defection.

Aside from fighting them all down the line business-wise, as the executive types put it, Dwight had joined a commune, started wearing their garb, and—the unforgivable sin—was living with a woman without the benefit of matrimony.

And just last night, alone in the house, the others off somewhere, lying nude with June on a thick rug before a roaring fire in the parlor of the old house, he had learned that the Coles had even more to be concerned about.

June had been talking in a low voice. Hardly listening, mesmerized by the leaping flames and his own musings, he turned his face to her. "I'm sorry. What did you just say, Junebug?"

"I said, I'm pregnant."

Dwight gaped at her. "Pregnant?"

"They used to call it quick with child." Her elfin, monkey grin flashed. "Though I must say that I don't feel quick at the moment."

"You're sure? Why didn't you tell me?"

"I wasn't sure. The doctor made it sure for me today. And I didn't want to tell you until I *was* sure. I'm two months pregnant, lover."

"Then you did stop the pill?"

"I told you I was going to. You remember the argument..."

Dwight remembered. One night Caroline, Bob's old lady, had read an item in the paper that some doctors were beginning to suspect that the birth control pill increased the incidence of cancer in women. There had been a heated discussion afterward, with Bob, their antireligion member, arguing that it was nothing more than propaganda put out by the Catholic Church.

"... told you that night that I was going off the pill," June said accusingly. "You weren't listening to me, you're always off somewhere in your head!"

"I was listening, babe, I was listening."

Tears glistened in her black eyes. "You don't want the baby!"

"I want the baby, Junebug. Believe me, I want the baby."

He turned toward her, propping himself up on one elbow. He ran his palm across her flat stomach, the tips of his fingers just brushing the black thicket of pubic hair.

June claimed she was part Eskimo. She was dusky enough, her hair black as night, and her eyes had a slight slant. Yet he doubted her claim. June was chameleonlike in her emotions, her thinking. She adapted to her surroundings like an actress preparing herself totally for a part different from her real personality. Dwight had been with her for over a year, and he still wasn't sure he would recognize her true personality if it ever surfaced. Her past was a mystery; she had simply appeared one day on the streets of Fairbanks. It was all a part of the fascination she held for him.

Right now the Eskimos' fight was their fight as well, so she laid claim to Eskimo heritage. It was even quite possible that she really believed the roles she assumed for herself. Dwight had often thought that she could adapt to any role; but since she was so serious and sincere about it all, and because he loved her, he didn't mind.

He made a listening funnel with his hand on her belly and put an ear to it. "I don't hear a word from Dwight, Junior."

"Oh, you big ninny!" She aimed a playful punch at him. "*Two* months!"

His hand on her stomach moved lower. June drew in her breath, eyes fluttering closed, and she arched against his hand.

He probled her with a gentle finger.

June moaned. Lower lip caught between her teeth, her head rolled from side to side. "Yes, lover, oh, yes!"

She opened her thighs to him as he got upon his knees between her legs. Gazing down at that lovely body, the full breasts slightly flattened now by their own weight, Dwight mused on how easy it was to turn her on. A touch, a word, any suggestive move, and she was ready for him.

And look, he thought with a grin, gazing down at his own engorgement, at who's talking!

He had barely penetrated her, ready to go all the way in with one thrust, when he remembered and paused, appalled at himself.

June's eyes opened wide. In some alarm she said, "What is it, Dwight? What's wrong?"

"You know, your condition ... for a moment I forgot."

"My condition?" For a moment or so she looked blank. "Oh, for God's sake, Dwight, you won't have to worry about that for months!" A worried frown creased her brow. "And then I'll be so big and fat and ugly that you probably won't love me any more."

"I'll always love you, babe. To me, you'll be even more beautiful."

"You're a bullshit artist, Dwight Cole," she said. Then her voice changed. "Now come on, I want you in me, all the way. Just like you would have before I told you anything."

His fears eased, he went at it with gusto. June thoroughly enjoyed sex and she let him know it. She was a noisy lover, a thrasher, a screamer, a thumper, and a quick comer.

She had two orgasms before his own passion crested. As she felt him begin to throb in her, she wrapped herself around him and crooned, "Yes, lover, that's it! That's it, come on now!"

Still inside her, he said with gusting breath, "The way that went, you suppose we might be blessed with twins?"

"Boy, somewhere down the line you must have failed your biology lessons."

Laughing, he rolled off her. "I wasn't very old when I found out that it was much more fun to learn all I needed to know about biology from actual practice, rather than from books."

"Well, at actual practice you do okay." She kissed him wetly. "But of the end results you know from zilch."

On the riverbank Dwight laughed softly to himself, the tension draining out of him at the memory of last night, and the knowledge of his impending fatherhood.

Impatient now to be with June, he turned and strode quickly back to the house.

He found her on the rug before the fire, on her back, head up on a cushion, hands folded over her stomach.

Dumping his jacket, Dwight stretched out beside her. He tapped a forefinger on her crossed hands. "How's Junior?"

"Junior's fine." She turned luminous eyes on him. "The question is, how are you?"

He said lightly, "I'm okay, babe. I just needed some cold air to blow through my head. I know, I shouldn't let my family get to me so easily..."

The slam of the front door brought Dwight's head up. He cocked an ear, listening to the sound of two voices. "Who is it, can you tell?"

"Sounds like Gordie and Theo to me."

Gordon Beasley and Theodore Calmer were their two unattached males. Not that they were gay. At least Dwight didn't think so.

There was the sound of something crashing in the kitchen, followed by a duo of giggles.

June smiled. "They sound stoned."

"If they are, I'm going to chew somebody out!"

Dwight got up. Opening the door to the hall, he shivered. The rest of the house was icy. There was no central heating. The rooms were heated either by a fireplace or an oil stove. The halls were always frigid.

He followed the sound of voices to the kitchen where he found Gordie and Theo at the table, sharing a bottle of Ripple. The stove wasn't on, but they weren't feeling the cold. They were both out of it. Dwight stood for a moment without their being aware of his presence.

Theo, a blond, moon-faced, good-natured slob of twenty-two, was just plain sloshed.

It was more than that with Gordie. Dwight had suspected for some time that Gordie was on something, and drugs, even pot, were strictly *verboten* in the old house. It was something that Dwight was dead set against. He had no moral scruples against pot; in his opinion it should be legalized. Not that it would be of any advantage to him; after a few early experiments with both he had sworn off drugs and liquor. He had no objections to anyone using drugs somewhere else. But not *here*. That old adage, "People who live in glass houses should not throw stones," applied to them, since, in effect, that was what they would be doing. If the cops raided the house and found even a smidgen of anything illegal, it was the slammer for all and throw away the key. The cops had been here, twice within the past six months, without finding anything, fortunately.

The trouble with Gordie, Dwight suspected, was that he was on something stronger than pot. He was a lanky, very tall, long-haired youth of twenty-three, prone to long, sullen silences, sudden rages, and sloughs of depression. Sometimes he ate like a horse, never gaining an ounce; other times he would go for days hardly eating at all. Yet they had no problem with food. They still received enough donations from SAS sympathizers for ample food, and there were plenty of jobs, full or part-time, to be had in Fairbanks, now that the pipeline had drained away any surplus labor force. Even the Fairbanks police force had been depleted by its members leaving to work for the pipeline at wages triple their police salaries.

Until last year, Gordie had been a student at the University of Alaska here in Fairbanks. During one of the coldest spells on record, in 1974, four students had streaked across the campus at 54 below zero temperature, wearing only sneakers. Two days later, Gordie had tried it—without sneakers. He had lost three toes. He had dropped out of college that week and never returned.

Dwight cleared his throat loudly. Gordie glanced around. His eyes had a blank, staring look and the muscles of his face sagged, as if he wore a mask constructed of some material that had begun to melt and run.

He flapped a hand. "Hark, our leader approaches! Hail, O Great Leader!"

Dwight grimaced. "Don't talk garbage, Gordie." He stared at him closely. "What are you on?"

Grinning, Gordie flapped a hand at Theo. "Drinking a little *vino*, you know, with old Theo here, man. Right, Theo?"

Theo looked around with a loose-mouthed smile. "'at's right, Dwight. Just a jug or two of Ripple, is all."

Dwight, staring at Gordie, didn't believe it for an instant. He wanted to rip the parka from Gordie, roll up his sleeves and examine those skinny arms for needle tracks. But that would never do, not at this time. Besides, he was probably popping pills, if anything.

"You know the rules, Gordie. No hard drugs. No drugs of *any* kind around here. If I catch you at it, you're out on your tail."

Gordie's blue eyes widened innocently. "Man, old Gordie would never do anything like that. Know why?" He began to chant, "Great Leader don't 'low no drug-popping round here, no drug-popping round here!"

"All right, all right!" Dwight sighed heavily. "You guys better finish that bottle, then crawl into the sack and sleep it off."

He started to turn away and caught the tiny flare of triumph in Gordie's eyes. Dwight hesitated, wanting to hit out in frustration. Then he thought, Screw it, I'm not their den mother!

Before he reached the door, Gordie's indolent voice brought him up short. "I guess you didn't get your invitation to the party, huh?"

"Party? What party?"

"You know what party. The one I mentioned this afternoon, the one your sister came here to attend. Ain't you hurt your bigshot brother didn't send you an invite?"

His voice low and hard, Dwight said, "Don't have me on, Gordie. I don't need that from you."

Gordie's strident laughter followed him out of the room.

There was really no point in being angry at Gordie when he was like this. He was a good worker, a talented artist who designed and illustrated their posters and pamphlets and he was dedicated to their cause. Most of the time he could be quite nice. It was only when he got into these moods, drug-and/or alcohol-induced or not, that he was a pain in the ass; and Dwight didn't feel right about kicking him out of the house because of a clash of personalities. Essentially that was what it was.

From what he knew of Gordie's background, Dwight understood that he had been pretty much on his own since he was twelve, when his parents had been killed in an accident; after that he had been raised by an uncle who paid little attention to him, who had paid Gordie's way at Berkeley, and later up here, probably just to get him out of his hair. It must irk him more than a little that Dwight, no matter how he might be living now, had been raised in a family with money. Probably Gordie had never had more than a few hundred dollars at any time in his life.

Going into the parlor, Dwight grinned derisively at himself for all this understanding. And forgiveness. A Christlike figure he was not, and never would be.

June had already snuggled down in her sleeping bag when he reentered the big room, and was asleep, just her hair, eyes, and that short nose showing.

The fire had died down. Quietly Dwight piled on fresh fuel and sat hunched on the end of his sleeping bag, knees drawn up, arms around them. Buck, the half-grown wolf, padded into the room and squatted beside Dwight, nuzzling his hand. Absently Dwight fondled the wolf's head, staring pensively into the flames.

His half-brother's wife loved to give parties. For several years now it was about the only thing Louise had going for her. She had told him once, "The only thing keeping me sane in this godforsaken country, Dwight!" That had been when he was still one of the family.

He thought back to some of those parties, not enviously, not with particularly fond memories, but with wry amusement. He and Kelly rarely attended, but he had been at a couple before he turned his back on the Coles.

Poor Louise! He never could stand her, yet he had felt sorry for her on occasion. Will gave her a hard time.

Louise always made such elaborate preparations, looking

forward with great expectations; and more often than not the parties turned into drunken brawls, with Will leading the way. Louise's idea of what made a dinner party a success and what the Alaskans, and Will Cole, thought of as a great party were poles apart—and no pun intended.

Nine

"Will . . . please keep it down to a roar tonight. No arguments," Louise Cole said. "Just this once, please, dear?"

"What do you mean, Louise?" Will grinned at her. "Ain't I always the perfect gentleman and host? If anybody starts anything, it won't be me."

"Will . . ." Louise sighed. "Don't play games with me. You know what I mean."

"Then why in God's name did you invite all those oil company guys, if you wanted a quiet party?"

Louise made a startled gesture. "You're in the same business, you're all partners, for heaven's sake!"

"That means shit, Louise."

"Please, Will, you know I don't like that kind of language."

He cut her off with a chop of his hand. "We were at each other's throats at that meeting this afternoon."

"But does that mean that you can't sit down together and have a quiet dinner, like civilized people? That was business, this is a social evening."

He stared at her. "Louise, Louise, some things you never seem to learn." He shook his head. "But you're right, of course, and I'll try to behave. Now I'd better move my butt and get cleaned up."

"Thank God for that!"

Already moving toward the hall, shucking his parka, he ignored her comment. Louise stood staring after him long after he had disappeared.

So different, this Will Cole, so vastly different from the man she had married eighteen years ago. Oh, she supposed that she had changed, too; all people do. And they had been so young then, Will twenty-one, she just eighteen.

If only she had a daughter, maybe she wouldn't be quite so

unhappy, so lonely much of the time. A son of course would have been welcome, but a daughter . . . oh, my, a daughter to share things with would have been so nice! But it was too late now, she was past childbearing age.

It was not for lack of trying. She and Will had both wanted children. Will, especially, had wanted a son, so when Louise reached thirty without becoming pregnant, she had secretly consulted a doctor. After a series of exhaustive tests, he could find no reason why she should be barren, and had suggested that her husband have an examination. Louise knew better than even to suggest it to Will. By that time she and Will had grown apart, and the mere hint that he might be sterile would send him into a roaring rage.

She had thought, any number of times, of leaving him for another man, before she was too old to have children . . . yet there was all that money; and now it was too late.

Privately Louise believed that that horrid old man on the island was responsible. She had learned very soon after marrying Will that there was bad feeling between her husband and his grandfather, so Jeremiah Cole had sent up an edict to the Almighty that there would be no offspring for Will and Louise, and it had come to pass. She knew this was absurd, of course, yet it was a conviction that she couldn't shake.

How she hated Jeremiah Cole! It was indecent of him to live to such a great age; and he was still handing down edicts; any time he beckoned with a gnarled finger, either Joshua or Will came running.

If only he would die . . .

Louise clapped a hand over her mouth and glanced furtively around, fearful that she had spoken aloud.

She went into the dining room, then into the kitchen to check on dinner preparations. Both the maid, Lucy Ahvahana, and the cook, Mary Kagak, were Eskimos. Domestic help was almost impossible to come by now that the pipeline boom was on. A woman could earn more in a day working in a restaurant, even a greasy spoon, than she could in a week of housework. Or as a prostitute. Eskimo household help was about all that was available, and even they demanded outrageous wages.

It wasn't that Louise had anything against Eskimos in general, but she considered them indolent and mostly incompetent. She had to keep a constant vigil over her two. They weren't actually insolent, not by word or gesture anyway, but in talking to those expressionless faces and black, shoe-button eyes, one might as well be addressing a dish! Both women could speak English well enough, yet getting a grunt out of them was something of an accomplishment.

Everything seemed well under control, so Louise went into the "saloon." At least she had cajoled—bribed would be more apt—an off-duty bartender into moonlighting this evening. A white man, not an Eskimo.

"Tom, would you make me a martini? A strong one, please. I feel in need of a stimulant."

"Certainly, Mrs. Cole."

This room she called the parlor and Will called the saloon was only one example of the differences in their outlook on life. When Will built the house, he had given her carte blanche with the architects, builders, designers, decorators, et cetera—with one stipulation. This room was to be his to do with as he pleased. It was a long room, on the south front, opening off the entrance hall. At the time Louise had considered it a little enough concession, but she had been horrified at the end result.

That was another thing she blamed Jeremiah Cole for. In designing the "saloon," Will, she was positive, was trying to outdo what Kelly called the baronial hall in Cole House.

Will had recreated a barroom of the Dawson City Gold Rush days, only on a far more elaborate scale. Their guests exclaimed at how fitting it was—and how cute. Louise was certain that most of them were surely lying out of politeness, because she thought the room tacky, in appallingly bad taste.

The entire north side of the room was taken up by the mahogany bar, with a brass rail, and brass spittoons placed at regular intervals. Thank God very few people, only the boors, ever expectorated in them. Behind the bar were two glass shelves holding bottles of every kind of liquor imaginable. But also behind the bar, on the wall, highlighted by neon tubing the length of the top, hung an enormous painting of a voluptuous nude. Everything was visible, of course, especially the breasts, but that wouldn't have been so bad if the artist hadn't included a red, V-thicket of pubic hair at the loins. The woman in the portrait lay half on her side, one leg cocked in the traditional prostitute's position, and one hand suggestively near the pubic patch.

Thank God, the actual lips of the vagina hadn't been painted in!

Louise had tried to get Will to have the artist airbrush out the pubic area, but he had waved her away with a booming laugh.

The rest of the room was taken up by round tables with chairs for four at each, upholstered and comfortable at least; a player piano; and a large green felt-covered poker table in one corner where Will and his card-playing cronies played at least once a week.

The only saving grace was the fireplace, with a grouping of easy chairs and two couches before it, and a polar bear rug on the floor.

Louise took her drink and crossed the room to the fireplace. She arranged herself on the couch, careful not to wrinkle the long, black hostess gown. She took a healthy gulp of the potent martini, gazed into the blazing fire, and once again asked herself the question, the question that recurred every time she paused for serious thought: What had happened to her marriage?

The years had something to do with it, she realized that. They had married too young. The Cole men had all gotten married too young; even Joshua had been only eighteen. There was a rumor, never actually verified, certainly not by himself, that Jeremiah Cole had married young back in California and had deserted his wife to join the Gold Rush, marrying a second time after starting his fortune. Dwight wasn't married, but it was common knowledge that he was living with some slut, probably as close to being married as he ever would be.

But Will had been so alive and so . . . so vital when she first met him. And handsome . . . oh, my, he had been handsome! In addition, there had been the Cole money. Louise hadn't denied to herself, then or later, that the Cole fortune had had a great deal to do with it. She had been sick of genteel poverty; her father was an accountant and he never seemed to earn much more than an adequate income.

Her childhood and teens had been spent in San Francisco, that most cosmopolitan of cities. Then her father had been offered a job with Cole Enterprises in Alaska, at twice the salary he had been earning in San Francisco. One thing nobody had bothered to tell him—it took almost twice as much money to live in Alaska and that was long before the oil boom.

They had arrived in summer which, though short, had not been too bad, but then winter came. Louise never became accustomed to the relentless cold, then or now. Garages had to be kept heated twenty-four hours a day; furnaces ran on the same schedule. Usually their oil bills for heating ran over two hundred dollars a month. Ice fog in the mornings was like breasting blowing snow. Sometimes even in heated garages automobiles had to be left running all night or risk freezing. Often, an electric heating device had to be used to keep vinyl seat coverings warm so they wouldn't crack.

Natives in Alaska took the winters in good-natured stride. In fact, they seemed to accept it as a way of life. But not Louise, and she knew that she never would. She would have left that first winter, even if she'd had to walk out, if she hadn't met Will Cole, who was at the University of Alaska. Louise had just graduated from high school in San Francisco, prepared to enroll at the University of California at Berkeley, when her father was offered the position with Cole. So instead, she found herself attending the University of Alaska at Fairbanks.

Louise had been a good-looking girl, tall, well built, with that tanned, long-legged beauty that seemed a trademark of California women. And Will Cole was the catch of the campus, of all of Fairbanks. They made a handsome couple. Louise fell headlong in love, and her parents were more than delighted to give their daughter in marriage to Will Cole.

Thinking about it later, Louise was sure that she would not have allowed herself to be rushed so quickly into Will Cole's arms had she been older. But that was all hindsight. She had allowed herself to be talked out of finishing college and was installed in the big, two-story house Joshua offered to build for his son and daughter-in-law as a wedding present.

The first few years were good, except for the bitter winters. They shared things together, they loved together and talked together, and they had fun together.

Then Will, at twenty-three, graduated from college, and things began to change. Jeremiah took him immediately into the company. By the time he was thirty-four, Will Cole was, to all intents and purposes, running Cole 98. And last year he had assumed the presidency of the whole company, when ill health forced Jeremiah into semiretirement.

The higher Will went in the company, the less Louise saw of him. Because Will wasn't content to operate out of an office like a normal executive. Oh, my, no! He was in his office less than he was at home. He was out in the field almost every day, flying here and there. Often, Louise didn't see him for days at a time. The gap between them widened. The social life that Louise had envisioned for herself as a member of Fairbanks' most prominent family never materialized.

Will had little interest in a social life, anyway. His idea of a great social evening was a gathering of a few cronies in the house, sometimes even working men stinking of fish or oil, and playing poker and drinking all night. Louise's presence was frowned upon.

Not that she had any desire to associate with them. They stank of cigars and cigarettes and whiskey and just plain body odor, and every other word was gutter filth. Even Will, who had a college education and could speak excellent English, used gutter language with apparent enjoyment.

Early on, when she had scolded him for it, he had replied, "You just don't understand, Louise. When men are with men, they talk like that. If you don't like it, stay out of earshot."

And many of those "social" gatherings ended with Will throwing one or more of his poker partners out into the snow and drunkenly battling with them. What baffled Louise about this was that the very same man would likely be back again the following week. These people were incomprehensible to her.

Finally Louise confronted Will with it, on her thirtieth birthday, which Will, predictably, had forgotten. She said, "Dear God, I don't understand! Will, why did you marry me?"

The argument had been going on for some time, and Will, pale with anger and weariness, snapped, "To bear and raise me sons!"

Louis recoiled. "You make it sound like you married me for breeding stock!"

"Maybe I did, I don't know, and sometimes I doubt the wisdom of my choice. You certainly didn't bear me any sons, lid you? Louise..." He made a conciliatory gesture. "Do we have to do this? You are my wife, to all of Fairbanks you are my wife."

"And how about your women? Do you think I don't know about them? And if I know, don't you think all of Fairbanks knows as well?"

"I couldn't care less what the rest of Fairbanks thinks of my private life. It's none of their business."

"And me, it's none of my business?" she said quietly.

Will, just turning away from the bar after pouring himself a glass of Jack Daniel's, stared at her thoughtfully. "I suppose you could consider it your business, in a manner of speaking."

"In a manner of speaking? Will, I'm your wife!"

"That's what I mean by a manner of speaking. For the past few years, you've been my wife in name only."

"And whose fault is that? You're never home. And when you do drop in you reek of fish or oil or whiskey!"

"Louise..." He took a drink. "That's not all of it, you know it isn't. Speaking of fish, cold fishes, that is..."

Louise spun away, no longer able to look at him. "I can't help that. When I heard about you going with other women, I shuddered at the thought of you touching me."

"So? What's a man to do?"

"A man could be a gentleman, instead of a whoremonger, a drunkard, and a gambler."

"A gentleman! Jesus Christ in a wheelbarrow, Louise! In Alaska a man is a man, no more, no less. Or he's nothing."

"Your idea of what makes a man isn't mine."

"You know what your trouble is?" He swished the liquor around in his glass, eyes hard as flint. "You're an Outsider. I should never have married an Outsider. It's always a big mistake."

"There's a way to rectify that." She spoke without thinking, spoke out of a deep anger.

"A divorce?" He stared. "You're talking of a divorce, Louise?"

Louise took a deep breath, shaken by her rashness. "That way you wouldn't be saddled with a wife."

"No way, Louise, just no way," he said bluntly. "You're my wife. You belong to me, for better or worse, and I never let anything of mine go."

"What if I do it anyway?"

"You'd never get a divorce in Alaska. You know Granpap

would see to that. If you went Outside, you'd be without a dime from me."

She recoiled with a gasp. "You wouldn't! Not after all these years!"

"You know fucking well I would." Then he softened visibly. "I'm sorry, Louise. I don't mean to come down on you so hard. Maybe I made a mistake, maybe we both did, but it's made. Why can't we just go on as we have been? I'll try to be home more and . . . be more discreet. Besides, you don't have it so bad." He swept a hand around the house. "Believe me, there isn't a woman in Alaska who doesn't envy you."

It always came down to the material things with Will. Yet, am I any better? Louise mused.

She cringed to think of giving up the Cole money. She'd been too long accustomed to the good things of life. Maybe she didn't have children or the love and respect of her husband, but she had a comfortable, some might even say luxurious, life.

"And I'm not giving it up, I've earned it," she said aloud.

Startled by the sound of her own voice, she glanced around quickly. Only the bartender was in the room, and he was busy polishing glasses.

The doorbell rang. With a feeling of relief, Louise set her glass down and went to answer it. If she waited for the maid to respond, any guests waiting at the door could freeze to death.

The first guest was Joshua Cole. "Joshua!" Louise said, pleased. "Will told me you were in town and would be here tonight. I'm glad to see you. It's been ages."

"Hello, Louise."

They kissed briefly, and Louise helped him off with his outer layers of clothing and hung them in the hall closet.

She liked her father-in-law, perhaps liked him best of all the Coles. She hated Jeremiah, certainly, she wasn't sure of her feelings for Will any more, and she was always uneasy around Kelly. Dwight, she rarely ever saw, and had little feeling for him one way or another.

Josh had good manners, breeding, sophistication, and he could talk on different subjects all day without ever touching on the oil business. He was always well dressed and groomed. She could not recall ever seeing him without a tie. And he never used gutter language, at least not in her presence.

While the bartender made their drinks, Louise said, "I'm sorry, Joshua. Will isn't down yet. He just got home a bit ago and..."

"My dear, no need to apologize. Don't you think I know that son of mine?" He patted her hand. "The expression, late for his own funeral, was coined for Will."

"You know something, Joshua. I just remembered," she said in some astonishment. "Will was late for our wedding, almost a half-hour late."

Ten

Upstairs, Will Cole was taking his own good time. He was in
no hurry to meet the guests. He'd had his craw full of most of
them this afternoon. This whole thing was Louise's idea, not
his. Let them get a few shots of booze under their belts,
maybe they'd be easier to get along with.

He scowled, thinking of his wife. He was in the sunken tub
off the master bedroom, just one arm out of the steaming
water. The hand at the end of that arm held a glass of
bourbon and a cigar.

Will knew that he gave Louise a hard time, perhaps a
harder time than she deserved. She was well thought of in
Fairbanks, by the women at any rate, although he suspected
that some of the men laughed at her efforts to bring culture
and high society to Fairbanks.

Behind his back, of course. By Christ, they wouldn't dare
laugh at her in his hearing, not even if he agreed with them,
not even if he no longer loved her.

Love . . .

He didn't know if he loved her, or if he ever had. He didn't
even know if there was such an emotion as love, not as most
women defined it. Sexual attraction, yes, and there had been
a degree of that between them in the beginning, but the
years had deadened that feeling. There had been dozens of
women he'd been attracted to since he'd married Louise, and
he rarely passed up an opportunity. He didn't love Penelope
Hardesty, either, although the sexual attraction was still powerful. He grinned as a sudden thought crossed his mind—he
had been faithful to Hardesty since the first time he had
taken her to bed.

How long since he'd been to bed with Louise in the
Biblical sense? His scowl returned. They'd had separate

bedrooms for years, since that night she'd mentioned divorcing him. He grunted. Hell, that was almost five years ago!

He likely wouldn't have married her anyway if not for Jeremiah. Not that Jeremiah had picked her out for him; he knew that the old man had never cared for Louise.

"Doesn't matter whether or not I like the woman you marry, boy. You're the one has to live with her. Just marry young and have sons, carry on the Cole line. My only regret is that I never had but the one son. Bearing Joshua made your grandmother go barren on me. Could've married again. I often thought about it, but just never got around to it."

Well, in that respect, Will thought, my choice of a wife was a disaster. She'll certainly never bear me any sons now. Maybe he should divorce her, and marry again. Probably even Jeremiah would forgive a divorce if it resulted in a great-grandson to carry on the name. Maybe Jeremiah would look more favorably on him if there were sons. For some strange reason the old man had never seemed to have the confidence in Will that he should have. Jeremiah wasn't even paying him a salary in the same ball park as those oil company executives he met with today, and he was head of a conglomerate, not just a damned oil company!

Will was sure that the Cole line, the Alaska branch of it anyway, began illegitimately. Jeremiah had left a wife behind in the States in 1898, and had never bothered to send for her, or even divorce her. The old man had confided that to Will once when he'd had too much bourbon. What did the legal aspect of it mean to Jeremiah back then? In those days in Alaska a man was pretty much a law unto himself; whatever he had the guts and the strength to get away with, he could; and Will was positive that the old man had gotten away with plenty.

Will got out of the tub, padding naked and dripping across the bedroom, and cracked open the door. The hum of voices from downstairs told him that at least some of the guests had arrived. He could go down now.

Entering the saloon downstairs, a fresh cigar fuming, he was surprised to see that only one of the men from this afternoon's meeting was missing. Even some of the wives were along. Or girl friends. Maybe they thought that accepting a dinner invitation would smooth his ruffled feathers. Well, they sure as hell were wrong there. Likely, they came out of simple curiosity—to see how the Alaskan barbarian behaved in a social atmosphere.

Will was surprised to see Kelly standing to one side with Brad Connors. He crossed over to them. "I'm glad to see you, Kelly, but I thought Louise said you'd turned down the invitation?"

"I did, Will, but I changed my mind. That's a woman's prerogative, isn't it? Anyway, Brad told me he was flying up on business, as I decided to come along."

Will's glance went from one to the other, and he cursed himself for being stupid as something suddenly became clear to him. These two were having an affair. As his gaze turned knowing, faint color rose to Kelly's face and he knew that he was right. Nothing wrong with that, of course. Kelly was a woman grown, twenty-four, if his memory served, and entitled to a life of her own. He had wondered, idly, in the past why she wasn't already married. Yet the thought of her marrying, and to Brad Connors, a man intimately connected with Cole Enterprises, made Will faintly uneasy. If she married Connors and bore him a son, thereby giving Jeremiah a great-grandson, what would that do to his, Will's, chances of fully taking over Cole with the death of the old man?

Fearful that his thoughts might be mirrored on his face, Will nodded abruptly and turned away toward the bar across the room.

Louise spotted him and came toward him. Eyes blazing, she paused to whisper balefully, "Damn you, Will Cole, the first guests arrived a half-hour ago."

"Sorry, Louise, I dozed off in the tub." He held up both hands in a defensive gesture. "But I'll behave, I swear."

"You'd better," she said, and swept on past him toward the dining room.

And Will was in a heated argument not ten minutes later, before he'd worked his way through his first Jack Daniel's. It was with one of the executives he'd met that afternoon. He had never gotten all their names sorted out—they all seemed to be turned out by the same cookie cutter. The man was complaining about the hardships of living and working in Alaska.

"You guys make my ass tired," Will said. "You come up here from Outside and right away you start to bitch. You think I don't know that all you company execs get hardship pay? Seems to me you can put up with a hell of a lot of hardship for that kind of dough!"

Will felt a gentle tug on his elbow, and he turned an angry face.

Josh smiled at him softly. "Easy does it, Will. I promised Louise I'd ride herd on you."

"I don't know what you mean, Josh," Will said innocently. "Just a little friendly discussion among friends. Right, gents?"

"My God!" Josh breathed. "Look who's here!"

Will followed his gaze to the doorway where Louise was greeting two new arrivals. The girl was a raven-haired beauty, tall, with an exciting figure, about twenty-five or so. And the man was . . .

"Jesus Christ in a wheelbarrow!" Will exclaimed. "Bry Tucker! Who's the girl?"

"I have no idea."

"So that's what Tucker meant today out at the pipeline; he knew he'd be here tonight! Louise invited him without telling me." Will thumped the bar with his knuckles. "She can goof up in the damnedest ways." Then he began to laugh. "I have to admire the bastard's gall though, coming here as bold as brass, right into the snake's den!"

"Now, Will, don't go off half-cocked. It's Louise's party, don't spoil it for her."

Just then, Louise faced around, her clear voice rising above the din. "Dinner is about to be served, ladies and gentlemen. Those of you who have drinks may bring them to the table, and Tom will be serving more for those who want them."

"That wife of mine!" Will laughed again. "One thing you have to say for her, she has a great sense of timing."

To Joshua Cole's amusement, Will was docile as a lamb during dinner. He had been as correct in his manners as a crown prince when Louise hurriedly introduced him to Bry Tucker and his companion, Candice Durayea. The union boss could have been a visiting minister of state from the courtesy Will showed him. Will did say, in an aside to Josh: "Louise acts as if I didn't even know the bastard."

Of course, during dinner, it would have been difficult for any harsh words to be exchanged. Whether by accident or design, the two late arrivals were seated at the opposite end from where Will sat—a necessarily long table since it had to accommodate close to thirty people. Josh was inclined to think that the seating arrangement was by accident. He was fond of his daughter-in-law, and she possessed average intelligence, yet Louise could be extraordinarily dense when it came to Will or anything having to do with his business affairs.

As for himself, Josh was seated on his son's immediate right, since he was supposed to keep a tight rein on Will.

And that assignment, Josh mused, could be about as challenging a task as harnessing a team of timber wolves to a dogsled. He'd had little to do with the direction of Will's life since about age eight.

It was around then that Josh firmly decided that politics was his chosen career, and had informed his father that his mind was made up. He would never, under any circumstances, have anything to do with heading up Cole Enterprises, expecting an explosion.

Instead, Jeremiah had turned his attention to the grandson, starting an early indoctrination course, shaping Will the right way, so he could eventually head up Cole. Josh suspected that Jeremiah had been secretly relieved by Josh's declaration. The old man was, usually, a shrewd judge of character, and must have long decided that he, Josh, didn't possess the ruthless drive necessary to run the company.

There was something about the current relationship between Will and Jeremiah that was puzzling to Josh. There was a coolness, at times a hostility, between them, and Josh couldn't put his finger on the cause. Of course Will was high-handed and arrogant, especially since he'd been proven correct about oil in Alaska, but then the old man had been just as bad in his day. Will grumbled often that he wasn't paid what he was worth, and that he wasn't given a free hand in running the company. That could account for his unhappiness with Jeremiah, yet it seemed to Josh that the old man no longer trusted Will.

Joshua thought about his relationship with his son. It wasn't that he was not fond of Will. Sometimes he didn't *like* him, but he was fond of him. Yet he was forced to admit that he often didn't understand his oldest son. He could understand the drive for power; Josh had that himself—politics *was* power. And the accumulation of money he could also understand, although he had to admit that Will did that mainly for the benefit of the company, and for the sheer joy of doing it.

What Josh did not understand, would never understand, he suspected, was the wild streak in Will: the hard drinking; the womanizing; the sometimes shady, at least unethical business tactics; and the seeming compulsion to place himself in physical danger as often as possible. Will often boasted that he would ask no man in his employ to do anything *he* couldn't do, and went about proving it time after time.

I suppose, Josh thought, that he frightens me; there is something self-destructive about my son. He was like one of those heroes out of a World War I movie—a fighter pilot, with teeth bared in a savage grin, scarf fluttering out behind him in the slipstream, flying right into the face of death with guns chattering.

Josh laughed aloud at himself, shaking his head to clear it, and looked around the table.

Will caught his eye and growled, "I've had enough of this shit. Let's go into the saloon and have a brandy, Josh."

"Will . . ."

Ignoring him, Will stood up, scraping his chair back.

Down at the other end of the table, Louise said quickly, "Dessert is about to be served, dear."

Will muttered something under his breath and plunged on. Resignedly Josh got up, looked at Louise with a shrug, and followed him.

From behind he heard Louise's clear voice: "Ladies and gentlemen, if I may have your attention, please. Perhaps some of you might prefer a brandy to dessert. If so, the bar is open . . ." Her laughter tinkled. Only someone familiar with Louise would have noticed the desperation in her voice.

Josh chuckled to himself and strode on to the bar, ahead of the stampede. He leaned on the rail. "Will, you can sometimes be a trial to an old man."

Will looked at him, that charming grin slashing his face, amiable now that he'd shocked everyone and infuriated Louise. "Only sometimes, Josh? You sure it ain't more often than that?"

"I refuse to commit myself."

Will blew smoke. "A bunch of goddamned stuffed shirts

and Louise trying to impress them with fancy sauces and all that shit!" At a sound he glanced around. "And here they all come!"

They were suddenly surrounded by a half-dozen people yammering at Tom for drinks. The bartender calmly placed brandy snifters before Josh and Will, and then began working his way through the other orders. Will picked up his snifter and drank.

A deep voice behind them said, "Quite a room, this. I've heard about it. Glad I finally got a chance to see it. Pretty authentic re-creation, Cole. But why no pool tables? Hell, the recreation halls for our union members, both here and in Anchorage, have pool tables. Free to the membership."

Will stiffened and slowly turned to face Bry Tucker. "Because they didn't have goddamned pool tables back in those days. Pool was considered something played by sissies."

"Couple of truck drivers I know who are pool champs of the local," Tucker observed dryly, "might resent being called sissies."

"You're something else, Tucker, you know that? A man in your position has to have the gall of a truckload of monkeys to show up as a guest in my house!"

"Why not? Your lovely wife invited me," Tucker said with a broad grin. "I told you this morning that I'd see you sooner than you thought, didn't I? Can I help it if you don't check out your guest list with your wife? Besides, you were out to my bailiwick today. Ain't I entitled to the same privilege?"

Will glared at him for a moment, then threw back his head and bellowed laughter. Tucker looked momentarily startled, then joined in.

"Listen," Will said abruptly, "do you play poker?"

"Sure, I enjoy a game of poker."

"You any damned good?"

"*I* think so." Tucker grinned. "But then I guess you've heard how immodest I am."

"Will..." Josh tugged at Will's arm, drawing him aside. "I don't think that's such a good idea, a poker game tonight. Not after Louise worked so hard to make this dinner a success."

"I'm going to do nothing to muddy Louise's evening, Josh. Poker won't be until after the guests are gone, all except those I invite to play." Will's grin was savage. "This union bastard invaded my turf, Josh. He's going to pay for that."

When they turned back to Tucker, he had been joined by Candice Durayea. She's a marvelously lovely creature, Josh mused. Emerald green eyes, short black hair, a tall, lissome figure boldly outlined in a tight-fitting, dove-colored pants suit. And approximately half Bry Tucker's age. What was her interest in Tucker? Of course, he was cocky, strutting, giving off an aura of virility like a macho aftershave. Still...

She was speaking, "I understand there's a poker game later, Mr. Cole?"

Will looked over at her. "That's right, Miss... Miss Durayea, is it?"

"Candice Durayea, Cole. She's with me." Tucker draped a casual arm around her shoulder.

"So? Take her home, then come back. The poker game won't start until late."

"I don't think you understand, Mr. Cole," Candice said. Her voice had a husky, drawling quality. Without being obvious about it, she withdrew from Tucker's embrace. "I'm asking if I'm welcome to play."

"Play? You mean, play poker with us?"

"That's exactly what I do mean, Mr. Cole."

"She's good, Cole," Tucker said. "You might be surprised at just how good."

"That's possible. A lot of things surprise me, but that's not the point. We've never had a woman in one of our games."

"Why not, Mr. Cole?"

"I don't know." Will looked faintly startled. "I just never... I guess none ever asked."

"Wouldn't that make you out to be a male chauvinist pig, Mr. Cole?"

Will groaned. "Oh, Jesus Christ in a wheelbarrow! Don't throw those women's lib clichés at me."

"Are you afraid that a woman might beat you at poker, Mr. Cole?" Now her voice was taunting. "A blow to your male pride?"

"Of course I'm not afraid..." Will broke off, hitting the bar with a rap of his knuckles. "You want to play, play. The stakes sometimes get a little steep. Just be sure you have plenty of money."

"Oh, I have plenty of money, Mr. Cole." The green eyes

were mocking. "Maybe not nearly as much as the Coles, but
enough for an evening of poker."

Josh had been listening to the exchange with growing
amusement. Suddenly, he decided to stay around. It promised to be an interesting evening. He had a hunch it might be
a poker game to remember.

His thoughts were interrupted as the Eskimo maid
approached him. "Mr. Cole? Somebody want you on phone
in study office."

Will and Candice Durayea were still speaking as Josh left
the room. He went down the hall to Will's study and to the
phone on the desk. "Hello?"

"Will? That you, boy?" a thin voice asked.

Josh grunted. "No, Pap, this is Josh."

"Hellfire, I wanted Will, not you, Joshua. I thought you
were in D.C.?"

"I flew in today, Pap. The maid must have misunderstood
who you wanted. Just hang on, I'll get Will . . ."

The receiver crashed down on the other end.

In Cole House Jeremiah slammed down the telephone in
anger. He was sure that Will purposely avoided talking to
him. Once, the boy had been all too eager to talk to his
grandfather. How many times had he sat quietly, listening
enthralled as Jeremiah talked of the old days?

But no more, no more.

The old man sat in the wheelchair in his bedroom in
darkness, sipping sour mash bourbon. He would have liked a
cigar, but even if he had one available, the odor would likely
wake up his watchdog, who thought he was safely tucked in
bed. The doctors had warned Jeremiah that liquor and cigars
were bad for him, but then they'd been telling him that for
twenty-five years. He'd finally given up the cigars, because it
wasn't easy to smoke them without getting caught; but
Will still smuggled in a bottle of sour mash now and
then.

"What the hell, Jeremiah, you've been drinking sour mash
by the barrel since I can remember," he had said with that
devil-may-care grin of his. "And it looks as though you might
outlive us all!"

Some might think that his grandson smuggled in the sour mash in the hope that it would hasten his death. Once, Jeremiah would have scoffed at such a suggestion. But no more, no more.

That hadn't stopped his taking advantage of the whiskey Will supplied. A man his age should have at least one small pleasure left to him.

He wasn't supposed to be up this late, either. The doctors: "The more hours of sleep you get, Mr. Cole, the better."

Only a little after nine and he was supposed to be in bed! The damned doctors didn't seem to realize that a man his age didn't sleep well, just a catnap from time to time. Well, frig all the doctors! He'd made fools out of them for years and he was going to live one more year, damn their eyes! He was going to live to celebrate his one-hundredth.

The drink actually had little more effect on him than warm water, but it brought a little heat to his cold bones, and helped bring back the memories. He lived much of the time in the past now, anyway; his memories were more pleasant than reality.

It was funny about the cold. In his younger days, he seldom minded the Alaskan winters. He had seemed to have some sort of immunity to the cold.

But now, here in this heated house, he was always cold, cold deep in his bones.

He sat in the wheelchair at the window, staring out into the night . . .

. . . and he was back on the Chilkoot Pass in that bitter winter of '98. He had slept little during that arduous trek over the pass, striding on into the long nights up the 32-degree grade, past campfire after campfire where weary, shivering men huddled.

Many had believed the myth that a man could pack his own weight over the pass. Examples of their folly lay strewn on every side of the trail as they had lightened their loads item by item. Jeremiah, weighing two-twenty, had outfitted himself with a little over a hundred pounds. Necessities only: bacon, flour, dried fruits, tobacco, plus as few utensils as possible, a bedroll, and a few extra items of clothing. All in the pack on his back. In one mittened hand he carried a .30-30 repeating rifle, and a hunting knife in his belt. Of course, he had been in his prime then, just twenty-one.

"Keep your bedroll clean, Will boy, always remember that," he said aloud. "If it becomes inhabited, freeze the boogers out."

Startled by the sound of his own voice, he sat up, blinking. He was alone, Will wasn't here.

He sipped sour mash, and sank back once more into the past.

He had made it over the pass and to the gold fields. Contrary to the legends about Jeremiah Cole, he didn't hit it big right away. The best claims were already taken. He found a few nuggets, true, but not enough to make it worth the backbreaking labor. It was a myth that he had perpetrated for reasons of his own—he well knew what myths did to a man's image. And it would never do to let people know that he had failed to make a big strike in the Klondike. It was part of his philosophy. When he failed at anything, he kept it as secret as possible. Failure had a stink about it that lingered for a long time.

Besides, what man now alive could call him a liar?

Failing to make the big strike, he had worked at many jobs around Dawson City. Jobs were plentiful; men were interested in scratching for gold, the big strike, not in grubbing away at a job. And wages were good. He worked, hoarding his earnings.

He had gradually worked his way over to Fairbanks and made his big strike at Chena, in 1903.

"Did I ever tell you how I struck it big, Will, boy? The damnedest thing you won't believe it. I was in Fairbanks, you see, when this Irisher I knew came in from Chena. He was illiterate and wanted somebody to write a letter to his wife back in Ireland. I knew he was working a claim outside of Chena. I asked him how he was doing. Not too good, he says. It was hard going it alone. On the spot we made a deal. If I'd write his letter for him and help him put his hole down through the tundra to pay dirt, he'd deed me half-interest in his claim." The old man chuckled in the empty room. "Well, sir, boy, three months later we struck it. Bigger strike than the one I made in the Klondike. We took two million in gold out of that claim in two years time..."

Jeremiah's voice trailed off, his chin slumping forward onto his chest, and his glass dropped to the floor with a thud. He slept in the wheelchair, and in his dreams he once again saw those many campfires he had trudged past on his climb over the 3,500-foot peak of Chilkoot Pass.

Eleven

Will Cole was in a vile mood; a mood he tried, successfully he hoped, to hide from the group of men having lunch around the table in the boardroom, chattering and scolding one another like a bunch of quarreling chipmunks.

Will knew that he couldn't hide his grumpiness from Josh, who sat on his right. Josh had witnessed the debacle last night.

He was a poor loser, Will knew, at poker or anything else. Recognizing this about himself, he tried to cover it up, and he usually succeeded. The hell of it was, he seldom lost—at anything.

But last night a woman, goddamnit, had beat him at poker! Jesus Christ in a wheelbarrow!

His intention, naturally, had been to best Bry Tucker, but almost from the moment they sat down to play, the contest had been between Will and Candice Durayea. Tucker, and the two oil company men Will had been able to badger into joining the game, hadn't mattered in the least.

Candice was one hell of a poker player, a fact Will had soon grasped, and he had risen to the challenge. Man, woman, ape—a good poker player was a good poker player.

Candice knew cards, and before long Will sensed that she had a poker mind, one that could sniff out her opponents' hole cards. Will called it poker ESP. That was all right—he had that poker instinct himself.

But what had infuriated, and finally defeated him, was her ability to hide when she was bluffing. She sacrificed a few early antes by dropping out. Getting the feel of the other players, Will later realized. Playing with his usual boldness and flair, Will won most of the early pots. Then, suddenly, she started staying in, staying in the pot until the last card was dealt.

In one hand, after the cards were all on the table, Candice had two pair showing, twos and threes, and Will had a possible flush. Except he didn't—his hole card was the seven of spades.

They were playing a five dollar bet limit. Everybody dropped out until only Will and Candice were left.

It was Will's bet. "I don't think you have a full house," he said, and tossed in a five dollar chip.

"It'll cost you to find out, Mr. Cole. Matching your five and raising five."

He tried his damnedest to bluff her out of the pot, but she matched him bet for bet.

Finally he said, "All right, enough already. I'll match your five and call."

Calmly she turned over her hole card, a third deuce, and just as calmly raked in the pot, which had grown substantially.

But the topper was the last pot of the evening. It was growing late, and the oilmen were yawning, complaining that they had to fly back to Anchorage early in the morning, so all agreed that it would be the last hand.

Both Will and Candice had been drawing good cards the last few hands, clashing head to head on almost every pot, and so it was again.

The other players dropped out one by one. Will had a possible straight showing, and this time he had it. Candice had three aces and a ten showing. The fourth ace wasn't on the table. Could she have it? Will could detect nothing in her lovely face, and those green eyes were as calm as a mountain lake. He had been watching her carefully all evening. Always there was a sign to be found. Even the best of poker players gave themselves away somewhere along the way, if a man was sharp enough to catch it.

And now, as Candice shoved two five dollar chips into the pot, matching his and raising, Will noticed the faint tremor of her hand. She had the fourth ace, he was sure of it.

"It's your pot, Candice. You've got that goddamned fourth ace, I know it in my gut, and that beats my little straight." He turned his cards over.

She didn't have to show her hole card, not after he'd

thrown his hand in. Never let the other player know you've been bluffing, unless you're called. But Candice did. Smiling ever so slightly, she flipped it over.

A deuce, a goddamned deuce!

Will stared in disbelief as a bellow of laughter erupted from Bry Tucker...

A nudge from Josh brought Will back to the present and the boardroom. The luncheon was over; waiters were clearing the table.

Will sighed. Now, already in a disgruntled mood, he had to deal with this newly formed reform committee, all so uptight about whoring, drinking, and gambling in Fairbanks—as natural to men as breathing—so uptight that their assholes were all puckered. Worst of all, he had to listen to speeches now. Some of them were politicians. An aide from the mayor's office was there, as well as several others in city government, including two men from the police department. They bitched and moaned about the bad image the big crime wave was giving to the fair city of Fairbanks. The men from the police said they simply couldn't handle the workload; they were too shorthanded.

After the others were done, an interminable time, Josh said a few well-chosen words. He promised to do everything he could at the federal and state level, getting special legislation passed if necessary, allocating state funds, and exploring the possibility of assigning more state police to the area.

Finally it was Will's turn. He didn't get up. "I'll keep mine short, gents." He rapped the table with his knuckles. "You have my support, that goes without saying. You may use my name. You can say that Cole Enterprises is behind you one hundred percent. In addition, I will contribute some money toward financing your campaign. Red..." He nodded to Red Patterson by his side. "Make them out a company check for five grand... no, make that ten, and I'll sign it. What's more, I've already decided that I'm going to look into this personally, see if there's anything I can do." Now why did I say that, he thought in dismay; it's thievery along the pipeline that I'm burned about, not what happens here in town.

Murmurs of appreciation swept the table, but he wasn't off the hook yet.

Down the table a man with a long, dour face leaned

forward. "Mr. Cole, do you believe it's true what some of the newspapers are saying? That organized crime has moved into Fairbanks, into Alaska?"

Will squinted down the table, trying to peg a name to the face. Then he vaguely remembered the man being introduced as a minister of some kind. "Well, Reverend..." That should be safe enough. "I'm hardly the man to answer that question. We have two police officers here with us. That's their business, after all."

Everyone looked at the two policemen sitting side by side. They glanced at one another uneasily. Finally one cleared his throat and said, "I can answer that in only one way. In all our investigations we have found no evidence pointing toward organized crime in Fairbanks."

"And why should organized crime move in here?" Will sliced the air with his hand. "The mob moves in where they can put down roots and grow." He thought, I sound just like I know what the hell I'm talking about. "What kind of a situation do we have here? Another year, two at the most, the pipeline boom will be over, and we'll settle back into our old rut." He smiled. "Don't believe everything you read in the papers, gents. What vice and crime we have here belongs to the carrion that always gathers when there's a boom, when pickings are good for a time. Boom's over, they move on." He scraped his chair back. "Now you'll have to excuse me, I have a busy afternoon. Thanks for coming, and good luck with your committee."

With a wave of his hand he went striding from the room. Let Josh take care of getting rid of them. He'd done all he'd promised Josh he would do.

But now he knew he would have to act, go through the motions anyway. It was possible that Milo Fanti was behind the pipeline thievery, as the bulldozer operator, Chris O'Keefe, claimed.

Will told Cora that he would be unavailable for the rest of afternoon, and drove down to the Two Street district. He found a parking space two blocks away from Fanti's building and walked the rest of the distance, unrecognized in the throng.

As he walked, he mused on what little he knew about Milo Fanti, all secondhand information. He supposed that Fanti would fit the Reverend's definition of a rackets operator, and Will was reasonably sure that Fanti had, at some time or another, been connected with organized crime. Yet he was equally convinced that Fanti was strictly on his own here. Probably an outcast from the Mafia for breaking their code.

According to the rumors, Fanti had appeared in Fairbanks about a year ago, from Outside. Again according to rumors, the hustling fraternity next showed up in droves. Where before the prostitutes and the gamblers had been mostly freelance, soon there was an organized look about them. Will had often wondered if Fanti was behind Penelope Hardesty's operation, but he had never been interested enough to ask.

Someone had once pointed Fanti out to him in a crowd. A creepy-looking character—a small, dapper man, with dark, slicked-down hair, a swarthy complexion, black, shoe-button eyes, and a George Raft poker face. He would have been an asset to any gangster movie.

Fanti had an office on the second floor of an ancient building, over a sleazy bar. Will mounted the creaking wooden steps alongside the building. A plain wooden door at the top of the steps had the words, *Milo Fanti, Investments*, painted across one panel.

Will gave a snort of amusement. Investments indeed! He rapped hard on the door.

In a few moments the door swung open, and to Will's surprise, Fanti himself stood in the doorway.

"Milo Fanti?"

"Yeah."

"I'm..."

"I know who you are, Mr. Cole." Fanti's thin lips drew back in what could pass for a smile. "I've been more or less expecting a visit from you."

"Expecting *me*?" Will said in astonishment.

"I knew that we'd be meeting sooner or later. I even thought of going to your office, but then that would never do, would it?" The smile widened a trifle. He stepped back, motioning. "Come along to my office, Mr. Cole."

Still taken aback, Will followed him down the dingy hall. The small office was as disreputable as Fanti himself.

"A drink, Mr. Cole?"

"No, thanks, Fanti. I didn't come here for a drink. Tell me why you've been expecting me."

Fanti went around behind his scruffy desk, and Will sat on a short couch that sagged alarmingly under his weight.

Fanti leaned across his desk. "Mr. Cole, I'm going into business in Fairbanks in a big way. I already have about a half-hundred whores hustling for me, but I'm in the process of expanding. I'm buying two bars and I intend to open the back rooms to games, along with a bookie operation. The back rooms will run twenty-four hours a day, booze served around the clock."

"You don't beat around the bush, do you? Jesus Christ in a wheelbarrow!" Will had listened with amazement and growing bewilderment. "Why tell me all this? And I understand you've been here almost a year. Why wait until now to expand?"

"It takes time to set things up the right way. When I do something, I want it to be right."

"You still haven't told me why you're laying it all out for me."

"Because you're the power in Fairbanks, you and Cole Enterprises. You have the most clout of any guy in town."

"Are you offering me a bribe?" Will asked in a softly dangerous voice. "A cut of the profits, some deal like that?"

"Oh, heavens, no! I would never do a thing like that, Mr. Cole."

"At least you have that much sense." Will leaned back relaxing a little. "But I'm still not clear as to why you're telling me all this."

"Because I want to reach an understanding. The boom is just heating up, men making more money than ever before in their lives. They are going to pour in here during their leaves. They'll want women, booze around the clock. They'll want to gamble. Agreed?"

"Oh, I agree with all that, right enough." Will suddenly bellowed with laughter. "Christ, you've got the gall of..." He leaned forward, eyes narrowing. "Let me ask you something, Fanti. There's a hell of a lot of thievery going on along the pipeline, material and expensive equipment disappearing. Even if the thieves are pipeline workers stealing on their own, they have to have a fence to go to. Are you involved in that?"

Without blinking so much as an eyelash, Fanti answered, "No, Mr. Cole. That's not my bag."

"I also hear that someone is peddling booze and drugs at the camps, even sending hookers out in campers. Know anything about that?"

"Again, no. I have enough to keep me busy right here in Fairbanks."

Will stared at him hard for a moment, undecided whether to believe him or not. Finally he said harshly, "I'll take your word for that, for now. But if I ever learn that you're behind any of it, I'll have your ass, Fanti. As for what happens here in town, I know somebody has to provide...uh, services." He grinned. "I'll admit that to you, privately, but don't expect me to say so publicly."

"Understood, Mr. Cole," Fanti said soberly. "What I ask of you is a quiet word in the right place, so that we won't get hassled every time we turn around."

"If I can help you there, I will, with one proviso." He leaned forward again. "Whatever is good for the pipeline workers, I'm for, so let's understand each other on that. No shady dealings. No crooked tables, watered booze. No con games played by the girls, or rolling of drunk customers."

"None of that, Mr. Cole," Fanti said almost primly. "I don't have to. The percentages are in my favor. I'm sure you're well aware of that. Besides, it wouldn't be good for repeat business."

"And the girls. Regular medical inspection. That's all we need, a VD epidemic. That could close down the whole pipeline!"

"Agreed, Mr. Cole. A clean operation all the way."

Will studied the man closely for a few moments, still far from satisfied, but he could only bide his time and see what happened. He said, "There's one thing you should know. I was at a meeting not an hour ago. A reform committee has been set up, to eliminate vice and crime in Fairbanks."

Fanti took it equably enough. "I've heard rumors, so I'm not surprised."

"Well, it's no longer a rumor. I've given them my blessing, plus ten grand, and permission to use my name on their literature. Nothing much else I could do. I have to live here after you're long gone, Fanti."

Fanti said impassively, "A man has to look after his own interests, Mr. Cole."

"You don't seem particularly concerned."

"I'll survive." Fanti shrugged. "Reform committees come and they go. A hazard of the business."

"If it's any consolation, your name wasn't brought up. If it gets to me that they're nipping at your heels, I'll let you know. Not as a favor to you, but because what you're doing provides a needed service."

"You'll have my thanks for that."

"No thanks needed," Will said curtly. "But one thing does still bother me a little."

"And what is that, Mr. Cole?"

"I'm still not convinced of your reasons for telling me all this. Now I'm wondering if you haven't been blowing smoke here today, setting me up some way as a patsy. You suspected that this reform group might start up, right?"

"It's something that a man in my business always suspects, Mr. Cole. But as for setting you up, how on earth could I do that, a powerful man like you? There's no way I could do that, Mr. Cole."

Of course I'm setting you up, *Mister* Cole, Milo Fanti thought after his visitor had left; but in a way you'd never suspect.

Fanti laughed aloud, a luxury he allowed himself only in private, and crossed to the small refrigerator installed in one corner of the office. He took out a can of beer and ripped off the tab, taking a thirsty gulp. He kept the refrigerator stocked with beer. It was his only vice, except for a woman when the need came on him, maybe once a week. Fanti didn't drink anything stronger. But he started the day with a can of beer for breakfast and consumed no less than two six-packs a day, evenly spaced out. His spare frame never gained an ounce. Doctors told him that he was one of the rare ones, with a metabolism that allowed him to eat and drink anything. Food, he could take or leave, but he loved beer.

Back at his battered desk, Fanti sat in the swivel chair, greedily swigging the beer and thinking about Mr. Holier-than-thou Will Cole. If Cole only knew that Penelope Hardesty's bedroom was bugged! Fanti had enough tape of what went on in that bedroom between Penelope and Will Cole to shock the pants off all Fairbanks residents about their most prominent citizen. And all without Penelope's knowledge, which made it all the more delicious.

It gave Fanti a kick that, with his bugs, he had reduced Penelope and Will Cole to a whore and her trick. Actually it was sheer good luck that she had connected with Will Cole.

As for Penelope Hardesty . . . some day he would humble and humiliate the snooty bitch. She had humiliated *him*. When she had the house running smoothly, Fanti had dropped around one evening, late—his weekly visit for his cut. On that night he had wanted more than just money.

Penelope had nipped that at once. "No way will I put out for you, buster. I'll run your flesh salon. But that's as far as it goes. I'm particular who I sleep with."

Remembering Cole's questions about the illegal activity involving the pipeline, Fanti laughed aloud again.

He was into more than prostitution and gambling. It *was* his trucks and his men running booze to the camps, and now and then a batch of broads, and he charged whatever the traffic would bear. Not too long ago, he had started handling pot, even coke and heroin.

More than that, he was partially responsible for the pipeline thefts. Not that he did the actual stealing or paid to have it done, but he was operating as a fence. The construction workers stole material and equipment from the pipeline, up to and including trucks and larger equipment, and Fanti bought the stuff for about a quarter of the market value and shipped it out of Alaska for sale elsewhere.

Now if Will Cole knew these things, especially about the fencing, he'd likely have a stroke. There was a good chance that Cole would eventually find out and come screaming. If and when that occurred, Fanti wanted to be fully prepared. He had to have enough ammunition not only to shut him up but also to assure his cooperation. With Will Cole behind him, Fanti knew that he would be virtually untouchable.

The tapes were not enough. Fanti believed he had a way to ensure Cole's cooperation. He prided himself on having an instinct for greed in a fellow human, and he had smelled it in Will Cole. Perhaps Cole didn't realize it, but it was there, and Fanti was certain that it wouldn't take a great deal to hook the man. Greed was a worse addiction than hard drugs.

For the first time in his life, Milo Fanti was involved in something big, and better still, entirely on his own.

For years he had worked for the Mafia, the Syndicate—whatever name the media applied to it in any particular year—but had never had anything really good going for him. Unless you were a blood member of the family, it was hard as hell to get up into the big money. You had to work your way up from the bottom, doing all the dirty jobs, and showing unswerving loyalty. And even then a man seldom got his hands on the heavy sugar. Those goddamn Moustache Petes gave all the good deals to their own blood, even if the bastards had all the intelligence of a Mongoloid idiot. And they discouraged any of their lesser men from having a little action of their own going on the side. That was where Fanti had gotten into trouble.

In New York he'd had a numbers operation of his own, nothing big, but a smooth, well-functioning setup. It went fine for two years, bringing him in a tidy sum. Then a disgruntled runner blew the whistle on him, and he was called on the carpet, ordered to break up his operation or end up with his feet encased in cement in the East River. Frightened, Fanti agreed to stop. As a further punishment, he was banished to Miami, and placed in charge of a gambling joint.

Fanti behaved himself for a year, but his itch for action soon overcame his fear, and he started a string of call girls. Within a short time he had a lucrative business going. He was congratulating himself when they pulled the zipper on him again. It seemed they had been watching him closely. Fortunately, the Syndicate dons were beginning to worry about their image. Instead of wasting him, he was tossed out of the organization, with a warning. If he ever again engaged in any activity in competition with the mob, he *would* be killed.

Fanti learned of the pipeline boom about to begin in Alaska, and that was how he came to Fairbanks.

Here, he wasn't in competition with the Syndicate. Fanti figured that he would have a couple of million tax-free dollars salted away by the time the boom was over; and if the natural gas pipeline was ever built, he would still be in business. If not, he would move on.

He had only one regret—that the big guys in the mob didn't know how well he was doing.

He finished the can of beer and reached for the phone. When a voice finally answered on the other end, he said crisply, "I just saw Will Cole. You're right, he's a plunger, and he's got greed coming out of his pores. Now it's your turn. I've got the line out, now you bait the hook and reel him in. I want him hooked solid by the time of the spring thaw and work on the pipeline picks up."

Twelve

The break Chris was looking for came from an unexpected source.

He knew better than to question the other workers too closely. If they suspected that he was snooping, he could end up with a shovel alongside his head. He decided that his best stratagem would be to grumble to each worker in turn that he would like a chance to pick up a few easy, extra bucks. There would be nothing unusual in that; despite the fact that the men were earning more money than they had ever dreamed of, most of them were always looking for a way to pick up a few extra dollars.

He broached the question in idle conversation to worker after worker, and received only a shrug for an answer, until he mentioned it to Ben Slocum.

By some strange twist of reasoning, Slocum had become friendly toward him since the fight they'd had the day of Will Cole's visit to the pipeline. Chris still did not like the Oklahoman and was not particularly flattered that his friendship was courted; but since he was not combative by nature, he did not rebuff the man.

Even after Chris was promoted to a better job with better pay, Slocum still remained friendly.

During an idle hour one afternoon, Chris approached Slocum. "How you doing, Ben?"

"Okay, I reckon, now that the cold weather's vamoosed. How're yu'all, Chris?"

"Aw, hell, I don't know." Chris scratched a toe across the softening tundra. "I just wish there was an easy way to pick up a few extra bucks. Seems like everybody is doing something on the side, except me."

Slocum looked at him with interest. "You're making more'n me these days, running that manlift."

"I know, but it strikes me that a man should make it while he can. I've just put in for ten days' R&R, starting Monday morning. I hear everything's sky-high in town. A little extra dough would come in handy."

"There is a way, man ain't too particular." Slocum peered about slyly, lowering his voice to just above a whisper.

"I guess I'm not overly particular, if I don't have to kill somebody."

"Nothing as bad as that." Slocum grinned, showing a broken tooth. "How about stealing? Got any compunctions about that?"

"It depends." Chris tried not to look too interested. "Stealing what and from whom?"

"From the pipeline, where else? And you steal whatever's worth stealing. That bother you?"

Chris appeared to think it over before he replied. "Not that much, if it'd be worth a man's time. What the hell, everything's cost plus, so who would it hurt?"

"Now you're talking." Slocum put his hand on Chris's shoulder, leaning close. His breath was sour. "You must have heard about all the stuff disappearing from the job?"

Chris nodded. "Yeah, I've heard. But to steal something worth anything, a man'd have to know where to sell it. For instance, you couldn't drive a stolen dump truck all over Alaska looking for a buyer."

Slocum lowered his voice even more. "Just after I went to work here, I stole a bulldozer and sold it. What do you think of that now?" Slocum's little eyes gleamed with pride.

Chris whistled softly. "I'd say that was something else! But how did you get rid of it?"

"Oh, I had a buyer all lined up before I stole it. I had a man in Fairbanks."

Chris just nodded, holding his breath, afraid to push it so far as to ask the man's name.

Slocum made an elaborate pretense of looking around. "You say you're going to Fairbanks Monday morning?"

"That's my plan."

"I'll go in with you. I have a couple of days coming to me. I need a round with a woman. The ones Fanti sends out here in campers are a sorry bunch, they purely are."

Chris arched an eyebrow. "Fanti?"

"Oops! I reckon I shouldn't have mentioned his name. But what the hey?" Slocum shrugged. "That's why I thought I'd go into town with you, introduce you to this guy, the guy to go to when you have something to sell. So you'll know then anyway. Name's Milo Fanti. But don't tell anybody I told you, most of all Fanti himself. I'm always supposed to check with him before I bring a guy around to see him. But I'll give him a call before we go in. I'm sure it'll be okay."

There were more questions clamoring to be asked, but Chris decided to postpone them. He had a bottle of Scotch stashed away in his locker. He'd take it with him on the bus. It was a long haul into Fairbanks. If he could get Slocum sloshed enough, he could ask his questions without arousing too much suspicion.

"That sounds fine with me. See you on the bus Monday morning, good buddy."

He clapped Slocum on the back and started back to his machine, a sour taste in his mouth. He wasn't cut out to be a snoop, an informer. Even if he didn't particularly like Ben Slocum, it went against the grain.

Spring had come to Alaska a little early this year. Some of the snow was melting in the lower elevations of the Brooks Range, and the solid ice in the river was groaning and creaking, preparatory to the spring thaw. Soon, wild flowers would be springing up, Chris knew. Wild life would be on the move. The day before he had seen a herd of caribou and numerous willow ptarmigan. The temperature was above normal. The coldest it had been for several days was 7 degrees above and the days sometimes nudged up into the forties. Now that the thaw had begun, they could start laying pipe again, and soon the work force would swell to near capacity.

Chris returned to his machine and went back to work. The manlift was on the order of an elevator, raising and lowering according to the need. It was mounted on a backhoe frame, with a platform. It was capable of swinging a full 360 degrees. Chris's job was to move the platform into position so two men could stand on it and drill holes in the large beams between two VSMs (vertical support members) which would ultimately support the pipe. In this area they were laying the pipe above ground so that the heat from the pipeline when

eventually put in use would not melt the tundra, and high
enough off the ground to allow wildlife to pass under the
pipeline itself.

There was nothing difficult about operating the machine.
Chris was very good with machinery, and it had only taken
him an hour or so to get on top of this one. It was easier
than running a bulldozer, and it had meant a jump in salary.

The nights were still long and it was dark at seven o'clock
on Monday morning when Chris walked up toward the area
where the bus waited.

Several men were already waiting outside the bus, smoking
and stamping their feet. Chris was among them before his
sleep-dulled senses caught onto the air of excitement. They
talked in low voices, shooting glances at the corner of a
nearby building where several other men were congregated.

Chris nudged the man next to him. "What's all the
excitement?"

"Haven't you heard? A man was killed last night. Murdered,
a knife in his back. An informer, the rumor is, an undercover
guy looking into dope."

"What's the dead guy's name?"

The other man shrugged. "Don't know."

Chris had been looking around at the group waiting for the
bus. Ben Slocum wasn't among them and Chris had a premonition, a premonition that grew into a cold gut feeling of
conviction as he hurried over to the group by the building.

He elbowed his way through the crowd, ignoring the
grumbles. A camp policeman kneeled on the ground beside
the body of Ben Slocum. Slocum was sprawled on his stomach, his face twisted around so Chris could recognize him.
The handle of a hunting knife protruded from his back.

Chris felt his stomach heave and he hastily backed out of
the circle, before the policeman could spot him and ask
questions. A few feet away, he leaned against the building,
fighting back the urge to vomit, as bitter gall rose to his
mouth.

It was too much of a coincidence, Slocum's being killed so
soon after their talk. It must have something to do with the
pipeline thievery. Slocum had done something to upset whoever was in charge. A disturbing thought edged into Chris's

mind. Had Slocum called Milo Fanti in Fairbanks, as he had said he intended doing, and told him he had a new recruit for him? And had he mentioned his, Chris's, name?

Did he dare approach Milo Fanti now? He mulled it over as he boarded the bus an hour later. If Slocum had given his name, he was in potential danger anyway. He might as well follow through, taking it a step at a time. There could be other reasons why Slocum was killed. He knew Slocum to be a greedy man; maybe he had stolen an item or two and peddled them to someone else besides his contact in Fairbanks.

The crowd aboard the bus grinding its slow way down to Fairbanks soon became boisterous. An hour late getting started, the pipeliners were subdued at first, sobered by the murder of one of their own. But the mood didn't last long. After all, it was R&R time! A couple of bottles were passed around. Chris took a token sip, but remained mostly to himself, staring out the window at nothing, brooding, trying to plan what he would do in Fairbanks.

It was beginning to look like he would soon regret his impetuous promise to Will Cole. He grinned mirthlessly, as he recalled an old Army saying: "Never volunteer for *anything*."

From the aisle he picked up a discarded edition of yesterday's Fairbanks *Daily News-Miner*. Two items snagged his attention.

The first was a paragraph on the lower right-hand corner of the front page: "Plane Crash in Wrangell Mountains: A small plane carrying tourists from Juneau to Taku Glacier Lodge crashed last evening on a mountaintop above the glacier. The plane carried six people, including the pilot. So far, no survivors have been found..."

Chris shook his head. The statistics on plane crashes up here were frightening.

The second article concerned pipeline corruption, and the recent spate of publicity. In the last paragraph of the article Chris found: "Will Cole, president of Cole Enterprises and vice-president of Cole 98, when asked to comment on all the stories about pipeline corruption in the Stateside newspapers, had this to say: 'Those stories are grossly exaggerated...'"

It was late afternoon when the bus reached Fairbanks. The others, tired from the long ride and most of them hungover, scattered to find lodgings. They would be lucky to find a cot somewhere, Chris knew, and would pay dearly for that.

Chris separated from them. Although weary, he wanted to walk for a little and clear his head. Carrying the small tote bag with toilet necessities, huddled in the mackinaw against the evening's chill, he walked down Two Street.

Second Avenue had always been the town's Skid Row, Chris understood. With the pipeline it had grown considerably, packed with tawdry bars and other similar establishments. Even this early, a few prostitutes approached him. Chris ignored them and strolled on. Some of the buildings, he noticed, had been thrown up in such a haphazard fashion they looked flimsy enough to blow over in the first strong wind. Even several tents had been set up on empty lots, advertising lodging at outrageous prices, some as high as fifty dollars a night. He had heard tales of men paying twenty dollars to sleep on a pool table for the night, ten to sleep under it.

He walked on, out of the main part of town, heading in the general direction of the university. Soon he could see it up ahead, a scattered group of buildings built on a high knoll.

The snow was all gone from the ground on this early spring day, but the trees were still as bare as skeletons. The area he was in now was mostly residential, middle-class prosperous; and Chris supposed that construction workers walking here were looked upon with the same suspicion as a wino wandering too far from Two Street. It was quite possible that a householder seeing him might put in a call to the police.

Chris quickened his step and turned off the street at the next corner, walked down a block, and continued on in the same direction the next street over. That was the last thing he needed—to be picked up and questioned by the police.

He didn't really know what he was doing here, but the walk had cleared his head of some of the depression and uncertainties brought on by Slocum's death. And Chris knew suddenly why he had walked this way. He had been told that the university was clean, with nice buildings, and plenty of open space between them, with none of the tawdriness that had crept over most of Fairbanks like a fungus.

Feeling much better, determined to do what he had set out to do, he turned back down the hill toward downtown.

By a stroke of good luck, he was able to find a bed for thirty bucks a night in a nearby rooming house—the occupant had been called away only a few minutes before Chris inquired. He was tired enough to fall into a deep sleep, even on a lumpy bed. In the morning he took a quick shower, changed from construction duds to the only civilian clothes he had, and went in search of breakfast. Having skipped dinner the night before, he was ravenous. He found a restaurant a few blocks from Second Avenue, and had a large breakfast: ham steak, redeye gravy, biscuits, three eggs, and a side order of hash browns. Almost all the restaurants in Fairbanks served food with a Southern flavor, a fact that always amused him. But the food was good, even though it cost him ten dollars.

It was after nine when he finished. There was a pay phone in the lobby. He debated with himself for a moment, then finally decided to make the call. After being routed from one person to another, he finally got Will Cole's personal secretary.

"Could I speak to Will Cole, please?"

"Mr. Cole is quite busy this morning," the secretary said crisply. "Unless it's important, I'm afraid . . ."

"It's important. Tell him it's Chris O'Keefe."

In a few moments Will Cole said gruffly, "O'Keefe? This better be important, I'm up to my armpits here."

Chris frowned at the receiver. Cole seemed displeased to hear from him. Was he backing away from his promise? Well, there was only one way to find out.

"I think it's important, it's about what we talked of that day on the job."

Cole was silent for a moment. "You mean you have some hard evidence for me?"

"I had a good lead that might have paid off. I'm on leave for ten days and I was going to follow it up." He went on to tell Will Cole what Ben Slocum had told him, and of Slocum being found murdered yesterday.

"You think his death has something to do with the pipeline shenanigans?" Will Cole said sharply.

"I think so. It's too much of a coincidence otherwise."

"It could just be that he had a quarrel with another pipeliner and got a knife in his back because of it."

"That's always possible, but I believe otherwise," Chris said stubbornly.

"Now let's see what you have, O'Keefe. This Slocum told you that he has been stealing stuff and peddling it to Milo Fanti and he was going to connect you with Fanti, right? And you *think* this Fanti might have something to do with his murder? Have I got it straight?"

"That's about it."

"Jesus Christ in a wheelbarrow, O'Keefe, that's not hard evidence! How can you expect me to act on that?"

"It's more than you had before," Chris said. "Can't you bring the police in on it now?"

"No, I can't. They'd laugh at me."

"Laugh at Will Cole?" Chris said with a touch of sarcasm.

"Don't mouth off to me, young fellow. The police here are understaffed, harassed, with their plate full of crime here in Fairbanks. The cops hate the pipeline, anyway. It's taken away their personnel, and created a basketful of problems for them. No, I need more to go on."

"So much for promises," Chris muttered.

"Will Cole keeps his word, O'Keefe. You bring me hard proof that Fanti is involved in the pipeline thievery and I'll hang him out to dry."

"Why should I? I'm not a cop!"

Will Cole's voice became more conciliatory. "I know, Chris. Look, don't think I don't appreciate what you're doing. If you help me put a stop to this business, I'll see to it that you're amply rewarded."

"I'm not doing this for money."

"Everybody is interested in money, Chris. It's what keeps the wheels greased." Will Cole was silent for a moment. "You going to keep on?"

Chris sighed, then said slowly, "I don't know. I'll have to think about it."

"Fine, you do that. I have to hang up now. I've got calls backed up to the men's room." Then his voice changed again. "If you do go ahead, watch your ass. If you're right about this Ben Slocum, you could wind up six feet under the tundra. I wouldn't want that to happen. Keep in touch, Chris."

Chris hung up slowly and wandered outside. Something about Will Cole's manner troubled him. Out at the pipeline he had seemed gung-ho for the idea, but now it struck Chris that he was dragging his feet. Had he lost his enthusiasm for the whole project? Or was there more to it than that? Of course, Chris realized that he could be reading something that wasn't there. Will Cole was a busy man, no doubt about that. Perhaps it was true that he was too busy to devote any time to it until there was more to go on—hard evidence, as he had put it.

At the same time, Chris had to wonder why *he* was involved. At the time, disgusted with what he had seen, it had seemed the right thing to do. But damnit, he was a construction worker, not an undercover cop! Casually questioning the pipeline workers was one thing, but now murder had come into the picture. If Fanti was behind Ben Slocum's death, he, Chris, could be putting his head on the chopping block if he approached Fanti directly.

He walked on, smoking moodily, trying to decide which way to jump.

Part of Chris's intuition was accurate enough—the pipeline thievery had assumed somewhat less importance in Will's mind. He was still determined to put a stop to it, but a new element had entered his life.

That new element was Candice Durayea.

He had received a surprise telephone call from her one morning two weeks after the poker game.

There had been a questioning note in his voice when he repeated her name. "Candice Durayea?"

"You don't remember me," she said sadly. "How unflattering, Mr. Cole."

"Oh, I remember you," he said hastily. "How could I forget somebody who whomped me at poker, a woman at that? No, if I sounded surprised, it was surprise at your calling me." He tried to assume a more formal note. "Is there something I can do for you, Miss Durayea?"

"No, but there's something I'd like to do for you."

"And what is that?"

"I'd like to take you to lunch, today."

He was surprised again, and then quickly wary. "Why?"

"No particular reason. Oh, I could say that I feel guilty about . . . whomping you at poker, but I don't feel guilty at all about that. I just have a feeling that we might enjoy one another's company. At least I'd like to find out. I know it's short notice. Maybe you have an important business appointment?"

As matter of fact, he did, but Will knew already that he was going to cancel. He thought it prudent not to let her know that. He lied, "As it happens, I was going to have lunch at my desk."

"Then you will come?"

"Jesus, you're direct, aren't you, Miss Durayea?"

"Candice, please. And yes, I'm direct. This is the era of women's liberation, after all. It's quite the thing, nowadays, for a woman to ask a man out."

"A married man?"

He could almost see her shrug. "If you don't care, I don't."

That was the beginning of it, and they'd had lunch a number of times since, and dinner twice. It had yet to go beyond that, something that had not happened to Will in a spell. These days, when he took a woman out, spent money on her, he expected his money's worth. He usually got it. If he didn't, it didn't particularly bother him. There were plenty of women around, and he didn't have time to spare for the courting game.

But somehow he had not made his move yet. It wasn't that he didn't want Candice Durayea; he wanted her so badly he ached for hours after being with her. She gave off an unmistakable aura of sexuality, and she was the most exciting woman of his experience. Yet he was fearful that she might spurn him if he made a premature move, and he knew instinctively that this would hurt. That was something else new in his experience—he had never been hurt by a woman, and had never before considered that he could be.

He had a date with Candice for lunch today, which was one reason he had been a little short with Chris O'Keefe. On any morning when he was taking her to lunch, Will was nervous and out of sorts until he finally sat across the table from her.

There weren't any really decent places to lunch in Fairbanks, not even a country club. The Fairbanks Country Club was a standing joke: a spavined wooden structure with the look of a honky-tonk, overlooking a nine-hole golf course that had grass about one month out of the year.

The times he had taken Candice to dinner Will had flown to Anchorage, but that was a trifle far in the middle of a workday. It was a nice day, so he drove Candice out to Chena, and they ate lunch in the restaurant across from the Malamute Saloon. The place had been a hotel during the Gold Rush days, and had been converted to a restaurant after the ghost town of Chena had been brought back to life as a tourist attraction. It was too early in the season for tourists, so they had the place pretty much to themselves.

As they sipped martinis, Will gazed across the small table at Candice. Her face was lovely, faintly triangular in shape, as exotic as an Egyptian princess of ancient times, the green eyes like emeralds to go with the diamond on her right hand, the tiny pearls in dangling earrings, the rubies encrusting the expensive, exquisitely thin watch she wore on her wrist.

"Candice, there is a question I've been wanting to ask you."

Even her shrug was elegant. "Ask anything you like, Will. I won't promise to answer."

"What do you see in Bry Tucker? He's at least twice your age."

She studied him amusedly. "You're not all that young yourself, Mr. Cole."

"I know and that only adds to my puzzlement."

"I like older men, Will. They know what it's all about." She smiled softly and her knee touched his under the table. "And older men, at least the ones I make it a point to meet, have money."

Will was wondering if the touch of her knee was inadvertent or on purpose. His pulse accelerated. "That brings up another question. Why are you here, in Alaska? You're a modern woman, a sophisticate. I'd expect to find you on Fifth Avenue, in New York, or on Rodeo Drive, in Beverly Hills."

"I've been to those places. I'm here because this is where the money is right now," she said straightforwardly. "I must warn you, if you don't know already, I'm expensive, very expensive."

Will was having a little trouble breathing. "I didn't know that all the money had fled from New York or Beverly Hills."

"Oh, it hasn't, but I find most of the rich guys there boring. Up here, there's an excitement, a raw, frontier excitement." The tip of her tongue ran around her lips and again the knee touched his.

"The men, you find them exciting?"

"Oh, definitely. Can't you tell?"

The waiter came with their lunch and neither spoke again until he was gone.

Then Candice said, "There's one other question I expected you to ask."

"What's that, Candy?"

She frowned. "Not Candy. I don't like Candy. Candy comes cheap and I'm not."

"Sorry. I'll try to remember that." He rapped the table with his knuckles. "So, what's your question?"

"Am I still seeing Bry Tucker?"

He had to look away, and coughed in embarrassment. "I thought of asking, but I didn't, for several reasons. I suppose the main one is that I didn't want to know."

"Didn't? How about now?"

He looked at her squarely. "Yes, I'd like to know."

"I haven't seen Bry since the day of our first luncheon. Bry was only a temporary amusement, a stopgap guy. He knew that, I warned him in the beginning."

"And me? How long for me?"

"I would say that more or less depends on you, Will Cole," she said gravely.

"I can take the afternoon off. How about you?"

"I'm free."

"Do you . . ." He coughed again, still on uncertain ground. Damnit, he was fumbling around like some school kid! "The motels in Fairbanks are full up. Do you have a place?"

"I have a place."

His expectations were more than fulfilled. Beneath that cool and elegant exterior, Candice had the passions and skills of a courtesan. Unclothed, her figure was everything he could have desired, and at his rough, demanding touch, she sighed, and the taut, controlled look vanished. She became languorous, the tawny skin seemed to take on a pinkish glow, and the green eyes grew heavy-lidded.

Will was in such an aroused state that he entered her at once. Now she became supple, her body showing a muscular strength and control that astounded him. She appeared to know intuitively exactly what move to make to intensify his pleasure, and yet to pace her own response to his. She attained a straining climax as his own began.

When they lay side by side, Will finally took time to inspect the apartment, at least the bedroom. His desire for her had been so powerful that he remembered the rest of the place only dimly—an impression of comfort and ease, but without a great many frills.

The centerpiece of the room, fittingly, was the bed—a king-size waterbed. He commented, "We don't see too many waterbeds up here, not in Fairbanks, at any rate. How do you keep it from freezing?"

"I keep the heat on twenty-four hours a day."

"That must be expensive."

"It is. But it's worth it, don't you think?" She laughed richly.

"You're fond of that word, aren't you?" he said dryly. "Expensive . . . you judge everything by that?"

"Just about. But don't you think it's worth it, my darling? The expense of me, *and* the bed?"

"Oh, you're worth it, whatever *it* is."

She said smugly, "You'll find out."

He reached for his jacket draped over a nearby chair, and dug out a cigar.

"No, darling. No cigars, not in my bedroom." She plucked the cigar from his fingers and deposited it on the nightstand beside the bed, making a face. "I can't stand the stink of cigars. Anywhere else, I'll suffer in silence, but I set the rules in my own bedroom."

Will opened his mouth to snarl at her—nobody told him when or where to smoke! Then he closed it again, as she used her lips and artful fingers on his body.

For the first time in his life Will Cole gave way to a woman's wishes. He sensed that this moment represented some sort of watershed in his life. This woman could make more demands on him in the future; and if he felt about her then as he did now, he would acquiesce.

Was she worth it? He didn't have the answer to that, but if the past quarter-hour was any yardstick, she very well could be.

Then he gasped, body arching off the bed, and all thought ceased.

After Will left her apartment, Candice Durayea, yawning, picked up the phone beside the bed. She held it resting on her bare stomach for a little while, a musing smile on her lips. Will Cole was quite a man, macho as hell, but that was all right.

She had to admit to herself, now, that she was more taken with him than with any man she had ever known, and that included quite a number.

For just a moment she considered not making the call, or at least admitting to failure. But that would never do—Candice had never failed at anything she set out to do.

She sighed, shrugged, and dialed a number.

When the receiver was picked up on the other end, she said, "It's okay, I've got him, just as I promised I would. But Will Cole's not stupid. I'll have to go easy for a while. It'll take me some time before I get him so hung up that he can't wiggle loose. But it'll happen, you can depend on it."

Thirteen

It was eight o'clock in the evening as Chris strolled down Second Avenue. Two Street was elbow to elbow with pipeline workers and hustlers, female, male, and some he wasn't sure of. Within two blocks he was offered everything from a joint to having his sexual needs taken care of in just about every way imaginable. Disgusted at what had happened to Fairbanks, at the same time somewhat amused, he spurned all offers and kept going until he found a decent-looking restaurant. A couple of drinks and a steak cost him twenty-five dollars. At least the drinks weren't watered and the steak was fair.

He still hadn't quite made up his mind about continuing his haphazard investigation. But he had been given the name of a bar on Two Street which, according to his source, operated games in the back room, and was owned by Milo Fanti.

So, after dinner, he went into the bar, had a quick drink, and a few words with the bartender, who steered him into the back room, where the walls were lined with slot machines. There were two crap tables, a roulette wheel, and two blackjack tables operating. Every table was crowded, all the slot machines in use. The crowd noise was like the roar of a cataract, and it was close and hot, thick with smoke and rancid with the odor of spilled drinks and unwashed bodies.

Chris had never been much of a gambler. He knew very well that the odds, even in legitimate casinos, were always in favor of the house; and God only knew how heavily the odds were against a player in a place like this. But he got ten dollars' worth of quarters from the cashier and took up a place before a slot when a player moved away.

He was down to three quarters when he heard a woman's voice say behind him: "Mr. Fanti?"

Chris turned slowly. A few feet away a woman was showing
a check to a slight, dapper man with slicked-down hair. The
man called Fanti examined the check, then nodded, initialed
it, and returned it to the woman, who hurried away toward
the cashier's booth.

Chris moved to intercept the man. "Mr. Fanti? Milo Fanti?"

"Yeah?" Fanti studied Chris with hard eyes. "Do I know
you?"

"No, we've never met. I'm Chris O'Keefe. I work on the
pipeline, out of Livengood Camp."

"So, what's the beef?"

"Oh, no beef, Mr. Fanti. I'd just like a few words with
you."

Fanti grunted. "So? I'm listening."

Chris motioned to indicate the crowded room. "Can't we
talk somewhere more private?"

Fanti eyed him narrowly, them shrugged. "This had better
be important, fellow. I'm a busy man. Come along."

Chris followed him to the back of the room. Using a key,
Fanti unlocked a small door, fumbled inside the next room for
a light switch. He motioned Chris in ahead of him, then
closed and locked the door after them. The tiny room had
once been a kitchen. It had been stripped except for a sink,
but ancient food odors still lingered.

"Yeah," Fanti said at Chris's look, "this was once a kitchen
before I turned the other part of the place into a casino, and
it still stinks. That way, any talks I have in here will be
shorter for that."

"You don't have an office?"

"Of course I have an office, but that's for business, not talks
with construction stiffs. Now, what is it you want from me?"

"Well, I heard from a . . . a friend, that you're the man to
see if I have something to sell."

"A friend? What's the name of this friend?"

"Well . . ." Chris drew a breath and said quickly, "Ben
Slocum."

Fanti's manner became cold and faintly menacing. "Slocum?
Isn't that the gink found dead up at Livengood yesterday
morning?"

Chris said quickly, "How'd you know about that?"

"Because it was in today's *News-Miner.* A man named Ben

Slocum was robbed and killed." Fanti scowled at him. "Unless you have some idea different than that?"

Chris knew that he was on dangerous ground, and he said carefully, "I don't know why he was killed. He was found dead shortly before the bus was to leave for Fairbanks, and I didn't stick around to learn any more."

"I see. So, you're telling me that this Slocum gave you my name?"

"Yes, he told me you were the guy to see if I had something to sell. He was coming into Fairbanks with me and he said he'd introduce us."

"He did, did he?" Fanti's eyes were like the flat surface of a mirror. "This stuff you have to sell, what is it?"

"Well . . ." Chris realized that he was getting in over his head. "I don't have anything yet. But you know . . . welder's tools, maybe a dump truck or a pickup."

"You mean, stolen goods, is that right?" Fanti said in a soft voice. "You're naming me a fence?"

"Not me, but that's what Slocum told me."

"Fellow . . . what's your name again?"

"Chris O'Keefe."

"Chris O'Keefe. I want to remember that. Now, O'Keefe, you have to be about the dumbest shit I've ever come across, bar none. You come in here, in my own place, and practically accuse me of being a crook! It's a good thing I'm an easygoing gink, or I'd take you to court for slander."

"I'm not accusing you of anything, Fanti, only acting on what somebody told me." Chris was on the defensive now, and it made him angry. "I just thought we could do business together."

"I'm not a fence, O'Keefe, and I don't take kindly to dumb construction shits accusing me. Now, I'm going to remember your name and your face. Everybody who works for me will get the word. Chris O'Keefe is not welcome in any of my establishments. In my business I have some rough types working for me, and if you show your puss around here again, you'll be sorry." Fanti unbolted and opened a small door to the alley behind the building. "Out, and stay out!"

Chris, steaming, found himself out in the alley, the door closed and locked behind him. Milo Fanti was right about one thing—he was a dumb shit. This had to be the dumbest thing he'd ever done in his whole life. At the same time he was deeply angry at Fanti, and more convinced than ever that the man was behind the pipeline thefts, and quite likely had given the word to have Ben Slocum killed. The motive he wasn't sure of. But Slocum had had a big mouth, and he could have talked out of turn. One thing seemed fairly clear—Slocum hadn't given his name to Fanti, or he wouldn't have walked into that alley alive.

A thought popped into his mind and he acted on it immediately. In the third bar he went into, the bartender found a copy of the Fairbanks *Daily News-Miner*. Chris ordered a beer and started going through the paper.

He found the item on the third page: "Pipeline Worker Found Murdered: Early yesterday morning at Livengood Camp, Ben Slocum, 41, was found dead of a stab wound. Slocum, a native Oklahoman, had been employed on the Trans-Alaska pipeline for seven months as a bulldozer operator. As of press time, the police can supply no motive for the crime.

"This is the fourth violent death of a worker since construction began on the pipeline..."

Chris stopped reading and swigged the beer. Milo Fanti had lied when he said he had read that robbery was the motive for Slocum's death. This could mean that Fanti had ordered Slocum's murder and told his hired killer, or killers, to loot the body to make it appear that robbery *was* the motive.

This small slip of Fanti's was certainly not proof to take to the police, or even to Will Cole. Fanti would simply laugh it off, claiming that he had heard about the robbery through a later newscast, or even a rumor, and had mistakenly attributed it to the newspaper.

But it was enough to convince Chris that Fanti was not only what Slocum had said he was, but a murderer as well.

Chris smiled grimly and sipped his beer. He had to admit that he wanted Milo Fanti to be guilty; the man had rubbed him the wrong way.

Chris was not a crusader; he had never been interested in causes as such. He had been content to drift, taking life as it came, enjoying himself. Now, for the first time, he felt a kinship with a country, a land, with Alaska, and he also felt a proprietary interest in the pipeline. That, he knew, was ridiculous on the face of it—he had worked on the pipeline for less than a year. Nonetheless, it was the way he felt, and men like Fanti were scavengers, vultures, feeding off the pipeline workers. And if he could do anything about it, Chris was determined to do it.

After all, he reflected wryly, he had eight days left. So why not devote the time to doing something worthwhile? Even if he failed, he would have the satisfaction of knowing that he had tried.

He finished his beer and left the bar.

It was now after eight, and Two Street was in full swing. As Chris made his way along the street, he heard sounds of a commotion in the next block, and he noted that the crowd was moving that way.

He quickened his step. They were out of the main tenderloin district now, and soon he saw the cause of the noise. Marching up and down before an old building were about fifteen young people, about an equal mixture of male and female. The building, Chris saw, was the union headquarters, Bry Tucker's union, and the one Chris belonged to.

The sidewalk, and even the street, was packed with pipeline workers. Many were drunk and all were muttering with outrage, heaping verbal abuse on the marchers.

Above the heads of the crowd, Chris saw Bry Tucker emerge from the union building and stand on the top step, face expressionless, hands on hips. Light spilled out of the doorway, dramatically outlining his imposing figure. The appearance of the union boss was a signal for heightened indignation from the growing crowd of construction workers. Chris could sense that they were working themselves up into an ugly mood.

The marchers were a motley bunch: long hair, beards, beads, patched jeans.

They were carrying placards hoisted like battle banners:

"Alaska for Alaskans!"
"Join SAS—Save Alaska from the Spoilers!"
"Save the Environment!"
"Pipeliners, Go Home!"
"The Pipeline Is Destroying Wildlife!"
"Ecology Now!"
"Pipeline Hardhats Are Destroying Alaska!"
"Shit in Your Hats, Pipeliners!"

One pipeliner in front roared out his rage and seized the offending placard from its carrier. "Go shit in your own hat, you hippie sonofabitch!"

He raised the picket sign high and brought it crashing down across the head of the youth who had been toting it.

This was the signal for a general free-for-all. Pipeliners closed with the youths, snatching signs and tearing them up. Then they waded in with fists flying. The youths tried to remain peaceful, but soon one returned a punch, and the others joined in. Most of the girls ran squealing to get out of the way. A few tried to fight and were batted away by the construction workers, eager to get at the young men.

Within seconds it had turned into a boiling melee. Chris stood back out of the way, having no stomach for it. He lingered for a moment, watching in wry yet somewhat sad amusement. There was justice on both sides, yet both factions went too far. The environmentalists were right in that much of Alaska was being plundered by the oil companies. Yet from what he had seen, little wildlife was actually being endangered; a few sane heads in the consortium had implemented a number of safeguards, among them raising the pipeline above the well-known game trails. On the other hand, the pipeline workers viewed the protesters as a personal threat to their jobs, and considered the environmentalists irresponsible, hippie freaks with scant regard for the march of progress.

The youths, of course, were no match for the toughened, battle-happy pipeliners, and were being wiped out. And Chris knew they couldn't expect to be rescued by the police. As short-handed as the police were, it would take too long for them to respond to a call; and even if they did arrive in time, Chris was sure that their sympathies would lie with the construction workers.

He started to move off, when he saw one marcher being ganged up on. It was a tall youth with a beard, the one who had been carrying the SAS sign. Two pipeliners were having at him, and even as Chris watched, yet a third joined in. The youth had been giving a good account of himself, but the addition of a third attacker was too much. He tried to retreat and succeeded in getting out of the mob, but just as it appeared he would make good his escape, the pipeliners, chasing him, caught him, banging him against the side of the building next to the union headquarters.

Then Chris saw light glint balefully off the blade of a knife. That was going too far. Aside from the unfair odds, the image of Ben Slocum lying dead of a knife wound was still too fresh in Chris's mind.

Without further thought he charged at them. Just as he reached them, he heard a grunt of pain and saw the knife drawn back, wet with blood. Without regard for niceties, Chris locked his hands together and brought them down on the back of the knife-wielder's neck. The man groaned and dropped to the sidewalk. Chris had already turned to the other two. Unprepared for an attack from another quarter, the pair were confused for just a moment, long enough for Chris to drop one with a one-two, a left to the belly, bending him over, and a powerful right to the jaw. The blow sent the pipeliner reeling back into the crowd, and then to the sidewalk.

As Chris whirled on the third man, the bearded protester ranged alongside him. The remaining pipeliner looked from one to the other uncertainly, then raised his hands, palms out.

"I'm not gonna take on two of you."

"Why not?" Chris said tightly. "There were three on one before."

The construction worker turned and walked quickly away. The fight was still raging, but only a few of the protesters remained on their feet. A glance up at the building steps told Chris that Bry Tucker had gone back inside.

Turning to the bearded man, Chris saw that blood was seeping through his shirt just above the elbow on his left arm. "Are you badly hurt?"

"I don't think so." The protester flexed the fingers of his left hand, and moved his arm up and down. He grimaced. "Everything seems to be in working order. I think it's just a flesh wound."

"Even so, I think it's time for you to fade away, and get that arm looked at. Your buddies have had it, anyway. You could end up with more than a flesh wound if you hang around."

The other's glance went to the melee. "I guess you're right, but it does bug me that we're getting the dirty end of the stick here. I've tried to instill in these peabrains that violence accomplishes nothing."

"Your guys, you mean? I'd say they had little choice. I saw a pipeliner get in the first lick. What would have been your advice, turn the other cheek?"

"A protest is more effective without . . ." He broke off with a sigh, then smiled slightly. "You're right, if we hadn't offered some resistance, they would have tromped us into the ground. I'm Dwight Cole, by the way." He held out his uninjured hand.

Chris shook it. "I'm Chris O'Keefe. You say your name is Dwight Cole? Any relation to Will Cole?"

Dwight was grinning openly now. "Will's my half-brother."

"Does he know what you're doing?"

"Oh, he knows and has disowned me," Dwight said in a dry voice. "I'm fighting him, and the pipeline, all the way."

"I'd say it's a little late to stop the pipeline."

"This one, perhaps, but we're keeping up the good fight. They're talking about another, a natural gas pipeline to the Outside."

"I know." As if by mutual consent, they started walking. "Hadn't you better get to a hospital?"

"June, my woman, will take care of it." He looked over at Chris. "We live just across the river. Would you like to come along?"

"Sure. If nothing else, I'll see to it that you get there. Delayed shock could hit you, and you'd pass out."

As they crossed the bridge over the Chena River, Dwight studied Chris in speculation. "I haven't thanked you for lending me a hand. Those three probably would have wasted me, if you hadn't interfered."

Chris said, "There's something I should tell you before we go any farther." He stopped to lean on the bridge rail. He took a pack of cigarettes out of his pocket, extended them to Dwight, who shook his head. After he had the cigarette lit, Chris said, "Just so I won't be under false colors here, I must tell you that I work for the pipeline. A bulldozer operator."

For a long moment Dwight was silent, staring at him with hard gray eyes. Then, unexpectedly, he laughed. "A pipeliner, huh? Fighting against your own? They won't care for that much."

Chris said uncomfortably, "I'm not well known yet, and I

doubt anyone there knew me. Except for Bry Tucker and I don't think he spotted me in that crowd."

Dwight's look turned quizzical. "Would you still have sided with me, if some of the pipeliners had recognized you?"

"That's a little hard to answer," Chris said ruefully. "I'd like to think that I would have."

"You're honest, at least." They resumed walking. After a moment Dwight said, "I suppose you think we're all a bunch of ecology freaks?"

Chris took his time answering. "Not exactly. You keep them on notice, that's for sure. Somebody has to defend the environment. I certainly can't say that I agree with everything you stand for. You people go too far in many things, but then so do those on the other side. Let me put it this way... I think you take too hard a line."

"You have to spit in their faces, Chris. Otherwise, they won't listen to you..." He broke off, motioning. "Here's the house. We'll continue this discussion after the warrior's wound is tended to."

Chris glanced around. They were standing in the yard of a two-story, wooden structure at least fifty years old. The house hadn't been painted in a long time, and the weather had turned it the gray color of driftwood. It seemed to lean slightly to the west, in danger of slowly collapsing to the ground. The yard was littered with debris, and an abandoned automobile sprawled like a corpse near one corner of the house.

"Doesn't look like much, does it?" Dwight said beside him. "I was able to buy the house and lot before the boom sent real estate out of sight. In those days ecology was more popular and our coffers overflowed, in a manner of speaking. But the donations have almost stopped and I've never gotten enough to fix it up. Anyway, it serves its purpose, living quarters for some of us and headquarters for SAS."

He started for the house, Chris behind him. The door wasn't locked. As Chris followed Dwight inside, he was assailed by the odor of decay. He was struck by the incongruity of the situation—a member of one of the wealthiest families in Alaska living in conditions approaching squalor. Dwight Cole, Chris concluded, was either a fool or a fanatic. Of course he could be a mixture of both.

He followed Dwight down a dark hall and into a parlor, in

which a fire blazed in a fireplace. A young woman rose from where she sat on cushions before the fire.

"June," Dwight said, "meet Chris O'Keefe, who, like a knight of old, just came to the rescue of your old man."

She gave a small cry. "Dwight, you're hurt!"

"It's nothing serious, just a scratch. But maybe you'd better clean it up, keep away any infection."

She tore the shirt away from the wound. "It looks like a knife cut. At the demonstration?"

He nodded. "The pipeliners got a little carried away."

"Those bastards! I should have gone with you."

"Oh, that would have been great, you the way you are." With his uninjured arm he hugged her to him, and beamed at Chris. "The old lady's pregnant. And careful about badmouthing the pipeliners, babe. Chris is one of them."

She pulled back to aim a baleful glare at Chris. "I thought we decided never to have one in our house?"

"Any reasonable man makes exceptions, babe. Besides, if he hadn't waded in, I could be in much worse shape. Now go fetch some disinfectant and do your magic." He patted her gently on the backside. As she started off, he added, "And bring us a couple of Cokes."

As June left the room, Dwight swayed, going pale, and would have fallen if Chris hadn't rushed to support him.

"Like I said, delayed shock," Chris said, as he helped the bearded man to the room's one couch. "You need a good, strong drink."

Dwight looked up from the couch, frowning. "I don't keep booze in the house. I stopped boozing when I started all this. We have enough problems without SAS's leader boozing or doping . . ." He paused, swallowing. "On the other hand, I *could* use a drink about now." He raised his voice, "Junebug?"

She popped back into the room. "Yes?"

"That bottle of Scotch we stashed away last New Year's, bring it and some ice cubes, instead of Cokes." He glanced at Chris. "Sorry, nothing to mix it with."

"On the rocks will be fine."

Dwight looked again at June, who hadn't moved. "Well, babe?"

Her face got a stubborn look. "You have a rule against liquor served in the house. I should have thrown that Scotch out long ago."

Dwight snapped, "Damnit, June, don't rasp me! I've had a day and I need a drink. A reasonable man breaks a rule now and then, even his own. Just bring the bottle and the ice."

"Seems to me we're awful reasonable all of a sudden," June muttered, but she went back into the hallway.

"She's right, of course," Dwight said somewhat sheepishly. "But what the hell, it's not every day a guy gets cut with a knife. But if you ever tell anybody I had a bottle of Scotch hidden away, I'll deny it up and down and sideways."

Chris grinned. "My lips are sealed, now and forever more." Despite his first impression, Chris was beginning to like Dwight Cole.

Dwight lowered his voice. "And if one of my people comes in, I'm going to claim that *you* brought in the bottle, strictly for medicinal purposes."

Chris said solemnly, "Right, strictly medicinal."

June came back with a bottle of unopened Scotch, two jelly glasses, none too clean, and a container of ice cubes. Also, she had a wet cloth, a bandage, and a bottle of disinfectant. While she tore Dwight's shirt off his left arm, Dwight used the right to dump ice cubes into the glasses, then filled them to the brim. He gave one to Chris.

Dwight held his high. "Up the pipeliners!"

"I can't drink to that," Chris said, "but I will drink to a broken leg each for the trio that attacked you."

"Hah!" June muttered. "That's too good for them, the destructive pigs! That's all they know how to do, destroy the environment, as well as people."

"Now, Junebug, no lectures to our guest." Dwight's gray eyes had a twinkle. He drank from his glass, then winced as June doused his wound liberally with disinfectant. "Ouch, babe! Damnit, that hurts worse than the knife did."

"You sure they didn't do this with their fangs?" she said acidly. "A bite from one of the pipeliners could turn you into a werewolf."

At a padding sound behind him, Chris glanced around. He started, almost dropping his drink. "Speaking of werewolves, what in the hell is *that?*"

Dwight roared with laughter. "Don't spook, Chris. That's Buck, a wolf I've raised from a pup. He's tame as a kitten, he won't hurt you." As the animal came to him, Dwight rubbed the wolf's ears briskly. Dwight's voice became bitter. "I found him near the pipeline. A dump truck had run over and killed his mother and the pup was starving. I brought him home to raise. Not only is the pipeline screwing up the environment, the damned machines run over anything that moves."

Chris eyed the wolf dubiously. "Buck?"

"Yeah. As in *Call of the Wild*. Did you ever read the book?" Dwight's voice was amused. "I thought it fitting. Jack London wrote pretty good about the spoilers up here."

To Chris's surprise, June didn't leave the room after she had tended Dwight's arm. She didn't take a drink, but she did resume her seat on the cushions, closely following the discussion that now began.

Dwight started it. "So you think we're wasting our time, do you, Chris?"

Chris shrugged. "I'd think that's a judgment you have to make. You've accomplished some good, agreed, but you've gone about as far as you can go. You told me yourself that the donations are drying up. How can you continue without funds?"

"We'll manage," Dwight said firmly. "We take part-time jobs, then give most of our earnings to SAS."

"That's commendable, I'm sure, but are you accomplishing anything worthwhile? Like with that demonstration today?"

Dwight poured himself another drink. Already his color was high, his speech becoming slurred. Unaccustomed to alcohol, he could get drunk in a hurry. Chris hoped that he wasn't a belligerent drunk.

"If we accomplish nothing else, we keep the bastards on notice. They know we're still here, checking on them."

Chris sipped at his drink. "I think you'd do better to scale down your demands. You might accomplish more."

"No way. Granpap once told me about horse-trading. 'Whatever you're selling, boy, ask the moon. You may have to come down some, but the other fellow'll know you put value on what you're selling. Always ask for more than you expect to get.'" Dwight was grinning. "I'm sure he'd have a stroke if he heard me use that adage to justify what we're doing, but it applies." He leaned forward. "That's what they said about Selma and the other black demonstrations that they were demanding too much all at once, but I'm sure that even the worst diehards will admit now that if the blacks hadn't demanded every right coming to them, they wouldn't have gained as much as they did."

"That was somewhat different. They were asking for rights long denied them, and they're people, not things."

June said vehemently, "We're not just talking about 'things' here. We're talking about the wildlife of Alaska."

Surprised at her interruption, Chris glanced over at her. Before he could frame a response, two youths sauntered into the room. Dwight jumped to his feet, staggering slightly. He threw an arm around each of the new arrivals. "Gordie, Theo! I want you to meet a friend of mine, Chris O'Keefe."

Chris stood and shook hands.

The one called Gordie said, "Man, you are one big dude!"

His eyes had a glazed, staring look, and it crossed Chris's mind that he was stoned on something. Pills, maybe speed.

"He a new recruit to the cause, Dwight?" Theo asked.

"Hardly." Dwight laughed. "I've been trying but I don't think it'll work. He's a pipeliner."

Gordie bristled. "A pipeliner? In our pad?" He turned his head aside and spat. "Shit, we'll have to do a thorough cleaning after he leaves."

Stung, Chris retorted, "From the looks of this place, it's a little late for that."

Gordie tensed, hand sneaking into his jacket pocket.

"Whoa now, whoa!" Dwight put a big hand on Gordie's shoulder, restraining him. "Chris just saved me from being wasted by three pipeliners, big suckers who would have left me little more than a grease spot on the sidewalk."

Chris relaxed with a faint smile.

"Dwight..." Gordie sniffed, then stared at the Scotch bottle on the coffee table. "Are you swilling booze? What happened to the rule of no hard liquor around here?"

With a loose grin Dwight said, "So I broke a rule..."

Chris interrupted, "I brought the bottle of Scotch along, tempting him."

"No need to lie for me, Chris. Thanks, anyway. I came damned close to getting killed, Gordie, so I'm getting smashed." He became a touch belligerent. "Are you going to make a big deal of it?"

"No way, O Great Leader, no way." Gordie held up his hands.

Dwight nodded stiffly. "Okay then. Help yourself, if you want, you guys."

"Naw. That stuff kills your brain cells, didn't you know that, man?" Gordie took a wine bottle from his pocket. "Theo and me, we'll stick with good old Ripple."

They all sat down, the two newcomers on the floor. Dwight turned to Chris. "As I was saying, we're fighting to save the environment. If somebody doesn't fight the spoilers, the exploiters, they're going to foul Alaska until nobody can live here. Kill the wildlife. Destroy the tundra. And all so people like my brother can get richer!"

"I don't think it's that bad," Chris said.

"It ain't? Shit, man, they're making a cemetery out of this beautiful country!" Gordie said explosively.

Chris looked at him with barely concealed dislike. "Are you a native Alaskan?"

"Naw, man, I'm from Cal-i-forn-ia. But I've been up here two years, though."

"So why are you so concerned with Alaska?"

"Where I come from don't matter. I'm wherever the battle is." Gordie drew himself up proudly. "I was in the oil spill hassle down in California."

With a shrug Chris turned his attention back to Dwight. "There're other bad things going on, out at the pipeline and here in Fairbanks, that should concern all Alaskans, just as much as the environment."

"And what is that?"

"Booze, drugs, and hookers are being trucked out to the pipeline. Equipment is being stolen and peddled to somebody here in town. And look at the town itself. It's overrun with hookers, gamblers, and dope peddlers."

Dwight shrugged negligently. "That's not our concern."

"Well, it should be. It's destroying people and I should think that would be just as important as the environment. I know I'd sure as hell like to nail the bird behind it all."

"You mean Milo Fanti?" Gordie was grinning.

Chris stared at him. "What do you know about Fanti?"

"Everybody knows about old Milo. Big Mafia guy once, you know."

"Not everybody knows about him, at least not enough to nail his ass."

Gordie squinted at him suspiciously. "Nail him? What's that mean, man? What are you, some kind of fuzz?"

"No, not at all," Chris said quickly. "I'm no cop. I'm just a pipeliner worried about the bad things going down along the pipeline. Just like you people are concerned about the environment."

Gordie stared a moment longer, then shrugged, his suspicions apparently allayed. "Well, old Milo is in it up to his greasy hairline."

"Do you know that for a fact? Or are you repeating rumors?"

"No rumors. Hell, man, I've done jobs for him several times."

"Such as?"

"You know, such as driving a panel truck out to the camps, pushing all kinds of good shit. Milo pays good bread."

"Would you swear to that in court?"

"Swear to it in court? Man, what are you on? I swear to nothing in any fucking court!"

"Wait a second!" Dwight shook his head, as though coming out of a fog. "What am I hearing here? Let me get this straight, Gordie. You've been running drugs out to the construction camps?"

Gordie glanced at him with some apprehension. "Sure, Dwight. We need all the bread we can get, don't we, and nobody pays better for less work than old Milo."

"You stupid idiot!" Dwight was suddenly raging. "I've put up with a lot from you, but this is going too far."

He raised a hand as if to strike out. Gordie backed up a step, and said in a whining voice, "I don't know why you're on my case, Dwight. I gave the cause most of the bread."

"Whatever else we are, we're not criminals!" Dwight roared. "We break the law all the time. The pigs are always throwing us into the slammer."

"There's a difference between pushing dope and civil disobedience . . ."

A loud knock sounded on the front door, and Dwight broke off, listening.

June jumped to her feet. "I'll get it, lover."

Dwight rounded on Gordie again, his voice lower now. "Like I said, I've put up with a lot from you, Gordie, and I'm giving you a last warning... If I ever hear of you pushing again, I'll turn you over to the cops myself! Is that quite clear?"

Gordie, clearly frightened now by Dwight's anger, held up his hands. "Okay, okay! I still don't see what's so terrible about it, but you're the boss."

They all turned as June came back into the room. There was another woman with her, a rather slight woman, with long, shimmering blond hair; yet she had a stunning figure displayed attractively by beautifully cut clothing. She was about twenty-four, Chris judged. She came directly down the room toward Dwight. She was undeniably feminine, yet there was an assurance about her manner and bearing that, even at first sight, struck Chris as slightly intimidating.

"Dwight, I heard about the demonstration, and that some people were hurt. Are you all right?" She broke off with a gasp at the sight of Dwight's torn sleeve and bandaged arm. "You *are* hurt!"

She reached out toward the injured arm. Dwight caught her hand and held it. His light laughter had a touch of embarrassment. "I'm fine, Sis, really I am. It's just a scratch."

"Have you seen a doctor?"

"No need. June cleaned and bandaged it."

"You still should see a doctor." Her voice took on a cutting edge. "I knew that sooner or later, you'd be hurt in all this foolishness!"

"Please, Kelly, no lectures, okay? We have a guest, the guy who stuck his nose in when three pipeliners were thumping me. Chris O'Keefe, I'd like you to meet my sister, Kelly."

Kelly gave Chris a brief, disinterested glance out of cool gray eyes.

That explains it, Chris thought dourly; a Cole. Born to wealth and privilege, and with that always went a bred-in arrogance, a feeling that the rest of the world didn't quite measure up. Chris had encountered this attitude in wealthy people before. He had noticed it in Will Cole, but in him it had seemed natural. In a woman it seemed... well, unwomanly, as illogical as that sounded.

Kelly was saying, "Are you sure you're okay?" She took a step toward her brother.

"I'm okay, I'm okay." Dwight took a step back and staggered slightly.

Kelly looked at him with widening eyes, then glanced at the half-empty bottle of Scotch. "Why, you're smashed!" she said in astonishment. "Is this the Dwight who scorns liquor? It seems this is a day for surprises."

"I'm surprised myself," Dwight said with a lopsided grin. "But you know what they say . . . a brush with death always makes a man think of mortality, and all that."

Kelly sniffed. "It's about time you were thinking about something aside from your damned SAS. Well, since I find you're not only all right but drunk, I'll leave you with your buddies." Her glance swept around contemptuously, the contempt including Chris as well.

Gordie said, "Yeah, we wouldn't want to hold you up from an important party somewhere."

"That's enough, Gordie." Dwight's eyes suddenly hardening, he nodded curtly to Kelly. "But he's right, Sis. We wouldn't want to keep you from anything important."

Kelly made a weary gesture. "There's just no give in you, is there, Dwight? I was concerned for your welfare. That *is* why I came by." She said crisply, "Goodbye, Dwight. I swore to myself that the last time I was here would be the last, but I came today anyway. This really is the last time; next time you'll have to ask me."

She turned on her heel and marched out.

Dwight, his face suddenly stricken, mouth open to speak, took a step after her. Then June touched his arm and said something in a low voice. He stopped in his tracks, and remained silent, unmoving.

The slam of the front door caused Chris to jump slightly. He said, "I'd better be on my way, too, Dwight. I have an appointment," he lied.

"Chris . . ." Dwight tried to smile. "I'm sorry for the family scene. I know it's sticky, a stranger being in on a family squabble. I'm so used to it, I forgot you were even here."

"That's okay, Dwight, don't sweat it," Chris said lightly. "Nice to have met you. No doubt we'll bump into each other again." He grinned. "Only let's hope it's not in quite the same way."

He left quickly. Kelly Cole was just getting into a dusty sedan parked in the yard, causing him to wonder why a Cole would be driving something other than a Cadillac or a

Mercedes. She started it with a clash of gears and spurted dust as she accelerated.

Chris lit a cigarette and started toward the street. In a moment, to his surprise, he saw the sedan backing up the street. She stopped alongside him and pushed open the door on his side.

"Can I offer you a lift?"

He bent down to peer inside. "I have aways to go, Miss Cole. I can walk uptown and hail a cab."

"Where are you going?"

"I'm staying in a rooming house not far from the college."

"That's where I'm going. I am staying overnight with my brother. He has a house close to the college."

"Well... all right," he said hesitantly. "If you're sure it's not too much trouble?"

"No trouble. It's the least I can do for the man who saved Dwight's hide. Despite our not getting along, he still is my brother."

There was a moment of silence after Chris exited the house.

Gordie was the first to speak. "Man, did you tell big sister off! She had it coming, her high and mighty ways."

Dwight turned on him savagely. "You keep your rotten tongue off my sister, you hear me? My family is my own affair. I'll go along when you badmouth Will. But that's as far as it goes, understood?"

"Sure, man, sure." Gordie held up his hands, palms out. "I just thought..."

"I don't care what you thought, asshole! And another thing... if I ever hear of you running errands for Milo Fanti again, I'll toss you out of SAS for good. O'Keefe is right about that. That man is as much our enemy as the oil companies."

Gordie shook his head, baffled. "I don't follow you there, Dwight. We need the bread, you know that."

"If you're busted for pushing dope, people will put us in the same bag with Fanti and his crooked deals. That would be all we'd need to turn everybody against us. We'd have to fold our tents and leave Alaska for good."

Fourteen

In the car with Kelly Cole, Chris was wary, though it soon occurred to him that he may have misjudged her. He felt her physical presence almost immediately. She was a damned attractive woman. She drove recklessly, having to brake sharply a number of times, and her skirt rode up her legs, which were splendid, and Chris wondered how she would be in bed. This thought brought him up short. He was not a man whose thoughts turned to bed the minute he was in the presence of a beautiful woman for the first time.

Neither spoke for a few minutes. Kelly didn't even look at him for the first few blocks. Chris lit a cigarette and studied her profile furtively. Where at first her features had seemed rather too sharp and cold, the nose a trifle long and forceful, now in the dimness of the interior of the car, her face appeared softer, rounder, more vulnerable.

She spoke first. "Are you a member of SAS?"

Chris laughed. "Hardly. I work for the pipeline, a heavy equipment operator."

She spared him a surprised glance. "A pipeliner? Yet you saved Dwight from being beaten up?"

He shrugged. "I don't like to see anybody ganged up on. Fair's fair, no matter which side you're on."

"Well, I do thank you for coming to his assistance. I've been expecting him to get hurt and he probably deserved it. Still, I hate to see it happen." She drove a block in silence. "Tell me, Mr. . . . O'Keefe, is it? Do you approve of what Dwight is doing, or what he stands for?"

"Both, I approve and disapprove."

"Would you mind explaining that?"

"Your brother and I started arguing about that, almost from

159

the moment we met, it seems. He gets rather steamed up about it."

She was nodding, a slight smile on her face. "Yes, Dwight has all the fervor and zeal of a missionary."

"Anyway," Chris said, "I agree that there is right and wrong on both sides, but these SAS people demand too much, so much that they often hinder the pipeline, and add unnecessary expense. After all, the pipeline is a fact of life now. It's there and it's badly needed. Your brother has yet to learn that compromise is necessary in this world."

"Oh, God, do I know that! Do I ever!" She gave an angry shake of her head, causing her hair to ripple.

Strangely, Chris felt that this sudden and unexpected meeting of the minds was drawing them closer together, creating an intimacy, where before there had been a feeling between them that could easily have turned into active hostility, even enmity.

Kelly went on, "In some respects, I suppose refusal to compromise a position is a family trait. My half-brother, Will, is as bad in that respect as Dwight."

"I've met Will Cole," Chris found himself saying.

Again she looked at him in surprise. "Have you? On your job, you mean?"

Chris hesitated a moment before replying, but his hunch that Will Cole was, suddenly and inexplicably, reluctant to act prompted him to say, "Not exactly. I met him at the pipeline, yes, but our meeting came about for another reason." He told her then what had transpired between Will Cole and him.

When he had finished, Kelly was frowning. "That doesn't sound like Will. God knows we don't get along too well, but usually when he gives his word about something, he sticks with it. He is busy, naturally, with many distractions. I must confess that I don't keep up with the company business, and all I know about what you've just told me is what I read in the newspapers. I have heard Grandfather grumbling and snorting about all the corruption, thievery, and suchlike. You know, although Will is now president of Cole, Grandfather is still chairman of the board and he calls the shots, when it comes to anything important."

"No, I didn't know that."

"Perhaps I shouldn't have told you, but then it's no great secret. In fact, I thought it was pretty much common knowledge." She gave him a troubled look, gnawing her lower lip. "Are you still going to continue with your investigation?"

He laughed shortly. "It's hardly an investigation, not as inept as I seem to be, but I plan to keep nosing around, at least for the next few days, until my leave is over. I feel guilty about the murder of Ben Slocum, although I didn't particularly like the man, but I still have an uneasy feeling that I may have inadvertently contributed to his death. And I still feel as strongly about what's going on out at the pipeline as I did when I first approached your brother."

"Is there any danger to you?"

"I doubt it." Chris thought of Fanti's threat. "Oh, there might be if I really stumble across anything. In case that happens, I'll run to the police, yelling 'help!'"

"I'm worried about Dwight. Even if he isn't directly involved, too many people would like nothing better than a chance to connect him with crime, including Will. Where did you say you were staying?"

"Turn left at the next cross street, and it's the third house down on the right."

Kelly didn't speak again until she had pulled up before his rooming house. Rummaging in her purse, she produced a pad and pen. "I don't live in Fairbanks. I live on Cole Island, near Juneau, with Grandfather and my father, when he's not in Washington. I'm going to give you my phone number there." Scribbling, she tore the top sheet from the pad and gave it to him. "If you don't get the cooperation from Will that you think you should, call me at this number. Will you do that?"

All at once he was excited by the prospect of seeing, or even talking, to this woman again. "I most certainly will." He hesitated, then held out his hand, suddenly awkward. "It was nice meeting you, Miss Cole."

She studied him gravely, those gray eyes all of a sudden large, seeming to probe his very soul. Then she smiled, a full smile this time. "I think Kelly would be better than Miss Cole, don't you, Chris?" She took his hand, and for just an instant her smaller hand seemed to snuggle warmly in his. "Do call, please? If nothing else, just to talk. Okay?"

*   *   *

Will's affair with Candice Durayea had intensified with each passing day, assuming more and more importance in his life, to the point of interfering with his working life. It was not that he saw much of her during the day, although that sometimes happened when he could make some excuse to get away, but she intruded into his thoughts at odd times, sometimes even during an important business discussion.

He had never thought that he would become so involved with any woman. Although he knew it was a cliché, she was like a fever in his blood, a fever abating only when he was with her. In calmer moments he was a little frightened by the depth of his feeling for Candice. He could only hope that it would subside with time, as it always had before. Yet when he was with her, he was often swept by a feeling of desolation at the very thought that there might come a day when she would no longer be a part of his life. He had never even come close to feeling this way about a woman. Could it be because he was approaching middle age, soon to be forty? He had heard that the older men got, the more inclined they were to become hopelessly infatuated with a woman.

The thing was, he could find little fault with her. Usually, after an initial sexual encounter, he began to search for faults—imperfections of physical beauty; character flaws; sexual turn-offs. All this, he realized, was preparation for dumping them.

None of this had happened with Candice. She was flawlessly beautiful, her personality suited him perfectly, and she was as splendidly satisfying in bed as she had been on that first afternoon.

There was one thing about her that some men might find unsettling—she was expensive. But she had warned him about that.

No one could ever accuse Will of being stingy, or even frugal; money was made to be spent. He had always spent lavishly on himself, but never on a woman. He had been lucky, he supposed; he had never had a woman who demanded much.

That could well be why he loved to spend money on Candice; like a father with a lone child born late in life, he was overindulgent. He did indulge Candice's every whim, he thought her childish delight in fine jewelry and expensive furs a part of her charm, "cute," as much as he disliked the word.

Candice had one trait that could be considered a flaw: she loved to gamble. Will also liked to gamble, of course, but it was usually confined to a poker game with cronies, high stakes or low. But Candice was such an accomplished poker player that poker, she told him early on, "has lost most of its kick for me. You know what the shrinks say. 'A compulsive gambler has an unconscious desire to lose.' I don't know if that applies to me or not, Will, but the kick for me comes from playing with the odds heavily against me, knowing that I might lose. I suppose that makes me a little kinky, but next to a good bed romp with a guy I like, I like a fling at roulette or at the crap table."

Will thought it *was* a little kinky, but he did love to watch her shoving hundred dollar chips onto a crap table, her color high, her eyes blazing, her body tense, and her shudder as she lost or won, it didn't seem to matter. She would give a shuddering sigh, her hips jerking as though she was getting off on it. And in bed afterward, she was insatiable.

He finagled three days off and flew with her down to Reno in the Cole private jet. At the end of the three days, she had lost twenty thousand dollars, and fucked his brains out. Despite his salary, Will was always close to the bone with his own finances, and the twenty grand was money he could ill afford to lose. But he figured it was well worth it. It was three days in his life he knew he would never forget.

Candice, after the jaunt to Nevada, started nagging him about playing at Milo Fanti's place in Fairbanks. Will was reluctant. Fairbanks was, in essence, a small town and a loss of the proportions of the Reno trip would soon be all over town.

"That's a poor excuse, darling," she said. "How many times have you told me that you don't give a rat's ass about what people think? It's not as if you're a banker, or someone's money manager. You're rich, Will. You're expected to do outrageous things." She stood close and warm against him. "Remember Reno?"

Oh, yes, he remembered Reno.

He went, of course. He did choose a week night, and a

time after midnight, hoping for a sparse crowd. It was a vain hope; the place was crowded, and hot and smoky.

They managed to find a spot at one of the dice tables. Candice held the spot while he went for three thousand dollars in chips.

As he returned to the table, she was waving frantically, almost jumping up and down. "Hurry, baby! The dice are mine next!"

She didn't like to bet unless the dice were in her hands. "I don't get the same kick unless they're in my hot little hand, a part of me."

The stickman pushed the dice down the table as Will elbowed his way in beside her. She scooped the dice in, blew on them, kissed them with pursed lips, and rattled them between her cupped hands.

Will stacked the chips beside Candice. She pushed five one hundred dollar chips onto the table.

Will rapped the table with his knuckles. "Roll 'em, baby!"

She rolled a seven. She crowed, clapping her hands. "Let it ride!"

She rolled a four, and made her point on the third roll. She let her winnings ride, and then rolled another seven. Will had been betting a few chips with her, but his primary interest was in watching her delight. Other bettors around the table now began backing her. Candice continud to let her winnings ride. She rolled yet a third seven.

Clapping her hands, she shouted, "Let it ride!"

The stickman was frowning. "I'm sorry, miss. The table limit is five thousand. You're already over that. I'm afraid . . ."

"That's okay, Sam. For Mr. Cole and his lady, we'll raise the limit."

Will glanced down the table to see Milo Fanti's darkly smiling face. Fanti winked at him and turned away from the table.

On the next roll, Candice crapped out. She groaned, slumping, as the stickman raked in the huge pile of chips.

Candice straightened, turning to Will with a blossoming smile. "Don't worry, darling. I'm hot tonight, you can see that. Fanti jinxed me, coming around when he did. Just wait until I roll again."

But the one brief flash of luck was gone. Each time the

dice came around to Candice again, she lost, and after three more rolls Will's three thousand in chips had disappeared.

When the last chip was gone, Will took Candice's arm. "That's it for tonight, sweetheart."

She looked at him with luminous eyes. "Please, Will? Just one more stack of chips? My luck is about to change, I can feel it."

He hesitated, then finally shrugged, and turned away toward the cashier's booth. Why was he letting her have her way again? Never before had a woman manipulated him as Candice seemed able to do. But what the hell! It was only money.

At the cashier's booth he said, "Will you honor my personal check?" If the cashier refused, Will would have an easy out.

But the man smiled, and said, "Any time, Mr. Cole. Mr. Fanti gave me explicit instructions. Your checks are always good here."

Shrugging aside a feeling of uneasiness, Will scribbled a check for another three thousand. He wasn't even sure he had enough money in his account to cover it.

The second stack of chips lasted longer. It was almost three in the morning before they were all gone.

"I know, darling," Candice said, picking up her purse with a sigh. "It's time to go. I was sure that my luck would turn. Oh, well," she brightened, "next time."

"Sure, next time," Will said dryly.

They encountered Milo Fanti on their way to the door. "Leaving so soon, Mr. Cole? The night's young."

"The night may be young, but we lost six grand," Will said grumpily, "and that ages a man considerably."

"A man in your position shouldn't have to worry about losing," Fanti said. "Next time you may win, who knows? Your note is always good with me, Mr. Cole. Any time."

Will didn't know if he should feel grateful, or punch Fanti in the teeth. He said merely, "I'll remember that, Fanti."

Will was determined that it wouldn't happen again, but the rest of the night with Candice was such an erotic experience that his resolve faltered. As he dressed to leave for the office, he said, "This was some night, Candice, even if it did cost me six thou."

She stretched and smiled lazily. "The thing you have to ask yourself, Will, is was it worth it?"

He had no answer for her at the moment, but when she pressured him to return for another try at the tables, his resistance began to weaken. She didn't speak of withholding sexual favors, but there was a marked coolness about her, a slight withdrawal, that started to get to him.

A week later he took her back to Fanti's place again. This time she lost the five thousand he brought along with him in short order, and went through ten thousand more, which Fanti advanced to Will for his IOU. "No hurry about repaying the paper, Mr. Cole," Fanti said with a somewhat feral smile. "What's a few thousand between friends?"

Will cursed himself for being abysmally stupid, for letting Candice seduce him into it. It was a foolish thing to do—to go into debt to Milo Fanti. Most of all, he cursed Jeremiah for being too tightfisted to pay him a decent salary. How could a man live nowadays on fifty thousand a year?

He was overdrawn at the bank—the bank manager would be on his ass the minute the last check came in—and he had the marker to Fanti to pay off. Will knew that he had only one option. On Jeremiah's retirement he had given Will, Josh, and Kelly ten shares of stock in the company, with Jeremiah still retaining the other seventy. The old man had never gone public with the stock, managing to hold onto full control even during the rough periods. In Cole Enterprises' present healthy position, the shares of stock were worth top dollar.

At the time of giving them the stock, Jeremiah had fixed a beady stare on them, and said, "The stock will be in your names. You can sell it, do anything you want with it. After all, you're family and you're entitled. But I trust you won't. If I ever hear of any of you selling one share of that stock, you'll be Lord God sorry. If for some reason, any of you need money, and I can't think of one, you can come to me for a loan. If any of that stock gets into the hands of them not in the family, I'm going to be upset, almighty upset."

Will could just feature himself going to the old man for a loan to repay a gambling debt!

His only out was to sell some shares of stock, for enough money to pay Fanti's marker and make up the deficit in his bank account. If he did it quietly enough and then repurchased the stock later, even if he had to pay a premium for it, the likelihood of Jeremiah's finding out was very small. Except for his contacts with Will, Jeremiah was pretty much isolated from the world. Even if someone learned of the stock transaction, they wouldn't be very likely to run to Jeremiah with the information. Of course Will could borrow against the stock, but that would still leave him in debt.

The day following the night at Fanti's, Will made the transaction, selling two percent of his stock for enough money to pay his debts and add a healthy sum to his bank account.

That same afternoon he went to Fanti's office. When Fanti ushered him in, Will immediately dropped a bound stack of hundreds onto his desk.

"There's the dough I owe you, Fanti," he said. "I want my IOU back."

Fanti looked gravely at the money. "There wasn't all that much hurry, Mr. Cole."

"I don't like to be in any man's debt."

"Very well." Fanti opened his desk drawer, took out the IOU, and handed it to Will. "Just remember, any time you need fresh money, you're always good for it with me."

Will tore the IOU into bits and let them flutter into the wastebasket. "That won't be necessary again."

Fanti had a knowing smile on his face. "A man never knows when he might be in need of money."

"You going into loansharking now, are you?" Will said.

Fanti tried to assume a wounded expression. "Now that's not nice, Mr. Cole. Did I charge you interest?"

Will was determined to stay away from Milo Fanti henceforth. His resolve didn't last long.

The next afternoon he received a call from Chris O'Keefe. Will debated for a moment when Cora told him who was calling, but he finally accepted the call. He had given his word to act if and when O'Keefe had something for him.

"Well, O'Keefe, have you come up with anything?"

"I have certainly learned enough to satisfy me that Fanti is behind the dope peddling and whore running to the camps."

Will frowned. "What have you got?"

"I met a guy who told me that he'd been hired by Fanti a number of times to push dope to the pipeline workers."

"Would he be willing to testify to that?"

"Well, no, but it seems to me that if the police learn about him and pick him up for questioning, he might be willing to make a statement to save his own hide."

"That's pretty flimsy, O'Keefe. Who is this guy?"

"A guy named Gordie Beasley."

"Well, I admit that it probably should be followed up. Where could he be found?"

There was a brief silence on the other end. Finally Chris said, "He's staying with your brother across the river."

Will was incredulous. "Living with Dwight? You're talking about one of his goddamned hippies! Jesus Christ in a wheelbarrow! Dealing dope is as natural to that bunch as breathing! I wouldn't believe one of them on a bet."

"Well, maybe so, but I happen to believe he was telling the truth," Chris said defensively. "There was no reason for him to lie, the way it came up. Your brother was furious with this Gordie, and I'm fairly sure the guy wouldn't lie and put himself in jeopardy with Dwight."

"It wouldn't surprise me if Dwight was dealing himself, and tried to lay it off onto Fanti."

"I don't think you really believe that, Mr. Cole."

"Who are you to tell me what I believe? How did you meet Dwight, anyway? No, I don't want to know. Dwight is no longer a member of my family, and anybody who has anything to do with him is in the same bag, as far as I'm concerned."

"And that includes me, I suppose?" Chris's voice was tight with anger now.

"If the shoe fits, O'Keefe, if the shoes fits." Will took a breath. "And that's all you have for me?"

"I guess it wouldn't matter if I had any more, would it? It strikes me that I've been wasting my time. You're no more interested in doing anything than anyone else."

Will snapped, "That's not true!"

"Isn't it? Well, it doesn't matter. I have to report back to the pipeline in a few days, so I wash my hands of the whole thing. I can't say that I'm happy to have known you, Mr. Cole."

Before Will could get in another word, Chris O'Keefe hung up. Will stared at the receiver in anger and disbelief. Who did the arrogant young pup think he was, talking to him like that?

He slammed down the receiver, lit a cigar, and strode to the window, smoking and scowling over the Chena at the spot where Dwight lived with his eco-freaks.

Slowly, his fury diminished, and his conscience began to nag him. He had promised Chris O'Keefe that he would act, and he was forced to admit that the young man had tried. Certainly he had come up with signs pointing right at Milo Fanti, although they did not constitute hard evidence, nothing he could go to the police with.

But he just might be able to throw a scare into Fanti. He began to grin with pleasure, realizing the extent of his dislike for the man. If he could frighten Fanti enough to get him to stop his operations along the pipeline, it would go far toward accomplishing what he had promised himself, and others, that he would do.

He left the building without telling Cora, and drove down to Two Street.

Although it was short of noon, Fanti answered his knock. Will wondered, fleetingly, when the man ever slept; he knew that Fanti was up most of the night at his gambling places.

Fanti gave him a slanting smile. "Mr. Cole, back so soon? Not that it isn't always a pleasure."

"This isn't like yesterday, it's something else altogether."

Fanti's face went still. "Oh? And what might that be?"

"We'd better talk in your office." Will grinned unpleasantly. "I don't think you'd want somebody inadvertently overhearing what I have to say."

"Very well, Mr. Cole."

Fanti led the way into his office, closed the door, and went around behind his desk, lowering himself into the chair. "Now, what is this that I wouldn't want overheard?"

Will took out a cigar, unwrapped and lit it, taking his time.

Fanti sat without moving, face without expression, his hands on the desk before him, palms down.

Will blew smoke. "Do you recall our little chat, the first

time we met? About dope pushing and whores trucked out to
the pipeline camps, and the thievery?"

"I remember, Mr. Cole," Fanti said quietly. "I have a good
memory for false accusations made against me."

"False, are they?" Will leaned forward suddenly. "Do you
know a hippie punk by the name of Gordie Beasley?"

"The name is not familiar to me, no," Fanti said steadily.
"But then I don't associate with hippies. They seldom have
money enough to patronize my establishments."

"He never ran errands for you?"

"Errands? What errands would a punk run for me?"

"Pushing dope at the camps," Will said harshly.

"Oh, now really, Mr. Cole." Fanti grimaced. "You come in
here with some story like that and what do you expect from
me? To break down and confess to all sorts of misdeeds?"

"It's not a story, this Beasley is ready to tell all to the cops,
to save his own hide." Even as he spoke, Will wondered if he
was putting Gordie Beasley in danger. But what the hell did
he care about one of Dwight's buddies?

"Tell him to go right ahead. I don't know why he told you
this cockamamie yarn. Probably some LSD hallucination."

Will drew on his cigar, studying Fanti closely. On the
surface the man seemed unperturbed, but then who could
tell from that poker face? Some gut instinct told Will that he
had struck a nerve. He decided to push the bluff further. "I
got word, from yet another source, that you're fencing stolen
pipeline equipment. And that's exactly what I warned you
about at that first meeting."

Fanti raised his eyebrows a fraction. "This from another
dopehead?"

"No, it isn't. It came from a reliable pipeline worker, but I
don't think I'll tell you his name. You might have him put
away. There was a pipeliner murdered a few days ago."

"Are you laying that onto me as well?" Fanti asked in a soft
voice.

"Let's just say it wouldn't surprise me a whole hell of a lot
if you were behind it. But I'll admit that I don't have proof of
that. About the rest, I do."

"You have nothing, Mr. Cole," Fanti said flatly. "You're
bluffing. I thought you were a better poker player than that."

Will's temper stirred. "Bluffing, am I? Well, we'll see who's bluffing." He came to his feet. "I'm going to keep a close watch on the pipeline from now on. If there are any more shenanigans, it's your ass. So call my bluff, *Mister* Fanti!"

He had taken two steps toward the door before Fanti spoke. "Don't leave just yet, Mr. Cole. You've shown me your cards, now I'll give you a look at mine." His voice was still soft, but commanding now.

"What?" Will gaped back over his shoulder.

Fanti had taken two items from his desk—a small cassette and a cassette player. "Sit down, Mr. Cole, there's something I'd like for you to hear." He was fitting the cassette into the player.

"Why should I listen? What is it?"

"It'll be to your advantage," Fanti said in his soft voice. "Believe me, it will."

A feeling of apprehension gripped Will, passing over him like a chill. Unwillingly he resumed his seat as Fanti pressed a button.

Two voices, against a scratchy background, could be heard:

"God, I needed that! I know, a cliché, right? But true, how true. I haven't been to bed with a man since I came to this town. Seem strange to you?"

"A little, yeah."

A red rage rose in Will—the voices were unmistakable. He roared, "You sonofabitch, you wired Hardesty's bedroom!"

Will came off his seat, lunging for the cassette player. In one smooth motion Fanti raked it into an open desk drawer, and his other hand snaked up above the level of the desk, holding a revolver.

"Don't think I won't use this, Mr. Cole," he said calmly. "I won't kill you, no, but I'll cripple you. Believe me, I will."

Will skidded to a stop, trembling badly, but from fury, not fear. He got himself under a semblance of control. "You slimy bastard, what do you expect to gain from this? Blackmail?"

"Not at all, just the opposite. All I'm seeking is a little cooperation from you, Mr. Cole."

"I'm to close my eyes to what you're doing and you won't use that tape, is that it? Jesus Christ in a wheelbarrow! No way, Fanti, no way. Broadcast it to the world. It won't do me that much damage. People know me as a womanizer, a whoremonger, even my wife."

"But that isn't all, you see. I have in my safe photostatic copies of the checks you wrote when you purchased chips in my establishment, also a copy of the IOU. That could dirty you some."

"It might damage me some, yeah, but I'll take my chances. People who know me know I'm no saint. And I've done nothing criminal, anyway."

"I have something else that I think might interest you." Once again, Fanti brought his hand up from behind his desk, holding stock certificates this time. "Recognize these, Mr. Cole?"

With a sick feeling Will did. He said, "Where did you get those, Fanti?"

"Bought them through a broker in Anchorage, a guy I've been paying to keep an eye out for something like this. It cost me a heavy premium, but I was glad to pay it. I now own two percent of stock in Cole Enterprises." He was gloating now. "I figure that I can only stand to benefit in the end, aside from other considerations. Cole stock keeps appreciating." He bounced the certificates on the desk, eying Will slyly. "How do you think Jeremiah Cole would react should he learn that two percent of the stock in his precious company, stock once belonging to his grandson, now belongs to one Milo Fanti, and that his grandson signed an IOU to that same Milo Fanti to the tune of ten grand?"

Will knew very well how the old man would react—he'd be out on his ass, no longer associated with Cole Enterprises. In a dead voice he said, "What is it you want, Fanti?"

Fanti smiled. "Don't sound so down, Mr. Cole. What I want can be of mutual benefit. There is a lot of money to be made as long as the pipeline construction continues. Why shouldn't you share in it? Who can it hurt? Things will continue as they have been, and insofar as I can see, the pipeline is getting built. Somebody is going to rake in all that money, so why shouldn't it be us?"

"You still haven't told me what you expect from me."

"Your cooperation and support. I want you to drop this investigation into what's happening along the pipeline." At Will's look of surprise Fanti smiled coldly. "Oh, yes, I know about it. This Christopher O'Keefe, he came to me. Oh, he didn't tell me he was in cahoots with you, but I'm not stupid. I want him out of my hair."

Will said quickly, "I don't want anything to happen to him, like the other worker who was killed."

"Nothing will, so long as he sticks to working the pipeline." Fanti spread his hands. "As for the other guy, I told you, I had nothing to do with that."

Will was silent. He didn't believe Fanti for an instant, but his mind was in such a turmoil he didn't want to call him on it. He had never felt so helpless in his life. What made it even worse, it was his own damned fault for letting Fanti get the edge on him. And he had no choice but to go along. Besides, he rationalized, Fanti was right. Corruption along the pipeline was so widespread that he had never had any hope of doing much more than jamming a finger into the dike, while it burst out somewhere else.

Fanti was going on: "The other oil companies aren't in the least interested in doing anything about it. All they're interested in is getting oil flowing through the pipeline, no matter what the cost. All the other executives are getting paid almost twice as much as you are, Mr. Cole. Why shouldn't you have a few perks of your own?"

Will grunted in surprise. "You seem damned well informed, Fanti."

"I made it my business to learn everything about you, Mr. Cole. When I set up business here, it didn't take me long to learn how much clout Cole Enterprises, and you, have in Fairbanks, in Alaska. With you behind me, or shall we say, not against me, I can operate freely. The other people, reform groups and the like, are no more bother than . . . what do you call those pesky insects up here? No-see-ums?"

He smiled tightly. "Without your leadership, they mean damn all, just pests. All you have to do is be too busy to see them, or when forced to, tell them you're doing all you can. What can they do alone? You know yourself that I'm running a clean operation, no rough stuff, no crooked games. If one of my people steps out of line, *I'll* come down on him hard, without getting the cops into it."

Will had doubts about the "clean" operation, but he had no real proof of shady dealings. "How about the stolen stuff? You are fencing, aren't you?"

"I am, I'll admit that now. I lied to you about that, but there's big bucks in it. So who's hurt if a dump truck is stolen? The worker who steals it gets some dough, which he probably spends here in Fairbanks. And there's always another dump truck to replace it, or the money to buy a replacement."

"So nobody's hurt, right?" Will said sourly.

"Right! Now you're getting the picture."

"Nobody but the taxpayer."

For the first time Will saw a true expression on Fanti's face—that of utter disbelief. "Ah, come on, Mr. Cole, you have to be putting me on! Everybody rips off the taxpayer and the best example of that is the cost-plus contracts on this pipeline."

Will smiled grimly. "How well I know. That's why I've been trying to do something."

Once again, Fanti's hand dipped below the level of the desk, and Will had to wonder what other goodies he had to show.

"The way I figure it, Mr. Cole, it's going to continue even if you did succeed in putting me out of business. Some other gink would take my place, maybe somebody far greedier than me. The way it stands now, there's dough enough for all concerned, and best of all, it's tax free."

Now Fanti raised his hand above the edge of the desk. It held a stack of hundreds, neatly bound. Will estimated that there was at least ten thousand in the bundle. He couldn't keep his gaze off the money. His throat went dry and his heart began to pound.

Fanti thumped the stack of bills on the desk, his eyes bright. "Now, if you happen to come up short, now or at any time, just let me know. You'll find that I'm generous to my friends."

Will had to struggle to get the words out. "No, thanks just the same." The last time he was in Anchorage with Candice she had seen a diamond bracelet she desperately wanted. He had halfway promised to get it for her. "You leave me no choice but to back off, Fanti, but that doesn't mean that I'll take dirty money from you."

"Dirty money?" Fanti raised an eyebrow. "Well, it's up to you, of course. But if you ever change your mind . . ."

Fanti returned the money to the desk drawer and closed it with a sound of finality.

With an effort Will forced himself to turn away. Leaving the office, Will felt that he was slinking away in defeat. Sunk in despair, disgusted with himself, he walked down the dingy hallway with dragging footsteps.

When the door closed behind Will Cole, Milo Fanti made a beeline for the refrigerator. He took out a beer, popped the tab, and took a gulp.

He snorted with glee, and had to restrain himself from doing a little dance step.

He had him, he had Will Cole by the balls! All he had to do was squeeze a little and Cole would scream.

Fanti knew that he didn't have a complete lock on him yet, but it wouldn't be long. Cole actually had to accept money from him before he had him completely, but he would before long. Dirty money, was it? He'd never seen a man's eyes shine so with greed as had Will Cole's when he'd eyed that bundle of C-notes.

Now Fanti felt that he could relax a little. He could operate without fear from now on, with Will Cole there to cover his ass. As for Cole's avowal that he wouldn't stand still for any rough stuff, he would come around there, too. Fanti had seen it happen before. A man got involved in something criminal, claiming that he wouldn't be a party to anything violent; yet when the easy money began to pour in, he was quite willing to look the other way, if anything threatened to cut off that flow of money.

Not that he had anything like that in mind at the moment, but it was sometimes necessary in his business. For instance, if that pipeliner, O'Keefe, came back nosing around in his, Fanti's, business, he would have to be dealt with.

Finishing his beer, Fanti pulled the phone toward him and dialed. When it was answered, he said, "Will Cole was just here. I've got him in my pocket. Now it's up to you to keep him spending money."

Candice Durayea gave a gusty sigh. "That's good, I suppose, but I'm not sure how happy I am. I like the guy, you know."

"So what does that have to do with anything? You like a guy who spends big bucks on you, am I right? And from what you've told me, Will Cole is doing just that."

"I know, Milo, I know. It's never bothered me before, but this time it does."

He said tauntingly, "Attack of conscience, babe? *You?* That hardly fits your image." He made his voice harsh. "And don't lay that guilt crap on me, okay? You just keep doing what you do best."

"Oh, I'll keep it up," Candice assured him. "I like the good life too much to turn off the money tap. Just see to it that Will isn't hurt badly, all right?"

"So long as he stays in line, we'll all be okay. But if he balks, I'll have to sting him a little."

Fifteen

Now that the short summer was here, work on the pipeline quickened. Men worked longer hours; leaves were shorter and less frequent. On some of the more urgent jobs, pipeliners labored around the clock, putting in twelve-hour shifts—golden time, double and triple time. The money flowed like a river of gold.

This resulted in some restlessness and discontent, and men snarled and spat at one another, sometimes engaging in fisticuffs, usually as brief and violent as a summer storm. Horny, thirsty, pockets full of money and no place to spend it. It was too much to ask of a man, especially the young and fiddle-footed. Men quit, were quickly replaced. The family men there to make a quick killing and scamper home with it were, in the main, content.

Chris was content enough. Oh, not the money; that interested him very little. But he liked the feeling of doing an important job well, the feeling of being useful. He had only one regret—he ached to do something about his failure to do anything about the thefts, and the other criminal activities of Milo Fanti's.

He observed an example of Fanti's work firsthand two weeks after he returned to work. Late one night, three campers slipped up to the camp. Out of the campers tumbled whores, quickly pairing off with men, after money was exchanged—a hundred dollars a pop. At the rear of one camper, a man set up shop, selling bottles of liquor and sticks of marijuana at exorbitant prices as fast as he could make the exchange.

Chris had no moral objection to booze, broads, or even pot, and he knew how tough it was on the men stuck out here for so long. But the trouble was, the workers were bleary-eyed and fagged out the next day, their work sloppy and careless. Mysteriously, all those in authority, including the camp policemen, did a vanishing act prior to the arrival of the campers, and Chris knew that someone was being paid off. He didn't know if any hard drugs were being pushed; he didn't see any indication of it.

This decided him. He had to finish what he had started out to do. He knew it would be a waste of time to complain to the job superintendents, or the union representatives, about the campers or the sloppy workmanship the next day. He would either be fired or get his head cracked open.

And it was abundantly clear by this time that Will Cole wasn't going to keep his promise; he was going to sit on his hands.

Remembering Kelly Cole, Chris had to wonder about the things she had said to him. Was she any more reliable than her half-brother?

At least he had a piece of evidence now. He had jotted down the license numbers of the three campers, with descriptions of the drivers.

He decided to give Kelly a call.

But that presented another problem. There were no private telephones at the camp, not even pay phones. All calls in and out had to be routed through the camp switchboard. Chris didn't want to risk being overheard. For all he knew, all calls could be monitored.

The next day was Friday. A short time before his shift was over, he approached Cody Brant, the job boss. "Mr. Brant, I have to go into Fairbanks tomorrow. It's urgent, personal business."

Brant frowned. "Damnit, O'Keefe, you know how busy we are right now!"

"I know, but I'll be back Sunday night at the latest. I'll take the bus in in the morning. I'll just be in Fairbanks overnight."

"Well, okay," Brant said reluctantly. "But if you don't report for work Monday morning, your paycheck will be waiting for you." He jabbed a thumb against Chris's chest. "There's been too damned much goldbricking, understand?"

"Understood. Don't worry, Mr. Brant, I'll be back on the job Monday morning."

*   *   *

Since the bus started on time the next morning and the road had been improved a little since the spring thaw, Chris arrived in Fairbanks in the middle of Saturday afternoon. There had been places along the way where he could have made his call, but he would have been forced to wait overnight anyway for a bus to take him back to camp, so he continued on to Fairbanks.

He closeted himself in a telephone booth with a stack of quarters and called the number Kelly Cole had given him.

The phone was answered by a man. "I'm sorry, Miss Cole is not at home just now. She went sailing this afternoon, and won't be back for at least three hours."

Chris thought for a moment. "Will you please tell her that Chris O'Keefe called? I'm calling from a pay phone and can't give her a number to call me back. But I will call her again. Please tell her to be expecting my call."

"Very well, sir."

Leaving the booth, Chris felt at loose ends. How was he going to spend the time? He certainly wasn't going to call Will Cole. He finally decided to cross the river and visit with Dwight until it was time to call Kelly again. It might be interesting to find out how SAS was doing.

Dwight answered the door himself. His bearded face went dark when he recognized Chris. "What are you doing here?" he demanded truculently.

A little taken aback by Dwight's attitude, Chris said, "I was in town overnight and I just thought I'd drop in for a chat."

"I wouldn't think you'd have the nerve after what you did."

"What *I* did? What the devil are you talking about?"

"I'm talking about Gordie."

"What about Gordie? Make sense, will you, Dwight?"

"You repeated what he told you about pushing dope along the pipeline. You told *someone*. He was damned near killed last week, he was just lucky he wasn't. Two goons waylaid him in an alley, beat him up, then left him for dead with a hunting knife in his back. The knife just missed his heart by a hair."

"I'm sorry about that, Dwight, really I am. I don't like Gordie, but I sure wouldn't want to see him hurt. How do you know what was behind it? Maybe he was mugged."

"The last thing he remember is one of the goons telling him that the boss didn't like squealers."

"And by boss, he meant Milo Fanti?"

"Who else?" Dwight relaxed into a more friendly manner. He motioned Chris inside and led him into the parlor. To Chris's relief, there was no one else present.

Dwight said, "Are you trying to say that you didn't pass on what Gordie said to Fanti?"

"Now why would I do that? Honest to God, Dwight, I didn't mention Gordie to Fanti . . . oh, Jesus Christ!" Chris suddenly remembered. "But I did tell someone else, never dreaming it would get back to Fanti!"

"Who? Who did you tell?"

Chris sighed. "Will Cole. I told your brother."

Dwight tensed visibly. "Will? Why on earth did you tell *him*?"

Chris hesitated, uncertain as to how much to reveal. "I've been doing some investigating for your brother, into the corruption along the pipeline."

"Investigating?" Dwight scowled. "I thought you were a bulldozer operator?"

"I am, but I got sick of some of the things I saw going on. I ran into your brother out at the pipeline one day. He said he was interested in putting a stop to it, also. So we made a sort of pact. I would see what I could find out, come to him with it, and he'd act." He added sourly, "Only he doesn't seem to be doing much."

Dwight snorted. "The only thing Will is interested in is what's good for Will. But that still doesn't explain how he passed on Gordie's name."

"Well, when I was here that day and learned that Gordie had pushed for Fanti, I told your brother about it. Why the hell he should then turn around and tell Fanti, I have no idea. He should have sense enough to realize that Fanti might react just this way."

Dwight's laugh was bitter. "It wouldn't surprise me a whole lot if he isn't in cahoots with Fanti."

"Oh, I find that hard to believe. Why should he be? Surely he doesn't need the money?"

"I doubt that there's enough money in the world for Will. He's the original big spender."

"I'm unhappy with him, true, but I just don't believe that a man in his position would be in cahoots with a hoodlum like

Milo Fanti. He'd be risking everything, if he was ever found out."

"He could be doing it partly for kicks. When I lived at home, I saw Will do foolish things, risk his neck time after time, just for the hell of it. Then, I admired him . . . no, I idolized him. But I grew up, got a little sense, and saw that the things he did were stupid. Shit, don't listen to me, Chris. We don't get along, I hate his bloody guts." Dwight laughed shortly. "Besides, who am I to judge him? In some respects I'm just as bad. We Coles, Chris, are not altogether nice people."

It was on the tip of Chris's tongue to ask if that applied to Kelly, but he said instead, "Is Gordie going to be okay?"

Dwight nodded. "He's healing fine. In fact, this may do him some good. He's being forced into withdrawal from whatever he's been on. We've got him hidden away, but I can take you to see him if you like." Dwight looked at him questioningly.

Chris shook his head. "I don't think that's such a good idea. There's no love lost between us, and he'd think me the worst kind of hypocrite, if I come with the sympathy bit. Besides, I don't have time right now. I have an important appointment shortly. . . ."

This time Kelly answered the phone herself. "Chris! I've been waiting for your callback. You know, I've been hoping all along that you'd call me."

The sound of her throaty voice, and her frank pleasure at hearing from him, sent a tingle racing along his nerve ends. "You told me to call you if I wasn't getting cooperation from your brother."

Her voice went flat. "Oh, yes, I did, didn't I?"

Chris felt a leap of delight. Had she been waiting for him to call on a personal basis? No, that couldn't be. Kelly Cole and a construction stiff? That was the stuff of dreams—the impossible dream. He laughed harshly.

"What, Chris? What did you say?"

"Nothing, just clearing my throat."

"Oh . . ." Her voice flattened even more. "So what's the story? Isn't Will cooperating with you?"

Chris said cautiously, "I'm not sure how to answer that. He *is* your brother."

"Chris, forget our relationship for the moment. Something must be bothering you, or you wouldn't be calling. Now, what is it?"

"Well, I've talked to him only once since our conversation, but something isn't right."

"Explain, please." She laughed lightly. "Grandfather has a saying, one of a great many, I might add. He says that if a man is any good, trust his gut feelings. More often than not, he's right. Is this a gut feeling you have?"

Chris shook his head sharply. She had a knack for knocking a man off balance. "Well, partially, I suppose, but there's more to it than that."

She said impatiently, "Then tell me about it. This is long distance, it's costing you."

He told her about the near-fatal attack on Gordie and his conviction that Will Cole had passed Gordie's name on to Fanti.

"You're sure Will did that?"

"Not one hundred percent, no, but I don't know how else Fanti could have found out that Gordie talked to me. I certainly didn't tell him, and I'm sure Dwight didn't. Of course there is the possibility that Gordie mouthed off to somebody else, but I think the chances of that are pretty remote."

She was silent for a long time. Chris was beginning to wonder if she'd left the phone. When she did speak, her voice was firm, almost commanding. "Grandfather must be told about this, and it has to come from you, Chris. You must come down to Cole Island."

Her tone and manner stirred his temper. "Now hold on, lady! I have a job. I'm risking it as it is, and I'll damned sure be fired if I don't show up for work Monday morning."

"This is more important than any job."

"To you, maybe, but it's not your job that's in jeopardy."

"Chris, Grandfather may be old and retired, but he carries a lot of weight still. He'll see to it that your job is safe."

"*You* say that, but how do I know he'll agree? Your brother made me promises he didn't keep."

"Grandfather is not Will Cole," she said coolly. Then her voice warmed. "You're right, I guess I am being unreasonable, Chris, but I promise, personally, that you won't lose your job."

Privately, he didn't think her promise was worth shit, but what the hell? He'd been fired before, they wouldn't be getting a cherry, and the thought of seeing Kelly Cole again did something to his pulse rate. "Since you put it that way, how can I refuse?"

"Chris, I'm glad!" She became brisk. "I'll handle everything from here. Take a cab out to the airport. I'll alert a Cole jet to expect you. It will fly you to Juneau. I'll send a launch over from the island, and Perkins, the launch operator, will pick you up at the terminal, then ferry you here. It'll be late when you get in, and Grandfather isn't allowed up that late. But I'll wait up and we'll have a late supper..."

"Wow! You do things on a grand scale. I'm overwhelmed."

"What? Oh..." She laughed without taking offense. "I guess I was putting it on a little thick. It's what comes of being born to privilege, Chris. You snap your fingers and your every wish, well, almost every wish, is granted."

"Many more wishes than three, I'd imagine."

"Oh, yes, many, many more." She laughed again.

"Doesn't that tend to make you a touch spoiled?"

"How very perceptive of you." She added in a dry voice, "Wouldn't you like to be spoiled, Chris?"

"It might take some getting used to, but I imagine I could grow to like it."

As Chris hung up, replaying the conversation back in his mind, it struck him as rather strange, especially for a conversation with someone he was speaking with for only the second time. He decided that he'd better play it cagy until he found a handle on Kelly Cole.

Something of the same warning bell was sounding in Kelly's mind after the conversation. She knew that she had come on a little strong with Chris, but she hadn't been able to get him out of her thoughts since their brief meeting. It wasn't that he was simply handsome, although he was certainly that—rugged good looks that were strongly reminiscent of James Coburn's saturnine charm—but it seemed to her that a spark had been struck between them. It may have been her imagination, but it seemed to her that he had experienced the same attraction. In any case, she was looking forward to seeing him again. She had manipulated the meeting, something she had never done in her life. Far from feeling ashamed of her maneuverings, she was unduly proud of herself.

A glance at her wristwatch told her that it was still early—Grandfather would likely be up.

Detouring through the baronial hall, she picked up a bottle of bourbon. Since Will wasn't seeing as much of Jeremiah as he once had, Kelly smuggled him a bottle of Jack Daniel's now and then.

The door to Jeremiah's room was cracked open slightly, but no light spilled out. This wasn't unusual, since he often sat in the room in the dark for lengthy periods.

She knocked lightly on the door, pushing it open farther. She said softly, "Grandfather?"

"Kelly?" said the thin voice. "Is that you, girl?"

She pushed the door wide and went in. "I thought maybe you were asleep."

The wheelchair creaked as he turned it about from the spot by the window. "Nope. Just sitting here, dreaming about the old days."

"I brought you a bottle."

"How'd you get it past the watchdog?"

"I didn't see Hank around. He must be asleep."

He grunted. "That fellow sleeps more than I do, that's for Lord God sure." His voice gathered strength. "You'll find a glass in the bathroom, girl. Turn the light on if'n you want."

"It's all right, I can find my way."

Kelly went into the bathroom off the bedroom, closed the door to turn on the light, and found a clean glass. Bright light hurt Jeremiah's failing eyes. She poured about a half glass of the bourbon, and carried it and the bottle back into the bedroom.

She gave the glass to her grandfather, who took it in both hands and raised it to his mouth. While he drank, Kelly pulled a footstool up before the wheelchair and sat down.

"Ah-h, nectar, pure nectar of the gods." Jeremiah smacked his lips, and gave a breathy sigh. "Thank you, girl, and thanks for dropping in on an old man. Appreciate it."

"Grandfather . . ." Kelly paused, trying to frame her words. "There's a young man coming here tonight, Christopher

O'Keefe. He's a pipeliner. I asked him to come and talk to you. I think it's important that you see him."

Even in the dark, she could sense his wariness. "You know I don't see people nowadays, girl, especially strangers. You know how I am. I can be talking perfect sense one minute and wander off into a fog the next."

"I know, Grandfather." She reached out to touch his hand lying atop the lap robe. "But he'll understand, I'm sure he will. I do think you should listen to what he has to say."

"Say about what?" A note of hope crept into his voice. "Is he your fellow? Come to ask for your hand? I thought you young people didn't go for that these days? Besides, it's Joshua he should see, not me."

Kelly laughed softly. "He's not my fellow, Grandfather. I've only seen him one time. I do like him, more than I have any man on such short acquaintance. But it's about the pipeline, the company, that he will talk about."

"The company?" Jeremiah said sharply. "What does a pipeliner know about my company?"

"Actually, it's about . . . well, about Will."

"What does he know about Will?"

"I think it should come from him, Grandfather. I don't know all the details."

"I'm a mite surprised at you, girl. Never knew you to spare a thought to the company."

"I don't often, that's true," she admitted. "I probably wouldn't have this time, if Chris hadn't brought it to my attention."

"Why didn't he go to Will?"

"That's just the point, he did."

Her eyes had grown accustomed enough to the darkness now so that she could see him, dimly, and she saw Jeremiah draw himself up alertly, into a semblance, almost a parody, of the Jeremiah Cole of old. His voice grew deeper, crackling a little, as he said, "What about Will?"

Instead of answering directly, she said, "Grandfather, I've never questioned you or Will about what's happened between you. I figured it was none of my business. But once you were very close. The last few years there's been a coolness between you. Could you tell me the reason for that?"

He was silent and unmoving for so long that she began to

think he wasn't going to answer. When he did begin to speak, his voice was so low that she had to lean forward to hear. "The boy is not responsible. He's too indulgent of his appetites. I've always had appetites and catered to them, but the company always came before anything else. To run an empire, a man has to have that in mind first, all else comes second. That's not always so with Will."

"But you might have thought of that long ago. Will hasn't changed all that much, that I can see."

"I know, girl, I know. But I hoped that he would straighten out as he began to get on. I had doubts about him when I put him in charge of Cole 98, but he did a damned good job there. Yet, even then he would get a wild hair in his ass and go sniffing off after something. Then, it didn't matter all that much. Hell, Cole 98 could run itself, anyway. But heading up the whole shebang is something else again. I had my doubts when I put him in charge." Now his voice turned bitter. "I had no choice, girl. Lord God, who else could I use? Your daddy ain't interested, never was. And Dwight, he's turned his back on all of us. The only choice was to put someone other than family at the head of Cole, and I knew nobody I could trust. So, Will was it."

He stopped, as if he had run down. Kelly was deeply moved, but she could think of nothing to say, and she sensed that he wasn't through unburdening himself.

Jeremiah proved her right, as he went on, his voice tired now, quavering and weak. "There's something else, girl, something I ain't never breathed to a living soul. Will, he's sterile. He can't never sire me a great-grandson. I was hoping for that, at least, a boy who would grow up and take over."

"Will can't have children?" Kelly gasped, trying to grapple with it. "How did you find that out, Grandfather? Did Will tell you? Or Louise?"

"Will? Hah!" The old man snorted softly. "The boy would never tell me something like that, even if he knew. Which I doubt to hell and gone. As for Louise, she doesn't talk to me, never has. She hates me into the ground. But it was through her that I found out, in a roundabout way. She wanted children, I'll give her that, so she went to several doctors, trying to find out why she had none. There was nothing wrong with her, so it has to be Will."

"But how did *you* find out?"

"From one of the doctors. I paid him handsomely for the information."

"That wasn't nice, Grandfather," she said in reproof.

"Never said I was nice, especially about something as important as that." His fading voice gathered a little strength. "Lord God, girl, don't you know how much I want a great-grandson before I kick off? You're my last hope, girl. I keep hoping you'll find a beau and get married. Maybe this Chris fellow who's coming to see me?"

"Grandfather, when and if I get married, it won't be because *you* want me to, or just so I can provide you with a great-grandson you can mold into another Will!"

"I didn't mold him, girl, that's just the way he turned out."

"You had a hand in it," she said coldly. "He's been under your wing since before I was born."

"That's true, I can't deny that." Jeremiah heaved a windy sigh. "And I reckon I have to shoulder some of the blame." His voice turned wistful. "Lord God, he was bright and quick, picking up on everything as a youngster. He listened all ears when I yarned to him about the old days, always at me to hear more, then boasting that he was going to be just like me. What happened to that boy I told yarns to?"

"People grow up, Grandfather. They grow up and change, become somebody else." Kelly cringed inwardly at the banality of the cliché. But what else could she say to a dying, bitterly disappointed old man? For there was no denying that he was dying, clinging stubbornly to life from day to day. She felt an ache of sorrow. Without thinking she said, "I guess you haven't heard. Dwight is soon to be a father."

"I have no wish to hear about him. He's a traitor to the family. He turned his back on us, and I'll deny any child he has, just like he did us."

Jeremiah went silent, and Kelly could see his chin fall onto his chest. She was about to get up and tiptoe out of the room when he began to speak again.

"Did I ever tell you about the spring flood of nineteen-ought-six, boy?" he said in a musing voice. "Millions of tons of ice came piling down from upstream when the Chena began to break up, with trees and whole houses riding on its back..."

Kelly knew that he had slipped away, back into the past, and believed that Will, a young Will, was in the room. Kelly had not listened to Jeremiah's reminiscences as much as Will and Dwight, but she had heard many of the tales, this one included. Yet she sat on, not wishing to upset him by sneaking out. He might notice her absence, he might not, but she didn't want to chance it. He would nod off to sleep soon, anyway.

". . . the bridge was the first to go. It was built on wooden pilings in those days, which snapped like matchsticks, and the bridge floated away whole on a big ice floe. The bridge went almost every spring back then. But that was the worst spring flood I ever saw. Slabs of ice acres wide and as tall as a man were thrown up onto the banks, knocking over wagons, boats, houses, even some store buildings.

"And then, as the ice began to melt, the water came boiling up over the banks of the Chena, going as far over as Sixth Avenue."

Jeremiah chuckled. "The mosquitoes, Lord God, the mosquitoes that year! They swarmed in the millions. The folks could clean up after the flood, rebuild if need be, but not much they could do about the mosquitoes but burn Buhach and splash on citronella. Everybody in early summer that year smelled to high heaven of citronella. I recollect that the girls all lined their cotton drawers and stockings to protect themselves from mosquito bites . . ."

Jeremiah's voice trailed off, his head slumped down onto his chest again, and the whiskey glass, empty, thumped to the floor.

Kelly got up and tiptoed out, leaving him asleep. He had told her once that he could sleep just as well in the wheelchair as in his bed.

Sixteen

It was late when the Cole jet arrived in Juneau. It was still daylight; at this time of the year there were only about four hours of darkness out of twenty-four. But it was cloudy and raining, as gloomy as twilight, and Chris could see very little of Juneau.

Perkins was a tall, skinny, taciturn individual of about fifty. All the way to the dock he spoke scarcely a dozen words. About all the response Chris got from him was a grunt, and he finally gave up talking to him. His driving reminded Chris of an old Texas description of a bad driver: "He don't drive, he loose herds."

The open Jeep had no side windows and Chris was damp and cross by the time they reached the docks. The launch had a cabin, but Perkins kept the windows wide open, and spray whipped in through the windows. Chris huddled in his mackinaw, and was soaked through by the time they reached the island. Perkins herded the launch as he had the Jeep—plowing through the choppy waters of the sound at full speed.

Fortunately it was only a half-hour trip to Cole Island, which loomed up like a green sanctuary through the mist. It was larger than Chris had expected, stretching out of sight both to the north and the south, and a tree-shrouded hill bulked up through the rain several hundred feet high. He had to admit that the scenery along the sound was spectacular—majestic mountains rising to the right, and one island after another on the left.

It must be nice, he reflected sardonically, to be rich enough to afford your own island.

A small, secluded bay lay on the east side of the island, with a wooden dock jutting out like a long finger. Two sailboats, sails furled, bobbed where they were tethered to the jetty, and there was another, larger launch tied off. In fact, it looked more like a luxury craft, a small yacht. Another Jeep was parked at the landing.

Perkins reduced the motor's roar to a muttering growl, and brought the launch neatly alongside the dock. Without a word Chris started up the ladder to the dock.

"Wait until I secure the launch, Mr. O'Keefe, then I'll take you up to the house." It was the longest speech Perkins had made since Chris got off the plane. "It's a far piece up to Cole House."

At least this Jeep had windows. Chris got in, waiting for Perkins. It *was* a far piece, close to two miles. At least here Perkins drove at a more sedate pace. Chris saw no other buildings until Cole House came into view through the driving rain. There were several outbuildings to the rear of the main house, a long, low rambling structure which didn't impress Chris particularly. Although large enough, it didn't strike him as the ornate structure befitting a man who could afford his own island.

Perkins braked the Jeep to a stop before the steps, and Chris ducked out, hurrying up the steps and to the door. He banged the brass knocker.

Kelly opened the door herself, and Chris's breath caught at the sight of her. Whether by design or not, she wore a champagne-colored lounging outfit, not quite sheer enough to reveal the details of her figure, but so close to it that Chris could *imagine* he could see everything, right down to the pubic pelt; and the total effect was far more provocative than if she had been totally naked.

Realizing that she had been speaking, he broke out of his daze. "I'm sorry, Miss Cole." He passed a hand over his eyes. "I've been up since six this morning, and things are a little foggy about now."

"I said, you're soaked through. Come in, come in." She took his hand and pulled him inside and closed the door. "You're going to have to get out of those wet clothes." She glanced behind him. "Where's your luggage?"

"What you see is what I have," he said with a faint smile. "I didn't expect to be gone more than overnight, and brought nothing but a razor and toothbrush."

She said, "You flew down."

He peered at her. "Of course. You told me to, don't you remember?"

"I know, but I heard on the news while I was waiting for you that there was a plane crash up north of Anchorage. Four people were killed." She shivered.

"Well, I'm sorry to hear that, but a plane crash is not that rare up here. Anyway, what does that have to do with me?"

"Nothing, really. It's just that I'm absolutely terrified of flying, and every time there's a plane crash . . ." She clapped a hand to her mouth, her gray eyes widening. "Now what caused me to say that? You're one of the few people I've ever revealed that to!"

Then she gestured sharply, and stepping back, she studied him with a finger at the corner of her mouth. "Will keeps some clothes around to change into when he's here. You seem about his size to me."

Wearing Will Cole's clothing didn't appeal to Chris all that much, but Kelly was right, he was soaked through. "Okay, if that's the best we can manage."

She took his hand. "Come along to the baronial hall. There's a fire going, and you can have a drink while I look for some clothes."

She led him down the hall. Chris was more impressed by the inside of Cole House than he had been by the log-covered exterior. The furnishings, although heavy and dark, had an expensive look, and the room Kelly led him into was even more impressive, with its many couches, huge fireplace, and the dark mahogany bar at one end, with a glittering array of bottles on the back bar. Even the dark and bloody hunting scenes framed on the walls seemed appropriate.

Kelly said, "Help yourself to a drink, Chris. I'll be right back."

Chris hung his mackinaw over a chair close to the fire, warmed himself front and rear for a few moments, then crossed down the room to the bar. He found a bucket of ice cubes and a bottle of Chivas Regal on the back bar. He poured a liberal portion of the Scotch over ice, and returned to the couch before the fire.

His clothes began to steam from the blazing fire, and he detected a rather pungent odor from the clothing. By the time Kelly returned, with garments draped over her arm, the combination of the fire and the Scotch had worked some magic on him. At least he had stopped shivering.

Kelly placed a checkered flannel shirt and dark corduroy trousers over the arm of the couch. "All I could find were Will's hunting clothes. I thought he had other clothes here, but then he hasn't been coming out to Cole Island as much as he once did."

"Those will do fine." Chris drained his glass and stood up, reaching for the garments. "Where do I change?"

She motioned with her head. "That door over there, it opens to a bathroom."

Chris took the clothes into the bathroom and changed. They fitted well enough, but he still felt strange wearing Will Cole's clothing. He hung his own wet things over the shower door.

When he came back, Kelly had a fresh drink for him and a balloon glass with a splash of brandy for herself. She said, "I'll have the housekeeper wash and iron your clothes in the morning. It's so late, everyone's gone to bed, Grandfather as well. I told him you were coming, and he very much wants to talk to you, but he sleeps so little, I don't want to wake him now. You can talk to him tomorrow afternoon."

He took a sip of his drink. "Why not in the morning?"

"That's not the best time for him. He's like a bear in the morning." She smiled. "He says it takes him a half-day to get his blood circulating again. You may already know, but Grandfather's very old, coming up on one hundred. He's feeble, and sometimes his mind's not too clear, but you'll find he's very sharp when he wants to be."

Chris thought again of mentioning that he had a job to get back to, but she already knew that.

As though reading his thoughts, Kelly nodded. "I know, you're thinking about your job. If you lose it, I'll see to it that you get another, probably a better job. So, don't worry, Chris."

"I'm not worried," he said with a shrug. And it was true. Being here with Kelly Cole was preferable to the job, any job, and he determined to take matters as they came, and worry about his job later.

He sat down beside her on the couch, a careful distance away, and worked on his drink. The silence that ensued for the next few minutes was companionable, as easy and undemanding of small talk as if they were old acquaintances. Staring into the leaping flames, Chris became drowsy, and it took an effort to rouse himself when he heard her soft voice.

"I'm sorry, Kelly, I was dozing." He gave her an apologetic grin. "It's not that the company's boring, I'm just knocked out."

"I understand. What I asked was, are you hungry?"

He wasn't all that hungry, yet her company was more alluring than going to bed, alone, even as weary as he was. The trend of his thoughts was uncomfortable. Watch it, Chris, he told himself; to hope for her to go to bed with you is expecting too much. He said, "I could eat. Something light would be fine. You did say all the help had gone to bed."

"Oh, I can cook, not gourmet food, but the basics I can manage. How about an omelet?"

"An omelet sounds great."

Kelly got to her feet. "You relax, have another drink if you like. It should take only a few minutes."

He looked at her. She was standing between him and the flames, and this time he didn't need his imagination to see the bold outlines of her figure. He tore his gaze away. "Be sure and wake me if I doze off."

Her smile was enigmatic. "I'll wake you."

His tumescence and the workings of his fevered imagination were enough to keep him awake. Kelly Cole held an enormous appeal for him, more than any woman he had ever met. Chris had never been in love. He had felt affection for a number of women over the years, and had enjoyed them sexually, yet he had never met one he wished to marry. In fact, he had seldom thought of marrying. He was still young and there were other women to be enjoyed, yet he did want to marry eventually. Chris was an only child and both his parents had died in a car crash when he was only fourteen. He had spent the remaining years of his adolescence with an aging maiden aunt, who was now deceased as well. He had a few cousins, on his mother's side of the family, scattered around, but he was the last O'Keefe, the last of the line . . . unless he had a son.

He sat up, laughing scornfully at himself. Good Lord, was he actually thinking of Kelly as his wife? She was probably the wealthiest woman in Alaska, and that, combined with her good looks, would give her a license to pick and choose. So why on earth should she consider a construction stiff? It was unthinkable on the face of it, but undeniably there was a strong current of physical attraction running between them, and he was positive she was aware of it as he.

"I forgot to ask..." Kelly poked her head through the doorway. "Tea or coffee?"

"This late, I prefer tea. Coffee would only keep me awake."

"How about English tea, and a dash of rum?"

"Sounds great."

A short time later she came into the room carrying a tray, which held a plate and a steaming pot of tea. The omelet was speckled with mushrooms, and the tea and rum had a kick like an aroused mule. Chris ate hungrily, while Kelly sat silently, gazing into the flames.

He finally set the tray aside, pouring a second cup of tea, and sat with it cradled between his hands.

"Chris, do you sail?"

"Sail? Like in a bathtub, with a bed sheet flopping in the wind?"

"Hardly that," she said, smiling. "I have two sail-boats, both good-sized, and sailing is one of the things I do best."

"I worked as a deckhand on an oil tanker once for almost a year. I'm not all that crazy about the sea, but this tanker was a big mother, almost the size of a football field, and it didn't bother me too much. But a sailboat, I don't know."

"I don't sail on the ocean usually, just on the sound. The water is usually quite calm. The weather report said the morning would be clear, if breezy. I thought we might take one of the boats out for a couple of hours in the morning."

"We? I'll be about as useless as those well-known tits on you know what."

"You'll learn what you need to know. Who knows, you might even like it. Sailing clears your head of everything but the moment." Those gray eyes were suddenly intent on his, and the small space on the couch between them seemed, to Chris, to vibrate with sexual tension. Then it was gone as Kelly looked away. "Besides, I don't need much help. I can sail the twenty-two-foot sloop on my own."

*   *   *

Chris slept like the dead until a rap on the bedroom door woke him at nine o'clock.

When he finally responded, Kelly said beyond the door, "It's a beautiful day, Chris. Your breakfast will be ready in fifteen minutes. I'll be down at the dock getting ready. We sail at ten sharp, sailor. Don't be late."

Chris shaved quickly and got dressed in the clothes he had worn yesterday. He found them, dry and freshly ironed, draped over a chair at the foot of his bed, and he had to wonder if Kelly had crept in with them. The thought of her being in the bedroom with him, even with him dead to the world, excited him enormously. He was beginning to wonder if she had lured him here for a purpose other than talking with Jeremiah Cole. He wondered if he *would* ever see the old man, but he found that it really didn't matter.

After eating a huge breakfast, he stepped outside and quickly walked the two miles to the dock. The weather prediction was accurate—it was a clear, sunny day, a few white clouds frolicking like sheep above the mountains east across the sound. The sun was hot, but a brisk breeze made the morning pleasantly cool.

Kelly was busy aboard the smaller of the two sailboats. Whatever she was doing was a mystery to Chris and he wasn't inclined to inquire. She straightened up to stare over at him on the dock, where he stood inspecting the craft dubiously.

"I've been waiting for you," she said crossly. "It's past ten."

"You told me to have breakfast and I did." He eyed the lettering on the side of the boat with a cocked eyebrow. "*Lodestar II?*"

"It's named after the mother lode Grandfather found in Chena. The one over there, the first one I bought, is *Lodestar I*, named after his discovery in the Klondike. Get in, get in!" She gestured impatiently.

He stepped on board and experienced a sinking feeling as the boat rocked under the impact of his weight. "Is this thing really safe? It seems rather frail to me."

"People have sailed around the world in sailboats no larger than this one."

"But I don't plan on sailing around the world."

"You sit up there, in the bow, while I unfurl the sail."

"Can't I do something to help?"

"Like the TV ad says, I'd rather do it myself." She turned

a laughing face to him. "Seriously, Chris, I've found it easier, and safer, not to involve an utter novice. So, sit."

He made his way to the front of the boat and sat, watching her curiously. Her laughter was gone now, as she went about getting the boat underway. She raised the sail and watched as it caught the wind, then settled down in the stern with the tiller.

"You can come up here with me now, Chris," she called down to him.

Chris quickly clambered back to her, and just in time, as the boat began to move.

"Watch the boom," she said. "It can knock your ass over teakettle. Keep a wary eye on it at all times. Sometimes I may be too busy to warn you."

Shortly they were tacking before a stiff breeze out of the northwest, and *Lodestar II* was soon moving along at a good clip. The only sounds were the creaking of the rigging, the whistle of the wind, and the slapping of the water against the hull.

Chris studied Kelly at the tiller. Apparently all this was serious business with her, and there was an air of supreme confidence about her. Clearly she knew what she was doing and was good at it. She wore a green sweater, and a gray, wrap-around skirt that folded back in the breeze, and showed him tanned, beautiful legs. Her hair blew back in the wind, and where before her features had been serious and intent, now she was relaxed, smiling openly in contentment; yet Chris had a hunch that, for the moment at least, he didn't exist for her.

To test her, he said softly, "Kelly?" She showed no awareness of hearing him. He raised his voice. "Kelly?"

She looked at him, her eyes slowly coming into focus. "Yes, Chris?"

"Doesn't this thing have a motor?"

Her gesture held contempt. "Motors are for landlubbers. What's the fun in that? A sailor isn't really a sailor unless he can get away from the dock under full sail."

"Somehow I'd feel better if there was a motor to fall back on."

"Come on now, admit it, Chris." Her eyes sparkled. "Isn't this the greatest?"

He considered for a moment. Now that he was past his

initial reservations, he concluded that sailing was rather fun, and told her so.

"I love it," she said simply. "It's one of my two true passions."

"What's the second, a man?"

She didn't look at him. "No, tennis."

He was silent, thinking that a life with two such passions would be rather empty.

In a flash of intuition, Kelly said, "I know, you're thinking, poor little rich girl, nothing to do with her life but play games, right?"

"Something like that, yes."

"Yet, if I were a professional tennis player, a *champion* tennis player, if I had a shelf of sailing trophies, you'd think differently, wouldn't you?"

"Well . . . probably," he said cautiously.

"I'll have you know that I probably could be both those things, if I applied myself. At least, I've been told that by people who know about such matters."

"Then why haven't you?"

"Two reasons. One, I'm not that competitive. And two, because I am who I am, people would think me a dilettante. No matter how many honors I won, people would tend to dismiss it, saying I bought the honors."

"It seems to me I've heard of other wealthy people being champions in various sports, and they were thought none the less for it."

"I suppose there are some." She shrugged. "But those few are competitive by nature. My idea of competition is this—" she waved a hand around—"competing against nature, the sea, the wind. Against myself. *I* know how good I am, that's enough for me." She slanted a look at him. "You asked about men. Yes, I have a . . . uh, friend. But it's no grand passion. I sleep with him occasionally and enjoy it." The gray eyes suddenly glinted with mischief. "That admission surprise you, Chris?"

It did, a little, yet he wasn't about to admit it. "No plans for marriage then?"

"That, of course, is none of your business, but I'll answer it anyway. No, no plans for marriage. If there is a guy out there for me, I haven't found him as yet. Chris, tell me about yourself. I just realized something. I've unburdened myself more to you in just a few minutes that I ever have before, and yet all I know about you is that you operate a bulldozer for the pipeline."

"A manlift. I operate a manlift at the present time, if that matters," he said with a smile. "What else can I tell you, Kelly?"

"I want to know all about you, your likes and dislikes, where you grew up and the places you've been. In short, your oral autobiography. We have plenty of time, we'll be out here for a while. If you get hungry or thirsty, I have an ice chest in the cabin with wine and sandwiches."

Chris was a little hesitant at first; he had always been reluctant to talk about himself, finding other people far more interesting. But Kelly showed such genuine curiosity that he soon found himself talking freely. Once, he stopped to fetch the ice chest and they shared tuna sandwiches and a bottle of white wine.

When he finally glanced at his watch, Chris realized that he had been talking for two hours. "Good Lord, I've never rattled on that long before about myself! But you did seem to be interested. Or else you're a damned good actress."

"An actress I'm not, Chris. I've never been very successful at hiding how or what I feel, and you can believe that I was very interested. You have had a varied life, to say the least."

He said dryly, "A checkered career, I believe they call it, and not in a flattering way."

"In other times, you might have been called a soldier of fortune."

He laughed. "Hardly that, Kelly."

"One thing you haven't told me. What's your ambition in life? You can't knock around the way you have been forever."

"Oh, I don't know." He grinned lazily. "You just gave me an idea. That soldier of fortune role sounds pretty good, I just might make it my life work. It has a romantic ring to it. From movies I've seen and books I've read, soldiers of fortune do all right with the ladies."

"Not after they get a little long in the tooth."

"Ouch." He feigned a wounded look. "That's a low blow, lady. But to be serious, I suppose it is about time I was looking around for something more permanent. I probably will when the pipeline's finished. One thing I do know, I like this country. In all my wanderings I've never found a place that appealed to me so much."

"Does that mean you'll be staying on up here?"

"I think I can safely say yes to that."

"And I think I'd like that, Chris," she said gravely. She sat up suddenly, looking about. "Oh, oh! I do believe we've stayed out a little too long. I've been so absorbed in your life story I haven't noticed that the weather's changed on us."

Chris also looked around. The clouds hovering over the mountains to the east had not only thickened but had become black and threatening, and even as he looked they blotted out the sun, and it became chilly at once. In addition, the wind had picked up, becoming quite strong. "I see what you mean." He looked again to the east and saw a rain squall move down the mountains toward the water.

"The weather does that often up here. We're going in. Watch the boom, Chris."

"Can we beat the storm in?"

"I'm going to try. We have a good chance. At least the wind is in our favor and blowing up a gale."

Chris ducked as the boom whistled over his head. He held the tiller while Kelly adjusted the sail, then dropped back down into the cockpit. She moved the tiller and they heeled over as they came about. In doing so, the sailboat tipped so far on its side that Chris was positive they would capsize. In alarm he glanced at Kelly and saw that she was laughing, spray running down her face like tears of happiness. He had never seen her face so alive, and he knew in that instant that he was in love with Kelly Cole.

Gradually the boat righted itself and began to fly toward the distant island. To Chris, the sailboat seemed to skip over the water. The rigging creaked, the bellied sail sang, and the water hissed like sea snakes as it divided and sped by the hull on both sides.

Kelly laughed aloud and took one hand from the tiller to grope for his. She squeezed, and shouted, "Isn't this absolutely marvelous?"

"It's great." He glanced behind them. As fast as they were moving, the rain was moving faster, a solid sheet of water now, drumming on the surface, and gaining steadily on them. "But if we don't beat the rain, we're going to be soaked."

"Who cares?" She nodded her head. "If you're afraid of a little rain, there's always the cabin. It's cramped, but it should keep you dry."

Chris remained where he was. If she could stay out here in the wet, he'd be damned if he'd scoot for shelter! Maybe it was macho bullshit, but he had the feeling that somehow he would be diminished in her eyes if he ducked into the cabin.

He could see the island clearly now, and could make out the long finger of the jetty. He looked back over his shoulder. The wall of rain, black as night, was less than a hundred yards behind them. It caught them before they were halfway to the dock. The force of the wind drove the raindrops against them like pellets, and they were both drenched by the time Kelly maneuvered the sailboat against the dock.

She pointed to a rope coiled on the deck, and shouted against the roar of the wind and the rain. "Tie us off while I take care of the sail!"

Fingers wet and stiff from the cold, Chris uncoiled the rope and awkwardly tied the boat to an iron ring on the dock. By the time he was finished, Kelly had already rolled the sail around the mast and lashed it securely.

She was damned efficient at this, he thought admiringly, and wondered how she'd be at tennis, a game he'd played only a few times in his life. He decided then that he would be better off if he didn't let her lure him into a game.

Dripping water, they clambered onto the dock. Kelly said ruefully, "I should have taken some transportation down to the dock this morning. Stupid of me. It's a long hike back to the house. I don't even have a slicker on the *Lodestar*."

"Who laughed at the rain a bit ago?"

"That was different. We're on land now."

"And the longer we stand here, the wetter we'll get." He put his arm around her. "Let's head for the house."

"No, that's not necessary. There's a cabin over there."

She pointed to a grove of pines along the shore on the right, then tugged at his hand. "Come on."

They ran together off the end of the dock, then veered right about fifty yards along the narrow strip of rocky beach. Chris could see nothing through the driving rain until they entered the grove and then he saw it—a small, weathered log cabin completely hidden in the trees.

As they paused under the overhang over the door, Kelly

said breathlessly, "Grandfather built this to stay in when he was on Cole Island supervising the construction of the big house. I'm really the only one who uses it any more, when I want to be alone for a bit." She laughed up at him.

She opened the unlocked door and Chris followed her inside. It was dim, the only light coming through the small window in one wall. At one end of the room was a fireplace, with a stack of firewood beside it. The rest of the small room held a couch, two chairs, a small desk, a liquor cabinet, and two walls of books.

Kelly said, "There is no electricity, but there is a shower and a bathroom, with hot water, off there." She indicated a door at the end opposite the fireplace.

Chris was not listening, his interest caught by something across the room. He walked over to an easel, holding an unfinished picture. There were several other paintings, finished, in a rack beside the easel. "What's this?"

"Damn," she said faintly. "I forgot about those being left out in here."

He looked around. "Did you paint them?"

She looked suddenly shy, and stood mute, her color high.

He turned about for another look. The one on the easel was finished enough so that he could tell it was of a wild section of coastline, a glowering sky of cloud and storm, the surf crashing high, churning angry foam across huge rocks. There was a primitive look about it, like it had been painted in another, far distant age, and Chris had the fancy that a sea monster would rise out of the surf momentarily.

He took two finished canvases from the rack and crossed over to the cabin window.

Kelly said in a small voice, "Chris, I wish you wouldn't."

He ignored her. At the window he held the paintings up to the light one at a time. Both were seascapes: one of a sailboat flying before a storm much like the one that had driven them ashore; the second was the tip of an island lashed by a storm. In both he detected the wild, untamed quality that came across to him in the unfinished one.

He looked at Kelly. "Do you always do seascapes?"

She still had a bashful, almost embarrassed look. "I do landscapes, too, and an occasional still life."

"No portraits?"

She hesitated for an instant. "No, I've never quite dared."

"Because no one knows about your painting, that's it, isn't it?"

"Daddy knows. He's the only one."

"I don't know anything about art, not even what I like, but there's a power here that's almost frightening."

"You really feel that?" Now she sounded eager.

"Hell, yes. It comes off the canvas like a fist in the gut." He eyed her quizzically. "You've got all that stored up in you, lady? How long have you been at it?"

She raised and lowered her hands. "Off and on since I was sixteen."

"But why all the secrecy?"

"I . . . I was afraid people would think I was godawful."

"And just this morning you told me you do nothing but sail and play tennis."

She shrugged. "This is just a hobby, something to fool around with."

"Some hobby," he said dryly. "I'd bet a bundle that any art critic would go into raptures if he got a peek."

"Oh, I'd never do that. It'd be . . . oh, like putting myself and my feelings on display."

"Some feelings. Wow!"

"Enough of that," she said briskly. "I have dibs on the first shower. While I'm at it, see if you can get a fire going, okay?"

She was standing very close to him, looking up into his eyes. The small confines of the cabin, the rainstorm, Kelly's closeness, the paintings and their startling revelations into her being—all created a sense of isolation from the rest of the world and a feeling of intimacy that was too much for Chris.

He put his arms around her, pulling her against him, and sought her mouth. Her lips parted to his kiss. She tasted of the wine they had drunk. She made a small sound deep in her throat and squirmed to get closer. Even through their layers of clothing, Chris could feel the contours of her body, and his tumescence was instant and full.

Finally she pulled back slightly to gaze up into his eyes. Her own were huge and luminous. "Oh, my," she said huskily. "Oh, my." She disengaged herself from him. "My shower first, okay, Chris?"

He stood without moving, breathing heavily, as she walked toward the bathroom door. As she started in, she glanced back at him, an unreadable look.

Chris was torn between desire and dismay. Had he been too precipitous? At least she hadn't slapped him, but then a slap to punctuate a stolen kiss was an old-fashioned concept nowadays. And there *had* been an implied promise in her last words...

He shook himself, laughing ruefully, and turned away to the fireplace. There were newspapers and a small pile of kindling, so he got a fire going without too much difficulty.

He stood back, warming himself before the blaze, turning slowly. Finally he removed his shirt, which was soaked, then his boots; his trousers, being corduroy, weren't quite so wet. All the while he was aware of the roar of the shower in the other room. He had ceased shivering when he heard the water stop. He turned, staring at the closed door. When it didn't open at once, he turned his back on it.

A few moments later he heard a small sound, and faced around again. Kelly stood in the open door. Chris said, "Is it my turn now?" He took two steps and skidded to a stop, sucking in his breath. "Jesus!"

Kelly was naked as a needle. Her slight figure was breathtakingly lovely, from the rather small, upthrust breasts, down across the firmness of belly, to the blond pubic triangle, where his gaze lingered.

Blood pounding in his temples, he raised his gaze to her face. She was smiling slightly, apparently unself-conscious of her nudity. Now she came toward him with the lithe grace of a cat.

"Am I too brazen, Chris? Do I embarrass you?"

When he did not answer, could not answer, she said simply, "I want you, Chris. Of course, we could go through the coyness of the seduction game, but it isn't a game that I like very much."

"When you want something, do you usually get it?" he said through a dry, aching throat.

"Not always." She had reached him now. She placed her hands on his bare chest, stroking gently. So close, he could feel the heat of her body. "Don't you know that, in this day of the liberated woman, women often come on to men?"

"I've heard that, but it's never happened to me, except with..."

"Whores?" she said softly. "That makes you out to be a male chauvinist, doesn't it?"

"Whatever."

"Do you think that of me, Chris?"

"Of course not," he said roughly.

He crushed her to him, his kiss rough and demanding. The hardness of her nipples poked against his chest like probing fingers. He picked her up, his big hands around her waist, and bore her to the couch.

Stretching her out, he stared down at her, and said in a growling voice, "I want you, too, Kelly Cole."

He unzipped his trousers and stepped out of them, then removed his shorts. Kelly, gaze fastened on his hard readiness, moved restlessly.

Chris dropped to his knees beside the couch. His head dipped, and he drew his tongue across a nipple. One hand moved across her stomach to her Venus mound, and cupped the wetness he found there. Kelly tensed, moaning. Her hands stroked his hair, then clenched behind his head, forcing his mouth harder against her breast.

He loved her with his lips and tongue and stroking fingers, exploring her body, searching out the touch-buds of her passion, bringing into play all the skills he had learned over the years. He ached and throbbed, yet he made himself wait, prolonging it as long as possible. Everywhere he touched, her flesh leaped like an erratic pulse. She writhed and tossed under his ministrations, making little murmuring sounds of pleasure.

"Chris, please..." She looked at him with eyes out of focus. "Please, Chris, you're torturing me!"

Still he waited, still he carressed her, until her body was as familiar to him as his own, until she began to tug at him with urgent hands.

Finally he got upon the couch with her. Kelly opened to him with a stuttering cry. As he entered her, her head arched back, the tendons in her neck standing out. He held her pinned to the couch with his hands on her shoulders, as their love rhythm synchronized. It was only seconds before his orgasm began. Kelly convulsed against him, crying out. She reached up blindly, her hands behind his head, bringing his mouth down hard on hers.

As their mutual ecstasy subsided, they lay intertwined, her thighs, soft now and lax, a sweet cradle.

"Ah, God!" Kelly opened her eyes and stared into his,

inches away. Chris could see the twin images of himself swimming in her eyes.

Then she turned her face aside, eyes fluttering closed. He stroked her moist hair, and she whispered, "Dear Chris, dear, sweet Chris."

After a little Chris moved away to sit on the end of the couch and to light a cigarette.

Kelly said, "You know what?"

"What?"

"It's stopped raining."

"So?"

"We can get dressed and go up to the house. Grandfather should be up and stirring."

"What's the rush?"

"You're the one wanted to get it over with, so you can return to your job."

He grinned down at her. "Things have changed somewhat." He put out his cigarette and stretched out beside her.

Kelly gave a small shrug. "Well, I'm certainly in no hurry, if you're not."

"That depends on what the hurry is about." He propped his head on one elbow and ran his gaze over her.

"Oh, ho!" She gave a yelp of laughter. "For someone as easily embarrassed as you were when I came in here without a stitch, you've suddenly became a bold fellow, Mr. O'Keefe."

"There's something about you that brings out the ribald in me."

"Ribald, is it?" Her eyebrows climbed. "I've always liked that word, but no man ever used it to me before."

"Get used to it, it seems to fit you." He suddenly became serious, his gaze intent on hers. "Kelly, I think that I've fallen in . . ."

"No, don't say it." She shushed him with a finger across his lips. "Not yet, not just yet."

"Why not?"

"Because. I have some things to sort out first."

Seventeen

"Grandfather," Kelly said, "I'd like you to meet Chris O'Keefe."

Chris took Jeremiah's extended hand. "I'm delighted to meet you, sir."

"Likewise, I'm sure." Jeremiah glared at Kelly. "Where've you been, girl? The day's almost gone."

Kelly grinned. "You know you never get going until afternoon, Grandfather. I took Chris sailing." She directed her gaze at Chris and winked, wondering what her grandfather would say if she told him what they'd been doing the past hour. She felt a weakness invade her extremities as she thought of that past hour. She seemed to feel Chris still inside her.

"Sailing," Jeremiah grumbled. "A pastime for sissies."

"That's what Chris thought, but I'll bet he's changed his mind. A storm came up while we were out, and unless I'm badly mistaken it scared the pee-wadding out of him."

"Bring us a drink, girl. Man can't talk without a glass in his hand. What do you drink, young fellow?"

"I'm a Scotch drinker, mostly."

"Scotch!" Jeremiah snorted softly. "That's a drink for foreigners. A good American drinks his own product, sour mash and the like."

Kelly said, "Not only is Grandfather a male chauvinist, Chris, he is also a patriotic chauvinist as well. He absolutely refuses to buy or use anything not made in America."

"Labels," Jeremiah growled. "Man does or says something other people don't agree with, label him. To women today, a man's a male chauvinist if he doesn't act according to the way they think he should." He gestured. "Why don't you fetch the drinks, girl?"

Kelly laughed. "You see, Chris? Women are only good for making drinks, cooking, scrubbing floors."

"And giving a man great-grandsons," Jeremiah called after Kelly as she left the room. He was smiling slightly. "Kelly is a damned fine girl, Chris." His voice dropped to a whisper. "But how can a man turn an empire over to a woman? They ain't cut out for it."

Jeremiah lowered his chin onto his chest, his eyes closing. His eyelids were blue-veined and thin as tissue paper. Chris could see the eyeballs moving behind them.

Just as he thought the old man had dozed off, Jeremiah opened his eyes and looked at Chris, his stare piercing. "Where you from, boy?"

"I was born and raised in California."

"How about your folks?"

"Both parents were killed when I was fourteen."

"Brothers, sisters?"

"None. I was an only child."

"Orphan, are you?" Jeremiah grunted. "Nothing wrong with that, I was one myself. A man either survives and grows strong for it, or he falls by the wayside." He peered, squinting. "My hunch is, you're one of the survivors, eh?"

Chris gave a self-deprecatory shrug. "Well, I've survived so far at least."

"I came from California, too, young fellow, back in ninety-eight. But I was born in Ohio, came west when I was only fifteen. I worked at this job and that before I left for up here."

"I've heard that you made your first strike around Dawson City, after coming over the Chilkoot. You must have been pretty young to have made that trek all alone."

"Just past twenty," Jeremiah said with a proud grin. "But I was a tough youngster. Had to be to make it over the pass that winter of ninety-eight. And I'll tell you a little secret . . ." The old man leaned forward with a conspiratorial air. "I didn't really make my first strike in the Klondike. I struck out there. It was in Chena, where I hit it . . ."

Past him, Chris saw Kelly enter the room and pause, listening.

"The Klondike was pretty much staked out when I got there. I did stake a claim, but the color was piss-poor. So I worked around Dawson for a spell, then moved on to Fairbanks, and it was there that I hit pay dirt..."

Kelly came on into the room, carrying three glasses on a tray. "Why, Grandfather, I didn't know that! All these years I've thought, along with everyone else, that you made your first million in the Klondike."

"It was none of your business, girl," Jeremiah said in a grumbling voice. "People wanted to believe I hit it in the Klondike, I let them believe it. A smart man never denies legends about himself."

"But you kept the members of your own family in ignorance all these years."

"Will, he knew about it. Nobody else seemed too interested in the truth, family or otherwise."

"Here's your drink, Chris. Scotch, like you wanted. And here's your Jack Daniels, Grandfather." She gave them each their drinks, then held her own glass up. "And this, Grandfather, is a vodka tonic, *Russian* vodka."

Jeremiah grunted. "Drink what you want, girl. Vodka's a female drink, anyway." He took a greedy pull at the bourbon, then looked directly at Chris, gray eyes intent. "And speaking of Will, young fellow, what is it you have to tell me?"

Chris hesitated, looking at Kelly. "I don't know how much your grandaughter has told you..."

"She told me nothing, said it all had to come from you."

Chris nodded, took a thoughtful sip of his drink, then lit a cigarette and began to talk. He started at the beginning, from the moment he talked with Will Cole at the pipeline, and told it all, in chronological order, right up to the moment he took the Cole jet in Fairbanks yesterday. Jeremiah listened without interruptions; Kelly went away once to replenish their drinks.

After Chris was done, Jeremiah said slowly, "I care damn all about the corruption and thievery along the pipeline. Far as I'm concerned, this damned oil will be the ruination of Alaska, but Cole 98 *is* an oil company, and Will convinced me we should be in on the pipeline. Now you tell me that the boy is involved in the stink. Lord God!"

"That is only a surmise on my part, sir," Chris cautioned. "I have no direct proof of his involvement."

Jeremiah seemed not to hear him. His face had suddenly taken on the gray, skull-like look of death. His voice was barely audible. "I'll have to think on it. I'm tired now, we'll talk again tomorrow."

Kelly frowned. "But, Grandfather, Chris has a job to go back to..."

Chris cut her off with a gesture. "I've stopped worrying about that."

Jeremiah raised his head to stare at him with hooded eyes. "Of all the things you might worry about, boy, a job ain't one of them. I'll see to it that you don't suffer, my word on it."

As he got to his feet and followed Kelly from the room, Chris reflected wryly that the Coles were hell on giving their word.

After she had closed the door, Kelly said, "What made you stop worrying about your job?"

"I've discovered something more important."

She gave him a roguish look. "Such as?"

"If you're fishing for a compliment, lady, forget it." He looped an arm around her shoulders. "Right now, lunch is important, I'm famished. It's been awhile since those sandwiches on the boat."

"It strikes me that you have a pretty strong appetite."

"We construction stiffs need a lot of food," he told her with a grin. "Besides, at camp they feed us well. Why, a man can have three steaks at a sitting if he wants that many. Crustless tuna sandwiches won't do the job."

"I don't know whether we can afford to keep you around for long..." Kelly broke off as a tall, thin man in hospital whites came down the hall. "Hank, Grandfather is napping now. Don't disturb him for a while. If he wakes up and asks for us, we'll be around the house. Or maybe," she flashed a sly grin at Chris, "maybe out at the tennis courts."

The man called Hank nodded stiffly. "Very well, Miss Cole. But the doctors don't approve of your grandfather sleeping in the daytime. That's why he can't sleep at night."

"I'll give you the answer Grandfather would give you to that, Hank," she said coldly. "Fuck the doctors!"

Hank stiffened, his long face flushing red, and he turned on his heel and strode back down the hallway.

"Grandfather has wanted to fire him for months, and I'm beginning to agree with him. But we have to have somebody around to tend him and they're all alike, these nurses."

"Why not a lady nurse, instead of a man?"

"We tried that for a while, and you know what happened?" She laughed, a burst of bawdy mirth. "Grandfather patted rumps and pinched boobs until they were black and blue, and they all quit. At least *that* he doesn't do with the boys."

"Now there's a man after my own heart. He's what...ninety-seven? And he still has an eye for the ladies?"

"He's ninety-nine, Chris."

"He's my kind of man. I hope I can still have that much interest in women when I'm that age."

"And so do I, so do I." She hugged his arm to her side. "Now let's see what we can scare up for you to eat."

"About what you told that nurse, the tennis. Kelly, I'm not a tennis player."

"But you can learn. I'll teach you." She dimpled up at him. "Besides, didn't I tell you I wasn't competitive? Playing a novice, I won't have to compete."

Jeremiah Cole did not send for them the rest of the day and evening, and Chris said no more about having to return to his job. He played several sets of tennis with Kelly that afternoon. She had a volley like a rifle shot, and hit the corners with the accuracy of a sharpshooter. She ran him right into the ground, and beat the hell out of him.

"Enough! Enough already!" He held the racket up before his face and approached the net. "Since I'm your guest, I'd think you'd have some mercy. I told myself this morning that I'd never play tennis with you. I should've listened to myself."

She was flushed and she was laughing with the same unabashed pleasure he'd seen on her face when they sailed that morning.

"Not competitive," he grumbled. "Look at you. You're in seventh heaven. I think you got off on beating me."

Kelly took his arm. She smelled of honest sweat and woman, and it was an effective aphrodisiac. She said, "Now I suppose you're hungry?"

"Well, it *is* about dinner time and I've just had one hell of a workout."

"It figures. I told Annie to prepare the biggest steak she has on hand, along with baked potato, Italian green beans, an enormous salad, and a half-gallon of ice cream. Since I didn't know your favorite flavor, she's making vanilla, so you can add whatever flavor you want."

"Sounds great. Hey!" He did a double take. "That sounds suspiciously like the dinner menu at camp."

"How do you think I planned it?" She hugged his arm against her side, and he could feel the shape of her breast. "I called the head chef at your camp."

He shook his head. "You're something, you know that? You do know how to treat a guest."

"Special guests, yes. And you know what we're doing after dinner?"

"I'm afraid to ask."

"I'm going to show you what I really get off on."

Shortly after lunch the next day, Jeremiah sent word by his male nurse that he wanted to see Chris. Kelly accompanied him. Inside the old man's room, she said, "Is it all right if I listen in, Grandfather? Or is it strictly man-to-man talk, nothing for a lady's delicate ears?"

Jeremiah was quite alert today, with more color in his face, and his eyes glinted as he scowled at her. "It doesn't matter to me, girl. It'll be business talk, sort of, so stay if you want. You brought him here, after all."

"That's right," Kelly said with some smugness. She took Chris's hand. "And he's my fellow, to use your words, Grandfather."

Chris grunted in astonishment and aimed a glance at her. She looked back at him innocently.

Jeremiah said, "Now that's good to hear. All I can say is, it's high time."

More than a little annoyed, Chris started to speak, then shut up as Jeremiah leaned forward, his gaze intent on Chris's face. "I want you to go to work for me, young fellow. I'll pay you as much or more than you're earning on the pipeline."

Chris made another small sound of surprise. "Well, I appreciate the offer, sir, but doing what? I've had experience at this and that, but . . ."

"Some of what you'll be doing you're already doing."

"Investigating, you mean?" He snorted. "Hell, any dummy can do a better job at that than I'm doing!"

"I don't agree. You don't strike me as a man who underestimates himself, so don't do it now. Besides, there'll be far more to it than that. Sure, you'll continue in that direction. I still don't care about the pipeline, as I said, but at the same time I don't want any mud to stick to Cole Enterprises, or the Cole name. And for that reason, I want you to check on Will at the same time. You'll be reporting directly to me, not Will. When he finds out what you're doing, he'll no doubt blow, given his temper. Just tell him to check with me, when that happens."

"Oh, he'll blow all right," Chris said grimly. "I know him well enough by now to know that much."

"I'll handle him, just tell him you're working for me directly, not the company. Anybody else asks, tell them the same thing. Tell them you're a . . . a troubleshooter, with my full authority. Now, about those license numbers you gave me yesterday." Jeremiah took a slip of paper from his pocket and gave it to Chris. "I made some calls to Juneau, and there are the names and addresses of the vehicles' registered owners. Talk to them, come down on them hard. Find out who they're working for, use any means you have to. Threaten them, frighten them, bribe them. I'll open an account you can use for that. Learn what you can about this Milo Fanti, and if Will is cooperating with him in any way. But do not, under any circumstances, go to the police or anyone else. Bring all the information to me. Then we'll decide how to handle it."

"That's a tall assignment," Chris said, reading the names on the sheet of paper.

"It is, but I think you're the man to handle it. I've been accused of making snap judgments on people, but I've been wrong damned few times in my life."

Kelly said impishly, "I inherit that, at least, from Grandfather."

"I suppose I should be flattered, but I'm not sure just *how* I feel. This is all happening so damned fast."

Jeremiah's lips formed a faint smile. "Get used to it, young fellow. If things work out as I hope, your head'll be spinning like a top."

Chris stared at him, wondering what he meant, but he was afraid to ask.

Jeremiah pounded his fist on the arm of the wheelchair, a gesture faintly reminiscent of Will's. "One thing I want you to understand, Chris... if whatever you dig up can help toward stopping the finagling going on at the pipeline, fine and dandy, but that's not the main thing. The main thing is to learn what Will is up to. Lord God, my grandson, my own blood!" His voice trailed off and chin slumped forward. There was a brief silence before he looked up, his eyes unfocused, and he said in a dreaming voice, "Boy, did I ever tell you about the time, back in nineteen-ought-six when I . . ."

"Grandfather," Kelly interrupted gently. "Not now. And Will isn't here."

Jeremiah scowled irritably. "Damnit, girl, I know Will ain't here!" Then he sighed. "Was I about to wander off again?"

"I'm afraid so, Grandfather." Kelly stood up. "We'd better go now, Chris, it's time for him to nap."

They were halfway to the door when Jeremiah said, "Girl, when are you two getting hitched?"

Kelly laughed softly. "Now that *is* going a little too fast for Chris. Heavens, I haven't even asked him yet!"

Jeremiah laughed abruptly, the first time Chris had heard him laugh, and it was the full-bellied roar of a much younger man.

Outside, in the hall, the door closed behind them, Chris turned to Kelly. "I thought you told me you had things to sort out first?"

"That's true, but I got them all sorted out."

"You did it damned fast."

"I was awake most of last night, thinking about you, Chris, about us. I realized that I was in love with you," she said simply. "I think I fell in love with you that day I drove you home from Dwight's."

They had started walking down the hall. "Just like that, huh? And then you just decided you wanted to marry me? You once told me that you got most things you wanted. You think that's the case this time?"

"No, it isn't. Inside I'm quaking, terrified of what you may say." She took his arm and turned him to face her. "I don't know what prompted me to speak out like that in there. You *do* love me, Chris? I know you started to tell me so yesterday."

"That much is true, yes," he admitted. "But maybe I have some things to sort out as well. I can see a truckload of problems ahead."

"The money, you mean?"

"That's a part of it, yes. You're an heiress to Lord knows

how much money, and I don't have the proverbial pot."

"And you're afraid of what people will say?"

He thought for a moment, then shook his head. "No, that doesn't bother me all that much. What people think of me has never concerned me. But it's what I may think of myself."

"There's one thing that's always baffled me. A woman can marry a man with gobs of money, and few people think less of her for it. But turn it around and the man is considered a gigolo."

Chris shrugged. "That's the way the world is, Kelly. But like I said, that doesn't bother me, because if we were to get married, I wouldn't be living on your money, I'd pay my own way. And there's the problem, don't you see? I'm a construction stiff. When the pipeline's finished, I may want to move on to another project in some far corner of the world. Then what would you do, go with me?"

"If it came down to that, yes." She frowned. "But you told me you liked Alaska."

"I do, but liking it doesn't cut it, if there are no jobs."

"Chris . . ." She touched his hand. "There will always be a job for you with Cole. Now don't say it!" She covered his mouth with her fingers. "It wouldn't be a sinecure, you'll earn your keep. That's one thing Grandfather insists on, that all Cole employees do the job they're paid to do, relatives or not. That's one reason he's upset with Will."

He studied her intently. "There's something else . . . I know this is the age of the liberated woman, but I'm old-fashioned about one thing. I believe in women 'raising the consciousness.' I get that right? But I still think a man should do the proposing."

"I didn't actually propose, Chris, and as I said, the words just popped out." She stepped back, hands on hips and stared at him challengingly. "So go ahead, if it will ease your macho pride!"

He stared. "Go ahead what?"

"Ask me to marry you."

"Jesus!" He began to laugh, shaking his head. "You're some kind of weirdo, you know?"

He reached out, pulled her into his arms, and kissed her.

After a moment she drew back to look up at him with shining eyes. "Does that mean what I think it means?"

He said gravely, "Will you marry me, Kelly Cole?"

Eighteen

One of the two names Jeremiah Cole had dug up, Chris discovered, belonged to a former pipeliner, a man by the name of Bert Dawes. A dump-truck driver, he had been fired from the pipeline for being drunk and disorderly on the job, rehired and fired yet a second time when he had gotten so drunk that he ran the truck he was driving into a bulldozer, totaling the truck.

Chris found him living in a trailer park on the outskirts of Fairbanks. One of the first things Chris had done after returning to Fairbanks, with the thousand dollars Jeremiah had given him as an advance against salary, was to buy a business suit; white shirt, tie, the whole bit. It would hardly do, he reflected wryly, for a man in his new position to run about dressed in construction duds. The second thing he had done was to rent a car, which he had driven up to the camp to pick up his personal belongings. True to Brant's warning, his paycheck was waiting for him.

On his way back into Fairbanks, Chris pulled into the trailer park, found out which trailer belonged to Dawes, and drove down the line to it. Washing hung on the lines strung between trailers, and dogs and children of all ages raced about the trailer park, which had the dismal look of a dumping ground, not a single tree or flower in sight.

Sitting before the trailer which housed Bert Dawes was a dilapidated camper. Stopping his car, Chris compared the license number with the ones he had copied down at Livengood Camp that night. This was one of the campers, no doubt of it.

He approached the trailer and knocked on the door. When there was no response, he knocked again, louder. He was about to conclude no one was in, when he heard a grumbling voice within, then heavy footsteps. The door swung open and a burly man, with a red face, glaring brown eyes, and a stubble of graying beard, glowered out at him.

"What do you want, bud? I warn you, if you're peddling something, I'll kick your butt out to the highway."

"I'm not a salesman. Are you Bert Dawes?"

"What of it?"

Chris flinched at the man's beery breath. He said, "I want some information. I'll make it worth your while."

"Information about what?" Dawes growled.

"May I come inside? I'd rather not talk out here where we can be overheard."

Dawes stared at him blearily, swaying slightly. Then he shrugged meaty shoulders. "What the hey, come on in."

The inside of the trailer was a mess—dirty dishes on the sink, the remains of food giving off a stench, and empty beer cans on the floor. Down the short corridor to the left, Chris saw an unmade bed with gray sheets.

Dawes shambled to the table at the other end and sat down, picking up a beer can and sucking on it. "Can't offer you a brew, bud. This is the last one I've got."

Chris slid into the dining nook across from him. "Is that your camper outside?"

Dawes squinted at him belligerently. "What are you, a repo guy? Just because a man misses two payments is no reason for the goddamn bank to repossess!"

"No, no, nothing like that. I told you that all I was after was information. *Is* that your camper?"

The man's suspicions lingered for a moment, then he shrugged. "What the hey, yeah, it's mine."

"And last week you drove out to Livengood Camp, loaded with hookers, booze, and for all I know, hard drugs. Is that right?"

Dawes reared back. "What the hell is this? You a cop? Get the hell out of my trailer!"

Dawes started to get up, but his beer belly snagged for a moment on the table. Chris reached across, clamped his hand around the man's wrist, and forced him back down into his seat. "No, I'm not a cop, and I mean you no trouble, personally. In fact, I'm willing to pay you for the information."

Chris knew that he had struck the right chord as Dawes's eyes glinted with sudden greed, and Chris realized just how shrewd Jeremiah was. Jeremiah had told him, "A bank account will be opened in your name, boy. Ten thousand to start. Call it a slush fund." The old man's eyes had danced with cynical knowledge. "Never underestimate the power of a buck when you need to find out something. It can open a man's mouth like nothing else I know. Do you know what police work is, the nitty-gritty? It's not chasing down clues, putting puzzle pieces together. It's the barter system, old as time. You swap something for a piece of information here, a piece there. You trade a lower fellow's freedom for him tattling on somebody above him. Or else you pay for the information. That'll do it every time."

He'd talked to Jeremiah Cole only three times, but Chris was impressed by the bits of wisdom stored in that ancient brain.

Dawes was speaking. "What information you after?"

"I want confirmation from you that Milo Fanti hired you to make that trip," Chris said bluntly.

Dawes recoiled, his watery eyes blinking in fear. "Bud, you have to be crazy! Or you think I am. If I told you something like that, Fanti would grind me up in a cement mixer!"

Chris carefully hid his glee at this unthinking admission. "The way I see it, Dawes, you have a choice. I'm going to bring Fanti down, with or without your help. And when that happens, if you don't help me now, you're in shit up to your eyeballs, *bud*. You'll be brought down with him, and that means a nice jail term for you."

"People have been after Fanti's butt since he moved in here," Dawes said in a blustering voice, "and he's still in business."

"This time there is a difference, I'm working for Cole Enterprises. With the company behind me ..."

Dawes gave a weak sneer. "Will Cole, you mean? The way I hear it, he's in on it."

Chris said carefully, "Can you prove that?"

"Hell, no, I can't prove it. Why should I?"

"For your information, my authority comes from Jeremiah Cole, not his grandson."

"The old man?" Dawes whistled, and greed flickered again in his eyes. "I thought he was dead."

"Far from it, Dawes. And you know what money and power he has behind him." Chris leaned forward. "Look at it this way. I know all about you. You'll never get another job

with the pipeline, but if you'll sign an affidavit swearing that
Fanti hired you, I'll pay you one thousand dollars."

Dawes wet his lips. "The thousand dollars won't save my
ass from Fanti, if he finds out I've done something like that."

"Fanti may have means of retaliation up here in Alaska, but
he has no mob connections down below, in the Lower 48.
Take the money and run, Dawes. You can get set up down
there. You're finished up here, anyway."

Dawes frowned in thought, then his eyes turned crafty. "I
can sell the camper, get a few bucks after the loan's paid off.
If you'll spring for plane fare to LA, plus the grand, it's a
deal." He laughed uneasily. "Coach fare is okay, I won't hit
you up for first class."

Chris despised the man for his penny-ante greed, but he
kept his feelings from showing. "It's a deal." He stood up.
"Now let's write out the statement, and then find a notary to
make it official."

The owner of the second camper was more amenable.
Through Jeremiah's source in Juneau, a check had been run
on both men. Dawes had no criminal record, but the second
man, Jake Furness, had a record going back to his teens: car
theft, breaking and entering, and suspicion of drug dealing.
He had served short prison sentences on the first two charges,
released for lack of evidence on the third, but now he was in
danger of going down as a three-time loser, which would
mean a long term in prison.

A little man, with a ferret face and frightened eyes, he
could hardly wait to cooperate with Chris, then snatch the
thousand and run. He didn't ask for plane fare. Chris knew
that the man's affidavit, in view of his criminal record, would
carry little weight in court, but that was not the reason he
wanted it.

Jeremiah had been explicit about that: "No police. No
matter what you find, I don't want the police in on it, boy.
Not yet, anyway."

Elated by his success thus far, Chris drove to Dwight's
place across the river. Now that his mind was free for a few
moments from other concerns, his thoughts turned to Kelly.
She had made him promise to call her every day and so far he

had, the sound of her voice and the words of love they spoke like a welcome oasis at the end of a hard journey.

She was always on the edge of his mind now. She was in his heart and soul, his bone and sinew, all the time, and he was astounded at the intensity of his love for her. Perhaps he should have been dismayed that she so inhabited his waking moments, but he wasn't. She was a strong-minded woman, even willful, and he wasn't a fool. She had gone after him with a singleness of purpose that would have been frightening in anyone else. But somehow in Kelly it was a virtue, and he was flattered, not in the least intimidated.

His initial reservations that the differences in their life-styles would be too great a chasm to bridge had receded. Those reservations had still been in his mind when he proposed to her, but the way in which he missed her since he had left Cole Island told him that he would never be completely happy without her to share his life. Whatever their differences, they could be overcome; they were two intelligent, strong people and they would find a way.

As he pulled the rental car up before Dwight's old gray house, Chris shoved all thoughts of Kelly into a small corner of his mind where he had made room just for her. And he fancied that he heard her hoot of laughter, and taunting voice: "You can't get rid of me that easily, buster! You'd better watch it, I'll pop out when you're least expecting me!"

He was laughing heartily as he got out of the car. He choked it off, glancing around to see if he'd been observed. Anyone seeing him would think he was out of his skull.

As he mounted the steps, two bearded young men came out the front door. They cast sidelong glances at him as they passed. Chris saw Dwight standing in the open door.

Dwight said, "Chris! I'm delighted to see you."

Dwight held out his hand and Chris took it, saying, "I was just struck by something, Dwight. All the times I've been here, I've never seen anyone, except Gordie and his friend that one time. Yet you told me this was headquarters for SAS."

Dwight shrugged. "Oh, they come and they go." His eyes searched Chris's face. "What can I do for you?"

"How is Gordie?"

"He's coming along okay. Still not allowed up, it takes time to heal, the doctor says."

"Would you take me to him? I'd like to talk to him."

Dwight hesitated. "Sure, why not? Come on in."

"He's *here?*" Chris said in astonishment.

"He couldn't hide out forever. Besides, it was costing money we couldn't afford, paying for room and board and nursing care. Here, June can tend him, she's good at it, and there're always people around in case he needs something. Fanti wouldn't dare send his goons in here."

"I wouldn't bet on that," Chris muttered.

Dwight didn't hear, having already turned away, motioning for Chris to follow him. At the end of the hall were the stairs. Dwight led the way up to the second floor and to a room at the end of the hall.

As Dwight started to open the door, Chris stayed him. "If you don't mind, I'd like to speak to him alone for a few minutes."

Dwight looked at him narrowly. He said slowly, "It's okay with me, but I'll have to check it out with Gordie."

Without knocking he opened the door. "Gordie, there's someone here to see you."

Gordie was propped up in bed, reading a paperback book. As he saw Chris, his narrow face closed up. "The big dude from the pipeline. I have no business with him."

Chris approached the bed. "But I have some with you. I think you should at least listen to what I have to say."

"I don't see why. You're the cause of my being racked up like this."

"That's not true. Not directly, at any rate."

Gordie raised and lowered his thin arms. "What the hell! You can't do me any harm with Dwight here."

"Chris would like to talk to you alone, Gordie," Dwight said.

"No way!" Gordie reared up, then winced and fell back onto the pillows, his face graying. "You're not leaving this guy in here alone with me!"

"Gordie, all I want is to talk. How can that hurt you?" Chris said reasonably. "I just think it's better for everybody concerned that Dwight not be involved."

Gordie was silent for a moment, his gaze going from Chris to Dwight and back again. He had been pale when Chris had seen him before, but his pallor had deepened, and he seemed even skinnier, if that was possible.

"Okay, okay," Gordie said suddenly. "Anything to get you out of my hair."

Dwight started to turn away, then hesitated. "Don't forget, Chris, he was hurt pretty bad."

"I won't hurt him, I have no reason to."

As the door closed behind Dwight, Chris pulled a straight chair up to the bed and sat down, his hands braced on his knees. "Gordie, you're finished in Alaska, surely you know that. If Fanti sent those hoodlums after you once, he will again. He won't let up until you're wasted. And you can't hide away forever."

Gordie said sullenly, "What's that to you?"

"I'm prepared to offer you a thousand dollars for a signed statement. That's more than enough for plane fare to the States, and some left over to keep you going until you find something else."

Gordie gave him a suspicious look. "Statement? Statement about what?"

"An affidavit attesting to the jobs you did for Milo Fanti."

"Man, you belong in a rubber room!" Gordie gaped at him in disbelief. "There's no way I'll do that! Fanti will kill me for sure."

"You're not listening to me. He's going to kill you, anyway. You know he's not going to give up, he has to make an example of you. My way, you get paid, and once you're out of Alaska, he can't touch you. In fact, if you leave secretly, he'll probably conclude you're dead anyway."

"To do that makes me a stool pigeon."

Chris grinned mirthlessly. "Come on, Gordie, you've been seeing too many late movies on the tube. You know you don't give a good goddamn about that."

"But if the pigs get their hands on a statement like that, it's the same as a confession. Into the slammer I go."

"You have my word. The police will never see it."

"Tell me something, man. What's in this for you, a pipeliner?"

"I'm no longer a pipeliner. I'm working for Cole Enterprises. For Jeremiah Cole, not Will Cole."

"The old man?" Gordie squinted. "Man, if you're working for him, a thousand ain't much bread to a man like that."

"Don't get greedy, Gordie," Chris said harshly. "A thousand is all you get. I already have sworn statements from two other guys, yours is only insurance. It's a grand or nothing, and you'll always be looking over your shoulder for Fanti's hoods. You'll be afraid to step out of the house."

Fear crawled across Gordie's face. He was silent for a little, studying Chris closely. "What I can't figure is, if not the cops . . ." He raised his head off the pillows. "You're going to flash it before old Milo, ain't you?"

He's more intelligent than I gave him credit for, Chris thought. He said, "Not unless it becomes absolutely necessary. I have the other two, and they've already hightailed it out of the state, so they're now out of danger. Their affidavits should be enough for my purpose. Now, it's nitty-gritty time, Gordie. Either take the deal or not. Otherwise, I'm walking out. Right now."

He got to his feet and started toward the door. His hand had touched the knob when he heard Gordie's breathy sigh.

"Okay, okay, I'll do it. I don't have a hell of a lot of choice, do I?"

Chris turned and walked back to the bed, taking the notebook and pen from his coat pocket. "Now you're being smart. I'll go for a notary after you've dictated your statement and we'll make it official."

After he left Gordie's room, Chris met Dwight at the bottom of the stairs. "Are you going to tell me what this is all about, Chris?"

Chris weighed his answer carefully. "I think it's better that I don't, Dwight."

Dwight combed his fingers thoughtfully through his beard. "I could be making a big mistake, but somehow I trust you. But if this backfires on SAS, or Gordie, I'll pound you into the ground like a fence post."

"If anything happens to Gordie, it won't be my doing, not if he follows my instructions." He started past the other man, then stopped, facing him fully. "Kelly and I . . . your sister and I are getting married, Dwight."

Dwight's face went slack with consternation. "You're *what*?"

"We're getting married."

"Jesus! I didn't even realize you knew Kelly. Oh, that's right, you met her here, didn't you? That was bloody fast, wasn't it?"

With a straight face Chris said, "Sometimes it doesn't take long, I guess. I do love her."

Dwight smiled suddenly. "Well, congratulations, Chris!" He seized Chris's hand and pumped it. Then his smile died and he shook his head gloomily. "I probably should offer my condolences, not congratulations, your marrying into the Cole family. Now don't take me wrong. Kelly is the best of the lot, if that means anything." He stared at Chris appraisingly. "I think I may adjust to having you for a brother-in-law, but, Jesus, are you in for a lot of heavy flack! Probably from Josh, certainly from Will. About Jeremiah, I don't know..."

"Your grandfather knows. In fact, that's why I'm here today. I'm working directly for Jeremiah now."

Dwight became still. "Doing what?"

Chris shook his head. "I'd rather not say, at the moment. I'll tell you about it eventually. But I would appreciate it if you didn't let on to Will."

Dwight snorted softly. "Not bloody likely, but I sure would like to see his face when he finds out you're marrying Kelly."

Chris was pleased when he drove away from Dwight's. He now had, with the three notarized statements, enough evidence to cause Milo Fanti considerable worry, probably enough to cause him to suspend his operations along the pipeline, when it was all laid out for him. That was a moment Chris was looking forward to with relish.

But he had yet to achieve his primary objective, to uncover any connection between Will Cole and Fanti. He had carefully questioned the habitúes of Two Street, and no one would admit to seeing Will in or around Fanti's office. He had learned that Will had been seen gambling, accompanied by a woman, in Fanti's place, but since Will was a known gambler and womanizer, that was of no help.

Chris thought of calling Jeremiah for guidance, but he finally decided against it. The old man had shown faith in him, and Chris had a hunch that Jeremiah might think he was admitting failure if his advice was sought. And from what Kelly had told him, Chris knew that Jeremiah Cole scorned failure.

After mulling it over for the rest of that day and night,

Chris decided he had only one option: to confront Fanti with what he had and play it by ear.

He knocked on the door at the top of the outside stairs shortly past noon the next day.

He was unprepared for Fanti himself opening the door. The dapper little man gaped at him in astonishment. "You! What the hell are you doing . . . ?"

Fanti's hand darted under his coat, and Chris moved, crossing the few feet between them in a single step. He seized Fanti's left arm and twisted, spinning him around, and bending the arm up between his shoulder blades. Fanti yowled in pain.

Chris had already sent a glance down the dim hall and saw no one else. He said, "Drop the gun, Fanti, or I'll break your arm!"

"You punk, what do you think you're doing?"

Chris twisted the arm higher. "Drop it!"

"All right, all right!"

In a moment Chris heard the thump as the gun hit the floor. He slammed Fanti face up against the wall, spotted the gleam of metal on the floor, and gave the gun a swift kick, sending it spinning down the hallway.

"We need to talk, Fanti. And don't bother to tell me I won't get away with it. I *am* getting away with it. Is the open door your office?"

Fanti bobbed his head in agreement. Still holding the man's arm bent up behind his back, Chris propelled him down the hall to the open door, shoved him inside, followed him in, and slammed the door, pushing home the bolt.

He grinned companionably at Fanti, who was standing by his desk, rubbing his arm and glaring at him. Chris said, "I'm surprised you don't have a couple of your hoodlums body-guarding you."

"I don't need a bodyguard," Fanti said in a snarling voice. "There's nobody in this town stupid enough to think they can get away with something like this. I'll have you taken care of before you can get three blocks from here."

"Yeah, I understand you're good at that," Chris said, still smiling. "But then I am stupid, like you said once, remember?"

"You're going to regret this, pipeliner," Fanti said, voice now soft and deadly. "So say what you've come to say, and get your ass out of here."

As Fanti started around behind his desk, Chris moved in quick strides, crowding him against the wall. The space between the desk and the wall was narrow. Chris pinned Fanti to the wall with one hand, and began pulling out drawers with the other, and riffling through the contents.

Fanti turned livid and tried to squirm free. "What the hell are you doing? You have no right to go through my desk!"

Chris pushed him hard against the wall. "I'm only interested in one thing in your precious desk. Ah, there it is!"

He had found a small, flat automatic. Plucking it from the desk drawer, he dropped it into his jacket pocket and stepped away, making a sweeping gesture. "Now that your fangs are pulled, you can sit."

Fanti's swarthy face was cold with fury. He was a very humiliated man, and Chris had to wonder if he was pushing too hard. But what the hell, he'd come here to rattle the man, and this was as good a way as any.

His movements as jerky and controlled as a mime's, Fanti sat down behind his desk.

Still standing, Chris took copies of the three affidavits from his pocket. Keeping Gordie's in his hand, he spread the other two out on the desk for Fanti's inspection. "I have three statements from men who have been working for you, running dope, liquor, and whores to the pipeline camps. This one," waving Gordie's statement, "I'm not going to show to you at this time. The other two men are already out of the state, out of your reach, but this guy is still around and scared shitless you'll wipe him out."

His face expressionless, Fanti read the statements. "Never heard of either of these ginks," he said flatly. "All lies, of course."

"It won't wash, Fanti. That's enough to put you in deep shit with the police, if I go to them."

"Why don't you?"

"That's not my purpose."

"You're going to Will Cole, then?" Fanti sneered. "You'll be wasting your time, he won't do anything."

Chris concealed a leap of elation. "How do you know?"

"I know, take my word for it."

"I wouldn't take your word for the time of the day," Chris said contemptuously.

"You'll only be making trouble for yourself."

Chris shrugged. "I'll take that chance."

Fanti's gaze was thoughtful. "If you collected that garbage to show to Will Cole, why come to me first?"

"Because you're the one I want to stop. You're the bad guy, and any connection Will Cole has with you is immaterial."

"Immaterial, is it?" Fanti sneered again, then looked down at his hands on the desk in thought. "I'll show you just how immaterial it is, you dumb shit."

He got up and crossed to the far wall, where a small refrigerator rested on a shelf. He moved the refrigerator aside, revealing a wall safe. Chris took the chair across from the desk and sat tensely, scarcely daring to breathe, as Fanti worked the dial. It appeared to Chris that his bluff was going to work. Unconsciously he crossed his fingers and hid them between his legs.

Fanti took several papers from the safe and a small cassette. At his desk, he spread everything out, then took a cassette player from a desk drawer. "Now I'm going to show you why it would embarrass both you and the guy you're working for if you go to him with those statements."

Inserting the cassette, he played it, and Chris listened without comment to the scratchy tape of the voices of Will Cole and a woman as they made love.

Switching it off, Fanti looked across the desk. "Well?"

"Well what?" Chris shrugged elaborately. "So Will Cole is a woman chaser. What else is new? That might be of some interest to me if I peddled pornographic tapes."

"Have a peek at these." Fanti held out three pieces of paper.

Chris examined them one by one. Two were photostatic copies of checks made out to Milo Fanti and signed by Will Cole; one was dated several weeks ago, the second more recent, and together they totaled just under thirty thousand dollars. On the back of each, just below Fanti's endorsement, was the notation: "For gambling chips in the sum of the face value of check." The notations were in Fanti's cramped handwriting.

Chris glanced up. "These notations, you made them before the checks went through the bank?"

"Right. And if you're thinking it's evidence of my running illegal games, who's going to turn me in? Will Cole?" Fanti gave a bark of laughter. "Wishful thinking, pipeliner."

Chris studied the third document. Again it was a photostat-ic copy, this time of an IOU made out to Milo Fanti and signed by Will Cole, in the sum of ten thousand dollars.

Chris dropped the documents back onto the desk. "So? Again, all that proves is that Will Cole dropped a large piece of change in your establishment. It's no news flash that he is a gambling man."

Fanti smiled unpleasantly. "Do you think Will Cole would want this to get out, to the public, most of all to his own board and that old man on Cole Island? That he signed some paper for ten thou to the very man he's supposed to be out to get?"

"It might embarrass him, sure, but that still doesn't mean he won't go after you full throttle if I show him what I have."

"I have another little tidbit for you, O'Keefe." Fanti hand-ed Chris another document, with the sly look of a poker player showing his trump card.

This one was the record of a stock transaction handled through a stockbroker in Anchorage recording a sale of two percent of shares of stock in Cole Enterprises, sold by one Will Cole, owner of record, for a substantial sum. The new owner of record was Milo Fanti.

Chris concealed his elation, keeping his head down. This was what Jeremiah had been seeking. It might not be actual proof of Will's corruption, but Chris knew how the fact that his grandson had sold stock in Cole to a known rackets boss would affect the old man. Along with his feeling of triumph, Chris also experienced a fleeting sadness. Although he did not like Will Cole, he did have a sneaking admiration for him, and the sight of any man tumbling from a pedestal into the mud was never something to bring instant joy.

Fanti said impatiently, "Well?"

Chris looked up, his expression carefully guarded. "Well what, Fanti? Are you telling me, straight out, that you've been bribing Will Cole?"

Fanti said sanctimoniously, "Bribery is a crime, O'Keefe. I'm admitting to nothing like that. Draw your own conclusions."

"Nothing you've shown me here does anything to negate the proof in my pocket that you're guilty of illegal activities along the pipeline. And I've hardly started on my investiga-tion. I have no doubt but that I can find workers willing to sign statements that you're also fencing stolen pipeline equipment."

"I must be talking to myself here." Fanti made an elaborate pretense of looking around for someone in the office. "You take all the stuff you want to Will Cole, he won't do shit for you."

"There's one thing wrong with your reasoning, Fanti." Chris smiled broadly. "You're laboring under a misapprehension, I'm afraid. I'm no longer working for Will Cole."

"You're not? Who then?"

"I'm working for another Cole, Jeremiah."

"The old man?" Fanti blinked. "Hell, he's senile. Will Cole's running the company."

"Jeremiah is far from senile. And as for Will Cole running the company, you're forgetting a couple of facts. Jeremiah is still chairman of the board, and he is the majority stockholder, your two shares notwithstanding."

Fanti's dismay was evident. "But why would old man Cole concern himself?"

"Because he doesn't like what's coming down. Unlike some others, he's bound and determined to do something about it. And you're one thing he's going to do something about. That's why I came to you. I'm here to give you fair warning. I agree with Will Cole in one respect . . . what you do here in Fairbanks, so long as it's straight, is of no concern. The workers need your services. We don't wish to see Fairbanks turned into a church social town. But what you're doing along the pipeline has to stop. Don't be greedy, Fanti. You're making a buck here, be satisfied with that."

Fanti didn't reply, just started at him balefully, his thin lips drawn back in a snarl.

He didn't speak until Chris got to his feet to leave, then he said harshly, "I think you've bitten off too big a chew here, pipeliner. You may be working for old man Cole, but his grandson still has the clout, and we've gotten to know each other pretty well."

Chris knew there was no longer any chance of keeping Will Cole in the dark, and he said cheerfully, "Then why don't you check with him? But if you don't back off from the pipeline, Fanti, you're in trouble."

Fanti said viciously, "You think I'm the only gink working

the pipeline? If I let myself be scared off, the others'll just move in."

"You're not the only one, true, but you're the biggest. I believe in starting at the top. I'll be going after the others next." He took the automatic from his pocket, hefted it in his hand. "Just so you won't get any ideas, I'll leave your toy outside the door."

He turned on his heel and went out without another word.

Milo Fanti sat quite still for a few minutes after the pipeliner left, his thoughts boiling with frustration. Just when he thought he had everything all sewed up, with clear sailing ahead, *this* had to happen.

He scooped the documents from his desk, returned them to the safe, locked it, and got a beer from the refrigerator. He drank half of the beer in a gulp, then snarled, "Goddamn all the Coles to hell and gone," and hurled the beer can at the wall, beer splashing down the wall like spilled paint.

He snatched up the phone and dialed Cole's office with a shaking finger.

"I'm sorry, sir," Cole's secretary said in a formal voice. "Mr. Cole is in conference and cannot be disturbed."

"I don't care if he's in conference with God," Fanti snarled. "This is urgent. You tell him Milo Fanti has to talk to him right *now*."

After a moment Will Cole came on the line. In a guarded voice he said, "Fanti, I thought we'd agreed you'd never call me here . . ."

"There's no longer any need to keep it under our hats. The cat's out and it's going to run squalling all over Fairbanks, unless you can put a gag on it."

"What *are* you talking about?"

"I'm talking about that construction stiff, O'Keefe. He was just in here, and he's got proof of what's going on at the pipeline. This gink spells trouble with a big T, Mr. Cole."

He heard Will Cole's sharp intake of breath. "Chris O'Keefe came to see you? I thought he'd dropped all that business. If he's still nosing around, it's not my doing."

"This time he's nosing around on orders from the old man."

"Jeremiah? He's working for Jeremiah? How could that have come about? He must be lying to you, Fanti!"

"He's not lying, take my word for it." Succinctly he told Will Cole the substance of his conversation with O'Keefe, omitting the fact that he had shown O'Keefe documents incriminating Cole himself.

"Jesus Christ in a wheelbarrow!" Will exploded. "I can't believe that Jeremiah would care enough to involve himself in this! And his reason baffles me."

"I don't know his reasons, Mr. Cole, but you'd better do something."

"I'll do something. I'll take care of it."

"You'd better or we're both in deep shit."

"I said I would, didn't I?" Will roared. "Now just relax, Fanti, and let me handle it." He banged down the phone.

Fanti hung up slowly, far from being reassured. He sensed that, behind all the bluster, Will Cole was a frightened man.

Whether that assessment was right or not, Fanti decided to pull in his horns. No more campers with goodies would be sent out to the pipeline, until he saw which way the wind blew. And he'd better back away from buying stolen pipeline equipment as well. There was a quality about Chris O'Keefe that said he wasn't a man to be ignored. Fanti hoped that Will Cole would win out. He didn't look forward with great delight to the possibility of having O'Keefe on his ass forever.

Nineteen

"And that, sir, about covers it." Chris had just finished his report to Jeremiah. Sitting beside him, Kelly gripped his hand tightly. "There's nothing directly tying your grandson in with Milo Fanti, but everything points in that direction."

"This stock transaction," Jeremiah said tonelessly. "There's no doubt about that?"

"I don't see how Fanti could have faked it, if that's what you mean."

"I don't either, since all it would take is a phone call to Anchorage to verify it. Lord God!" Jeremiah sighed, his eyes closing. "The boy must have needed money bad. He knows how I'd react if I found out he had peddled his Cole stock. Looks like everything has finally caught up with him." His voice faded to a whisper.

Kelly moved involuntarily. "Grandfather, are you all right?" She started to get up.

Jeremiah's eyes snapped open. "Sit still, girl, I'm fine. Just low in spirit, mighty low. The boy has long been a disappointment to me, but this . . ." His glance went to Chris. "He knows about what you're doing, Chris. He's been calling here, but I wouldn't discuss it with him. I told him if he wanted to talk to me, do it face to face. I'm expecting him any time now."

"I'm sorry, sir." Chris spread his hands. "I figured the best way to put a damper on Fanti, at least temporarily, was to confront him with what I had. I'm sure he got in touch with your grandson the minute I left his office."

"It's all right, boy, don't fret it. Will had to know sooner or later. Lord God, it's a mess, ain't it?"

Kelly, studying the old man in the wheelchair, felt compassion for him. Physically he looked little different, but knowing

231

how strong he was on family, she realized that he was suffering deeply, even if he had long been turned off Will. She said, "Grandfather, what do you plan to do, about Will, I mean?"

"I'm thinking on it. Chris, boy..." He looked directly at Chris. "You've done a good job, done what I asked of you. I want you to keep at it. I wasn't all that concerned about this corrupter, this Fanti fellow, at first, but now that I've learned that he's managed to smear his mud on Will, I want you to keep after him. Maybe you can't stop him completely, but I want him stopped at anything that affects Cole, and that includes the pipeline."

"You still don't want the police in on it?"

"Nope," Jeremiah said without hesitation. "Two reasons. First off, I doubt they'd do much, or even want to. They care damn-all about the pipeline, and they've just about washed their hands of it. Second, if they do do anything, more'n likely Will's name would come into it, and that would mean that some of the mud would splash on Cole. That, I don't want..."

"And Will, your grandson?"

Jeremiah's lips tightened. "I'll handle Will from now on. You just concentrate on this rackets fellow..." He broke off as the sound of an approaching vehicle penetrated the room. He wheeled the chair over to the window and peered out. "Yep, there's the Jeep and Will now. Kelly, you and Chris leave. I want to speak to the boy alone."

As they started out of the room, Jeremiah spoke again. "Girl, when you two getting married?"

Kelly looked at Chris. "Why, I don't know, we haven't really talked about it. Chris?"

Chris took her hand. "Any time is okay with me."

Jeremiah nodded. "The sooner, the better. You two talk it over today and let me know after Will leaves."

Outside the old man's room, Kelly looked up at Chris with an impish smile. "You feel like you're being rushed a little, darling?"

Chris nodded, but he was grinning. "I've felt that since the first day I set foot on the island, but what the hell? In fact, I'm all for the soonest. When I'm away from you, I'm not sure this is all happening, not sure but that you may change your mind in my absence."

She took his hand as they walked down the hall. "Never, my darling. That will never happen. Now that I've found you, I'll never let you go. And if that sounds like a threat, it is."

Before they reached the end of the long hall, Will Cole came striding toward them. He began waving a finger before he reached them, his face darkening in a scowl. He roared, "You sonofabitch, how dare you go to Jeremiah behind my back?" He poked Chris in the chest with a stiff forefinger.

Chris batted the hand aside, and said coldly, "Don't try to bulldoze me, Cole. I don't have to answer to you for anything."

"When it involves my family, you have to answer to me. Damned right you do. I don't know how you managed to worm your way into the old man's good graces. That's what I'm here to find out."

Kelly said, "I'm responsible for that, Will. I asked Chris to see Grandfather."

Will stared at her in bafflement. "You? Jesus Christ in a wheelbarrow, what business is it of yours?"

"I'm a Cole, although I sometimes think you refuse to admit that fact. When something affects the family or the company, it affects me."

"The company?" He sneered. "Why the hell don't you stick to your tennis and your other playthings and stay out of my affairs?"

Kelly was unfazed. "Grandfather is waiting for you, Will. I think you'd better go on in to see him. He has some things to say to you."

"And I sure as hell have some things to say to him!" Will plunged on down the hall with angry strides.

Jeremiah sat quietly in the wheelchair, facing the door, his hands folded in his lap. He had no liking for what he had to do, yet he had no choice. Waves of despair threatened to overwhelm him, and he felt like weeping for the first time since Joshua's mother died.

For long, hard years he had struggled to build an empire and had succeeded beyond his wildest imaginings. But what good was it if there was no one left behind with the strength and will to run it after he was gone? Early on, he'd had great hopes for Will, only to see those hopes gradually eroded.

He felt the great weight of his years pressing on him. Did

he have the strength left for one more try? He had to make the effort, for a new hope had been ignited. This boy, Chris, there was a strength and intelligence in him. True, he wasn't blood, but if he married Kelly, he would be family, and perhaps that was the best he could hope for now.

As he heard the angry thud of Will's footsteps approaching the door, Jeremiah rallied his failing resources. He drew himself up, and his eyes burned with the old indomitable fierceness as the door banged open and he confronted his grandson.

Will wasted no time. Even as he charged across the room, he said in a furious voice, "I want to know just what the hell you think you're up to, Jeremiah? Hiring this goddamned construction worker to nose around in my business!"

"*Your* business, boy?" Jeremiah said softly. "I hired him to look into all this corruption, especially this rackets fellow, Fanti. Is that your business, Will?"

"You know me better than that, Jeremiah."

"I thought I did," Jeremiah said sadly. "But I just don't know any more."

"Jesus Christ, Granpap! I was the one talked to O'Keefe first, got him started on it."

"Then why didn't you act on what he came to you with?"

"Because he came to me with doodley squat. He found out nothing that I could use."

"Funny, I thought differently when he came to me. And now that he's working for me, he has signed statements attesting to just how rotten this Fanti is."

"Yeah, I'd like to see those affidavits. If they're authentic, I'll act on them."

Jeremiah stared at him for a moment. "How did you know about those affidavits, boy?"

Will blinked, face reddening. "Why, I . . . I heard it, somewhere."

"You heard it from Fanti himself. He called you and told you, didn't he? Didn't he, Will?"

"All right, goddamnit, yes! He got into a panic and asked me to help him."

"And what did you tell him?"

"I told him nothing. I don't owe him anything."

Jeremiah, staring directly into his grandson's eyes, caught

the evasiveness there, and knew that he was lying. He said, "But you did owe him an IOU for ten thousand."

"So I lost some dough in his place. I gamble some, you've always known that, Jeremiah."

"And to pay off the IOU, you sold some of your Cole stock."

"Not to Fanti directly," Will said quickly. "I sold it to a broker in Anchorage, and the bastard turned right around and sold it to Fanti."

"You know what I told you when I gave you that stock, that if it ever got into the hands of someone outside of the family I would be upset."

"I know, Jeremiah, but I was caught by the short hairs. I needed the money and I knew I couldn't come to you for money to pay off a gambling debt."

Jeremiah nodded. "You're right there."

Will took the offensive. "If you'd pay me a decent salary, a salary even close to what other executives in my position get, I wouldn't always be short."

"Yes, you would, Will. No matter how much money you earned, you'd always live to the hilt."

"I recall back during the days when you were younger, Granpap, you spent money right and left."

"I ain't going to deny that. But no matter what I did, I was always careful never to dirty Cole Enterprises, or the family name, like you've been doing."

"I've done nothing to dirty Cole. Whoever told you that is lying! There's no proof of anything like that."

"Not legal proof, maybe, but I know it in my own mind. Even if I didn't know it, your unloading company stock is something I won't put up with." He sighed. "No, I've made up my mind, boy. You're demoted, as of this minute. You can still run Cole 98, like you did before, but not the whole company. And even there, you're on probation. Any more of the kind of thing you've been doing and you're out entirely."

Will stared, his face turning scarlet. "You can't do that to me!"

"Oh, but I can. I'm still chairman of the board, don't forget, and the board members will vote my way. You know that as well as I do."

"You'd do that to your own blood?"

"I ain't happy about it, but I have no choice."

"This will ruin me in Alaska. Everybody will wonder why you're doing it."

"You should have thought of that before."

"Jeremiah, don't do this to me, please," Will said desperately. Staring into Jeremiah's unyielding eyes, his shoulders sagged in defeat. Then he straightened up, eyes burning. "I won't stand still for it. Christ, I won't! I'll get a job somewhere else, with some company that appreciates my ability, and will pay me the money I'm worth."

Jeremiah said calmly, "You're a grown man, Will. You do what you think best for you. But I have to warn you . . . you leave Cole for another job, you're completely on your own. And by that, I mean you'll get the traditional dollar in my will, and that's all."

"You wouldn't do that!" Will looked stunned. "Hell, I'm your grandson, Jeremiah!"

"I'll do her, boy. I did it to Dwight and I'll do it to you. You leave Cole Enterprises, you leave the family."

"Well, I won't beg you to change your mind. I would never do that."

"I respect you for that much, at least. So, what's your decision? Stay or leave?"

"You give me no choice," Will said bitterly. "I'll take over Cole 98. Who're you putting in as head of Cole?"

"You'll find that out when the time comes."

Will said emptily, "I guess there's nothing left for me to say, is there?"

"I think she's all been said, boy."

Will, a beaten man, turned away with dragging footsteps. It took all of Jeremiah's willpower to prevent him from calling him back, and arranging some kind of accommodation.

Hand on the doorknob, Will faced around. "At Cole 98, how much autonomy will I have?"

Jeremiah said firmly, "As much as I, and the new president, give you, Will. If you behave yourself, you'll be all right. Step out of line again, and you'll be come down on hard."

Will gave him an embittered look and went on out of the room.

Jeremiah sighed, slumping in the wheelchair. The confrontation had drained him, emotionally and physically. But most of all he felt a deep sorrow. If he had needed any confirmation of wrongdoing, Will's hangdog expression, his giving up so easily, were more than enough. Whatever else he was, Will was a fighter. He was guilty of *something*, that was abundantly clear.

Jeremiah waited, not bothering to ring the bell to summon Kelly. He knew that both she and Chris would be in shortly, eager to hear the details. He sat in the slumped position, resting, until he heard footsteps on the other side of the door. Then he sat up straight, the old fierce look on his face.

They came in together, Kelly in the lead. She started to speak, then stopped and came quickly to him. She touched his cheek with gentle fingers. "Was it bad? You look terrible, Grandfather."

"I'm all right," he said gruffly, and pushed her hand away.

Kelly gave him a lingering look, then shrugged and went to sit beside Chris in front of the wheelchair.

"I'm not going into all that was said in here. The only thing you need to know is that I'm removing Will from the presidency of Cole."

Kelly drew in her breath sharply. "How did he take that?"

"About as you'd expect . . . no, that ain't exactly true. After some blustering he backed down and took it like a whipped dog."

Kelly nodded. "That, you wouldn't expect from Will."

"And it only proves, to my way of thinking, that he's involved with this Fanti fellow. I may be making a mistake letting him take over Cole 98 again, but Lord God, he *is* my grandson!"

"He isn't leaving the company then?"

"He threatened to, but when I didn't back down, he decided to stay."

Kelly looked at him in speculation. "Who are you putting in his place as president of Cole?"

Jeremiah smiled faintly. "Your fellow there."

Chris grunted as if struck. "Sir, you can't be serious! You're putting *me* in that spot? People will think you're . . ."

"Finally senile, as they've been thinking for some time? More'n likely, but then *they* have nothing to say about it, do they? What do you think girl?"

Kelly took Chris's hand and squeezed tightly. "What do I think? I couldn't be more delighted!"

Chris jumped up in agitation. "Damnit, I think you're both

crazy! I've never even been a job foreman on a construction job, much less the head of a company the size of Cole. I know absolutely nothing about it."

"You'll learn fast enough," Jeremiah said complacently. "Don't fret about it, Chris. It's my decision and what I say goes. If there's any static, it'll land on me."

Chris was shaking his head. "Not necessarily. If I screw up, and the odds are all in favor of that, I'll catch flack right and left. They'll say I married Kelly not only for her money, but for the cushy job of Cole president."

Jeremiah said dryly. "The money you knew about already, yet you're going to marry her."

"That, I can cope with . . . I think. But this is different, don't you see that, Jeremiah? Hell, I only had a year of business school after college, then I dropped out. Seeing some of the world seemed more important to me than an MBA."

First time the boy's called me by name, Jeremiah thought with satisfaction. "Thing people don't realize is that being president of a large company ain't all that complicated, not once a company's built, anyway. And the way I built Cole, I didn't install too many chiefs and not enough Indians, as all too many companies do. The people in the lower executive positions are capable and can handle day-to-day operations. The president of Cole is there to make the decisions nobody else can. Like Harry Truman said, the buck stops there. And a college education ain't all that important, to my way of thinking. Godalmighty, I didn't even finish high school and look where I made it to. Colleges turn men out like cookie cutters . . . one bite in the ass and they're finished." Jeremiah grinned fiercely.

"Think of the President of the United States, boy. How many times have we elected men to office who had little or no experience in that direction, and yet they grew into it. Old Harry is a prime example."

"You're simplifying it, Jeremiah," Chris said angrily, "and you damned well know it!"

"Don't think so." He squinted at the pacing Chris. "Lord God, you know how many fellows would kill for a job like this?"

"I'm not interested in how many guys want this job." Chris stopped pacing to stare at Jeremiah narrowly. "Does it give you a charge, old man, to play God, dispensing largess?"

Jeremiah smiled benignly. "I can see why you might think that, and it may have happened in the past, but any time I ever did something for somebody, they deserved it. And this time, boy, I'm doing it because I want Cole Enterprises in capable hands after I'm gone. More, I want it in the family."

"You mean, if I wasn't marrying Kelly, this wouldn't be happening?"

Jeremiah hesitated, then nodded. "I'll be honest, boy. That's about the way of it."

Chris stared from Jeremiah to Kelly before saying slowly, "I have a feeling here, a feeling that I've been manipulated all the way. Kelly goes on a hunt for a husband, then you put that husband in as head of Cole."

"Darling, you can't really believe that!" Kelly said quickly. She jumped to her feet to cross to him. "I love you and that's the only reason I'm marrying you. It's true that Grandfather has been bugging me to find a husband for a long time, but I've always told him that when I marry someone, it'll be because *I* want to, not just to please him."

Jeremiah said, "That's true, Chris. Take my word for it. I've been at her and at her, but this is the first time she's ever thought enough of any fellow to get hitched."

Again, Chris looked from one to the other. "I suppose I have to believe you."

"Thank you, darling!" Kelly threw her arms around his neck and kissed him.

Jeremiah said impatiently, "Well, boy? What do you say? Look at it this way. What do you have to lose?"

As Kelly took her arms from around his neck and stepped back, still looking up into his face, Chris said, "I can think of a number of things I could lose. Your respect, both yours and Kelly's, and my own self-respect, if I fall on my face."

"It won't happen, Chris," Kelly said fervently. "Believe me, it will never happen!"

"In the face of that much faith," Chris said dryly, "what can I say but yes?"

"Good, boy, good!" Jeremiah said briskly. "Now, one more thing. The wedding, when is it to be? Next Sunday week all right with you two? If it's all right, I'd like for you to get the announcements out, girl."

* * *

He held himself erect until the two young people left the room, then sagged, chin falling onto his chest. Lord God, he was bone-tired! The last hour had taken a lot out of him. How easy, how very easy, it would be to just let go and slip down into eternal darkness. For some time now he had been clinging to life by sheer will alone. If he let up for just an instant, he would be gone.

Not yet. Lord God, not yet! He had to live to see his empire in safe hands. Most of all, he had to live to celebrate his one-hundredth. He had sworn, hadn't he? Jeremiah Cole never went back on his word.

He dozed and was back into the past, during that terrible winter of 1898, on Chechako Hill on the Klondike, where he had sunk his first shaft, working until his fingers were raw, and all to no avail.

"The ground was frozen to bedrock, Chris, boy," he muttered. "I had to sink her thirty feet down. You had to use fire, you see. A fire about six feet by four was built on the frozen ground and you'd let her burn eight hours. Then you'd dig out what dirt had thawed, hardly ever more'n three feet at a time. Then you'd do her again, again and again, until you reached bedrock. Two months I put in on that Lord God hole in the ground and not a trace of yellow did I ever find. . . ."

Twenty

Josh, in from Washington for two weeks, learned about the coming nuptials the next day, at the breakfast table.

Kelly had just introduced Chris. Josh masked his surprise fairly well, he thought, at finding a man staying overnight at Cole House. He couldn't recall Kelly ever having an overnight male guest before. True, Brad Connors had stayed the night on numerous occasions, but he was a Cole employee, in a manner of speaking.

As they sat down to eat, Josh said warily, "What do you do, Chris?"

"Well, I did work for the pipeline . . ." Chris hesitated, with a glance at Kelly.

Kelly got that impish grin that always gave her away when she was about to do something outrageous, and Josh braced himself for what was coming, without having the least idea of what.

"Chris is a Cole employee, Daddy. He's working <u>directly</u> for Grandfather."

This time Josh didn't conceal his surprise. "He is? Doing what, if I may be so bold as to inquire?"

"All in good time, Daddy. There's something else I think you should know first." She leaned forward. "Chris and I are getting married a week from Sunday."

"Getting married? You two?" Josh said in a stunned voice. It was the shock of his life. For some time now he had wondered when his daughter would find a man she loved enough to marry. Kelly and he had always been close, and she confided frankly in him, keeping him familiar with her private life; and to be told now that she was marrying a man he had never even met until this morning was like a slap in the face.

Kelly was going on, "I know it must be a shock to you, Daddy, coming at you like this. You hadn't even met Chris, but then we just met a few weeks ago. And you *have* been in Washington most of the time."

"There's always the telephone," he said. "And if I recall correctly, you've talked to me at least twice in the last ten days."

"I know, but it's all been so sudden. We didn't really decide until a few days ago."

Anger was beginning to build in Josh now. He glanced across the table at Chris O'Keefe. He had seemed a nice enough young man at first—handsome, clean-cut, intelligent—but now he was assuming a different aspect in Josh's eyes. A fortune hunter, a goddamn gigolo, all old-fashioned words. Yet they fit. Why else would a pipeline worker be marrying Kelly Cole, if not for her money and the position being her husband would bring him?

"Daddy," Kelly said in a warning voice. "You've always been cool, a quality I've admired in you. Don't blow that cool now and say something you'll regret later."

Josh looked down at his plate and took a bite of ham. He chewed thoughtfully, examining the situation. Finally he nodded slowly. "You've concocted the right scenario, my dear, as we government planners are so fond of saying."

"What did you mean, Daddy, concocted the right scenario?" Kelly demanded. "You made it sound like I'd planned it all this way."

Nothing more had been said about the coming marriage during breakfast. Now Josh and Kelly were strolling together down toward the dock.

Josh said dryly, "Didn't you? You worked everything out so that I would be confronted with a fait accompli, and then told me in the presence of your young man, so I'd have to choke on my own bile or risk alienating you, and then have a chance to calm down before we talked privately. When there's a deadlock in the Senate, a hot and unresolved debate, we recess. A cooling-off period, we call it."

"Daddy, don't handle this like a political debate. This is my life we're talking about!"

"Don't you think I know that? But I have the feeling I've been manipulated here."

Kelly laughed suddenly. "You know, Chris said something of the same thing, that Grandfather and I were both manipulating him."

"Then I have to credit him with spirit and intelligence. Did you?"

Kelly hesitated. "To be brutally frank, I suppose I did, in a way."

"In a way? It's not like you to equivocate, Kelly."

"I'm not. It's just . . . well, Daddy, you have to understand Chris. I'm a wealthy woman, an heir to power and position as well. For that reason he was reluctant to . . . well, court me, to use an out-of-date word, afraid that I'd think just what you did, that he was a fortune hunter. Oh, yes, I knew what you were thinking! Eventually Chris might have adjusted to the idea and gone ahead. I couldn't wait, for many reasons. For one, I was terrified of losing him. So I went after him, in naked pursuit."

"I should have thought that would have spooked him."

"It would have most men, I know. But you have to get to know Chris. He's an unusual man, I'm finding that out more every day. I think he even admires the way I went after him. One thing you must understand, Daddy. I made sure that he loved me, before I made a move."

"I'm afraid to ask how you learned that," he muttered. "You said Papa also manipulated him. What does that mean?"

She was shaking her head. "That will have to come from Grandfather."

"He seldom confides in me."

"You'll find out soon enough, I'm sure," she said with her impish grin.

"Well, if all you tell me is true, I guess I can accept Chris, once I know him better. Kelly . . ." He stopped walking, took her by the shoulders and turned her to face him. "The main thing is, are you happy?"

"I have never been so happy," she said with shining eyes. "I never dreamed that I would ever find a man I could love as much as I love Chris."

*   *   *

Will learned about the marriage of Kelly to Chris O'Keefe from Louise.

In the days immediately after his meeting with Jeremiah, he was moody and withdrawn, inwardly seething with outrage and humiliation. So far at least, Jeremiah had taken no immediate action, and so far as Will knew, no one had learned of his demotion. Silence from Jeremiah could mean that he had changed his mind, but being well aware of the old man's iron determination, Will seriously doubted it. He could not remember an instance of Jeremiah's changing his mind once a decision was firmly made. Will expected an announcement in the newspapers any day.

When it didn't happen on the third day after the meeting, he decided to take advantage of the delay. So far, he had not taken a dime from Fanti. Why not do so while he had the chance? When Fanti learned later that he was no longer head of Cole, that much of his clout had been taken away, he would be furious. But what could he do?

He was just getting up from his desk when Cora buzzed him. "Yes, Cora?"

"Mrs. Cole is on line three."

"Tell her I'm too busy... no, wait, I'll take it. But I'm going out after I talk to her, and won't be available for the rest of the day."

He punched the button, changing lines. "Louise? What is it? I'm snowed under here." He hadn't yet told her of his demotion, and wondered if she'd learned about it from another source.

"I just had a call from Kelly, Will."

He tensed. "What did she want?"

"She had a bit of startling news. Will, she's getting married!"

"So? That comes as no big shock. I guess she and Brad Connors have been shacking up for some time."

"Oh, no, it's not Brad."

"It's not? Who then?"

"It's somebody I never heard of, a man named Chris O'Keefe. Do you know him, Will?"

Jesus Christ in a wheelbarrow! The rage that had simmered in Will all week threatened to explode. His fingers tightened around the receiver and it was all he could do to keep from hurling it at the wall. And then another thought edged into his mind. Was this what was behind Jeremiah's removing him? Was he putting O'Keefe in his, Will's, place? No, it wasn't possible! He had long suspected that the old man was becoming senile, but surely he wouldn't put a construction stiff in as president of Cole.

Will became aware of a voice drumming in his ear, and he realized that he had forgotten that Louise was on the phone. "What? What are you saying, Louise?"

"I said, the wedding is this coming Sunday, at Cole House. That's awfully short notice, but Kelly said that they had decided all at once..."

"I'll just bet they did," Will said through gritted teeth. "Well, I'm not going, damned if I will!" He thumped his fist on the desk.

"Not going?" Louise said in a startled voice. "But, Will, she's your own sister! How can you *not* go?"

"I'm not going to witness her making a fool of herself. I know who this O'Keefe is, Louise. He's nothing but a pipeline worker. He's latched on to a good thing with Kelly. He's a goddamned fortune hunter! I always credited her with more sense than that."

Louise was slow in responding. "But if that's the case, all the more reason for us to go. If we don't go, the family will be upset. We have to stay close to protect our own interests, Will!"

"You mean, kiss ass, Louise? Watch this fortune hunter fawn over Kelly? Don't worry, she's not a complete fool. When he starts to bleed her dry, she'll wake up to what's going on, and that'll be the end of Mr. O'Keefe."

"Will, we're going if I have to drag you. Think of the talk it'll cause if we stay away. All of Alaska will be buzzing!"

"Since when did you drag me anywhere, Louise? I'm not going to this damned farce of a wedding!"

He slammed down the phone and strode out of his office, ignoring the intercom as Cora buzzed him again—Louise calling back, he was sure.

Will hadn't talked to Milo Fanti since his galling encounter with Jeremiah; he had told Cora not to put Fanti through if he called, and if he barged into the office, not to let him in.

Consequently he wasn't surprised at Fanti's glower when he answered Will's knock. "Mr. Cole, I'm not pleased with you. You've been giving me the run-around, not answering my calls. I haven't heard word one from you."

"I've been out of town," Will said brusquely, brushing past him. "I'm here now, so simmer down, Fanti. Let's talk."

Inside Fanti's office, Fanti said, "Now tell me what's happening with your grandfather. Did you get him to back off?"

"Of course, didn't I tell you I would?" Will lied with a straight face. "He just wanted to throw a scare into you. All you have to do is cool it for a couple of weeks, let things quiet down, and you're back in business."

Fanti looked at him sharply. "Do you know how much money I can lose in two weeks?"

Will waved a hand airily. "Don't be greedy, Fanti. You're doing all right here in Fairbanks."

Fanti studied him narrowly. "What I don't understand is why he got involved, hired this pipeliner. I thought he was retired, completely out of the company?"

"It's Kelly, my half-sister," Will improvised. "They're sweet on each other, she and the pipeliner. He told her what was going on and she trotted right to the old man, got him all worked up. But Jeremiah has a short attention span. A couple of weeks and he'll have forgotten all about it."

"He'd better," Fanti grumbled. "Two weeks more of laying off is going to cost me."

"It's going to cost you more, right now."

Fanti grew still, looking at him with half-closed eyes. "What does that mean?"

"I'm doing you a big favor, getting Granpap off your back. As the saying goes, one hand washes the other."

"How much?"

"I figure ten grand for now."

"Now who's greedy?"

"You offered me ten grand once, for just cooperating with you. Then I refused. Let's just say I've changed my mind."

"How do I know that I can start up again in two weeks?"

"I guess you'll have to take my word for that."

Fanti grunted. He looked down at his hands on the desk. Will took out a cigar and lit it. His heart was beating erratically, and he didn't know whether it was from concern over Fanti's falling for his bluff, or from his, Will's, finally accepting a bribe. But why should he feel guilty about that? He had the name now, at least with Jeremiah, so why not play the game? He recalled something a man once told him. A well-known official high up in state government had been accepting bribes for years, and had finally been caught. He had told Will with a twisted smile: "It's always easier after the first time, Will. You get hooked, like a drug addict. Even the thought of giving it up gives you withdrawal pains."

Fanti finally looked up. He stared at Will out of hooded eyes. In a soft voice he said, "You'd better not be fucking me around, Mr. Cole. I'm not stingy, but ten grand is a chunk of cash and I always receive full value for my money. *Always*."

"You'll get full value," Will said steadily. He was not intimidated by any threat Fanti might make, fully confident that he could handle him.

He watched the rackets boss cross the room to the shelf where the refrigerator sat, and push it aside, revealing a small wall safe. It was the first time Will had known of its existence. He squinted, narrowing his vision, as Fanti began dialing. He saw the man dial 8 right, then 15 left, and then Fanti moved his head fractionally and Will could no longer see the dial. He filed the two numbers away in his mind for future reference. Fanti carefully blocked Will's view of the interior of the safe, as he swung the door open and reached inside. He took out a bundle of bills, then closed the door, spun the dial and moved the refrigerator back into position, before returning to his desk. In a gesture conveying faint contempt he tossed the bundle of money on the desk before Will.

Fanti said, "There's the ten grand. No receipt requested."

"Thanks, Fanti." Will got to his feet and picked up the money, putting it into his pocket without counting it. "I'll be in touch."

"Oh, we'll be in touch," Fanti said softly. "You belong to me now, Mr. Cole."

Will, his thoughts jumping ahead, did not hear the last remark. Excitement churned in his blood. He had not talked to Candice since Jeremiah had handed down his edict; he hadn't been in the mood and he hadn't had the money. Now he had the money and he was sure as hell in the mood!

He called her from the first pay phone he came to, praying that she would be in. As her low, vibrant voice said, "Hello," his knees went weak.

*   *   *

Dwight, of course, already knew about the marriage. When Kelly called him, he said, "Yeah, I know about it. Chris told me a couple of days ago."

"Oh? I didn't know that."

"Congratulations, Sis. I like old Chris, he's a nice guy. Be good to him."

"I intend to be," she said somewhat tartly. "I wanted to invite you to the wedding, Dwight."

"Does that include Junebug?"

She hesitated. "Of course, if she wants to come."

"Wouldn't her presence cause a few people embarrassment?" he said with an edge of malice.

"That doesn't matter. I'm the one getting married and I'm the one inviting her."

"Thanks, Sis," he said affectionately. "You're a good kid, you know. But I was putting you on, more or less. June has no intention of going."

"How about you?"

"I'm no longer a member of the clan. Both Will and Jeremiah have disowned me, remember?"

"But this is *my* wedding, not theirs. I want you there, Dwight. Will . . . I'm not even sure he'll be there, anyway."

"If I needed an inducement to get me there, that would do it. But I won't be there. Thanks for asking me, anyway."

"Dwight, damn you! Won't you ever learn to compromise? There'll never be a chance at reconciliation if you don't bend a little."

"How about Will? How about Jeremiah?" he said in a bitter voice. "Some bending on their part might be nice."

"Just because they're like they are doesn't mean you have to be. Dwight, I want you there!" Her voice rose.

"I'm sorry, Sis. No way," he said quietly. "I do hope that Chris understands that my absence is in no way a slur on him."

"Goddamn you, Dwight Cole!" she said in a voice that sounded close to tears. She hung up.

Dwight replaced the receiver slowly, sorrow welling up in him. Perhaps he *should* bend a little. Who would it hurt? But then Will's scathing words and Jeremiah's iron rejection swam back into his memory, and his resolve hardened. No, they didn't want him in the family and he would oblige them!

"Dwight . . ." June touched his arm. "Maybe you should go."

"Not without you, Junebug."

"Don't do that to me, don't lay that guilt trip on me," she said in distress.

"I'm sorry, babe, I didn't mean to." He cupped her face between his hands and kissed her lightly. "Actually, you have little to do with it. I made my bed before I met you, Will and Jeremiah locked the door on me, and I've reconciled myself to it. If I went to Kelly's wedding, it would only open up the whole enchilada again."

Kelly dreaded telling Brad Connors about the marriage, but it had to be done, and she refused to take the coward's way—by mail or even a phone call. It had to be done face to face. She called him and they agreed to meet for dinner in Juneau.

Her face gave her away, she realized that the instant he looked at her. His eyes changed and he seemed to retire within himself. They were dining late and the restaurant was only half full, for which Kelly was grateful.

He waited until the waitress had taken their drink orders and had left them alone. Then he leaned forward, elbows on the table, staring directly into her eyes. He said tightly, "All right, Kelly, let's have it. Something's bugging you, I can always tell."

"You always could do that, I know." She took a deep breath. "Brad, we've never made each other promises or commitments, have we?"

His face was still, his eyes never leaving her face. "I'm not quite sure how to answer that, Kelly. I'll admit that it's never been put into words, but I've always felt a commitment to you."

"But ours wasn't the great love of all times."

"*Wasn't?* Past tense, Kelly?"

"Brad . . ." She sighed. "You're making this extremely difficult."

"Good! All right. I'll make it easy for you. You've found someone else?"

"Yes," she said.

"A man you're having an affair with? Or someone you love?"

"A man I'm going to marry, Brad," she said simply.

He got a stunned look, and had to grope for words. "Marry? You're going to get married? But I always thought..."

"No, Brad," she interrupted. "I've never said I'd marry you. I've never said I loved you."

"But I love you, I'm sure you've known that. Doesn't that mean anything?"

"Of course it does. Dearest Brad, it means a lot to me." She reached across the table to touch the back of his hand.

He jerked his hand back violently, as if her touch burned him. "But apparently not enough."

"I'm sorry you feel this way, Brad. I suppose I must shoulder some of the blame. But I do hope that we can remain friends."

"Friends," he said with elaborate irony. "That sounds like a quote from a Hollywood gossip column. When a famous couple gets a divorce, they tell the press that they will always remain friends. Who's the man you're marrying?"

"Chris O'Keefe."

He frowned. "Chris O'Keefe? I've never even heard the name."

"No, I don't suppose you would have. Until recently Chris worked on the pipeline."

"A pipeliner? How long have you known him?"

Kelly felt herself flush. "A few weeks."

"A few *weeks!*" he said incredulously. "You're marrying a man you've known a few weeks? And a construction worker at that!"

"Don't be a snob, Brad, it doesn't become you. I love him. It wouldn't matter if I had known him a week or a year."

"He's after your money, naturally."

She shrugged. "We expect people to think that, but it happens that he loves me, as well. Wait until you meet him, Brad. You'll like him, I know you will."

"Never!" he said explosively. He leaned forward, lowering his voice to a venomous whisper. "I could kill the fortune-hunting sonofabitch!"

Kelly was filled with dismay. She had anticipated a shocked reaction, but not this much bitterness and anger. "I never expected this from you, Brad. I thought you were more civilized."

"Civilized? *Civilized?* The way I feel at the moment, I'm not far removed from a redneck brawling in a honky-tonk over his woman."

"Brad, I'm not your woman, I never was. We had an affair, we enjoyed each other. You must accept that."

With anger receding slightly, he said glumly, "I suppose I must, but don't expect me to do it with grace." He gave a bark of laughter. "All that time I wanted to ask you to be my wife, but I always held back because of what you represent, Kelly. How wrong can one man be? I'm a respected attorney, I earn damned good money. Now I learn that you picked a construction guy over me for a husband."

"It wouldn't have mattered, Brad," she said softly. "I would never have married you. I didn't love you enough."

Sunday dawned bright and clear, a beautiful day for the wedding.

Even on such short notice, well over a hundred people attended. It would have been Kelly's preference to restrict the guest list to members of the family, and Chris concurred with her. But Jeremiah would not have it that way: "It ain't every day that my granddaughter gets married. I want all the biggies here." He had added mysteriously, "Besides, I have my reasons for a packed house."

A catering company was hired, plus additional service people, and a gaily striped awning was put up on the lawn before Cole House, just in case the weather was inclement. Two bars were set up, and the liquor flowed freely. All morning Perkins plied the launch back and forth to Juneau, and by two, the schedule time for the ceremony, the assembled crowd was abuzz.

Finally it was time. Josh, splendid in morning clothes, came to fetch her. His gray eyes glowed with pride and his voice was husky as he said, "My dear, you look absolutely ravishing. This is supposed to be a sad day in a father's life, but the sight of the happiness on your face is enough to make *me* happy."

She dimpled up at him, squeezing his arm. "You know

what they say, Daddy. You're gaining a son, not losing a daughter."

"I know." He nodded gravely. "I wouldn't have thought so a few days ago, but I've gotten to know Chris quite well this week. Not only do I think you've made a fine choice, but I find myself liking the guy."

"Too bad most of the guests out there won't be thinking the same. Speaking of which, did Will and Louise show up? The last time I spoke to Louise, she said Will refused to attend."

"Oh, they're here. Will is as grumpy and sullen as a bear with his paw caught in a trap. What's happened between him and Jeremiah? He keeps muttering something about what Pap has done to him. Do you know what he's talking about?"

Kelly hesitated. "I know, Daddy, a part of it anyway. But I think it should come from Grandfather."

They were exiting the house now, and Kelly saw Chris waiting under the awning, tall and handsome and hers, all hers. From that instant on, her entire attention was focused on him—until the vows were said and he turned to take her into his arms for the bridal kiss.

Then the mob of people, which had been relatively quiet during the brief ceremony, began to chatter and crowd around, offering congratulations and faces to be kissed.

All at once Jeremiah, who had stationed his wheelchair near the temporary altar, raised his voice. "Quiet down, all of you! I want your attention for just a few minutes. I have an important announcement to make."

A sudden and dramatic silence fell, and Kelly reflected wryly that Jeremiah's "announcement" was no doubt more important to most of the guests than the wedding, and she had the absurd notion that that was the reason they were here.

Jeremiah sat erect and stern, his voice sonorous as he spoke again. "I wish to announce a change in the chain of command of Cole Enterprises. After my granddaughter and her new husband enjoy a week's honeymoon, Chris O'Keefe will return to assume the position of president of Cole Enterprises..."

As a concerted gasp swept over the assemblage, Kelly's gaze sought out Will, standing to one side. All color drained from his face, and he swayed, catching at the back of a folding chair. Then blood surged back into his features, and he opened his mouth as though to bellow his outrage.

Jeremiah forestalled him: "Due to a difference of opinion, Will's and mine, my grandson has tendered his resignation and will once again resume his duties as vice-president of Cole 98 . . ."

They honeymooned on board *Lodestar II*. Kelly said, "We could take the other one, it would certainly be more comfortable, but I think *Lodestar II* would be more romantic, don't you, darling? Since that is where it all began."

Chris, still slightly dazed by the rapidity of events, said, "That's hardly where it began, but whatever your little heart desires. Who am I to argue?"

The weather remained benign; in fact, the whole week was sunny and warm, with only one brief rain squall to mar it. The small cabin was cramped, but they made do. They spent a great deal of the week anchored in secluded coves along the sound heading south, sailing on only when the whim struck them. Kelly knew the area intimately. She knew which coves were almost totally isolated, which ones had tiny beaches where they could sun and swim in the quiet waters, more often than not in the nude.

It was a perfect time, and Kelly's happiness was complete. She had not been sure if she could share her life with another person, since she had always been independent, but her fears soon ceased. Of course, she realized that a week's time, and a honeymoon at that, was scarcely a true test, but they seemed to complement each other in most ways—in their views on many wide-ranging subjects, in their likes and dislikes. Chris even came to share her love of sailing, and was a competent sailor before the week was out.

"But tennis, no way," he said with a grin. "You're never going to get me hooked on tennis, nor will you be able to con me into playing you again."

"A tennis partner, I can always find," she said contentedly, snuggling into his arms. Since the bunk beds were so narrow, they had brought along a voluminous sleeping bag and placed it on the deck between the bunks. They had just finished making love, and now lay impossibly entwined, breathing and

pulse rates slowing back to normal. She reached down between them to cup his organ, which had performed so
magnificently only moments ago, and now lay flaccid in her
hand. "But this, I can't always find. At least I've never found
one like it before."

"The better to turn you on, darling," he said lazily.

During the week they made love between the bunks, in the
cramped cockpit, on the narrow, deserted beaches, and even
in the water, frolicking like pagans. No doubt their wanting
each other almost every waking moment would eventually
lose its intensity, but Kelly intended to enjoy it to the hilt. In
fact, she wallowed in it, this new sensuality that Chris had
managed to awaken in her.

One thing happened the second evening away from Cole
Island that she feared would mar their week. Due to the
small space aboard the *Lodestar II*, they had brought along
very little luggage—only toilet necessities and two changes of
clothes. She noticed that Chris brought along a new attaché
case, but she didn't question him about it.

On the second evening, anchored in a snug cove, after they
had made love, twice, Chris lit the Coleman lantern and
settled into the small dining nook, attired only in his shorts.
Kelly, sated and almost asleep, watched him curiously, until
she saw him open the attaché case and take out sheaf after
sheaf of stapled papers.

She sat up, staring. "What on earth is all that?"

Chris looked over at her with a smile. "My homework,
papers Jeremiah gave me to take along. Financial statements
of all the corporate entities of Cole, profit and loss statements, briefs from the various vice-presidents with sugges-
tions for improvements, a prospectus or two outlining new
investment possibilities, predictions of future areas to consider, the whole shmeer. All put together by accountants, attorneys, and the vice-presidents themselves.

"Many things, Jeremiah says, that your half-brother neglected
to look into. The whole story of Cole Enterprises is in here,
Kelly."

She said in awe, "My God, you sound like an executive
already! And you're going through all that on our *honeymoon*?"

"In between, sweetheart," he said with a grin. "It won't
interfere, I'll see to that."

Each evening Chris devoted at least two hours to a study of the contents of the attaché case. Watching him, Kelly was fascinated by his ability for total concentration. Head bent over the papers and haloed by the glow of the lantern, his eyes raced over the pages, and she had the feeling that nothing else existed for him in that moment. And yet, if she spoke to him, he would look up with a flashing, loving smile, without the slightest hint of annoyance, and become equally intent on whatever she wanted or asked of him. Before the week was out Kelly realized that he brought the same concentration to love. When they made love, there was nothing else on his mind.

Kelly was astute enough to recognize this talent of his as a plus for their relationship, and yet a tiny bit of jealousy nagged at her when he was absorbed in the papers. Jealous of a few pieces of paper? It was ridiculous on the face of it, but there it was.

She would not have dreamed of confiding this in him, but on the third evening, with one of those startling thrusts of perception, he suddenly glanced up, caught her gaze on him, and grinned. He said gently, "This is going to be my work, Kelly, and you're going to have to get used to it. When we get back, it will get worse, much worse. I'm going to be working a ten-hour day, a seven-day week, for God knows how long. I'm going to have to run just to keep in place. But I wouldn't have it any other way and I don't think you would, either. There'll still be time for you, I promise that. It might help you a little, if you got involved in some of it with me."

She was startled. "Involved in company affairs. *Me?*"

"Why not?" he said reasonably. "You needn't get directly involved, but you should know something of what's going on. No matter what you might try to tell yourself, Kelly, Cole Enterprises is largely yours. Will is no longer a large factor, your grandfather has seen to that. Dwight is out, and your father as well, if what I've learned is true. So who does that leave?"

"You," she said, looking at him in challenge.

"I'm a surrogate, in a way," he said with a shrug. "I'm working for you, *through* you, to be strictly accurate. And for that reason alone you should get to know some things. If for no other reason, because I'll need someone to talk to, to

confide in, someone I can trust. Who knows?" He grinned.
"How do you know you won't like it until you try it? Didn't
you say something like that to me about sailing? Well, I've
come to like it."

"All right," she said in sudden decision. "I suppose I should
get involved, learn something else besides tennis and sailing
and painting. Wait! Is that the reason you want me involved?" She peered at him in sudden suspicion.

He assumed an innocent look. "Do you think I'm that
devious?"

"I'm not sure, you could be," she said slowly. She got up,
naked, and came to the table. "But a word of warning . . . if I
get bored, forget it, buster!"

"*I* certainly won't get bored, if you come over here like
that," he said in distress. "Can't you put something on? How
can I concentrate on anything else?"

"Sometimes, Chris O'Keefe, I think you have some strait-
laced Puritans in your lineage."

"It's a matter of priorities, sweetheart," he said with a
straight face, but there was a twinkle in his eyes.

"Priorities, my ass!" But she found a robe and put it on
before sliding into the nook across from him. "Okay, Mr.
Executive, where do we start with my education?"

"With this." He slid several stapled sheets of paper across
to her.

"What is it? I'd rather you told me about it than reading it.
Just say I love the sound of your voice."

Refusing to respond to her needling, he said gravely, "It's a
report from an Alex Durand, VP of the Cole fishing fleet. You
know that I think the environmentalists, like Dwight and
SAS, go much too far, yet they often have a valid point. The
catch from the fishing grounds is getting scarcer year after
year, yet Cole Canneries demand more and more product,
and refuse to lower the quotas of each boat in the fleet. Kelly,
we have to let up a little. If we catch fish faster than they can
spawn, soon there'll be none left to catch. That's what this
report is all about. Durand recommends reducing the quotas
for a while. This report was sent to Will, and you can see how
he reacted."

He opened the report to the last page. Kelly leaned
forward to read: "Durand, you sound like an eco-freak to me.

There's no place at Cole for a man like that. No reduction in quotas. Will Cole."

Kelly glanced up. "I'd expect something like that from Will, but I'm afraid Grandfather would agree with him."

Chris shook his head. "You're wrong. I discussed a few things in these reports with Jeremiah. This was one of them. He realizes that times have changed, although he probably wouldn't admit that to most people. He told me that any decision I make in a matter like this is mine alone, he won't overrule me."

She gave him a sharp glance. "The two of you've become very chummy, haven't you?"

"We understand each other pretty well, I believe. Don't you approve?"

She said hastily, "Oh, I approve. Just a little surprised, is all."

He was frowning down at another paper, and she said, "You seem to have picked up on all this fast enough."

"Not as fast as I'd like. Not as fast as I should. Some of these are legal documents. Do you know that attorneys write in a language incomprehensible to the rest of us? I think they do it on purpose, to perpetuate their species." He sighed. "Soon as I have time, I'm going to have to sit down with Brad Connors and have him interpret some of this legalese."

"Oh, oh!" She drew in her breath. "Chris, you remember that I told you I was having an affair when I met you?"

"Of course I remember. What about it?"

"Brad Connors was the man."

He looked at her. "I see."

She shook her head from side to side. "I'm not sure you do. To be fair to him, I told him I was getting married and who to."

"How did he react?"

"Badly. To me it was an affair, nothing too serious. Oh, I suspected that he was half in love with me, but then I've found that men often have to convince themselves of that, to soothe their conscience, I suppose. I've never seen Brad lose control of himself like he did that day."

"Threatened you, did he?" Chris said tightly.

"Not me. You. He said . . . Chris, he said he would gladly kill you!"

"Did he?" He was looking at her almost absently. "Well, we have to get together. There's no help for that. I think he'll come around. He has a good thing in Cole, he'd be a fool to blow it. He doesn't have to like me for us to work together. If he hates me, that's his hangup." His face hardened. "But he'd damned well better not let it interfere with his work for us, or he and that firm of his will be in need of a new client!"

Twenty-One

Some bad news awaited them on their return to Cole Island. Jeremiah was in bed with pneumonia, and Josh had a doctor staying in the house until the old man was better.

"Or worse," Josh told them glumly. "The doctor says it can go either way, but the odds are on the bad side. Pap is old, kids, very old, and pneumonia is usually fatal at his age. The will is there and he's fighting back, but we just don't know. He took to his bed right after you left on the boat." His smile was twisted. "It seems that that one burst of energy, willpower, or whatever it took, to make that announcement about you taking over, Chris, drained him."

Chris was filled with dismay, but was careful not to let it show. "I suppose there's no chance of talking to him then?"

"The doctor absolutely forbids any visits at this time. And that means it's all on your shoulders, Chris. Don't expect any help from Pap." Josh's look was understanding. "He did say one thing to me before they put him into an oxygen tent. 'Tell the boy that he's on his own. I trust that boy, Joshua. Any decisions that he makes will be okay with me. And if anybody calls up here bitching to me, tell them that I'm behind Chris one hundred percent, no matter what he decides.' And he added to me, 'I've made my last company decision, Josh. It's going to take all I've got in me now to see my one-hundredth.'"

Chris shook his head ruefully. "Damn, it's going to be hard enough as it is. Without his help, I don't know."

"I'll give you what help I can, Chris," Josh said warmly. "But I know damn-all about running the company. As the saying goes," he grinned, "'if you can't stand the heat...'"

Chris looked at him keenly. "I know that my becoming head of Cole is as much a shock to you, Josh, as it was to everyone else. We left so soon after the wedding I had no chance to discuss it with you. What do you really think?"

"How can I answer that, Chris? It's a hell of a jump from construction worker to president of a company like Cole. All I can tell you is, you have my best wishes and support. After all, you *are* part of the family now."

"I know that Will stormed off the island right after Jeremiah's announcement. Have you heard anything from him?"

"Not word one and I'm not likely to, either. But I very much doubt you'll have any strong support from him. The contrary, in fact."

Chris nodded glumly. "We'll have to have a face-to-face, thrash it out the best we can."

"You can always fire him, Chris. You have the authority, you know."

"Not unless he leaves me no choice."

"Speaking of talks, there are a couple of matters I want to discuss with you. Not about Cole Enterprises, per se, but political issues on which I need to know how you stand. I may need company support. I never had it from Will. Separate status for Alaska, and the moving of the state capital from Juneau to Anchorage. Or Willow."

"I've heard something about such a move, to Anchorage, but to *Willow*? Hell, I passed through there when I came to Alaska, on the way from Anchorage to Fairbanks. It's no more than a wide place in the road."

"At the last count it had around thirty people. It's a porkbarrel, Chris, the whole thing, yet it has some powerful people behind it. That's why I've always badgered Will to swing the weight of Cole behind my opposition to it, but he wouldn't do it. It all started back in 1960, and again in 1962, when the move was put to a vote of the people. It failed to pass both times, but in 1976, it did pass."

"I didn't realize that. Why hasn't the capital been moved, then?"

"Money," Josh said succinctly. "It's going to cost a lot of money. There's a bond issue in the works now, probably for the ballot in 1979, or sooner. They're talking about nine million dollars, Chris. I'm fighting against it tooth and nail and I need all the support I can get. I don't know how many times I've been asked why Cole Enterprises doesn't support me. My own family, for God's sake! Pap, he couldn't care less, and he's always left it up to Will."

Chris said instantly, "As soon as I get myself settled in, I'll make a press announcement, Josh. The official Cole Enterprises position will be unequivocal support for you on the issue."

Josh blinked, then smiled slowly. "You've got one fine executive trait, Chris. You can make instant decisions."

"Let's just hope I don't make some I'll come to regret." Chris lit a cigarette before going on. "About this other thing. Separate status, you called it? I've heard there was some kind of a movement for secession, but it strikes me as rather off the wall. I assumed that it was something proposed by a bunch of kooks, not held as serious by anyone with any intelligence."

"It may have started out that way," Josh said soberly. "But the idea is gaining momentum, especially now with the prospect of all that oil money pouring into the state, of which the federal government will get a big chunk in taxes. Also, it looks as if we're not going to be allowed to export oil, the only one of the states not allowed to do so. When the pipeline is in operation and the money starts coming in, some important people are going to get behind it. Out of selfish motives, I'll agree. That's Will's line. Why should we let the Lower 48 have a big chunk of *our* money? It's not a serious issue right now, but it will be within a couple of years. I've seen it coming for some time. To stave it off, a countermovement is going to have to start soon. I'm going to spearhead it. If I'm still in the Senate." He grinned ruefully. "I've been warned that if I come on strong against separation, I may not be reelected."

Chris was shaking his head. "It still strikes me as pretty weird. Christ, look what separation would do to the armed forces. I'm not up on politics, but it strikes me that it would open up a whole can of worms in respect to the balance of power between a state and the federal government."

"All those things and more, Chris. But it's coming."

Chris sighed. "Well, let me think about that one for a little, okay? You're putting me on the hot seat here, Josh, and I have yet to sit behind the president's desk, wherever that's going to be."

* * *

Anchor Town—Anchorage. A boomtown, scrambling to spend the new oil money, building in all directions, rapidly becoming an urban and commercial sprawl.

There was a joke that Chris had heard innumerable times: the best thing about Anchorage was that it was located only a half-hour from Alaska. Living in Anchorage, you might as well live in Kansas City, but thirty minutes away by car or by private plane, you could be in country wilder than most people in the Lower 48 had ever seen.

His first executive decision was to run the company from Anchorage instead of Fairbanks. The headquarters building was in Anchorage, and the vice-presidents of all the companies, with the exception of Cole 98, had their offices in the Cole Building. Even the VP of Cole Airlines was in the Anchorage building, although the airline operated primarily out of the Fairbanks airport.

Chris arrived in Anchorage on a Sunday, and as he had done that day in Fairbanks, he spent hours walking through the city. He arrived unheralded; the company personnel had been alerted that he was the new president, but he didn't want anyone to know he was in the city; they would learn that soon enough when he walked into the building early Monday morning.

The only time he had been in Anchorage was the day he arrived in Alaska and on that day he had only passed through.

He walked, his thoughts occupied with the coming weeks. Aside from settling into the job—and dear God, was *that* going to take some settling—he had to have serious talks with any number of people. Will Cole, Milo, Fanti, Bry Tucker, Brad Connors, Dwight, et cetera. The confrontations, for the most part, weren't going to be pleasant, yet he had to establish his authority with them, as well as with the company employees.

He started his walk downtown, at the park strip. The day was cloudy and gray, Cook Inlet the color of steel. The weather was damp and raw—summer was over.

Anchorage was a boomtown, as was Fairbanks, yet there was a difference. Fairbanks had the look of a frontier town, while Anchorage was in the middle of a construction explosion, with new buildings shooting up everywhere. Since it was Sunday, the main street, Fourth Avenue, was almost deserted. The Anchorage *Times* building, and a number of banks—all closed. Farther along Fourth there was more activity, where the bars, pawnshops, and sex shops were located. All the bars were open; he knew they didn't close until five in the morning, and opened again at eight. Chris could smell the spilled beer and urine a block away. Eskimos leaned against bar fronts, or wandered about, all in a blank, sodden state of drunkenness. This area, at least, was in the Fairbanks mold. He cut over to Third Avenue, lined with fur shops, travel and rental car agencies, and the Anchorage Westward Hotel.

After a while he walked down a steep hill and into a residential district, probably the most expensive part of an exorbitantly expensive city. It was also, Chris knew, where the earthquake of 1964 had struck the hardest. All the buildings were relatively new, and quite expensive. Chris was amused to see a lot of plate glass and wood, the big windows facing the inlet. He wondered idly how much it added to the winter fuel bills, this ersatz mimicking of Southern California.

After another hour's walk it grew late and he was fatigued. He turned back toward the hotel, where he had a room for the night. There was an apartment in one of the new condominiums which belonged to the company and was exclusively for the use of the president; but Kelly didn't want him to stay there until she could share it with him. She was remaining on the island for a few days, until Jeremiah got better—or worse.

Chris arrived at the Cole Building—an impressive, modern, nine-story structure housing the executive and office personnel of the various Cole Enterprises—at seven the next morning. The building wasn't yet open and he had a brief argument with the guard at the door before he could convince the man that he was Chris O'Keefe, the new president. He asked directions to his office, which was located, naturally, on the ninth floor.

It was a large office, with a glass slab for a desk, a fully stocked bar, and an executive bathroom. The office occupied an entire corner of the ninth floor, with glass walls on two sides. Chris walked over to look out. It was a clear day and he could see snow-capped Mount McKinley, a hundred and seventy miles to the north, and much of downtown Anchorage

He whistled softly—it was an impressive view, very impressive!

But how was a man supposed to get any work done with such a view? He pulled the floor-length drapes closed, opened his attaché case, and spread the contents out on top of the glass slab, which held only an intercom system and a desk pad.

Shortly after eight o'clock, absorbed in the papers, he heard a timid knock on the door. He stood up, stretching, and called out, "Come in!"

The door opened to admit a tall woman of around fifty, wearing a severe face and dress to match. She said tentatively, "Mr. O'Keefe?"

He took out a cigarette and lit it. "That's me."

"We . . . we were informed that you were coming, but we didn't know exactly when. I'm sorry there was no one here to meet you."

"I didn't expect anyone. I came in around seven."

"I'm Harriet Bickham, Mr. O'Keefe, head of the secretarial pool. I'm sorry that we have no secretary for you, but since Mr. Cole seldom used this office, we never had anyone for him, but sent someone up from the secretarial pool when he needed something done."

"How do you do, Miss . . ." He tried to see if she wore a wedding ring. "It *is* miss?"

"I'm not married, Mr. O'Keefe, and I do prefer Miss over Ms."

"Fine, Miss Bickham. There will be some changes made. For one thing, I will be working out of this office, not Fairbanks. And I will need an executive assistant, as well as a secretary. Is there anyone suitable in the company, someone with extensive experience? Top salary, the final amount to be negotiated."

"I'll find someone for you, Mr. O'Keefe."

"Then I'll leave it in your capable hands, Miss Bickham. Meanwhile, send someone up to handle the desk outside permanently. Inform all executive VPs that I wish to meet with them tomorrow, both collectively and individually. No excuses accepted. And tomorrow afternoon I also want to meet with all department heads. Three sharp. It has to be tomorrow, Miss Bickham, because I'm flying to Fairbanks on

Wednesday." He pointedly looked at her empty hands dangling by her sides. "Aren't you noting all this down?"

"I do believe that I can remember all that, Mr. O'Keefe," she said coolly.

He threw back his head and laughed. "Fine! I do believe we'll get along, Miss Bickham."

Grudgingly she smiled, then laughed lightly, and he could see her visibly thawing and knew that he had won her over. He felt a flush of pride. Now if he could do half as well tomorrow with the others!

He didn't really know, after lengthy meetings with the executives of the company, whether he had won them over or not, but he did feel that he had earned a measure of their respect.

At first they were all wary, and not overly warm in their welcome, which was to be expected. He also knew from Jeremiah that Will had run a loose ship, letting all the VPs have their heads, unless some problem arose requiring his attention; he never interfered except as a last resort. Even after being elevated to president of the corporation, Cole 98 had remained Will's baby, the oil company receiving most of his attention.

But Chris had studied hard, going through all the reports available to him, and he came to the meetings with a good grasp of the day-to-day operations of all the companies, and the executives were impressed by that.

At the end of each meeting, separately and collectively, Chris left all of them with much the same final word: "There are still a hell of a lot of things I don't know, but I'll learn. I will make mistakes, and when I do, I want to be told about them. Nobody's ass will be scorched for that. On the other hand, I'm going to be more on top of things than Will Cole was, so if there is any sloppiness in any of your operations, tighten it up before I can get around to it, or then I *will* scorch some asses. I have no intention of being a hardnose, but I'm putting all of you on notice that I'm tightening the reins. How much or how little depends on what I learn after a more thorough study."

* * *

On the plane to Fairbanks on Wednesday morning, Chris was reasonably content. So far, it had been much easier than he had anticipated, yet he knew full well that there were many difficult days ahead. If he could make it through the meetings in Fairbanks without his head being handed to him, he figured that he was off to a good start.

He had called Kelly just before boarding the Cole jet and she had given him a bit of good news. Jeremiah had rallied and was out of danger.

"He's a tough old rooster, your grandfather."

"He's all of that, darling. In fact, just an hour ago, he asked how you were doing. I told him that you were under full sail, damn the torpedoes."

"I'm sailing right into the middle of several torpedoes in Fairbanks."

"You'll cope, my darling. When are you returning to Anchorage?"

"Probably this evening."

"Good! I'm flying up this afternoon. I'll have our place ready when you get back."

"How about you, will you be ready for me?"

"Oh, will I! I'll be ready to hop on you the instant you walk through the door."

On the plane Chris smiled to himself. No matter what happened in the end, he would never regret marrying Kelly. He loved her with an intensity that was an ache, a feeling he would never have thought possible.

It was shortly after noon when the jet touched down at the Fairbanks airport. A rental car was waiting for him, and he drove directly to the building downtown where Will had his office.

When he approached the desk of Will's private secretary, a large-busted woman of indeterminate age, with a face as stern and forbidding as a prison matron, she looked up at him with a frown. Chris plucked her name out of his memory.

"Miss Brewster, I'm here to see Will Cole. I'm Chris O'Keefe."

Her brown eyes frosted over. "I'm sorry, Mr. Cole is extremely busy at the moment, and can't be disturbed. Perhaps if you'd care to make an appointment?"

"I don't need an appointment," Chris said amiably enough.

"I'm sure if you'll let him know I'm here..." He pointed a forefinger at the intercom.

She pushed a button and spoke softly into the intercom box, but not too softly for Chris to overhear. "Mr. Cole, *he's* here to see you."

Her lips tightened and she sniffed audibly at the answer she received. "Mr. Cole says he can spare you a few minutes."

As he started past her, Chris said gently, "My name, Miss Brewster, is *Mister* O'Keefe. I really do think it'll be worth your while to remember that in the future."

Will Cole did not get up from behind his desk as Chris came in. With his gray eyes bitter and bleak, he used the big cigar in his hand as a pointer. "O'Keefe, the operator. I guess I underestimated you. Tell me something, operator, did you have all this in mind when you approached me that day out at the pipeline?"

"I'm not here to bandy sarcasm with you, Cole."

"Then why are you here?"

"I'm here to see if we can reach some sort of accommodation. I know you don't like me, I know what you think of me, and the feeling is mutual. In spite of all that, we have to work together now and then. As president of Cole and vice-president of Cole 98, it's necessary."

Will sneered openly. "You won't be president long. You'll fuck up somewhere, and soon. When you do, I'll see to it that you're out. I'm putting you on warning, I intend to fight you."

"Fair enough," Chris said steadily. "So long as it's out in the open. But watch that *you* don't fuck up meanwhile. For instance, stop holding hands with Milo Fanti."

"I don't hold hands with Fanti, never have. But let's suppose I do, what would you do?" Will said, the words a challenge flung down between them.

"I'll fire your ass," Chris said cheerfully. "Jeremiah has given me full authority."

"The old man has gone round the bend." Will thumped his desk. "He's senile and I'm going to see to it that he's so declared in court."

"You won't get anywhere. Jeremiah Cole is far from senile."

"I'd expect you to say that." Will blew smoke.

"To get anywhere, you'd need the support of the family and you won't get it. Not from Kelly, not from Josh."

"Josh, is it? You've gotten to my father, too, have you? You *are* some kind of an operator." Will thumped the desk with his knuckles. "But we'll just see what the courts have to say about whether Jeremiah is competent or not."

"Cole . . ." Chris sighed, scrubbing a hand across his chin. "Why go to all this trouble, dig the hole deeper for yourself? Why not do the job you do best, running Cole 98? You're damned good at that, I grant you that. It's what you like to do, anyway, you know it is. So why involve yourself with the rest?"

"Why?" Will almost spat the word. "Pull into my shell and watch Cole Enterprises fall apart with you running it? Not for a damned minute! Cole is my heritage and I don't want to see it go down the toilet."

"You don't know that it will. I might surprise you."

Will shook his head. "A construction stiff, a goddamned fortune hunter? I predict you won't last a month."

"Then I gather that you don't intend to work with me, that you intend to obstruct me in every way?"

"In every goddamned way I can, operator."

Chris made his voice harsh. "Then watch yourself, Cole. For I sure as hell will be watching you. And if you try anything shady, we'll go head to head."

Will grinned savagely. "Oh, I'd like that, O'Keefe. That's when we'll separate the men from the boys."

Chris locked stares with him for a few moments. Will drew on his cigar and sent smoke billowing toward Chris, obscuring his face.

Tight with anger, Chris wheeled and left the room. Just before he closed the door behind him, he heard Will's taunting laugh.

Going down the corridor past the bank of elevators, Chris got himself under control, smiling slightly. He had come out the loser back there, letting Will get to him. His admiration for the man increased a few notches; whatever else, he was a worthy antagonist.

At the end of the hall he paused before an unmarked door. This was the office Brad Connors used when he had business in Fairbanks, and Chris, having called Juneau before he left Anchorage, knew that Connors was in town. He knocked lightly on the door, then went in when a voice called out. Brad Connors began to frown when he saw who it was. He was behind a desk piled high with papers. He leaned back, his eyes hostile.

"Well, if it isn't the bridegroom," he said with heavy sarcasm. "To what do I owe the pleasure?"

"I thought it was time we had a talk." Chris took the only chair in the room, directly in front of the desk. He lit a cigarette and drew on it gratefully.

"A company legal problem?"

"Not exactly, Connors. Kelly told me about the...uh, relationship between the two of you."

Brad gave a bark of laughter. "Is that what she called it? We had an affair, O'Keefe." He leaned forward, his voice suddenly harsh. "Did she tell you that?"

"She told me, she told me everything."

"And because of that, you're going to see to it that my firm loses the Cole business? Well, I've been expecting it. I think we'll manage somehow without it."

"On the contrary. I have just the opposite in mind." Chris looked the attorney in the eye. "I want to know if you can put the past behind you, if we can work together whenever necessary, without your animosity getting in the way."

Brad shook his head, blinking. "You want to continue using the firm?"

"Certainly. You're the best there is, I've found that out, and Cole will continue to use the best talent available, if I have anything to say about it. Besides, I know that you're in the middle of a couple of legal problems right now. It would be foolish of me to upset matters."

Brad's look turned speculative. "You surprise me, O'Keefe. This is the last thing I expected."

Chris smiled briefly. "I hope to surprise a lot of people along the way. So, will you stay on, continue to represent Cole Enterprises?"

"Since you put it that way, it would be petty of me to refuse."

"Good!" Chris stood up, and said with some hesitation, "Would it be wrong of me to offer to shake hands?"

Brad shrugged. "Why not?" He also stood and extended his hand across the desk. "But don't expect me to say that the better man won. I'm not quite ready for that yet."

Chris laughed. "I think we'll get along, Brad. I'll be running the company out of Anchorage, in case you don't know that already. Fly down some day next week and we'll have a conference."

Outside, the day had turned gray and cold; the morning weather report had mentioned the possibility of the first big snowstorm of the season moving in tonight. Chris hoped that he could finish up here and get back to Anchorage before the airports were socked in. He also wished he'd brought along a mackinaw, or at least a topcoat.

On Second Avenue, he went into Bry Tucker's union building. Tucker was in, but the girl at the desk out front told Chris that he was in a conference.

"I do need to see him, I'm only in Fairbanks for the day. If you'll tell him that the new president of Cole Enterprises wishes to see him, maybe he can give me a few minutes. I promise not to take up much of his time."

After a moment's hesitation she picked up the interoffice phone and spoke into it. She got a look of astonishment on her face. Hanging up, she said, "Mr. Tucker will be right out."

In a moment the office door swung open and two men in construction duds came out, followed by Bry Tucker. He said heartily, "I'll take care of it, guys. That's what I'm here for, right?"

As the two men went past Chris, Tucker's gaze settled on him. He leveled a finger. "You worked the pipeline. Christopher O'Keefe, a dozer operator, right?"

Chris grinned tightly. "Not any more."

"Yeah, I heard the rumor, but wasn't sure I believed it." He motioned Chris into his office, closed the door, and went around behind his desk, an ancient piece of furniture dwarfed by Tucker's big frame as he sat down behind it. He squinted up at Chris. "Come up in the world, ain't you, bozo? That old man on the island must have finally gone round the bend."

"An opinion shared by many people," Chris said dryly, "but I fully intend to prove them wrong."

"Well, what the hell?" Tucker shrugged massive shoulders. "I always like to see my boys come up in the world. When they graduate to management, it's easier to deal with them if they once belonged to my union."

"Not true in my case, Tucker."

"We'll see, we'll see. What can I do for you, Mr. O'Keefe? Not that I'm not honored by a visit from the new president of

Cole." He clasped his hands on the desk, his eyes faintly mocking.

Chris took out a cigarette and lit it before answering, his glance moving around the office. It was the first time he'd been in here, yet he wasn't surprised at its Spartan appearance. Despite Tucker's reputation as a high roller, he was always careful to maintain a "just one of the boys" image with the union members. The only things out of ordinary in the office were several photos of Tucker on the walls, attired in boxing trunks, fists cocked aggressively.

Chris said, "I'm mainly here to acquaint you with the fact that I'm the new president of Cole, the guy you'll have to deal with from now on."

"Well now, I consider that right friendly of you," Tucker said amusedly. "As I recall though, most of Cole employees are nonunion, except your cannery workers. Unless," his smile grew, "you're here to finally agree to the whole company being organized. If so, I call that downright neighborly."

"I'm referring to the pipeline."

"The pipeline? You're as bad as Will Cole." The union boss was no longer amused. "As I told him not too long ago, the only say Cole has in the pipeline is as a member of the consortium, and a damned small member, at that."

"As you very well know, there's a vacuum in relations between the pipeline unions and the oil companies. Any time there are any labor problems, or contract negotiations, the oil companies cave in, no matter how far off the wall your demands are."

"I take that as a compliment, Mr. O'Keefe," Tucker said blandly, "to my abilities as a labor negotiator."

"Bullshit," Chris said bluntly. "They want the pipeline built at any cost and you take advantage of that fact."

"Tell me something, O'Keefe . . ." Tucker propped his chin on his raised hands, his eyes twinkling. "What do you think would happen if you, as head of Cole Enterprises, were to stick your nose into labor negotiations and caused a full-scale strike, shutting down the pipeline? Not only would the big oil companies come down on you, but the federal government would likely intervene, if any strike long delayed the construction of the pipeline. Cole may have clout in Alaska, but you mean shit down in the Lower 48."

"I wouldn't be too sure about that. There's been a hell of a

lot of bad publicity about how things are going with the
pipeline down in the States."

Tucker shrugged. "Most of that has come about through all
the crime."

"I'm doing what I can about that, too."

"Are you now? Promises, promises. I get that line of bull
from Will Cole."

"*This* promise is mine. I've already put the brakes on Milo
Fanti."

Tucker nodded meagerly. "I heard something about that,
but he's only a part of it. But every little bit helps, and on
that score you can count on my cooperation all the way. As for
the rest, we'll have to see, right?"

"Right. I'm just putting you on notice."

"Now I call that downright sporting of you, O'Keefe.
Unfortunately I can't return the favor. It doesn't pay to give
management advance notice of a strike."

"If your demands are reasonable, there won't be any
strikes. That's all I ask."

Tucker spread his clasped hands apart. "Oh, I'm a reasonable man. Everybody says so."

Chris snorted softly, admiring the man's audacity. Having
said what he came to say, Chris nodded. "In your own words,
Tucker, we'll see, right?"

Just as Chris reached the door, Tucker said, "O'Keefe? Are
you still a member of my union?"

"Yeah." Chris looked back over his shoulder. "I haven't had
time to do anything about it."

"Then I would suggest you see about a withdrawal card
before you leave the building." Tucker laughed. "It would
never do for you to sit down at the negotiating table with an
active union card in your pocket, now would it?"

At least he wouldn't have to go through a secretary this
time, Chris reflected with a grin, as he rapped on the door at
the top of the outside stairway.

Milo Fanti, opening the door, gaped at him in astonishment, which was quickly replaced by an angry scowl. "What
the hell? Didn't I warn you never to show up here again?" He
started to shut the door.

Prepared for just such a reaction, Chris shoved with all his strength, slamming the door back into Fanti, sending him reeling back a few steps. His hand darted under his coat.

Chris waved a finger playfully. "You won't need that, Fanti. Besides, it wouldn't look nice for the president of Cole Enterprises to stoop to taking a gun away from a hoodlum like you, now would it?"

Fanti blinked confusedly, but as the impact of Chris's announcement sank in, his hand came out from underneath his coat, empty, and he stared at Chris in disbelief. "You're what? The president of... you couldn't be!"

"Oh, but I am," Chris said cheerfully. "You mean you haven't heard? I thought everybody knew."

"But what happened to...?"

"To Will? I thought you'd be the first one he'd run to." Then he grinned slowly. "But then he wouldn't want you to know right off, would he?"

"That dirty, lousy..." Fanti broke off, his features becoming the usual, expressionless mask. "What do you want here, O'Keefe?"

"I heard from my... uh, sources, that you followed my advice and have been keeping a low profile along the pipeline. I like that, Fanti, it shows you've got good sense. Keep it up and we'll get along fine."

"It wasn't because of you, it was the old man getting the wind up," Fanti said sullenly.

"Same difference. If you become active again, you'll be in deep shit. I'm going to be a busy man and if I have to take time off from more pressing things to devote to your case, I'm not going to be happy, not happy at all."

Face still impassive, Fanti said, "Is that all you have to say, Mr. O'Keefe?"

Chris hesitated, trying to read the mask that was Fanti's face. "I guess that about covers it."

"Then you'd better leave now." Fanti sneered. "Other people besides executives are busy."

Fanti let his fury explode the instant he closed the door after O'Keefe. He slammed his fist repeatedly against the door, obscenities pouring from him in a vicious stream. It was only after the pain inflicted on his hand filtered through the anger that he regained a measure of control.

He almost ran into his office and dialed Will Cole's number.

Cole's secretary said coolly, "I'm sorry, sir. Mr. Cole is not in."

"Don't give me that same run-around," Fanti snarled. "You tell him that Milo Fanti wants to talk to him, or he'll be damned sorry!"

"That's just not possible, Mr. Fanti." She sounded intimidated now. "Mr. Cole left for a week's vacation just a short time ago. He's flown out of the state."

Flown out of the state, or flown the coop? For a moment Fanti was shaken. Then reason reasserted itself. Will Cole had too much at stake to run for a hidey-hole. Then the man's reason became clear to Fanti—he was putting himself out of touch for a few days.

He said, "Where did your boss go?"

"Mr. Cole said Nevada, but not where. He said he'd call and let me know where he's staying."

Frustrated, Fanti banged down the phone. There went the ten grand he'd given Will Cole a couple of weeks ago. At the time he had thought that at least some of it would come back to him through his own tables, but Cole hadn't been in his place once.

As another thought edged into his mind, he picked up the phone and dialed again—Candice's number. He let it ring at least twenty times, but there was no answer. She was with Will Cole, naturally. Fanti decided to demand that Candice get an answering device hooked up to her telephone, so he could at least leave a message.

He got a beer from the refrigerator and swigged it, and his anger gradually receded. As he mulled it over, he was glad he hadn't talked to Cole while he was still hot under the collar. It was better this way. Let the bastard blow the ten on the Reno tables, and on Candice. There was no doubt that he would; Candice would see to that.

Fanti decided to play a waiting game. He wouldn't even contact Will Cole. Eventually Cole would be itching for more dough, and he would come with his hand out. The last time had caught Fanti by surprise and he hadn't taped the transaction. The next time he would and he would have Will Cole by the gonads, have him hooked good.

Cole might no longer be president of Cole Enterprises, but he was still the top man at Cole 98, and the oil company was more involved in the pipeline than the rest of the company, anyway. Cole still had a great deal of clout, and Fanti was confident that he could get the man's cooperation if enough pressure was applied. Even that nutty old man wouldn't want to see his grandson go to the slammer, and he would see to it that the pipeliner backed off as well.

The pipeliner...

Fanti felt his anger boiling up again. Something had to be done about that gink. Fanti sat very still, thinking hard.

Finally he reached for the phone one more time.

The weather had turned really nasty, a chill wind blowing, and the leaden sky was spitting snow. It had been Chris's intention to pay Dwight a short visit before returning to Anchorage, but he settled for a phone call instead.

"Chris! Hey, it's good to hear from you," Dwight said. "Are you in Fairbanks?"

"For the moment, yes, but I'm flying back to Anchorage before everything gets socked in."

"I hope you didn't take it wrong, my not attending the wedding."

"Not at all. I understand."

"Kelly tells me that you are now the big man at Cole."

"Yeah, how about that?"

"I suppose congratulations are in order, but if the past is any gauge, we're going to be at each other's throat before long." Dwight chortled. "But I'll bet it did rasp brother Will's ass, your taking over."

"You might say that. Dwight, there's no need for us to fight each other. I sympathize with many of your aims, and I think we can reach a middle-ground agreement on many things. Just don't go too far."

"Hasn't Kelly told you? I'm not one to compromise."

"Dwight, a part of a loaf is better than none, as the saying goes."

"We'll see, we'll see. At least I think you'll be more inclined to cooperate than with Will."

"How's Gordie? Has he left for the States yet?"

There was a moment's silence before Dwight said slowly, "How did you know he's left?"

Chris swore at himself for asking the question. He said lamely, "I guess he must have told me."

"I don't know how he could have done that since he didn't know himself. I kicked him out of the house and out of SAS."

"Why did you do that?"

"He was back on drugs again. I caught him taking speed. What puzzles me, is where he got the money."

Chris sighed. "From me, Dwight, from me. I gave him a thousand dollars that day at your place."

"A thousand . . . ! What the hell for?"

Chris hesitated for a moment, then decided on the truth. "I got him to sign a statement implicating Milo Fanti in the drug sales along the pipeline. Knowing that Fanti would be after him when he learned, I gave Gordie the money to get out of Alaska, and enough to get started somewhere else."

"You could have let me in on all this," Dwight said coldly. "At least then we could have kept a closer watch on him."

"I didn't want to involve you any more than necessary."

"The thing is, I'm not even sure he left Alaska."

"But he must have. He'd be an idiot to stick around. Fanti would have him killed."

"In some ways Gordie is an idiot, Chris. Anyway, it's done, and I should've rid myself of him long ago. He's on his own now, wherever he is."

"I'm sure he's out of the state by now," Chris said with more conviction than he felt. He was calling from inside a bar on Two Street. Now he turned so he could see out the front window. It was snowing harder. "Dwight, I have to go, if I'm to get out of town before the airport's closed. Whenever you're in Anchorage, drop into my office. I'll always find time for you."

He hung up, fished another dime out of his pocket and dialed the Cole Airlines office at the airport. When the girl manning the phones answered, he said, "This is Chris O'Keefe. I'd like to speak to Jim Carson, please."

"I'm sorry, Mr. O'Keefe, I'm afraid that's not possible. He flew the executive jet out about thirty minutes ago."

Chris grunted. "He did? You mean he returned to Anchorage? He wasn't supposed to do that, he was to wait for me."

"No, not Anchorage. He flew Mr. Cole and . . . he's flying Mr. Cole to Reno. Mr. Cole said he was taking a week's vacation."

"I see." Chris was silent for a moment, his temper stirring. Will must have left the office right after Chris had confronted him. He has a lot of gall, Chris thought, taking off like that without a word to me. He said, "Is there another Cole plane available?"

"I'm sorry, all the executive planes are out, and there won't be a Cole Airlines scheduled flight available until tomorrow."

"How about other commercial flights to Anchorage? Do you know if there's any space available on any of them?"

"All flights to Anchorage are grounded, Mr. O'Keefe. A fifty-knot wind at the airport there. They hope that the storm front may have moved on by tomorrow."

"Shit! Uh, sorry. Thank you very much."

Chris hung up, gnawing on his lower lip in thought, his unhappiness with Will increasing. Then he laughed at himself. No use blaming his plight on Will. Even if the Cole jet was here, it wouldn't be allowed to fly into Anchorage.

He called the apartment in Anchorage. To his astonishment Kelly answered. "Kelly! You made it."

"I got here an hour ago. Good thing, too. I understand the airport's now closed down tight. I'm still shaking. Are you still in Fairbanks, darling?"

"Hell, yes. And you're right, all flights to Anchorage have been canceled."

"Chris, does this mean I won't be seeing you tonight?"

"Looks that way. I'm sorry, sweetheart."

"*You're* sorry? Here I am, all turned on at the mere thought of you. It's been almost a week, you know that?"

"I know, I know," he said dolefully.

They talked for a couple of minutes more, expressions of love that only increased Chris's frustration. After he hung up, he remembered the rental car parked up the street. Why the hell not? Alaskans were used to driving in snowstorms, and he was an Alaskan now, wasn't he? So long as the highway wasn't iced over, he should be able to make it okay. If Kelly, with her terror of flying, could fly up to Anchorage in this weather just to be with him, he owed it to her to make the effort.

The train between Fairbanks and Anchorage only ran two days a week—a twelve-hour journey at best—and this wasn't one of those days. Driving would take all night, maybe longer

Empire

with this weather, but it was better than chewing his nails here in frustration, thinking of Kelly waiting for him.

He reached for the phone to call her again, then decided against it. Let her be surprised.

Fifteen minutes later, with a full tank of gas, he was heading south in the rental car. The highway was two-lane, badly pitted, and the driving conditions were lousy. It was snowing harder now, a white curtain that the headlights only penetrated for about a car length ahead. At least the road wasn't iced over yet, but it could easily be before long—the temperature, in the thirties when he left Fairbanks, was dropping steadily. And if an ice fog formed . . . he shuddered to think of it.

The traffic was sparse, an occasional vehicle, mostly heading north. He kept the speed down; with the visibility such as it was, he could plow right into the back of a slow-moving truck. The windshield wipers kept up a monotonous droning, and it wasn't long before he had to fight to stay awake. He smoked cigarette after cigarette, and opened the window a crack now and then to let the cold air clear his head. He decided before long that he would be wise to drive with the heater off, and suffer the creeping cold.

He had driven some fifteen miles from Fairbanks, and was in a slightly hilly terrain, when he heard a roaring sound behind him. At first he took it for a low-flying airplane, until he glanced up into the rear-view mirror and saw the high beams of a truck coming up fast behind him. It took him a dangerous few moments to realize that the truck was not slowing down or pulling out to go around. Chris lightly touched the brakes, flashing his stoplights. It had no effect.

"Shit!" He tromped on the accelerator, peering ahead through the driving snow, praying there was no vehicle immediately in front of him. After about a hundred yards he risked another glance in the mirror—the truck had fallen back. Chris reduced his speed, relaxing a trifle. Maybe the driver hadn't seen his car in the heavy snow.

Then he saw the truck coming again. This time an air horn blared, and he saw the truck pull over to pass. Breathing a sigh of relief, Chris relaxed even more. The truck drew up alongside, and Chris saw that it was a huge dump truck. There were no markings on the cab door to identify it. To his surprise the truck hung alongside, not pulling on ahead.

Just as Chris prepared to drop back farther, to let the truck go on ahead, he saw the vehicle veer toward him.

He yelled, "You crazy bastard, what's wrong with you!"

The truck careened into the side of the rental with a rending crash of metal. For a moment Chris almost lost control. He fought the wheel. Just as he had his car under control, the truck moved toward him again, motor roaring.

It was an eerie scene, like something out of a science fiction movie—the truck some blind, unreasoning behemoth intent on destruction.

This impression was gone in an instant as the truck banged into the side of his car again, this time much harder. Again Chris fought the wheel, but a second shuddering impact was too much. The car left the road, which dropped off sharply at this point. The car was airborne for what seemed an eternity, and over his own racing motor Chris heard the truck's horn blaring, the sound fading into the night. At the last moment, thinking of fire, Chris switched off the engine.

Then the car hit, nosing down into the opposite bank of the ravine. Chris had willed himself to go limp, but even so the impact drove him forward against the confines of the seat harness, and then his head struck the top of the car.

Light burst in his skull, followed by a blinding pain, and unconsciousness.

Later, he was never sure how long he was unconscious, but he judged it to be only a few minutes. When he came to, all was still and quiet, only the sounds of metal cooling breaking the silence.

Gingerly Chris explored himself. Everything seemed to work—no bones broken, no bleeding anywhere. Even the sore area on top of his head was not bleeding. Almost without thinking, he keyed the ignition. The starter ground, but the motor did not start.

Realizing how stupid it was—if the motor started the car could burst into flames—he unbuckled the seat belt. The door on his side, he noticed for the first time, had opened on impact.

He got out carefully, his boots digging into the soft, wet earth of the bank. The icy wind set him to shivering at once, but it also cleared his head. Orienting himself, he trudged down the bank and up the other side to the highway. Halfway expecting to find the dump truck parked, waiting for him, he discovered the highway deserted. Although it was not yet night, the heavy snow was as effective in banishing light as full darkness.

It was much colder now, and he felt the slickness of ice under his boots on the roadway. He had no choice but to walk; standing here waiting for someone to come along, he could freeze.

Hands jammed into his pockets, cursing himself again for not bringing along a mackinaw, he started walking north. He doubted he could walk all the way to Fairbanks in this storm. His best hope was for a passing motorist, a good Samaritan. Failing that, he had to find an inhabited building, where he could call Fairbanks for help.

An unpleasant thought nudged his mind. Had that accident been deliberate? Had the dump truck been sent after him? No, it couldn't be, he decided. Such thinking led to paranoia. The truck driver must have been drunk. Or half-blind. Or both.

Plodding doggedly along, he was glad that he had not called Kelly to tell her he was driving to Anchorage. If he had not shown up at a reasonable time, she would have been out of her mind with worry.

It was another hour before he reached a house and was able to call for someone to drive him back to Fairbanks.

Twenty-Two

Kelly stood up, stretching tiredly. "That's enough for tonight, darling. Good heavens, it's after midnight!" She looked down at the top of Chris's head. They were in the apartment, and he was seated on the polar bear rug before the fireplace; nesting like a big bird, she thought, with papers scattered all around him.

"In a minute, sweet," he said distractedly. "Are you sure you understand about the acquisition?"

She shrugged. "I understand we're adding another steamer to the line, and we've just bought a tramp from some bankrupt steamship line in Seattle. And I also understand it's going to cost a fortune to refurbish her."

Head still bent, he said, "It'll be worth every penny. Hell, we have more freight business than the rest of our fleet can handle. Passenger business, too, for that matter."

"How about a nightcap, darling? A brandy?"

"Sounds good."

She stood a moment longer, stifling a yawn, gazing fondly down at his bent head. It was January now of the new year, and she was inordinately proud of Chris. The way he had taken over the reins at Cole was little short of incredible. He could have been born to the task. Naturally there had been any number of problems, but so far he had surmounted them, and a little discreet snooping by Kelly had told her that he had gained the respect of all Cole executives, with the exception of Will, of course. Even Brad Connors had admitted, albeit grudgingly, that he had come to respect Chris's ability.

And Jeremiah, still not completely recovered, was bragging proud: "Didn't I say the boy had good stuff in him? He's running things like he was my own blood!"

281

Kelly had commented dryly, "Don't I get any credit for finding him?"

"I'll give you credit when you give me a great-grandson. You just work on that, girl."

They had been active enough sexually, Kelly thought amusedly, recalling with a flush of pleasure their lovemaking. But the question of children hadn't been discussed, and Kelly was careful to stay on the pill. She had played with the idea of getting pregnant. However, she realized that this was not the time to mention having a child. The right time would come.

She was truly amazed by Chris's capacity for work; over the past year he had dug extensively into all phases of Cole Enterprises, exploring each company from top to bottom. He had gone out with the fishing fleet, he had ridden on the steamships plying the coast to Seattle and back, he had labored one whole day on the cannery assembly line, he had flown in every one of the Cole airplanes, and much to Will's displeasure, he had investigated every aspect of Cole 98. He told Kelly: "I have to give your half-brother credit. He's an unpleasant sonofabitch in many ways, but he knows how to run an oil company. The only fault I can find is that he tends to go off for days at a time and let the company pretty much run itself."

During the past few months, Chris had been gone almost as many days as he had been home. Kelly wasn't too happy about that aspect of it, but she didn't complain. With his usual perceptiveness, he had told her: "It won't always be this way, sweet. As soon as I familiarize myself with every phase of Cole Enterprises, I'll be home more. Be patient, Kelly."

She was patient. In fact, one facet of his hectic schedule was almost worth all his absences—the fierce lovemaking that ensued after he had been away for a few days.

Almost without thinking she placed her hand on his head, stroking his thick hair back. He looked up at her with a flashing smile, and winked.

"I'll get the brandy," she said.

He was still at it when she returned with two snifters of brandy. She arranged herself beside him on the rug and gave him one snifter. "Enough already," she said sternly. "You've done enough work for one day. You've put in your eighteen hours."

"You're right, I've done enough."

He spent a few minutes collecting the various papers, stowed them in the ever-present attaché case, and clicked it shut. He sighed, leaned back, and massaged his neck, rotating his head.

He took a sip of brandy, then peered at her over the snifter, a wicked gleam in his eyes. "Did you have something in mind now, Mrs. O'Keefe?"

"Can't a girl talk to her fellow without an ulterior motive in mind?" she asked with an innocent air.

"You always have an ulterior motive in mind, my dear," he said with a Clark Gable grin.

"But you do give a damn, I hope?"

"Oh, I do, I do." He leaned forward to kiss her lightly.

After a moment Kelly cradled his head on her breast and stared dreamily into the flames. She said, "You know, Chris, yesterday, when I stopped in your office, I met your executive assistant for the first time. You do have an eye for a pretty female, don't you?"

He raised his head to stare at her in amusement. "I picked you, didn't I? On second thought, don't answer that. Charlene Baker is a gorgeous lady, I agree. But much as I'd like to take credit for it, I had nothing to do with her selection. Miss Bickham did that. I instructed her to find me an efficient executive assistant, and Charlene is the one she came up with."

"Well, is she?"

"Is she what?"

"Efficient. What did you think I meant?"

"She's damned efficient." He grinned. "And I thought maybe you meant how was she in the sack."

"You!" She picked up a throw pillow and batted him alongside the head.

He laughed, ducking away. "Seriously, Charlene is extremely efficient. I've been having briefing sessions with her, when I have a minute or two to spare, much as I have with you. She has a mind much like yours."

Kelly, remembering what usually occurred after one of their own "briefing sessions," said tartly, "I hope that company business is all you've been briefing her on."

He peered at her solemnly. "Do I detect a hint of green suddenly?"

Kelly felt herself flush. "I suppose I am a little jealous, darling," she admitted. "She is an attractive woman."

He cupped her face between his hands. "I do believe I like it when you're jealous. I suppose I should play it cool and let you stew, but I won't. You have no reason to be the least jealous, my sweet."

He kissed her, and she came against him hard, the housecoat falling open. Lips locked together, they fell back onto the rug, as Chris's hands roamed freely over her body.

As always, it took only his merest touch to ignite her passion, but the intensity of her need surprised even Kelly. And then she realized the cause—her jealousy of Charlene Baker, unwarranted or otherwise, had acted on her like a spur.

Then all thought was blotted out, as Chris folded the housecoat back all the way and stretched her out on her back. He stood, shedding his clothes quickly, his gaze never leaving Kelly's nude figure. She watched him, her heart pounding, her breath coming heavily.

He kneeled between her spread thighs, his hands reaching for her breasts, stroking them, tweaking the tumescent nipples.

"Now, now, now!" she said in a guttural chant.

Silently he went into her with one long thrust, his torso descending on top of her. Kelly rose to meet him, shivering at the exquisite sensation as he filled her. She locked her arms around his neck and brought his mouth down to hers.

Already she was in shuddering transport, moaning deep in her throat. As he began to throb mightily in her, her hips rose in a final great convulsion.

A week later Chris looked across his desk at Charlene Baker, and Kelly's remarks about Charlene came into his mind. All at once he found himself looking at Charlene with new eyes. He had never once thought of her in a sexual connotation, and probably never would have, but for Kelly's brief flare of jealousy. But she was undeniably a damned attractive woman. She wore no-nonsense clothes in the office and had a cool, controlled manner about her, yet Chris realized now, with some astonishment, that there had been moments, moments when they weren't occupied with company matters, when she'd come on to him. Nothing blatant, just subtle signs that Charlene herself may not have realized she was giving out.

Chris hid a smile behind his hand, busied himself lighting a cigarette. Even if he were inclined to pick up on the signals, he would not risk it. Getting involved sexually with an employee, even one in the position Charlene occupied, could result in a messy situation, one that he certainly didn't need.

"Mr. O'Keefe?"

He came to with a start. "I'm sorry, Charlene, I was off somewhere. And isn't it about time we dispensed with the mister?"

Her cool blue eyes studied him gravely. Finally she said slowly, "I suppose you're right... Chris."

"Good! Now, what were you saying a moment ago?"

"I was speaking about this man, Milo Fanti, in Fairbanks."

Chris kept his face expressionless. "How come you know about Fanti?"

She gave a small shrug. "I imagine everybody knows of Milo Fanti. All I know are that rumors have it he's involved in dirty work along the pipeline. The reason I brought his name up, he called yesterday after you'd gone. Alice put him through to me. But he refused to talk to me, said he would only speak to you. He wouldn't even tell me what it was about." She looked at him in speculation. "He spoke as if he knew you, at least he had talked to you."

"I've met Fanti, yes," he said meagerly. Then he felt it necessary to add, "I met him while I was still working on the pipeline."

"Well, I did think it rather strange that a man of that caliber would be wanting to talk to the president of Cole."

For a moment he considered taking her into his confidence, but decided not. Too many people already knew about the connection between Will Cole and Fanti. He said, "He operates gambling establishments in Fairbanks, Charlene. It could be that one of our employees owes him a chunk of gambling money, and Fanti thinks that pressure from me might help him to collect."

"But gambling debts are illegal, aren't they?"

"I scarcely think that would matter a hell of a lot to Fanti," Chris said dryly. "Anyway, I'll return his call. Is there anything else, Charlene?"

"Not at the moment...uh, Chris," she said clearly still uncomfortable with the use of his first name.

"By the way, I'll be out of the office for a couple of days, starting this afternoon. But I'll be in touch with Alice, in case I'm needed for anything."

After Charlene left Chris turned his attention to the more urgent paperwork on his desk. An hour later, he leaned back, lit a cigarette, and let his thoughts turn to Milo Fanti. The last time he'd had any contact with the man had been that day last fall. To the best of his knowledge, Fanti had been keeping a low profile. Chris had checked along the pipeline several times, and there were no reports of criminal activity in the area where Fanti had been operating. Unfortunately the same could not be said for other sections of the pipeline, mainly north out of Valdez, but so far Chris had been unable to make any inroads in that area.

He debated ignoring Fanti's call entirely. The less he had to do with the man, the better. And yet...

He thumbed the intercom. "Alice, Charlene tells me that I had a call yesterday from Milo Fanti in Fairbanks. Did he leave a callback number?"

"Yes, Mr. O'Keefe."

"Buzz him for me, will you, please?"

He drummed his fingers on the desk until he heard the phone picked up on the other end and a cautious, "Yeah?"

"Fanti? Chris O'Keefe, returning your call."

"Oh, yeah! I was wondering..." Fanti cleared his throat loudly. "Well, I was wondering when I could go back in business along the pipeline. Things have cooled down now and I'm losing a bundle every day."

"Now that's tough, I weep for you." Chris gave a bark of laughter. "I do admire your gall, Fanti, after what I told you, asking permission of *me* to start up your cesspool operation again. Why do you think anything has changed?"

"Mr. Cole promised me that as soon as the heat died down, I could..."

"*Mister* Cole has no authority to promise you anything," Chris said, his voice cracking like a whiplash. "I thought I made that very clear. And don't bother going into your routine again. I don't care what you have on him, don't try to intimidate me with it. You peddle one ounce of dope, run one hooker, and your ass is grass. Now, I'm very busy. Goodbye, Fanti."

In his office in Fairbanks Milo Fanti hung up the phone with some smugness. He hadn't expected O'Keefe to accede to his demands, but the call set him up for later when he, Fanti, brought the big gun to bear. And he was going to load and cock it in a very short while.

Yesterday, he'd received a phone call from Will Cole—the first word he'd had from him since the bastard put the touch on him months ago. Cole said he would drop by to see him today. Fanti knew that the man had been snowing him all along. After O'Keefe's last visit, and his ultimatum, Fanti knew that nobody was going to give him the green light; he'd have to do it himself, by putting Cole's balls in the nutcracker and squeezing, squeezing until the guy's screams were heard all the way to Anchorage, and Cole Island.

Fanti had exercised patience, playing the waiting game he was so adept at, waiting for Will Cole to come to him again. He had been surprised that Cole had waited so long, until Candice told him that Cole had gotten lucky in Reno, winning a bundle; but even so, being the plunger, the big spender, that he was, it was to be expected that he would have been on his uppers long before now. Fanti had ordered her to pressure him good, to snap the lock on that pussy of hers if Cole got stingy with her. She had promised to do it, but Fanti had his suspicions about that. She was gone on Will Cole, that had been evident to Fanti for some time.

Well, it didn't make any difference—his patience had paid off. Will Cole was coming and with his hand out, what else? This time the little bug in Fanti's desk would be buzzing away, it would all be on tape, and *then* he would deal with Candice. He didn't like it when a man screwed around with him, but for a broad to do so...

Now that, he would not put up with, no way!

Will Cole breezed into Fanti's office, cigar fuming. The last few months had restored much of his confidence. Much to his surprise, O'Keefe had kept hands off, letting him run Cole 98 as he pleased, and had even given him a back-handed compliment once. Even more to Will's astonishment, and dismay, O'Keefe seemed to be holding his own. Of course things had been running smooth as silk. Wait until he was faced with a real crisis, a make-or-break situation, and then watch him fall on his ass! Then who could the old man, crazy or not, turn to but his own grandson?

Since Will had been behaving himself, maybe Jeremiah's ire would have lessened. Of course he was still gambling and seeing Candice, but the old man wouldn't mind that, so long as it didn't interfere with his job.

Will had to admit that his run of luck at the tables the last few months had been helpful, giving him enough money to satisfy Candice's expensive tastes. But a run of good luck couldn't last forever; last week he'd dropped a bundle and he'd soon be overdrawn at the bank if he didn't come up with a wad, and if that happened and Jeremiah, or O'Keefe, found out...!

But what the hell, a run of *bad* luck couldn't last forever, either. And that was why he was here today. He wasn't really as confident as he appeared; he had nothing to bargain with. Well, he'd bluffed Fanti out of his socks before, he could do it again.

Since Will had phoned yesterday with the time he would arrive, Fanti was expecting him, so he pushed the outside door open without knocking. Will had often wondered why a man in Fanti's business would operate behind an unlocked door. When he'd questioned him about it, Fanti had replied with a small shrug. "It's a matter of my image, Mr. Cole. People think of me as a Mafioso, which ain't true; as a thug, a hoodlum, which ain't true, either. But if I skulked behind some goon carrying a piece, or hid behind locked doors, I would only help *that* image along. But who would believe that about me if I go about my business like any other businessman? Besides—" his look turned sly—"I carry a piece under my arm and I'm good with it. If some nutcase does get it into his noggin to harm me, I've made it known along Two Street that any gink who tries anything will wish he'd never been born. And I'm a fair man, who'd want to kill me? I have no enemies, Mr. Cole."

Will wondered if the man really believed that. Fanti had any number of enemies—any pipeliner, well-liquored, and a heavy loser at Fanti's tables, would kill him without a qualm, given the opportunity.

But if Fanti truly believed his fairy tale, or was pushing the macho image, or was whistling in the dark, whatever, it was his problem, not Will's.

On this visit, Will was greeted by a black scowl when he sauntered into Fanti's office. "Do I know you, sir? Oh, you're Mr. Will Cole. It's been so long, I didn't recognize you."

"Sarcasm doesn't fit you, Fanti." Will grinned. "But you're right, I haven't been in touch as much as I should."

"Should? Not once since the end of last summer, as I recall." Fanti put his hands palms down on his desk. "Not only that, but I haven't seen you playing at my tables."

"Now there, you should consider yourself lucky as hell. I've been on a winning streak. It would have cost you a bundle."

"Was, Mr. Cole, that's the word. The past month you've lost your ass."

Will stared. "How did you know that?"

Fanti sighed. "Mr. Cole, as I told you on that first meeting of ours, I make it my business to know everything about you. Just like I know you've come to me for another handout. Right, Mr. Cole?"

Will nodded slowly, burning at the man's insolence.

"I can't hear you, Mr. Cole. Speak up! At least you can tell me right out."

Goaded, Will snarled, "Yes, goddamnit! I need some money."

"How much this time, Mr. Cole?"

"Uh, ten thousand should tide me over."

"Just like last time, eh? Just what can I expect in return, Mr. Cole? I'm a man who likes value for his money."

A faint uneasiness prodded at Will. Usually Fanti was soft-spoken, why was his voice louder than usual? But the thought of the money made Will's fingers itch, pushing him past caution. He rolled the smoldering Monte Cristo between thumb and forefinger. "The heat is beginning to die down, Fanti. The old man . . . Jeremiah, he's already forgotten about it."

"And the pipeliner, how about him?"

Will waved a hand airily. "Listen, he's in over his head, trying to run Cole. Hell, I give him another month, two at the most, and he's out. And right now, he's so busy fending off the wolves in the company, he has no time for anything else."

Fanti studied him levelly. "That's your considered judgment, is it, Mr. Cole?"

Will nodded. "Pretty much, yeah."

Fanti stared down at his spread hands on the desk. "Let's see now . . . if I pay you the ten thou, I'll be able to set up shop along the pipeline again. Is that it?"

"That's what I just said, wasn't it?" Will said testily

"No, it's not, Mr. Cole," Fanti countered, his voice softer now. "Just say I'm stupid. Spell it out for me. You told me before, after the pipeliner came to see me, that I'd be back in business shortly. It didn't happen."

"How'd I know my sister would be stupid enough to marry him or that Jeremiah would be crazy enough to jump him to head honcho?" Just reciting the indignities heaped upon him made Will's blood boil. He thumped Fanti's desk with his open hand. "When that happened, I had to keep a low profile. But now I can promise you, Fanti, that you can go back in untouched. You take care of me and I'll cover your ass." As he spoke the words, Will knew that he meant it. He'd been dumped on enough, from now on he was out for number one, out for everything he could get. And he could do it! He was smarter, tougher, than Chris O'Keefe would ever be.

Fanti was still staring at him. What he saw must have satisfied him, for he nodded suddenly and got to his feet. "I believe you, Mr. Cole, at least enough to take another chance."

He crossed to the far wall. At the thought of the money and the pleasure it would bring him, Will's blood ran hot, a feeling akin to sexual excitement. He actually felt himself getting an erection.

He watched carefully as Fanti spun the dial. This time he was able to catch the other two numbers and stored them in his memory. Fanti took out a bundle of bills, closed and locked the safe, and returned to the desk. With a contemptuous flick of his wrist, he tossed the bundle into Will's lap.

"Ten thousand, Mr. Cole. Count it."

"No need . . ."

"I insist," Fanti said in a grating voice. "I want no misunderstandings later."

Quickly Will counted, all hundred dollar bills. "It's all here."

"Ten thousand dollars?"

Will said irritably, "Damnit, yes!"

"For services rendered?"

Once again the warning pinged in Will's brain and once again he ignored it. The money in his fist was a potent drug, intoxicating his senses through mere touch alone. "For services rendered, Fanti."

Fanti waited until Will Cole left, then played the tape, listening intently. It was all there, every damning word!

Removing the tape with loving care, he stored it in the safe. Only then did he allow himself a beer. Popping the tab, he consumed it in two long gulps, then opened another.

Will Cole had lied to him, of course—again. Remembering O'Keefe's words just that morning, Fanti knew that he was not about to cooperate with Will Cole willingly. But now he would have to, he had no choice. That tape was enough to send his brother-in-law to the slammer and close the gates on him for quite a while.

Fanti finished the beer and then dialed the Cole Building in Anchorage. When O'Keefe's secretary answered, Fanti, vividly recalling the earlier conversation, covered the mouthpiece with spread fingers and deepened his voice. "This is Will Cole in Fairbanks. I need to talk to O'Keefe. It's important."

"I'll put you right through, Mr. Cole."

Fanti breathed a sigh of relief and waited.

"I hope this is important, Cole," Chris O'Keefe said. "You caught me at a bad time."

"O'Keefe? This is Milo Fanti."

"Fanti?" Chris said in disbelief. "I just talked to you not two hours ago! Where the hell do you get off passing yourself off as Will Cole?"

"Because I knew you wouldn't talk to me otherwise. Don't hang up now. Do and you'll be sorry."

"All right, Fanti. I'll give you two minutes."

"Will Cole just left my office here. I handed him ten big ones. In return he promised to open the pipeline to me again."

"Fanti, how many times do I have to tell you this? I don't give a rat's ass."

"I haven't told you all of it. I've got it all on tape."

"So? How does that change things?"

"He accepted a bribe from me, don't you see? That's a criminal offense. If you don't back off from me, I'm going to see to it that the old man gets a copy of the tape. If that doesn't do it, I'll send a copy to the *Daily News-Miner*, and to the cops."

"For the last time, the *very* last time, Fanti, let me try to set you straight. First off, you can't get to Jeremiah Cole, no way in the world. If you did manage, by some miracle I can't imagine, I'd kill you myself. Secondly, go to the papers or the cops, I couldn't care less. I can't seem to get through to you... Will Cole is expendable. He's fucked up too many times, I won't put up with it any more. And when I say *I*, I'm speaking for Jeremiah, and Cole Enterprises. And one more thing, something it seems you haven't thought through. Offering and paying a bribe is as much a crime as accepting one. Now, I sincerely hope that I've heard the last word from you, asshole."

The crash made by O'Keefe banging up the phone hurt Fanti's ear, but he sat for a moment with the receiver to his ear, a great rage building in him. It was too much, he couldn't take it any more!

Quickly he dialed Candice's number. When she answered, he said without preamble, "It's time to cut Will Cole down to size."

"What do you mean?"

"What I mean is, he just walked out of here with ten grand of my money, and I then learned I might have flushed it down the toilet for all the good it'll do me. Now here's what you're to do. Pack your bags, leave a message for him on that answering machine of yours, don't talk directly to him. I don't care what the message is, just let him know you've left for parts unknown, no return address. In short, it's all over, no more pussy for Mr. Will Cole, and no way he can find you."

A cry of distress came from her. "Milo, I can't do that, not that way! It would kill him."

"I doubt that very much. But if it does, fine and dandy. Just do it, bitch, don't argue with me!"

"Milo, please..."

"No please," he snarled. "Just do what I say or you'll be found in the Chena River. I brought you up here to do a job on him. You did fine, I'll grant you that, but you were paid well, and you got your kicks. Now the party's over. Forget you ever knew Mr. Will Cole and get your tail out of Alaska. No later than tomorrow!"

He hung up over her protesting voice, and immediately dialed another number, this time in Anchorage.

When a man's voice answered, Fanti said harshly, "I want Chris O'Keefe taken out as soon as possible. And this time I don't want any screw-ups, understand?"

After Fanti's call, Chris sat for a few minutes at his desk, ruminating. While it was true that he wasn't about to knuckle under to Fanti's demands, no matter what Will had done, he was nonetheless depressed by Fanti's news. He didn't doubt that Fanti had the tape; he had been more or less expecting something like this. But if it all came out, it would create a stink that would rub off on all of them. He felt sorry for Josh, even sorrier for Jeremiah. If it did happen, they would have to keep it from the old man at any cost; it wouldn't be easy.

Chris smoked, brooding. Finally he straightened up, cheered by one thought. What he had told Fanti was true. If the man turned the tape over to the newspapers or the police, he would be as liable for criminal charges as Will. For that reason, Chris was positive that Fanti, once he thought it through, would sit on the tape.

However, this was the end for Will Cole. He had to do something about him. If Will was this flagrant, sooner or later he would do something that could not be covered up. Chris sighed. Will had to be removed, kicked out of the company completely; there was no alternative.

But it would have to wait a couple of weeks. Something was taking place on Cole Island over the next two days—a TV crew was due to interview Jeremiah concerning his one-hundredth birthday, although it was still ten days away. The old man was still under the weather; the bout of pneumonia had weakened him considerably.

Chris grinned, remembering what Kelly had told him. Everyone had been surprised that Jeremiah had even consented to the interview. He had always scorned most interviews, but he had a special loathing for television—"Fodder for idiots"—and never watched it.

"But he said he thought it might be nice if the family had him on film. If nothing else, to show his grandchild some day. Yours and mine, darling," Kelly had told Chris. "The interviewer wanted to do it on Grandfather's birthday, but he said he would be too busy celebrating to be bothered with such a dadblamed nuisance as a blathering TV interviewer."

Kelly had flown down to Cole Island last night, so she could be there during the interview, the only one of the family present. Josh was in Washington, and Chris knew that if he was there, he would likely draw attention away from the main subject of the interview. So far, he had managed to duck most media interviews. The publicity he had received *without* interviews was bad enough: "Boy Wonder at the helm of Cole Enterprises!"; "Former pipeliner now directing Cole!"; "Many in the business community predicted Chris O'Keefe would flop as Cole president, but he has confounded all critics!"

Anyway, he couldn't do anything about Will until after the interview was aired, which was scheduled on Jeremiah's birthday. If Will was fired now, he'd be certain to raise a fuss and that could well overshadow the interview. After that was aired the stir created by Will's discharge would not have as much impact.

Chris intended to make himself unavailable for the next two days, just in case the media approached him for a comment to include in the TV segment. There was something he had been intending to look into for some time, but the weather had been too lousy until this week. Yesterday, the weather had shown a warming trend—if a temperature hovering around twenty degrees could be considered warm.

One of the recommendations he had received from a consensus of Cole executives had concerned setting up a real estate division of Cole Enterprises, not just office buildings and commercial structures, but farmland as well. The prospectus had predicted that Alaska was in for a big agricultural boom. It was not common knowledge down in the Lower 48 that Alaska had a potential for agriculture. The season for growing crops was short—from eighty to one-hundred-twenty days a year—but the long hours of summer sunlight, plus the subirrigation given off every summer by the thawing of the frozen ground underneath were a great advantage.

The agricultural possibilities were discovered in 1935, during the Depression years, when poverty-stricken farmers in the United States migrated to Alaska's Matanuska Valley north of Anchorage in search of a better life. Over the years since, the farming acreage had steadily increased, and other areas had opened up, until now well over a million acres of land were under cultivation.

Since it was Chris's intention for Cole Enterprises to diversify more and more in the future, now was a good time to begin. Although not cheap by any measure, it was his understanding that there were many acres of productive land not yet under cultivation in the Matanuska Valley, and this was the time to buy. Certainly it would never get any cheaper, not with the oil money ready to pour into the state.

Two hours later, after a brief stop at the apartment, Chris drove north out of Anchorage, bound for Matanuska Valley, where "cabbages as large as basketballs" were commonplace. He was driving a company vehicle this time, a high-wheeled Scout, with snow tires and everything else necessary in the event the weather changed suddenly and drastically, which was not at all unusual. On the driver's door was a decal: the capital letters CE, enclosed in a circle.

The valley, when he reached it, was covered with a blanket of snow, with nothing green in sight, but Chris knew that it had a look almost tropical in the middle of summer, when garden vegetables grew in profusion, all of an amazing size. Enough produce was grown here not only to supply Alaska's population, but much of it was being shipped to the Pacific Northwest and other points in the Lower 48. And that was one reason he had decided to involve Cole in agriculture. They would have a big advantage over the other growers. With their own shipping line, they could move produce down to the Northwest far more cheaply than the other farmers in the area.

The weather remained clear but cold and by the time he was ready to find a place to spend the night, Chris had inspected several tracts of potential farmland. A rough, preliminary survey had been made, and he had a map along showing the possible sites. Naturally it would be more convenient to purchase the acreage in a large chunk. All the sections he had so far inspected were smaller than he would like.

Now he was approaching what he decided would be the

last stop for the day. It was by far the largest area he had inspected, and well up the valley. He had passed the last farmhouse some miles back, and the land was a little rougher here, covered with shrubbery and some small trees. He pulled the Scout off the road and parked. By the dashlight he studied the map for a few minutes.

It was really too dark to do a thorough investigation, but since he was here, he decided to walk over a few acres; he could at least get the feel of it, and if he liked what he saw, he would return tomorrow and do a more thorough inspection.

From habit, he took the keys from the ignition. Then, lighting a cigarette, he got out of the Scout and walked down into a gully alongside the highway and up the other side. It hadn't snowed for almost a week, and a hard crust had formed on the surface of the snow, so the walking wasn't too bad. A hundred yards from the highway, he glanced back; he could no longer see the road or the Scout, but he could still hear the occasional car or truck passing.

He plowed on for another hundred yards. Soil samples had been taken here during the preliminary survey, and had shown up well. From what he could see, it would appear that not too much effort and money would need to be expended to clear the terrain and prepare it for planting. At his feet where he had stopped just the top of a shrub protruded from the thick layer of ice and snow. He bent down to tangle his fingers in the brown tendrils of the plant and tugged, not really expecting it to come loose from the earth.

A sound like the whine of an angry insect whistled over his head, followed immediately by a sharp, cracking sound. He looked back between his spread legs and saw, back on the bank of the ditch he had crossed, the dark bulk of a figure kneeling. Viewed this way, upside down and between his legs, there was a bizarre aspect to the figure.

At the same instant the meaning of what had just happened flashed to his brain—someone was shooting at him! He was already in motion before the thought was fully completed, throwing himself to the ground and rolling, just as another bullet puffed up snow from where he had stood a second ago.

He kept rolling, toward a frozen hump a few feet away, probably a clump of bushes covered with ice and snow. He rolled behind it, hugging the ground, as he heard the rifle crack yet another time.

His thoughts churned frantically. What was this all about? Could it be some hunter, mistaking him for game? He dismissed that notion at once. It was no mistake; he, Chris O'Keefe, was the target—someone was out to kill him. He flashed back on the dump-truck driver who had run him off the road. He had finally decided that the truck driver had either been drunk or a maniac, and then dismissed it. He had told no one about the incident, not even Kelly.

There was no dismissing it this time. Somebody was intent on killing him, and now he was sure this was the second attempt. Who was behind it? He had stepped on some toes since becoming president of Cole, but had he angered someone enough to bring about a murder attempt?

Milo Fanti popped into his mind. The other time he had infuriated Fanti, and an hour later had almost been killed. And just this morning he had angered Fanti again. Fanti would be the obvious choice. But Chris knew he couldn't prove it; and if it *was* Fanti, with all the hoods at his disposal, it meant that he, Chris, would have to look behind every bush from this time forward. His life would be in danger every moment. . . .

A bullet thudded into the other side of the mound, sending a shower of ice and snow into his face. Now was not the time to wonder who, now was the time to figure out a way to get out of this in one piece.

He assessed his options. On the face of it, he had none. Unarmed, he was pinned down here, helpless as a bug, and the rifleman could stalk him at his leisure.

He glanced to his right and then the left. Running to his right, into a growth of stunted pines, was a shallow depression, probably formed by water erosion. It wasn't too deep but it offered some concealment. If he could make it into the trees, which were about forty yards away, he might be able to circle back to the highway and the Scout. If there was some way of distracting the rifleman for a few moments . . .

It had grown darker now, but the question remained, did the added darkness offer much aid? The rifleman must have a night scope on his weapon, or he wouldn't have been able to home in on him. If he had not bent to pluck the shrub at that precise instant . . . Chris shuddered. He would be dead now, his brains scattered over the snowy ground.

He realized that it had been several minutes since the

rifleman had fired. He was probably waiting for Chris to show himself. And that gave him the glimmering of an idea. It wasn't much, but it just might distract the man long enough.

Careful not to show himself above his skimpy shelter, Chris wormed out of the mackinaw. The cold began to seep through his shirt immediately. Shivering, he bundled up the mackinaw, and threw it into the open, several feet to his left. Without waiting for the rifleman's reaction, he squirmed to his right, belly down, along the shallow depression, pulling himself along as quickly as possible by digging his fingers into the snow crust.

Before he had gone one body length, the rifle cracked. Chris tensed himself for the impact of a bullet, before he realized that he would have felt it before hearing the shot. Again, the rifle fired. At least the mackinaw had fooled the rifleman temporarily. But for how long? Would he be able to ascertain that the mackinaw wasn't a body, or would he come closer to investigate? Chris needed a few minutes' lead time.

He squirmed on, expecting discovery any second. Then he was into the small growth of trees, none much higher than his shoulders. Without pausing for breath, he came to his feet, and running half bent over, he hurried toward the road, circling a hundred yards south, so that he would come onto the road beyond where the rifleman was located.

The trees grew close together, and Chris careened off several, almost losing his balance. The disturbance his passing caused sounded unnaturally loud in his ears, and he was certain that his flimsy ruse would be discovered any moment. Just as he burst out of the trees on the lip of the gully, he heard the rifle crack again.

He lost his balance and tumbled over twice to the bottom of the ditch. Without getting to his feet he scrambled up the incline and gained the road. An empty car was parked right in front of him. He spotted a rental decal on the windshield.

He hesitated for an instant, then decided to risk it. The door was unlocked. He opened it, found the hood release and jerked it. He lifted the hood and groped under it, his fingers stiff and clumsy from the cold. Even with all the exertion his teeth chattered from the cold. He finally closed his fingers around a handful of wires. With one powerful jerk, he tore them loose. Turning, he threw the wires as far as he could into the trees he had just run through.

Then he ran all-out toward the Scout a hundred yards away. Breath sobbing, heart laboring, he collapsed against it, fumbling in his pocket for the keys. The road was empty of traffic at the moment. As his hand closed around the keys, he heard a shout behind him. Throwing open the door, Chris jabbed the key frantically at the ignition. It went in on the second try. As the starter ground, he risked a glance up into the rear-view mirror and saw a figure running hard at the Scout, the rifle bobbing up and down. The motor caught. Without ever taking his eyes from the mirror, Chris engaged the gears and floored the accelerator. Behind him he saw the rifleman drop to one knee, the rifle coming up.

The Scout was underway, fishtailing from the tire-squealing start, which probably saved his life. Crouched over the wheel, making himself as small a target as possible, Chris heard a thudding sound as a bullet whistled through the rear window. The angle was slightly upward, and the bullet thumped into the top a few inches to the right of his head. Looking into the mirror again, he saw a flash of rifle fire, but the second bullet missed entirely, and now he was drawing steadily out of range. Thankful there was no traffic, he whipped the speeding Scout left and right. And then he topped a slight rise and was down the other side, and the rifleman was out of sight.

With a shuddering sigh of relief, Chris sat up, reducing his speed. He lit a cigarette with shaking hands. Realizing that he was freezing, he turned the heat on full, but it was several minutes down the road before his shaking stopped. Fortunately the back window had not shattered; the rifle bullet had only made a puckered hole.

He drove at a steady pace toward Fairbanks, thinking hard. He didn't dare head back toward Anchorage. The car might be temporarily disabled, but the man was sure to be on the alert for a Scout coming back his way.

Chris considered calling the police, but even if they caught the man who had tried to kill him, Chris was sure he was only a hireling; and if he was to live with any peace of mind and move about unhampered, he had to get the man behind it all. If the police were brought in, they would likely want to provide him with police protection around the clock. How could he function in such a restricted routine? He determined to ferret out the culprit himself. It had become personal now; he longed to get his hands on the person responsible. How to proceed, was the question. He had to think it through carefully.

One fact was starkly clear—he had been incredibly lucky twice now. That luck could not run forever. As the saying went, three strikes and out!

Twenty-Three

Kelly was exasperated. The taping session was not going well.

Jeremiah was being difficult, of course; that was to be expected. But it was as if, after agreeing to the interview, he had now decided that it was a mistake, and he was making it as difficult as possible. He had not completely recovered—and never would, the doctors said—and he used his health as an excuse for his recalcitrance, a whining querulousness totally unlike him.

However, the interviewer, a dapper, cocky young man named Clive Palmer, was also making it difficult. "A young smart-ass," Jeremiah grumbled in an aside to Kelly.

The interview was being conducted in the baronial hall. The hot, blinding light, the tiny microphone clipped to his lapel—the physical requirements of the interview were reason enough for Jeremiah's complaints. But Palmer's badgering questions irritated the old man the most. Whenever Jeremiah launched into one of his anecdotes about the past, Palmer would interrupt him with impertinent questions, questions about his reputation for wildness in his younger days.

Palmer said, "There is a rumor, Mr. Cole, that you left a young wife behind in the States, when you came to Alaska in 1898, and that you never bothered getting a divorce when you remarried. Is there any substance to that rumor?"

Jeremiah glared. "What the goddamned hell does that have to do with the price of apples, young fellow?"

"Cut, cut!" Palmer snapped. "Hold the camera. Mr. Cole, you promised not to use any more profanity. We can't have that on tape."

"Then stop asking asshole questions!" Jeremiah snarled.

Kelly hid a smile behind her hand. She was unhappy at the

way the interview was going, yet she was delighted to see
that Jeremiah was still capable of holding his own.

Palmer sighed, scrubbing his knuckles across his skull,
disturbing the elegantly styled brown hair, and looked up at
Kelly in appeal. "Mrs. O'Keefe, *please!* Can't you order him
to tone down his language?"

"You don't *order* Grandfather to do anything. Besides, he's
getting tired. You've been at it over two hours now."

"And I'm lucky if we have two minutes of usable tape," he
said sourly.

"That's your problem, Mr. Palmer. When I gave my ap-
proval for this interview, I made the ground rules clear.
When he got tired, that was it. You can get a fresh start in the
morning. You knew it couldn't be done in one day. There're
comfortable quarters here for you and your crew, plenty to
eat and drink."

Palmer shrugged, then turned an ingratiating smile on her.
"Perhaps you might like to join me for a relaxing drink or
two?"

She froze him with a withering look. "Food and drink, I
provide, Mr. Palmer, but not entertainment."

"Just a friendly suggestion," Palmer said with a wounded
air.

Kelly was already crossing the room to Jeremiah's wheelchair. He was slumped, eyes closed, face gray with fatigue.

"Are you okay, Grandfather?"

He didn't answer until she had wheeled him out of the
room and started down the hall to his bedroom. "I'm okay,
girl. It's just that young whippersnapper, he grates on me like
sandpaper."

"It's the breed, Grandfather. They're all like that. They
figure that if they can rattle you, they'll drag something juicy
out of you in a moment of anger."

"Fooled 'em, didn't I?" Jeremiah gave a bark of laughter.

"You sure you want to go through with this? We can always
send them packing."

"And have that young pup think he got the better of me?
Nope, I can handle him. If word got around that the interview was called off, people would really think I'm round the
bend."

                    *   *   *

After driving most of the night, Chris stopped at a motel on the outskirts of Fairbanks, getting a room by bribing the woman at the desk outrageously. On the offchance that the rifleman might have gotten his car working and might come cruising along, looking for a Scout parked at a motel, Chris drove the vehicle up a residential street two blocks away and parked it.

He was emotionally and physically exhausted, yet he doubted that he would sleep much. There was too much on his mind; he still hadn't decided which way to jump. It was close to five o'clock when he stretched out on the bed, setting his watch alarm for eight o'clock.

He dozed off and on, coming awake from time to time with a violent start, his heart pounding, ears straining for the sound of a rifle shot. Once, in a shallow sleep, he dreamed that the door had crashed open, a dark, faceless figure looming in the doorway, a rifle coming up to bear.

At a few minutes after eight, he called his office in Anchorage, asking for Charlene.

"Chris, I've been trying to find out where you went! Don't you know that a man in your position should never be completely out of touch?"

"Never mind that." His voice was sharp with apprehension. "What's wrong? Why did you need to get in touch?"

"Brad Connors called yesterday from Fairbanks, after you'd left the office. There's a problem with the drilling crews up at Prudhoe Bay. It seems there's been labor unrest for quite some time, and Bry Tucker is up there now, working on organizing them. According to Mr. Connors, they're going to join up, unless somebody comes up to settle their grievances."

"That's Will's bailiwick."

"He seems to be unavailable, as of yesterday afternoon, anyway. And, again according to Mr. Connors, Mr. Cole appears to be a big part of the problem. It seems that this situation has been building and Mr. Cole was told about the grievances and warned that the men might organize if their grievances weren't settled. He told them that their complaints weren't legitimate, and if they joined the union, they'd all be fired."

"Hoo boy! Diplomatic as ever!" He was silent for a moment, thinking. "All right, Charlene. Run down Jim Carson for me. He's probably home, he's always on standby. Tell him to fly the jet to the Fairbanks airport. I'm in Fairbanks now. I'll be flying up there . . . wait, tell him to call this number before he leaves Anchorage." He read off the motel phone number. "I'll be here for another hour at least. Also call Brad Connors. He's in Fairbanks, you say?"

"He said he'd remain there until I could contact you."

"Then call him, tell him to meet me at the airport coffee shop at ten sharp. He can brief me there."

"What if Mr. Cole gets in touch?"

"Tell Will Cole to get stuffed. I'll handle it. Goodbye for now, Charlene. I'll call you."

He hung up the phone and went into the tiny stall shower. His mind was jumping with ideas and he stayed in the shower for a considerable time, thinking of pros and cons, of alternatives. He had dried himself and was standing before the mirror, thinking of shaving, when the phone rang. He decided to forego shaving for the day and went to answer the phone. It was Jim Carson calling. He had a brief conversation with the pilot. Afterward, he got dressed, and a glance at his watch told him that he had about thirty minutes before his meeting with Brad Connors.

He sat down on the bed, picked up the phone, and called Cole House.

They had gotten an early start this morning with the taping, and it was going well this time. A night's rest seemed to have relieved everyone's tensions. Even Jeremiah was amiable, and Palmer was a little more careful with his questions. Most of his queries now concerned Jeremiah's early days in Alaska, and Jeremiah was at his raconteur best, sharp and to the point, rambling hardly at all. Kelly had no prior experience with which to judge, but she realized from the rapt expressions on the faces of the crew, who must have seen it all, that his tales even engaged their attention.

Palmer was also intrigued. "Let's have a ten-minute break." He turned an enthused face to Kelly. "This is great stuff, great! It's living history. Your grandfather would have made a great actor."

Kelly merely nodded, looking at Jeremiah in time to catch his sly wink. Ham would be more like it, she thought with amusement; Jeremiah had been putting on his act for the members of the family for as long as she could remember.

The telephone rang and she went to answer it.

"Kelly? Hi, sweetheart."

"Chris! Darling, where are you? I expected you to call me last night."

"I was rather, uh, busy," he said guardedly. "I just didn't have a chance to call, Kelly, until long after you were in bed."

"Where are you?"

"In Fairbanks."

"But I thought you were going to inspect the Matanuska Valley?"

"I was there," he said tersely, and changed the subject. "How is the interview going?"

"Not too badly today." She looked back over her shoulder and saw they were about to start taping again. "In fact, pretty good. Yesterday was a disaster."

"Kelly, the reason I called . . . I'm flying up to Prudhoe Bay shortly. There's some kind of labor trouble up there and I have to handle it. The thing is, I may be gone . . ."

"Oh, darling, must you?" she said in dismay. "Can't Will handle it?"

"It seems he messed up somehow."

"How long will you be gone?"

"Since I'm not exactly sure what the problem is, I can't even hazard a guess. Kelly . . ." He cleared his throat hesitantly. "Kelly, last night I . . ."

Palmer's voice interrupted him. "Mrs. O'Keefe? We're ready to roll again."

"Be right there," she said with a wave of her hand. "Darling, I'm being paged, they're starting the interview again."

"All right. Kelly?"

"Yes, darling?"

"I love you, don't ever forget that."

"I love you, too, darling, you know I do."

It wasn't until she had hung up and was halfway back across the room that it occurred to her that something hadn't been *quite* right about the conversation. Chris had sounded . . . what? Harried? Well, yes, but he often sounded harried when in the middle of a company crisis. Afraid? Chris afraid? No, that wasn't quite it, either. What had he been saying when Palmer interrupted. "Last night, I . . ." Last night, what? Had something happened last night?

Her step slowed and she turned to go to the bar and call him back. Then she remembered—he hadn't told her where he was calling from. Anyway, it couldn't have been too important, or he would have finished telling her despite the interruption.

As she sat down outside the circle of light, Palmer was saying, "Now, Mr. Cole, you've told us about the gold strike in the Klondike. Fascinating, I must say. But how about the discovery of gold at Fairbanks?"

Jeremiah got a dreamy look on his face. "Well, sir, there was this Irish fellow, couldn't read nor write . . ."

Across the room the telephone rang. Kelly's first thought was to let the help answer it. Then she changed her mind; it might be Chris calling her back. She hurried to the bar and scooped up the phone just in time to hear the maid say, "Cole House."

"I've got it, Betty. Hello? This is Kelly O'Keefe."

"Kelly," said Will Cole's exasperated voice, "where the hell is that husband of yours? He ain't in his office and those idiots over there claim they don't know where he is."

"He's flying up to the drilling rigs, doing *your* job. He's probably already left. There's some kind of trouble up there."

"I know about the trouble up there, damnit! That's why I'm calling."

"If you knew about it, why aren't you up there handling it?"

"Because I was told to stay out of it, I'm not wanted up there."

Kelly laughed shortly. "That must really gall you, huh, Will? Chris having to do your job for you. Now, if that's all, Will, I'm busy here."

She hung up as he started to snarl, and hurried back across the room.

Jeremiah was just finishing up his tale of how he had made his gold strike near Chena. Palmer motioned to the cameraman. "Hold it a minute, will you, Pete?"

Kelly sat down beside him, as he scanned the yellow notepad in his lap. She looked at Jeremiah, who had closed his eyes against the strong light. She began to perspire immediately under the heat of the lights, but there were no beads of sweat on Jeremiah's brow. She remembered his telling her once that he was always cold nowadays. She said, "Are you about finished, Mr. Palmer? Grandfather is getting tired."

Without opening his eyes, Jeremiah said, "I'm fine, girl. Don't fret about me."

Palmer said, "Just about finished here. Just a couple more questions, sir." Putting on his sincere expression as he would don a mask, Palmer said, "You have lived a full and interesting life, Mr. Cole. On this, the occasion of your hundredth birthday, looking back on your long and full life, do you have any regrets? Or . . ." Palmer grinned engagingly, "do you have any words of wisdom for our viewers out there?"

"Regrets?" Jeremiah snorted softly. "Nary a one. I've done what I set out to do, to build an empire for me and mine. Words of wisdom? Just this . . . work hard, play hard. Whatever a man does with his life, he should give it everything he has in him. If there's one thing I've learned in this life, don't be a loser." As he spoke, Jeremiah sat upright, his hawklike face set in that fierce and indomitable expression. But as the words came out, he slumped, eyes closing, the very life force seeming to drain out of him.

Palmer gestured to the crew. "That's it, guys. And cut the lights."

As the blazing lights were switched off, Kelly went at once to the wheelchair. "Grandfather?"

"I'll be all right, girl. But you'd better wheel me down to my room now."

As she started to wheel Jeremiah out of the room, Kelly heard Palmer say in an aside to his assistant: "Let's just hope the old guy lives through his birthday, when we run this segment. Otherwise, this whole gig may be a waste."

Seething, Will banged the receiver down, after Kelly hung up on him. Sister or not, she was turning into a real ball-buster. He was strongly tempted to call her back and chew her out, but it would only degenerate into a shouting match.

He lit a cigar. This was not his week. When he'd heard about the labor trouble at the drilling rigs, he had been prepared to fly up and handle it. But then he'd been told that his presence there would not be welcomed, would only make matters worse. That had really galled him and he had thought of flying up anyway. Once, he would have, but the situation was changed now.

He felt hamstrung, helpless as a babe. It went against his grain to stand idle when action was demanded. Yet it *would* be a mistake to fly up now, with O'Keefe already there. It would never do to have a head-to-head with O'Keefe before the drilling crews. It would only give them another card to play.

All of a sudden he began to grin, blowing smoke. Let O'Keefe try to solve it and see how far he'd get! Perhaps this was the situation he'd been hoping for; this just might be the one that showed the operator up for the inefficient bastard that he was.

He laughed aloud, and thought of all that money he'd conned out of Fanti. Before this problem had surfaced yesterday, he had intended to call Candice and ask her to go to Reno with him. Flashing all that cash before her would light up her eyes like a pinball machine going wild!

Now he was free to go ahead; he would be completely out of touch for at least a couple of days. Let O'Keefe fall on his ass and come bleating to him for help! If they couldn't find him to iron out the mess, Will figured, maybe he'd finally get some of the appreciation he so richly deserved.

Using his private phone, he punched out Candice's number, his blood already running hot as he anticipated the sound of her husky voice. One ring, two, then a clicking sound: "Will, if this is you, you're listening to a recording. I'll call you at eleven A.M. sharp, Wednesday. I'll call on your private line. Do not leave a message." A second click and he heard only silence. He stared at the receiver in astonishment. When had she installed an answering machine? He hung up, then punched her number again, and once more listened to the recording.

He glanced at his watch. He had thirty minutes to wait. He didn't like it, not any of it. Something was wrong, he just knew it! A feeling of dread seized him.

He lit a fresh cigar and paced, finally going to the bar to splash bourbon over ice cubes, his hand trembling as he poured. It was early for a drink, but he needed it. He drank, pacing.

At eleven on the dot, his phone rang. He snatched it up. "Candice? Is that you?"

"Yes, Will, it's me." Her voice sounded faint and unsure, not at all like her.

"What the hell's going on?"

"I only have a few minutes, Will. My plane leaves in fifteen minutes."

Shock hit him like a dousing of ice water. "Your *plane!* Where are you going?"

"I can't tell you that. I'm not even supposed to talk to you. I was just supposed to leave a farewell message on the answering machine. But I couldn't do that to you."

"Who told you not to talk to me?"

"Milo Fanti. I suppose it doesn't hurt to tell you, since you're going to learn anyway."

"Learn what? Make sense. Candice, what is this shit?" All at once, he knew and he felt empty and desolate.

"I've been working with Milo all this time, Will. Or for him, however you want to put it. He sent for me to come up here."

There was such a roaring in his head that he could barely hear her.

"The thing is, Will, I never wanted to hurt you. You must believe that. It was not like the other times, the other men. I'm sorry for all that's happened. I know you'll never forgive me, but I never expected to come to care for you this much." She broke off for a moment, then said, "There's the final call for my flight. Goodbye, Will." Suddenly her voice sounded choked with tears. "I'll never forget you, please believe that."

Then she was gone, only the hum of the empty line in his ear, but Will sat on for some time. Gradually he came out of the gray fog of shock, a great fury driving him out of it. He had never known such a terrible rage, it seemed he was swelling physically with it, until he was in danger of exploding.

Milo Fanti had screwed him royally. All the time he had been manipulating him, like a puppet on a string! How could he have been so stupid as to let it happen? But that wasn't important now; first and foremost, Fanti had to pay, pay with his life. He was going to kill the sonofabitch. The thought of possible consequences never entered Will's head.

Suddenly his stomach heaved, and he barely made it into the bathroom. On his knees before the bowl, he vomited

until his insides felt like an open wound. Getting weakly to
his feet, he splashed cold water on his face. He looked into
the mirror and saw a white, suddenly gaunt face, and dull
eyes like twin bruises.

He thought of Candice. Even knowing of her perfidy, he
ached for her, and he knew that he always would. He had
never cared for a woman as he had Candice. He managed to
force her from his mind, and concentrated again on Milo
Fanti.

His fury consuming him like a fire, he plunged from his
office and barged past a startled Cora Brewster without
sparing her a glance.

By early afternoon the TV crew had all left Cole House,
and Jeremiah was napping in his room. The house was quiet
for the first time in two days and Kelly welcomed it. She built
a roaring fire in the baronial hall, and settled down with a
drink. She hadn't realized how much tension she had been
laboring under, worrying about how Jeremiah would stand up
to the interview. But everything had turned out well, and if
what she had seen was what was aired, it should be well
received. Jeremiah should be pleased when he saw it on his
birthday. She recalled what she had overheard Palmer say.
Grandfather *had* to live beyond his birthday, he just had
to . . .

The telephone rang. She glanced at it in irritation. She had
answered the blasted telephone enough! But there was always the chance that it was Chris.

With a sigh she went to answer it.

"Kelly? This is Brad Connors."

"Brad! How nice of you to call. Too bad you weren't here
for Grandfather's interview. It went well, I think."

"Kelly . . ." He drew a ragged breath. "Chris flew out of
Fairbanks bound for Prudhoe Bay this morning."

"I know, he called me." For some reason her heart began to
beat too fast.

"Kelly, I don't know how to tell you this . . ." His voice
had a raw sound. "I received a call from the airport a bit ago.
The control tower was talking to the pilot of the Cole jet.
The pilot broke off in midsentence, and the control tower
couldn't raise him again. And a report came in from a pipe-

line camp that a plane was observed exploding over the Brooks Range..."

An item in the Fairbanks *Daily News-Miner,* Jan. 27: "Milo Fanti, rumored to be a rackets boss here in Fairbanks, was found murdered in his office on Second Avenue shortly before noon. The police suspect robbery was the motive. His office safe was found open and empty. Fanti had been stabbed several times in the back. Since Fanti was armed, his weapon unfired and still in a shoulder holster, the police speculate that the killer may have been someone known to him..."

Book Three

"The future belongs to
Alaskans, if the chechakos don't find
a way to screw it up."

Twenty-Four

Kelly didn't find running Cole as difficult as she had feared. Of course, it would have been far more difficult without those "briefing sessions" Chris had given her. Naturally the number of things she did *not* know was mind-boggling, but she was determined to learn. Once she was into the swing of things, she began to thrive on it. Perhaps the best thing of all, it kept her mind off Chris—much of the time. It was mainly in the small hours of the night that she really missed him. She would awaken, warm, her mind and memory drugged with sleep, reaching across the big bed for him, murmuring his name. It was in those moments that the pain of missing him struck her like a dagger piercing her heart.

She had expected animosity and resentment from the company executives, not only because she had been jumped in over them, but also because she was a woman. But it didn't happen, except for Will, of course. He grew even more bitter as the days passed, and refused to accept any calls from her. When it was necessary to communicate with him, she had to do it through an intermediary, usually Charlene Baker.

When she expressed to Charlene her surprise over her apparent acceptance, Charlene said, "I imagine they haven't so much accepted you, as resigned themselves to it. After all, you *are* a Cole, the job is yours by right. It's different from Chris...your husband. Although he is your husband, he is not a Cole. Of course," Charlene smiled tightly, "their accepting you doesn't mean they approve, or that they aren't hoping that..."

"Hoping that I'll fall on my butt? I know, especially Will."

"Especially Will. You know, Kelly, I should warn you..." Charlene's color rose and she looked away in embarrassment. "Your brother is going to do whatever he can, I might even

315

say *anything* he can, to see that you do just that, fall on your butt."

Kelly said grimly, "Oh, I'm well aware of that."

"And that even extends to your private life."

"I know that, too. But I don't have much time for a private life these days."

She leaned back, tapping a pen against her teeth, looking at Charlene closely. Perhaps the most surprising thing of all was her discovery of how much help Charlene had been to her. She had anticipated as much hostility from her as anyone, but it had turned out just the opposite. Charlene had gone out of her way to be helpful, and Kelly was beginning to realize just how valuable the other woman must have been to Chris. She had a remarkable grasp of company operations, and could give instant, shrewd analyses of everyone in the higher echelons.

What was even more astonishing to Kelly, she found herself liking Charlene. Not only was she highly intelligent, she was a warm, perceptive person. Recalling how she had once felt about Charlene, Kelly wondered if this new liking had come about because there was, at the present time at least, no longer any reason for jealousy.

Now she said, "Charlene, I notice that every time you refer to Chris, you use the present tense. I take it that means you still believe him to be alive?"

"Yes." Charlene's look was challenging. "Don't you?"

Kelly flinched. "I want to, God knows, and I do most of the time, but sometimes my hope runs pretty thin. If he is alive, why hasn't he come back? Or at least gotten in touch with us? Do you have any explanation for that?"

"None whatsoever," Charlene said promptly. "But there has to be a good reason. As for my believing him alive, I have no logical reason for that, either. It's just a feeling I have, a strong feeling."

Kelly swiveled her chair around so she could look at the painting she had hung in the wall behind her desk. His face lit by soft light, Chris seemed to smile encouragingly down at her.

"That's a marvelous painting, Kelly. He seems so..." Charlene's breath caught, "so alive!"

"I know," Kelly said somberly. "Every time I have doubts, I look at it, and I know he's alive."

She faced back around. "Charlene..." She drew a deep breath. "Are you in love with Chris?"

Charlene looked startled, and then to Kelly's surprise, tears came to her eyes.

"I'm sorry." Kelly held up her hand. "I know I shouldn't ask that, it was impertinent of me. But I would like to know. I assure you that I won't resent it, whatever your answer might be. It won't destroy our friendship. At least I hope we're friends, something that I'll admit I would not have thought possible a few weeks ago."

Charlene met her gaze squarely. "I'd like to think we are friends, too, Kelly."

"I'll be frank with you, Charlene. Until I started working with you, I hated you with a passion."

"I felt much the same way," Charlene said with a rueful smile. "But I haven't answered your question, have I?"

"Don't, if you don't care to. On the other hand, maybe you just did answer it."

The other woman nodded. "Perhaps I did. I've asked myself if I loved Chris, but not until after he was gone, not really. Before that I was just happy to be with him, to work with him. To be honest, I suppose I am a little in love with him. I know I miss him a great deal."

"We're of one mind there."

"He's brilliant, sometimes overbearing and arrogant, but he can be utterly charming."

"Wow! Now that's some testimonial!" Kelly said with arched eyebrows. "But since I agree with every word, how can I complain?"

Although winter had loosened its grip only slightly on Alaska, another search party had been sent into the Brooks Range. It wasn't an official party this time, but one put together by Kelly herself, at great personal expense. She hired experienced mountaineers, outfitting them with every piece of equipment that would ensure their safety as much as possible and afford them the best chance of finding the wreckage of the plane, if any was to be found. Experts in aircraft crashes had told Kelly that, if the jet had exploded in midair, the likelihood of finding anything more than a remote fragment or two scattered over a wide area was small.

But Kelly had to know, or at least make the attempt. If Chris was dead, the thought of his mangled body lying out there in the wilderness until after the spring thaw was just too much.

Her bittersweet regret these days was that she hadn't allowed herself to become pregnant by Chris during the relatively brief time of their marriage. The thought of carrying a little Chris around in her body would have been a great comfort.

The search crew was gone into the Brooks Range for two weeks, an agony of waiting for Kelly. The leader of the crew, a man named Mack Browne, called her the moment he returned to Fairbanks.

"I'm sorry, Mrs. O'Keefe, I'm afraid we found nothing concrete. The only thing we know for sure now is that the plane did explode in midair. We found three pieces of the aircraft, two sections of fuselage, and part of an engine cowling, over a widely separated area."

"You found no . . ." Kelly swallowed, "no bodies?"

"One, we found one. From identification found on the body, it belonged to the copilot, Buck Roberts. Anything else to be found will have to wait until spring, I'm afraid, Mrs. O'Keefe, after the thaw. Whatever else is out there is likely covered with several feet of snow. There were a number of big storms after the crash, as I recall."

Will heard about the results of the second search in a secondhand manner; the investigators he had hired had a tap on Kelly's phones, both at her apartment and the office. He felt a measure of relief at the news, not that he had thought the search would be successful in the first place, but it was just an additional confirmation that Chris O'Keefe was out of the picture for good.

The one he had to work on now, the only person standing between him and the catbird seat, was Kelly. It was costing a small fortune to keep her under surveillance around the clock, and a running tap on her phones, but he figured it was money well spent. The investigators not only filmed her movements outside the apartment, but a timed camera had been placed in her bedroom. It had been no trick to get in and out, since Will had long had a key to the apartment, although he had used the place rarely.

Kelly would make a slip eventually, do something that would violate the morals clause in the old man's will, and then he'd expose her to the board of trustees. It had been his hope that she would screw up as president; in his opinion she already had made several bad decisions; but naturally everybody was protecting her. Did they think he was so stupid that he didn't know the executive decisions were being made by others, then giving her the credit? Let them try to protect her private life!

He grinned, blowing smoke. Yes, it was money well spent, and besides he still had Fanti's ten grand. After Candice had dumped him and run, Will had lost heart for gambling and women.

His grin died, as he thought of the dead Fanti. He'd had a rough time of it for a while there, afraid that a connection would be made between himself and the rackets boss. Jesus Christ in a wheelbarrow, how could he have been stupid enough to leave himself so exposed and vulnerable?

But the furor, what little there had been, soon died down and nobody came to Will. It would seem that Fanti was little mourned; the police were probably delighted to see the guy taken out of their hair. Will was sure that any number of people in Fairbanks would be willing to give Fanti's killer, if ever found, a medal for a job well done.

Every time Will thought of what Fanti had done to him, through Candice, his rage would boil up, his guts gripping painfully. He had hoped for a while that Candice, wherever she was, would read about Fanti's demise and return to Fairbanks. Will knew that he would take her back. Oh, he might punish her a little, even knock her around a bit, but he would take her back.

But as the days and weeks passed, he came to realize that it was a vain hope; Candice was gone from his life forever.

Well, what the hell, the world was full of women. And it was about time he had one, unless he intended to turn into a goddamned monk! It had been . . . what? Over a month since he'd bedded Candice last, and there hadn't been anyone else since. Certainly not Louise. She'd think he'd gone out of his head, if he so much as touched her after all this time. Not that he had any intention of *that*.

He punched the intercom. "Cora, I'll be out for the rest of the afternoon. I can't think of anything pressing that needs my attention. If anything pops up, let Red handle it."

He rode the elevator down to the garage and drove out in the Ford and down to Two Street, turning into the alley. He had to wonder at himself. He had always been circumspect in going to Penelope's place, and yet he had thrown caution to the winds whenever he visited Fanti. What would a head shrinker make of that? Probably say that it was a yen for self-destruction. He shrugged, dismissing it from his thoughts.

At the garage he thumbed the door opener, wondering if she had changed the frequency, or if she had changed the lock inside. But the door swung up, and inside, he found that the back door opened to his key.

He went down the short hall and toward Penelope's quarters. She wasn't there. Will made himself at home, as if the long months hadn't happened, pouring himself a drink and sprawling in his favorite chair, lighting a cigar.

He was wreathed in cigar smoke, two drinks warm and comfortable in his belly, when she came into the apartment. She wore a pair of revealing lounging pajamas. Without closing the door behind her, she glared at him, one hand on her hip.

She said dourly, "I figured it had to be you."

"Who else?" He grinned lazily. "It's been awhile, Hardesty."

"Whose fault is that, do you suppose?"

"Oh, mine, I don't deny it. I've been rather busy."

"You have indeed! Busy with a bitch named Candice. What happened, Will? I heard that she left town rather suddenly. Did she ditch you?"

Will felt a wrench of pain, but managed to keep his face expressionless. "I guess you could say that."

"Now you know how it feels."

Will waved his cigar. "Now we didn't swear eternal vows to one another, did we?"

"No, we never did that," she said in a toneless voice. "Do you expect to just walk back in here, as if nothing had ever happened, and pick up where we left off?"

"Tell me something, Hardesty. How come you didn't change

the frequency on the door opener? Why didn't you change the lock on the back door?"

A tiny smile tugged at the corners of her mouth. "I don't suppose you'd believe me if I said I'd forgotten?"

He said dryly, "I don't suppose."

For a moment he toyed with the thought of telling her that Milo Fanti had bugged her bedroom, then decided not. She might really get her back up if he let her know that he knew about her connection with Fanti. The bugs were probably still there, but he would find a way to make them inoperative; the detectives he had hired had given him a crash course in bugging.

He stood up, cigar still going. One good thing, with Penelope Hardesty, he could take the cigar into her bedroom. He said, "Why don't you close the door, so we won't be disturbed?"

"Mrs. O'Keefe," Alice said, "there's a lady calling from Fairbanks."

"Who is it?"

"She just said tell you that June, Dwight's girl friend, was calling."

"All right, I'll talk to her." Waiting, Kelly felt her pulse pick up a beat. Dwight's lady had never called her before, and all too many phone calls of recent months had been harbingers of disaster.

"Kelly?"

"Yes, June, how are you? Nothing wrong with the baby, I hope?"

"No, fine." Kelly heard the girl draw a ragged breath. "Kelly, it's Dwight!" June's voice suddenly climbed toward hysteria.

"What's happened to Dwight?" Kelly asked tersely.

"He's in jail!" June wailed.

"In jail? For what, demonstrating again?"

"No, for murder."

"For *murder*? June, you can't be serious!"

"I've never been more serious. He was arrested last night. He refused, you know, to let me call you, or anyone, for help. I just learned awhile ago that he's been officially charged with murder. Kelly, for God's sake don't tell him I asked you for help, he'll kill me!"

Kelly winced at the girl's choice of words. "All right, June, I won't tell him. But I can't believe he's charged with murder. Who's he supposed to have killed?"

"Milo Fanti."

"Milo Fanti? That's even more incredible! What possible reason could Dwight have to kill Fanti? And what brought about his arrest after all this time?"

"The police came to the house with a, you know, search warrant. They found some documents, tapes, I don't know what all, that they said incriminated Dwight."

"What caused them to show up with a search warrant? How did they know the stuff was there?"

"I pestered the pig at the desk at police headquarters. He finally told me they had an anonymous phone tip that the stuff was there."

Kelly was silent, thinking furiously. She wasn't sure whether this should be taken seriously or not; Dwight wasn't capable of killing anybody. Yet, he was in jail, a murder complaint lodged against him, and she knew that the Fairbanks police had long been annoyed at Dwight and SAS. They would probably welcome a chance to put him away.

June said, "What are we going to do, Kelly?"

"You go home, June. You shouldn't be running around, upsetting yourself. I'll handle it. I'll do everything possible. He is my brother, you know."

As soon as she broke the connection Kelly instructed Alice to find Brad Connors. He was in his office in Juneau.

He shared her astonishment when told of Dwight's arrest. "But it may be more serious than you seem to think, Kelly. The Fairbanks police department is a clean operation. No matter how much they might dislike SAS and Dwight, I very much doubt they would charge him without evidence to back it up."

"Will you fly up there and look into it, Brad? I'll meet you as soon as I can get there. Maybe we can at least get Dwight out on bail."

"Well, sure, I'll leave at once, Kelly. But criminal law is not my forte, you know. If Dwight is facing a trial, you have to get him a defense attorney."

"We'll face that when it happens. The important thing right now, is to get him out of jail."

"That may not be so easy to do. Judges are not inclined to grant bail on murder one, especially if the prosecution raises an objection."

Twenty-Five

Both Kelly and Brad Connors arrived in Fairbanks too late for visiting hours. They agreed to meet for breakfast the next morning and go to the jail together.

Kelly was already in a booth in the coffee shop when Brad came in the next morning, a newspaper under his arm. Grim-faced, he nodded without speaking and slid into the booth.

"Well, the ordure has hit the fan, to coin a phrase." He unfolded the paper and pushed it across to her.

Kelly gasped as she saw the glaring headline: "Cole Scion Held in Murder!"

"Oh, my God! If Grandfather were alive to see this!"

"How about Josh? I know they don't get along too well, he and Dwight, but they *are* father and son."

"I called Daddy in Washington. He's flying in later today. He's as shocked as we are, and doesn't want to believe it of Dwight, either. He asked me to do what I could until he could get here."

Taking a sip of coffee, Kelly skimmed the accompanying article, a phrase here and there jumping out at her: ". . . black sheep of the Cole family . . . prominent in the environmentalist movement . . . unpopular in Fairbanks . . . speculated that Cole's motive had to do with incriminating documents found in his possession . . . police refuse to divulge contents of alleged documents . . ."

And finally a paragraph that she read in its entirety: "So far, the only member of the Cole clan to make a statement to the press is Will Cole, vice-president of Cole 98, and half-brother to Dwight Cole. Efforts to contact other members of the Cole family have been unsuccessful. When asked to comment on the charge against his half-brother, Will Cole said: 'Dwight is no longer a member of our family, hasn't been for some years. In my opinion, nothing Dwight might do surprises me a great deal. This is only another example of his efforts to blacken the Cole's good name.'"

"Dear God!" Kelly slammed the flat of her hand down onto the paper. "Did you read what Will said?"

"I read it."

"Why would he say something like that? Although he doesn't say so in so many words, he might as well have come right out and said he thinks Dwight is guilty. Certainly that's what people will believe."

Brad laughed shortly. "I can't say I'm too surprised. Maybe Dwight can sue him for slander."

"It's not funny, Brad," she said angrily.

He sobered. "No, of course it isn't. But what else could you expect from Will? Just last week, he put in motion a court petition to get your grandfather's will declared invalid by virtue of Jeremiah being mentally incompetent at the time he dictated it."

"He's tried that once and failed."

"And I'm sure he'll keep trying."

She felt a stir of alarm. "Is there any chance he'll succeed?"

"I don't think he has a prayer. But then, who knows for sure? He just may get a judge who doesn't happen to like the name of Cole or anything it stands for. Unfortunately there are examples of incompetence among judges, as in any profession."

At the jail they were escorted into a small, nondescript room and left alone. The room had a small table, three uncomfortable chairs, and one high, barred window. The room was cold and stank of a disinfectant that made Kelly wrinkle her nose.

In a few moments Dwight was ushered in, the door slammed and locked after him. He was wearing faded jail denims. His step slowed when he saw them. "I thought it was June. How did you find out, Sis?"

She spread the newspaper on the table. "Just about everybody in the world knows by this time."

Dwight sat down, picked up the paper and glanced at the headlines. He laughed. "This whole thing is a joke, you know? The pigs are just hassling me. They like to do that."

Kelly said sharply, "It's no joke, Dwight. They have reason enough to arrest you or they wouldn't have!"

"They have zilch. Tell me, what do they have?"

"You tell us, Dwight."

He shrugged. "They came with a search warrant. I didn't object. What the hell did I have to hide? Then they found these papers and a tape."

Brad said, "What was in the papers?"

"Man, I don't know. Just some stuff they said came from Fanti's safe. Most of it concerns brother Will, I gather. Photostats of an IOU, checks, crap like that. Can you believe that? The stuff concerned brother Will and they arrested *me*! Oh, SAS was mentioned somewhere, I was told."

"Where did they find this material?" Brad asked.

"In the kitchen, can you imagine?" Dwight looked faintly embarrassed. "Hidden back behind a silverware tray in a drawer."

Kelly said, "But I don't understand why they arrested you. What motive do they think you had? Did you know Fanti?"

"I never had anything to do with him, Sis. I swear!" Dwight held up one hand. "Oh, I've badmouthed him a few times, about how his kind was spoiling Alaska as much as anybody, with his dope dealings and the like. But hell, it was all true and nothing more than other people said."

Brad said, "You said these things before witnesses, I suppose?"

"Well, yeah. But it was just talk."

Brad shook his head. "They must ascribe a stronger motive than that to you, Dwight."

"They say that I killed Fanti to protect brother Will!" Dwight wore a look of incredulity. "Can you feature that? That I would kill some guy just to protect Will's good name? That really gets to me. I told them that we hated each other's guts until hell wouldn't have it. They wouldn't listen." He snorted softly. "Cops! No wonder they're called pigs."

Brad studied him narrowly for a few moments. He said slowly, "Dwight, I have a feeling here. There's something you're not telling us. They have something else, I'll bet on it."

For the first time Dwight looked uncomfortable. His glance slid away and he shuffled his feet.

Brad bored in. "Well, Dwight?"

"They found an, uh..." His voice was little more than a mumble. "They found a hunting knife in the drawer with the other stuff."

Kelly breathed, "Oh, my God! The knife used to kill Fanti!"

"They can't know that for sure," Dwight said defensively.

"Dwight, Dwight," Brad said chidingly. "They're not stupid and neither are you. There's blood on the knife, has to be, and fibers from Fanti's clothing, if it is the murder weapon. It'll be easy to match all that up."

"But they can't tie it to me! If I killed him, it'd have my fingerprints, wouldn't it?"

"Fingerprints won't be necessary to tie it to you, Dwight. It was found on your premises, wasn't it? And undoubtedly the killer wiped his prints off it."

"I think somebody is setting me up here, framing me!"

Brad sighed. "Don't use that line with the police, Dwight. They hear it so often they automatically assume guilt."

Kelly interjected, "Who could by trying to frame you, Dwight?"

"The killer, who else?"

"But who, and why would he do this to you? Who could have planted that stuff in your house?"

"Hell, I don't know! I'm not all that well liked around here, you know that. And people come and go out of that house all the time. It's never even locked."

Brad leaned forward. "Fanti was killed between ten and noon of that day. Where were you during that time? Were you with anybody who could vouch for you?"

Dwight said glumly, "I'm afraid not. I'd heard that one of the game trails north of town was being blocked off by a section of the pipeline. I went up to check on it and didn't get back until late in the afternoon."

"You were alone then?"

"Yeah."

"Did anybody see you who might know you?"

"I don't know. Damnit, how do I know that?" Dwight said angrily. "I was thinking of other things, not worrying about an alibi!"

"How about now?" Brad said in a suddenly harsh voice. "Are you worried now, Dwight?"

Dwight looked startled. "Well, yeah, I'm beginning to be.

Why wouldn't I? You come in here and lay all this heavy stuff on me."

"Good! It's time you started to worry a little. We'd better go, Kelly. Our time is about up and we have to meet your father's plane." He got to his feet and directed his attention again to Dwight. "The reason I say it's time for you to worry is because you're in deep shit."

He strode over to rap on the door. Kelly sent a despairing glance at him, then leaned over to kiss her brother. "Don't worry, Dwight. It'll be okay. If you didn't kill Fanti, you really have nothing to worry about, do you? Daddy's flying in today. He'll be in to see you later."

The door had opened and Brad was already outside. As Kelly started after him, Dwight said softly, "Sis?"

She looked back. "Yes?"

"You said something last summer about there coming a day when I'd come to the Coles for help. Remember? Well, it looks like that day is here." His face twisted. "Help me, Kelly I'm scared!"

"We'll help you, Dwight. Did you ever think we wouldn't?"

Brad was already out of the building before she caught up with him. "Brad, did you have to say that in there? That was cruel."

He turned a grim face to her. "He needed a shock to bring him face to face with reality, realize what he's up against. He was taking this whole thing too lightly, Kelly. Maybe it was cruel, but it worked. Besides, I told him nothing that is not true. Your brother is in deep trouble."

"I know, I know."

They reached the car. Brad helped her in and went around to the driver's side. As they drove away, heading toward the airport, Kelly said, "I don't understand any of this. When I heard Fanti was killed, I assumed that it was one of his cohorts, a falling out of thieves, so to speak. But if that's so, why would they try to frame Dwight?"

He shook his head. "I thought all along that there was more behind Fanti's death than that. I've always thought that it may have been hooked up somehow with Chris's death. Maybe the same person who killed Fanti put a bomb on the plane."

"We don't know that Chris is dead!" she said hotly.

"Kelly..." He looked at her, his voice softening. "It's time you were facing reality as well as Dwight. This fantasy of yours about Chris being alive is just that, a fantasy. As long as you continue to delude yourself, you'll just keep making yourself miserable. It's been over two *months*, Kelly!"

"I believe he is still alive, I have to believe it! And I'm not the only one. Charlene Baker has the same feeling."

"Did you hear yourself, Kelly? You said you *have* to believe it. As for Charlene, I don't know what her reasons are. People's fantasies are hard to figure..."

"Damnit, it's *not* a fantasy!" she said explosively. Then she gestured wearily. "I don't want to talk about it, okay?"

Brad was silent until they parked the car in the lot at the airport. Then he caught her arm as she started to get out. "Kelly, give me a second, please? The plane isn't due for a few minutes yet."

Kelly grew still, but refused to look at him.

"Perhaps this isn't the best time to say what I'm going to say, but it's eating away at me. I love you, Kelly. I've told you that before. What we shared during those months were the high point of my life. I'll never forget. Now I need to know, if Chris is dead...wait!" He held up a staying hand. "You notice I said if. But I can't wait too long, like I did before. When this fantasy of yours is over..." She made an angry sound, and he tightened his grip on her arm. "No, you're going to hear me out, like it or not. I want you to know this. I want you to be my wife." He laughed suddenly. "Ironic, isn't it? I backed away from asking you before because of your money. Now you not only still have the money, but you're head of Cole Enterprises. But that doesn't matter any more. I love you and I want to marry you. This year, next year, whenever."

Despite herself, Kelly was moved by his eloquence, most of all by what she knew the speech must have cost him. She said gently, "Dear Brad, you are a nice man, and you've just paid me a great compliment. Don't you think I also treasure those times we had together? But there is one thing you must accept... I will never believe Chris is dead until I'm shown indisputable proof. When that time comes, God forbid it ever does, I think a part of me will die. I don't think you would want that person."

"I will always want you, Kelly. And you may not think so now, but that old bromide is true . . . time heals all wounds."

Perversely her anger flared again. "That's the thing I really need right now, bromides thrown at me!"

She wrenched her arm free of his grasp and was out of the car before he could stop her, almost running toward the terminal building. Just before he caught up to her, she remembered something. Brad, supposedly, had been the last person to see Chris alive.

She looked around at him. "I've never asked you, Brad. What did you and Chris talk about that day at the airport?"

He gave her a startled look. "Why, about the threatened walkout at the drilling rigs, what I knew about it, anyway."

"Anything else?"

"If you mean, did your name come up, no. We had a sort of unspoken agreement, Chris and I. We never talked of you, not since the one time after you came back from your honeymoon. Two men don't usually talk about a woman they both love, you know." He took her by the elbow and turned her to face him. "There's something I haven't told you, Kelly. You know, after you settled that mess with the drilling crews, Will tried to get me to call a meeting of the trustees. He said you settled it by giving the men everything they wanted, that it was an irresponsible executive action, not in the best interests of the company. He claimed that by settling it that way you broke the terms of the trust."

"And what did you tell him?"

"I told him that you did almost exactly what Chris told me he intended to do."

She stared. "Did Chris say that?"

"He most certainly did, that morning at the airport."

"Well, you might have told me," she said, annoyed. "It would have helped me in making my decision."

"Maybe I should have. But I figured that you should make company decisions on your own initiative, not with advice from beyond the . . ."

"Beyond the grave?" she said savagely. "Damn you, Brad Connors, you never let up, do you?"

Yanking her arm free, she strode on into the terminal. After a moment he caught up to her, and without speaking they made their way to the arrival gate. They had only a ten-minute wait before Josh came toward them with lunging strides. He had a disheveled look, hair rumpled, a dark shadow of beard on his face. Scowling, he stopped before them, bouncing a folded-up newspaper against one palm.

Without a word of greeting he said abruptly, "Have you seen or talked to Will?" He waved the newspaper. "About this statement he made to a reporter?"

Kelly said, "Then you know about it?"

"Hell, yes, they have newspapers in Washington. Look at this."

He unfolded the newspaper and Kelly read the headline: "Senator Cole's Son Held for Murder."

Kelly clucked. "I suppose it's to be expected that they would do that to you."

"That doesn't bother me half as much as that asinine statement Will made."

"I haven't tried to talk to him yet, Daddy. I thought we'd wait until you got here. You have any luggage?"

"No, I didn't wait to bother with it, Kelly. You have a car here?"

"In the parking lot."

"Then let's go."

On the way to the car and on the ride downtown, Kelly told her father everything she had learned, including the documents and tapes the police had supposedly found concerning Will, and the hunting knife. "I'm surprised that the reporter didn't ask Will about those documents."

Brad said, "It probably isn't common knowledge yet. The police aren't likely to let that out until they've questioned Will. Besides, any wise reporter would step gingerly around Will, as prominent as he is."

"Since Will was mixed up with Fanti, could *he* have killed him to protect himself?" She twisted around to look at Josh, in the back seat.

Josh shook his head. "Kill Fanti, yes, in one of his rages, but frame his own brother for it? No, not even Will is capable of that."

"Maybe I should fire Will. I do have the authority, don't I, Brad?"

"You have the authority, yes, but I wouldn't advise it. Not at this time. That would be an admission that you believe he's guilty, when the contents of the documents and tapes are finally revealed. And it will be, in court if not before."

Brad found a parking place before the building and nudged the car in. They got out, went inside the building, and rode up to Will's floor in silence, busy with their own thoughts.

Cora Brewster looked flustered when she saw them. "Senator, Mrs. O'Keefe! I think it's terrible about your son, sir!"

"Thank you," Josh said. "We'd like to see Will, please."

Cora Brewster fluttered her hands, and said in a rush, "I'm sorry, Senator. I'm afraid that's just not possible."

"Damnit, I'm his father!" Face flushing with anger, Josh thumped his fist on her desk.

"Oh, I'm sure he'd see you, Senator, but he's not here."

"Not here? Where is he?"

"I don't know, he didn't tell me." Cora Brewster spread her hands in a helpless gesture. "He said the pressure was too much, he had to get away for a few days. He promised to call in in a day or two." She brightened. "But his executive assistant, Mr. Patterson, is here. Perhaps he could help you?"

"Executive assistant!" Josh snorted. "Flunky is more like it. Come on, let's get out of here."

Josh took Kelly by the elbow and turned her about. As they rode down in the elevator, Josh growled, "Pressure, hell! It's all pressure he brought on himself."

Kelly said, "He probably knows what the police found at Dwight's, and doesn't want to answer questions about it."

"I don't know what's happened to him this past year," Josh said bleakly. "He's always gone his own way, but he's gone too far now. If he's allowed to continue, he's going down the tubes, and taking Cole, the family *and* the company, with him. So, when this mess with Dwight is settled, you and I, Kelly, have to sit down with Will and have a talk. If he doesn't behave, I think it might be best that he's eased entirely out of the company."

Brad said quickly, "That may not be so easy to do, Senator. He's going into court again, you know, trying to have your father's will declared invalid. If he's out of the company altogether, he may raise even more of a stink."

"Even that would be preferable to the stink he's causing *in* the company."

Kelly laughed shortly. "There is one thing we can be sure of... if Will goes, he'll go kicking and screaming."

"Pap said something to me on his birthday, knowing that his time was due," Josh said. "He said that the future belongs to Alaskans, if the chechakos don't find a way to screw it up. If Will has his way, we won't need Outsiders to screw it up, he'll manage to do it all on his own." As the elevator doors opened onto the lobby, he added, "Let's drive out to see Louise. Maybe she has some idea where he's gone."

Louise was in the saloon when she heard Will drive into the garage beneath the house. Since he hadn't shown up for dinner, or even called, Louise had sent the maids home, and merely picked at her own dinner. She had gotten up in the middle of it and came in here. She, who had once detested this room, came in here more and more often of late. After all, in here she had ready access to the liquor.

For weeks now she had gone to bed every night, sodden with gin. She was used to an empty bed; in fact, she preferred it, but it would have been a comfort, of a sort, to know that Will was somewhere in the house. Once in a while she would hear him come in quite late, but usually he was out all night. There had been a time, some weeks back, when Will had slept at home every night, usually coming home drunk and quarrelsome. But that period had passed and now he was following his old routine.

After several drinks the familiar, warm haze enveloped Louise, a protective cocoon against the harsh realities of her life. She recalled something Josh had said to her once about how many Alaskan wives became alcoholics. She was astute enough to recognize that she was becoming too dependent on alcohol, but what alternative did she have? At least it helped ease the aching loneliness. . . .

Will came into the saloon, carrying an overnight bag. He skidded to a stop when he saw her. "Well, Louise! I thought you'd probably be in bed."

"Hoped I'd be in bed, isn't that what you mean, Will?" she said in a slurred voice.

He said acidly, "Stoned again, I see."

She waved the hand holding the martini glass, slopping a few drops onto her dress. "It's something to do."

His mouth twisted in disgust. He took out a cigar and lit it before speaking again. "I'm going away for about a week. I need to get away."

"Nice of you to tell me, since you usually don't bother. I

heard on the news that Dwight was arrested. Is that the
reason you're going?"

"That has nothing to do with it," he said stiffly. "Dwight
means damn-all to me, one way or another."

"Where are you going, or is that privileged information?"

He hesitated for a beat. "I think it best you don't know."

"Best for me, or for you, Will? Who's going with you this
time?"

His lips tightened. "I'm going by myself."

"Turned down again?"

"Now what does that mean?"

"You think I don't know about your fancy lady, Candice
Durayea, and how she dumped you? You stayed home nights
for almost a month before you started tomcatting again.
Who's the new one, Will?"

"Why do you care, Louise? You haven't cared in a long
time."

"You have that correct, anyway." Then her temper flared.
"And whose fault is that, Will?"

He gestured wearily. "Let's not go through that waltz
again, okay? If you don't like the way I live my life, why don't
you leave? Get a divorce?"

It took a moment for the import of his words to penetrate
the haze. She gaped at him in astonishment. "A divorce? How
many times have you told me you'd never agree to a divorce?"

"A man has a right to change his mind and I've just this
minute changed mine. The last thing I need is a drunken wife
on my hands," he said savagely. "So get your goddamned
divorce. If you don't, I will!"

He picked up his bag and slammed out of the room.
Louise, still somewhat stunned, automatically picked up the
martini glass and raised it to her lips. Her hand froze as she
stared at the drink. Suddenly she laughed harshly and tossed
the rest of the drink into the fire. Still laughing, she watched
the flames leap as the alcohol splashed on them. . . .

"And so, you see, Joshua," Louise said, "I don't know any
more about where Will might be than you do."

She looked at the others on the couch, Kelly and Brad
Connors, and saw no censure there. She had told them, word

for word, what had transpired between her and Will in this room.

Now she stirred, getting to her feet. "I've forgotten my manners, I didn't offer you a drink. What would you like?"

When they gave her their preferences, Louise went behind the bar, made the drinks, and came back. She handed around the glasses and sat down opposite them in the wing chair.

Josh looked at her empty hands. "Louise, aren't you having a drink?"

"I haven't had a drink since I threw the dregs of that martini into the fire." She gave a scratchy laugh. "Oh, I don't suppose I'll become a teetotaler, Joshua. But I decided I'm going to need all my wits about me."

Josh stared at her over the rim of his glass. "Does that mean . . . ?"

"It means I'm not letting Will have everything his way." Her head went back. "Not after what I've put up with all these years. No, the shoe is on the other foot now. I'm going to refuse to divorce him. Let him try and I'll fight him tooth and nail. God knows, I have enough on him! Unless he agrees to a settlement, one I think I deserve, I'll fight him all the way."

Kelly clapped her hands together. "Good for you, Louise!"

"The way things are with Will right now," Josh said, "I doubt he could provide you with plane fare Outside."

"You think I'm wrong, Josh?" Louise found herself close to pleading. "Am I being too grasping?"

"Not at all, my dear, not at all," Josh said gently. He leaned across to pat her hand. "Anything you get from Will Cole you deserve. But unless I'm badly mistaken, the minute he learns you're going to fight him, he'll back off."

Will Cole wasn't completely out of touch. Before he left for Reno, he called Porter Reese, head of the investigative firm in Anchorage, and left word where he would be all week.

And it was true that he had left town to elude the police, at least for a few days, until he could get his head together. He wasn't overly concerned about the media; he could stonewall questions from that quarter. The police were a different matter.

The word that documents and tapes had been discovered in Dwight's place had shaken him to the core. He knew the police would get around to him sooner or later, and a week out of town would give him time to be better prepared. He had a few friends in the higher echelons of the city administration, and could probably have found out through one of these contacts what information the police had on him. He was reluctant to do that, afraid that it might arouse undue suspicion. He would be in better shape if he just ignored the whole affair until the authorities came to him, if they ever did. After all, he was Will Cole, and there was nothing all that damaging anyway, just evidence of a few peccadilloes: gambling and sexual antics.

His week in Reno wasn't as relaxing as he'd hoped. He had asked Penelope Hardesty to accompany him, and had been surprised and displeased by her refusal. She claimed that she couldn't trust anyone to run the house in her absence.

Will gambled without much interest, and was about even by the time he was ready to leave. He'd dallied with a showgirl and bedded a comely divorcee, but had found neither affair particularly exciting.

Then, the day before he was scheduled to fly back to Fairbanks, came the telephone call from Anchorage, a call that Will was sure would change his whole life around.

It was from Porter Reese. "Mr. Cole, we've finally got what you wanted. I think."

"What do you mean, you think? Either you have or you haven't."

"Well, she spent the night with a guy last night, all night. In her apartment. They left together this morning. And they didn't play tiddlywinks, either. That bedroom camera we installed got it all. Hot stuff."

For just an instant Will felt a twinge of conscience. Then he pushed it from his mind. Kelly was a big girl; she knew the terms of the trust. If she wanted to play around, she should be prepared to pay the consequences.

He said into the phone, "Porter, did you recognize the man?"

"Nope. Tim, when I showed him the film this morning, didn't either, and you know one or the other of us had been on her tail every minute. He's a bearded guy, a complete stranger to both of us. Think this is what you want?"

"Yeah." Will was silent for a moment's thought. "Here's what I want you to do, Porter. I'll fly back as soon as I can get a flight out. Tomorrow is Tuesday. Run the film over to Fairbanks. I'll set up a meeting with the trustees, as early in the morning as possible. I'll want you there, with the film. I may be late getting in, and not have a chance to view the film, so it'd better be what you say it is."

"It is, Mr. Cole. Take my word for it."

"All right, Porter. Call my secretary in the morning. She'll have the time of the meeting."

Will hung up and went about tracking down Brad Connors. He found him in the firm's office in Juneau.

"Will! Where are you? Kelly and your father have been trying to find you..."

Will cut him off. "Never mind that now. I want you to round up those other two trustees and set up a meeting for tomorrow morning at ten, in the boardroom of my building."

"Now look, Will," Brad said wearily. "I can't call them together every time you get a wild hair. And if this is like that other time..."

"It's not, Connors. This time I've got something that will convince you that my dear sister is morally unfit, under the terms of that cockamamie trust. Now, you set it up, okay?"

Twenty-Six

When Kelly walked into the boardroom, Brad and the other two trustees were already present. After Brad had introduced her to the other men, Kelly drew him aside. In a low voice she said, "What is this all about, Brad?"

Brad shrugged. "I haven't the least idea. Will called me yesterday from somewhere and said it was urgent that a meeting of the trustees be called. He said he'd fly back in time to attend. I thought of turning him down, like I did the other time, but he has a right to call a meeting. If he does it often enough, maybe he'll make a fool of himself so often he'll call a halt. And I figured it was a good way to get him back here."

"He still isn't here. His secretary told me that he isn't in the building."

"He'll be here. He called me from the airport a few minutes ago. He just got in. I'm sorry you had to come all the way from Anchorage again so soon."

"Oh, that's all right, Brad, I had to be here anyway. And Daddy's still in town. I called him and he said he'd be here this morning. Is it all right for him to sit in?"

"Of course. Oh, here he is now."

Josh strode toward them. His immaculate look was back, but Kelly noticed with a pang that his face seemed drawn, and he looked older. For years he had never seemed to change in age; now, almost overnight, he had aged ten years.

"Are you all right, Daddy?" She touched his arm.

He closed his hand around hers. "I'm not sure. I've been trying to get bail set for Dwight, all to no avail. At least I've hired a good defense attorney for him now. Maybe things will happen." He looked at Brad and said brusquely, "Now what is this business all about, Brad?"

338

"Like I just told Kelly, I'm in the dark. We'll have to wait for Will to enlighten us, I'm afraid."

Just then a hesitant cough came from the doorway. They all turned to see an inconspicuous, pudgy man of indeterminate age standing in the doorway, carrying a square case and a cylindrical object.

He came across the room. "Are you Mr. Connors?"

"That's correct," Brad said curtly.

"I'm Porter Reese. I operate a private investigation agency in Anchorage and I've been doing some work for Mr. Cole. He told me to meet him here this morning." He peered around the boardroom. "I don't see him anywhere."

Brad said, "He'll be here shortly. He called from the airport. He couldn't get a plane out from wherever he was until late."

Josh motioned. "What's that you're carrying?"

"A projector and a screen." Reese gazed about. "I might as well get set up, so we'll be ready when..."

"Just a damned minute!" Josh seized the man's arm. "Have you been spying on my daughter, taking pictures of her? If you have, I'll..." He clenched his fists.

"I'm sorry, sir," Reese said. "You'll have to put that question to Mr. Cole."

"I *am* Mr. Cole. Will Cole is my son."

"I know that. I know who you are, Senator," Reese said with a touch of smugness. "I make it my business to know everybody even remotely involved in a case."

"Case? What case?" Josh was breathing heavily, fists clenching and unclenching. "If you've done something to dirty my daughter's reputation..." He took a step toward the detective.

Brad stepped in front of him. In a low voice he said, "That won't help matters, Senator."

"Yes, Daddy, let the man do what he came to do. I have nothing to worry about," Kelly said steadily, but her thoughts raced frantically. Had she been followed, spied on, all this time, without even realizing it? She had never once thought that Will would stoop this low. How naïve she had been!

"Haven't you, Kelly?" Will's mocking voice said from the doorway. "And I heard what you said, Josh. Porter did nothing to dirty Kelly's reputation; she didn't need any help."

They turned to see Will lounging in the doorway, a cigar in his hand. His clothes looked slept in and his face was unshaven. He motioned with the cigar. "Go ahead, Porter. Get everything set up."

Josh said harshly, "What the hell is this, Will? What are you up to now?"

Will assumed an innocent look. "I just intend to show you some pictures, Josh. Thought maybe you might like to put them into the family album."

"And just where have you been? I've been trying to run you down for days. Dwight is in jail."

"I heard, Josh. But I don't see that it has anything to do with either of us."

"He's your brother."

"Not so. We disowned him, don't you remember? At least I did, and so did Granpap."

"I never did. He's my son and I'm not about to turn my back on him."

Will shrugged. "Then that's your problem. I still fail to see how it concerns me."

"That statement you made to the press, before you turned tail and ran..."

"Oh, I was misquoted. You know how reporters are. How many times have I heard you claim you were misquoted?" Will's voice hardened. "And I didn't run, as you put it. I had a few days' vacation coming and I took them."

Josh stared at him in disgust. "I never did understand you, Will. And I still don't."

"Nothing to understand, Josh," Will said ingenuously. "I'm just a clean-cut, hardworking fellow, trying to get ahead in the world."

Porter Reese said, "All set up, Mr. Cole."

The projector was set up on the end of the conference table and the screen was unrolled on its stand.

Josh gestured. "So what is this shit, Will?"

"Show-and-tell time, Daddy," Will said cheerfully. He stepped to the wall and hit the dimmer switch. "Everybody get comfortable, sit back and enjoy."

When everyone was seated around the table, Will said, "Start the show, Porter."

Kelly, sitting next to Josh, had her hands underneath the table, clenched tightly. She leaned forward as images began to flicker on the screen. The quality was poor, the pictures grainy, and the room the camera was focused on was too dim to make out many details. Then a light was suddenly switched on, and she gasped in shock. "That's my bedroom!"

Before she had finished speaking, two figures moved into camera range, herself and a tall, bearded man in rough clothing. The man had his back to the camera as they embraced hungrily.

"What the devil is this!" Josh roared. "Will, did you set up a camera in Kelly's bedroom? What a lousy thing to do. Your own sister! This is a new low, even for you."

Will's open hand thumped the table. "Goddamnit, it's not my morals that are in question here, it's Kelly's!"

Not a soul in the boardroom had stopped looking at the screen. The two figures, locked together, had managed to partially disrobe while Josh and Will argued. Now they moved apart. Kelly pulled her dress over her head and the man, back still to the camera, stepped out of his trousers.

"That's enough. Turn that projector off," Josh demanded. "Or I'll smash it, Will, so help me I will!"

"Porter, turn it off for a minute," Will said calmly. As the projector stopped whirring, he continued, "Perhaps you'd better leave the room, Josh. You, too, Kelly. Because I'm going to demand that the three trustees see the film through to the end. I'm not responsible for the cockamamie terms of that trust. But it stated clearly that Kelly, if she took over Cole, had to remain as pure as driven snow. Now, I want them to see just how pure she is. Then they'll have no choice but to oust her."

"Will, if you go through with this," Josh said in a choked voice, "I'll see to it that you're everlastingly sorry."

"Oh, I think not, *Daddy*. Your career is on the line here, too, if you push me. Think what would happen if copies of this film were to get in the wrong hands. Daughter of the eminent Senator Cole caught sleeping around . . ."

"I don't see anything so terrible about it, Will."

The overhead light came on and everybody turned to blink at the owner of the voice, standing in the doorway of Will's office off the boardroom. He was a big man, in construction clothes, with a beard obscuring the lower half of his face. He had an attaché case in one hand.

Porter Reese was the first to speak. "That's him! That's the guy we saw coming and going in Mrs. O'Keefe's apartment, the guy on the film!"

Kelly was already across the room, smiling, taking his hand. She said softly, "Good morning again, darling."

"Chris? My God, it *is* Chris!" Josh said in a stunned voice. He was also on his feet, hurrying across the room to seize Chris's hand. "You're alive! Thank the Lord!" He threw his arms around both Chris and Kelly.

Will, recovering, turned to snarl at Reese, "You stupid sonofabitch, that's her husband!"

Reese gaped. "How was I to know? I'd never met the man."

In a dazed voice Will said, "Gather up your equipment and get the hell out of here."

Chris, flanked by Josh and Kelly, came to the conference table. Kelly still clung to his hand, her gaze never leaving his face.

He said laconically, "Like I was saying, Will, what's so immoral about a woman sleeping with her own husband? However, I do think it shows rather poor taste on your part, invading a person's privacy like that. But then you've never been known for good taste, have you?"

"Go to hell, you bastard!" Will said in a vicious whisper.

"Not just yet, Will," Chris said genially. "I came close a couple of times. Too close, for my peace of mind. Somebody wanted me dead."

Will drew back. "I had nothing to do with that!"

"No, you didn't. But for a while there, I thought you did."

Josh said, "You didn't get on that plane, did you, Chris?"

"No, Josh, I didn't."

"Did you suspect there was a bomb on board?"

"No, I was shocked as hell when I heard about the jet blowing up. If I *had* known, naturally I wouldn't have let them take off."

Brad spoke for the first time. "But I saw you get on board."

"But I got off, Brad, after a few words with Jim Carson. You didn't watch us take off, did you?"

"No, but I assumed . . ."

"That's what I hoped everybody would think."

Josh glared at Kelly. "Kelly, did you know about this?"

"No, Daddy. The first I knew was when this bearded man rang my doorbell night before last. I came as close to fainting as I ever did in my life when I realized it was Chris."

Chris put an arm around her shoulders. "Again, I'm sorry, sweet. I'll try to make it up to you."

Josh made an angry motion. "I think you owe us an explanation, Chris."

"I do, yes, sir."

Porter Reese, the projector in its case and the screen rolled up, started out of the room, and Will got up to follow him.

Chris said tersely, "Not yet, Will. We have some things to clear up, aside from the reason for my vanishing act, so stick around."

"Why should I?" Will said with a sneer. "It looks like this is going to turn into a gushy reunion scene. Whatever else I am, I'm no hypocrite. I'm not overjoyed to have you back, operator."

"Oh, I'm sure not," Chris said sarcastically.

"And I have nothing to say to you."

"But I have a lot to say to you, Will. I won't try to keep you here by force..."

"I'd like to see you try!"

"... but if you walk out that door, you might as well keep going, for I'll send the police baying after you."

Will hesitated for a moment, his indecision mirrored on his face. But in the end he sat down—at the end of the table away from the others.

Chris turned to the trustees across the table. "I think we can dispense with your services, gentlemen. As you can see, your business here today is finished. But I'd like for you to stay, Brad."

When the two trustees had left, Chris lit a cigarette and leaned back. "Now. As I said, there were two attempts on my life, the second the day before I disappeared. The first time I figured it was an accident, a dump truck forcing my car off the road. But that day in Matanuska Valley was no accident. Some guy came after me with a rifle. I knew I had to do something. I couldn't be lucky forever."

Josh said, "Why didn't you go to the police?"

"I thought of that, but I had nothing pointing to anyone, just my suspicions of Milo Fanti. And I knew that if the rest of you learned about it, you'd insist that I have round-the-clock protection. Knowing you, Josh, I'd probably have gotten it. I couldn't function that way. Anyway, by then, it had become a personal thing between me and whoever was behind it."

He took Kelly's hand. "I did intend to tell Kelly, on the phone the next day, but she was busy with the TV interview. So I told Jim Carson to call and tell her that I was dropping out of sight for a few days. How was I to know that he would be dead a short time later? That was a real shocker. Then, right on the heels of that, came the news that Fanti had been murdered. I didn't know what to think. Maybe I had been wrong all along and there was somebody else behind it all."

"You could still have called me!" Kelly said. She was suddenly close to tears. "All that time, letting me think you were dead."

"I thought of it. Many times I picked up the phone to call, but stopped at the last moment. Kelly..." He took both of her hands in his. "You don't hide your emotions very well. If you had known I was alive, all anyone would have had to do was notice the change in you, and they would have known, too."

"You might have told me, Chris." This from Josh.

"Are you sure you wouldn't have let it slip, Senator? Seeing her grieving?" He glanced sideways at Kelly. "I assume you *did* grieve for me?"

"I'm not going to answer that. I think I'll let you wonder, as punishment for what you put me through."

Brad said, "She's not being entirely truthful, Chris. She never once believed you were dead. In fact, when anyone suggested otherwise, she went on the attack."

"Will you get on with it, Chris?" Josh said impatiently. "Didn't you catch Kelly up on everything last night, and the one before?"

"Not really." Chris gave her a sly glance. "We were too busy to talk much."

Kelly colored and jerked her hand away from his. "I was so glad that he was alive that I really haven't asked too many questions. And Chris said that he wanted everybody together when he went into details."

Josh said, "You must have learned what you wanted to know, Chris, or you wouldn't have surfaced."

Chris nodded. "I found out, yes. I uncovered one of Fanti's minions in Anchorage, a hardcase he'd hired to do dirty jobs before. I think I have enough on him to go to the police with, at least nail him on the first two attempts. I don't know if they'll be able to stick him with planting the bomb, or even if they'll be able to discover it *was* a bomb. But I was still stuck with one problem . . . who killed Fanti?" He directed a hard glance at Will. "I kept going back to you, Will. God knows you had reason enough."

Will bristled. "You're lying, O'Keefe. I had no reason to kill Fanti."

"Yes, you did. First off, I have a tape in here." He tapped the attaché case. "It records an illegal transaction between you and Fanti, which could have sent you both to jail. I also had a little chat a few days ago with a girl friend of yours, Will. Penelope Hardesty by name. She told me about a *former* girl friend, Candice Durayea, who worked for Fanti. Together, they screwed you royally." Chris grinned. "In a manner of speaking. Oh, you had reason to kill him, Will."

A glowering Will retired behind a screen of cigar smoke.

Chris said to the others, "All right, as to who killed Milo Fanti, when I heard that Dwight had been arrested because of an anonymous phone tip and that material had been found in his house, I was sure I knew the guilty party. . . ."

Once Chris knew who to look for, he wasn't hard to find. He found Gordie Beasley in a cheap hotel off Fourth Avenue in Anchorage. It had only taken a few questions of known dope pushers along the street to learn the name of a guy who had been flush the past two months, making big buys. By this time Chris, fully bearded and wearing cheap clothes, blended in perfectly with the sleazy atmosphere of Fourth. All he had to do was flash a roll before the pushers and whisper that he owed a large number of bucks to Gordie and wanted to find him to pay his debt. They were willing to talk. It seemed that Gordie's money well had run dry and he was no longer a lucrative customer. The prospect of his having money again was welcome. Actually the roll Chris had shown was a con man's flash—a fifty wrapped around a number of singles. The money he had taken with him was running low.

After knocking repeatedly and receiving no answer, Chris discovered the door was unlocked and he went in. It was a mean room, the only furnishings a narrow bed, one chair, a nightstand and a chest of drawers, and the room stank abominably. Gordie was sprawled on the bed, in his shorts. He was emaciated beyond belief. On the nightstand was a blackened spoon, a hypodermic needle: the paraphernalia of an addict, and Gordie was smiling in his narcotic dream. Both scrawny arms were scabbed on the undersides with the addict's chicken tracks.

Chris pried the room's one window open, letting in a blast of Arctic air, and sat down in the straight chair. He lit a cigarette and waited. It was a half-hour before Gordie began to twitch, muttering. The air from the window blew directly on him and he started to shiver long before he was fully aware.

Finally his eyes fluttered open. Chris leaned forward until his face was directly over the youth's.

Gordie's eyes were dull as he tried to focus when Chris spoke. "Hello, Gordie. You don't look like you're doing so good."

"Wh-at? Who are . . . ?" His head turned toward the window. "Jesus Christ, it's freezing in here!"

"Are you fully awake now? It was stinking in here and badly needed some fresh air. I'll close it now, if you'll stay with me so we can talk."

Gordie's eyes cleared as recognition dawned. "Hey, I know you, you're the construction stiff. The beard fooled me there for a minute."

"Right, Gordie. Chris O'Keefe. You seem lucid now, I guess I can close the window."

As Chris closed the window, he heard a rustling from behind and whirled about to see Gordie off the bed and going at a staggering run for the door. In two giant steps Chris scooped him up and turned back to the bed. Gordie's bones underneath the sallow skin felt as fragile as chicken bones. He struggled but his efforts were without strength. Chris dumped him on the bed and stood back.

"Now, you stay there, Gordie. We have some things to discuss."

Through chattering teeth, Gordie said, "Man, I have nothing to discuss with you."

"Oh, but you do." Chris sat down and leaned close. "Like, for instance, how much money did you cop from Fanti's safe?"

"Almost twelve grand," Gordie said with a touch of pride. Then he gaped, his eyes wild. "Man, how did you know about that?"

"Is that the reason you killed him, Gordie?"

"I didn't kill him!" The thin fingers plucked at the gray sheets. "Man, you're out of your tree. No way you can pin that on me."

"I have all the time in the world, Gordie. Do you? You're supporting a large habit now, aren't you? How many bags a day, Gordie? The word on the street is that you're busted, kiddo. No more dough for the sugar. How long since your last shot? An hour, two hours? It won't be long, will it?"

"I ain't telling you nothing," Gordie said sullenly.

"You will, I promise you. I have lots of time. Pretty soon you'll be strung out and begging to tell me anything I want to know."

The youth had more guts than Chris had credited him with. Within an hour he was twitching, scratching furiously, twisting and turning. Suddenly a cramp hit and he doubled up in agony.

"I have money, Gordie. I can be out and back with a fix within a half-hour. All you have to do is talk to me."

"Fuck off, man!" Gordie said through gritted teeth.

"Whatever you say."

Into the second hour Gordie was suffering horribly, and Chris knew that he must be used to shooting up several times a day.

"Please," Gordie whispered, "I'm dying!"

Chris said relentlessly, "You take care of me and I'll take care of you."

"You're a mean mother, you know that?"

"I'm whatever I have to be. Too many people are in trouble because of you. Dwight, for instance. You called the police, didn't you? You planted the stuff in the kitchen, right? You put the man who was your friend, probably your only friend in the world, into the soup."

"He's no friend. He threw me out of the house, out of the movement, like I was a piece of shit!" Gordie said in a raw voice.

"He was your friend, kiddo, until you no longer deserved to be. And this is how you pay him back."

Gordie grew still, staring at him with a crafty look. "I give you the real scoop and you'll fix me up?"

"If I figure you're telling me the truth."

"All right, I killed that sucker, but not for the money. I never once thought of money, until I walked into his office. He was standing before that open safe." Gordie's eyes glittered with macabre mirth. "He never even knew I was there until I stuck him. Since the safe was open, I cleaned it out after. I figured he owed me."

"Why did you kill him?"

"Man, like you said when you paid me to sign that statement, he would've offed me if he knew I was still around. When that money was gone, I knew I had to do something. He was no loss, everybody knows that. I did everybody a favor."

Chris said, "You didn't do Dwight much of a favor."

"The Great Leader had it coming for rousting me like he did. I never figured the pigs would do much more than hassle him a little, you know." Gordie got a crafty look again. "I didn't stash everything I got from that safe in Dwight's place. I saved back a real goodie. My bread was running out, and I figured that little tidbit would get me more. It's another tape, man, a little chat between old Milo and bigshot Will Cole. What's on tape would send Will Cole to the slammer. I figure he'll pay for that tape."

Gordie sank back onto the narrow bed, and was immediately seized by another cramp. Doubling up, clutching his midsection he gasped out, "A fix, man. You promised!"

"One more little thing you have to do for me, Gordie. I want all this written down, with your signature."

"A confession!" Gordie looked wildly around the sordid room. "You're crazy! I do that, they'll put me away forever!"

"Maybe not. You said it yourself . . . Milo Fanti won't be missed all that much. He wasn't the world's nicest guy."

Gordie rolled his head from side to side. "No way! You can't ask me to do that."

"In the end you will, Gordie. I have all the time in the world. But do you? Think how you'll be feeling an hour, two hours, from now."

Gordie made a lunge off the bed. Prepared for it, Chris caught him by the shoulders and pinned him back down. . . .

* * *

In the boardroom Chris said, "He signed the confession. I turned him and the confession over to the Anchorage police day before yesterday. I'm sure that Dwight will be released before the day's over."

Kelly said, "I haven't asked you, darling . . . did *you* buy dope for Gordie?"

Chris nodded. "I made good on my promise, yes. I figured it was the least I could do. I shudder to think what agony the poor bastard is going to suffer in jail. You can be sure that the police won't support his habit."

Down at the end of the table, Will rapped the wood with his knuckles. "It strikes me that your taking off like that, snooping around like some undercover cop, leaving Cole without a president, is an irresponsible action, and I think the board of directors should know about it."

"I was sure that Kelly would do a bang-up job and she did. I'm proud of you, sweetheart." He winked at her.

"That's a matter of opinion," Will said. "And you didn't know, when you took off like that, that she would take your place."

"Who else, Will? You? You know, the day I left, I had decided to fire you." Chris opened the attaché case and took out a cassette. "Because of this." He bounced the cassette in his hand. "This is the tape Gordie held back. He was going to blackmail you, Will. I already knew about it, Fanti called and told me the day before he was killed. I didn't turn it over to the police, since I figured it was company business. This is proof, Will, that Milo Fanti gave you ten thousand dollars that day, a bribe, in return for which you promised to open the pipeline to him again. It's all on here."

Will's face flushed red. "It's a damned lie! He faked it some way."

Chris shook his head. "That won't cut it, Will. You want me to play it now? Better yet, maybe we should let the board of directors hear it." He leaned forward suddenly, his voice hard. "You're finished with Cole, Will. As of today, I want you out of this building, out of Cole 98. If you take my advice, you'll leave Alaska altogether."

"You can't do this! Jesus Christ in a wheelbarrow!" Will

jumped to his feet. "Josh? Kelly? You can't let him do this. I'm family!"

Josh said, "Chris is only doing what Kelly and I were talking of doing last week."

"That's right, Will," Kelly said. "And Grandfather would have agreed. You seem to forget that I already knew most of this, as did Grandfather, and that he put you on probation. You've forfeited all right to family support."

"I'll fight you, all of you!" Will said furiously. "I'm still a Cole, and by God, I'll fight for what's mine by rights. You'll all be sorry for this day!"

He jammed the cigar into his mouth and started for the door.

Chris said, "Will?"

Will spun around. *"What?"*

"You know what's the most reprehensible thing you've done? Gordie told me one other thing. That day, after he killed Fanti, you were in the hall heading for Fanti's office, when Gordie ran out. You saw him, Will. You *knew* that Dwight didn't kill Fanti. Yet you sat on your hands and did nothing when he was arrested. I'm curious. If he was convicted, maybe even sent away for life, would you still have remained silent?"

Will glared, started to speak, then clamped his mouth shut, and stormed out. He slammed the door violently after him.

"Dear God," Kelly said, appalled. "Is that really true?"

"I'm afraid so, sweetheart."

Brad said heavily, "I'm sure he'll make good on his promise. Will won't take this meekly. He'll fight, with every means at hand."

Chris smiled tightly. "Well, at least he'll keep life interesting for us."

Josh got to his feet slowly. Kelly felt a pang of pity for him. His usual air of wry amusement was gone, he looked gray with fatigue and despair; she remembered that she hadn't seen him smile in days.

He came around the table to take Chris's hand. "Welcome back, Chris, in more ways than one. I think I'll go over to the jail and pick up Dwight. I would appreciate it if none of you ever tell Dwight about Will knowing he didn't kill Fanti. There's enough bad blood between them as it is."

"It won't go beyond this room, Josh," Chris said. "Tell Dwight something for me, will you? I hope he's learned something from all this, how to compromise a little. He owes me, tell him, and I won't forget to collect."

"I'll tell him," Josh said with a wan smile, and left the room.

Brad also came around to shake Chris's hand. "I'm glad to see you back alive and well, too." His glance went to Kelly. "And I think I can say it now and mean it, Chris, as much as it galls me. The better man won."

As the door closed behind Brad, Kelly said, "What was that all about?"

"Just a little thing we had going between us." Looking suddenly weary, he slumped in his chair, rubbing his eyes.

Kelly said solicitously, "Tired, darling?"

"Exhausted. I feel like I've been through the wringer."

She reached out to stroke his beard. "I think I like you with a beard. It gives you an air of distinction."

He grinned. "Thanks for the compliment, but I hardly think a beard would enhance the image of the president of Cole."

"Why don't we take off in the sailboat, Chris? For a week of rest and relaxation. A second honeymoon. We've both earned it."

He cocked his head to one side. "Don't tempt me. It sounds great, but this is hardly the time. I have a lot to catch up on."

Her mouth tightened. "I'll have you know that I've done pretty damned well, considering." She got up and moved to the picture window, staring out. She noticed, almost with surprise, that spring was upon them. Some of the skeleton-bare trees were sprouting green buds, and ice was buckling in the Chena River.

"Hey, I know you've done well, Kelly," Chris said behind her. "I said so a little while ago, didn't I?"

She faced around, her shoulders set in defiance. "I think I like what I've been doing."

"What's that's supposed to mean?"

"It means that I want to stay on. For a while anyway. For the first time in my life I feel useful."

Frown lines suddenly showed in his face. "There's hardly room at the top for two presidents."

"Oh, I don't mean that. But you should have two executive assistants."

"What about Charlene?"

"What about her? If you mean, can we work together, yes. We've become good friends. You need someone else, Chris. There's more than she can handle."

He looked thoughtful for a space of seconds. "Okay, if that's what you want. We can sure as hell give it a try. Wait . . . you said, a while. What did you mean by that?"

Without answering directly she said, "Chris, six weeks ago, the night after Brad read that crazy will to us and I had to decide whether or not to take over your job, I had a dream. Or at least I told myself it was a dream. I had taken two Dalmanes in order to sleep. I was disoriented, confused, and I was never sure. I dreamed that you came into my bedroom at Cole House, that you made love to me. Did you, darling? Or did I dream it?"

He was silent for a little. Then he smiled secretively. "I think I'll let you wonder about that. Maybe I'll tell you some day. Then again, maybe I won't."

"There is one way I can find out for myself."

"What way is that?"

"After you disappeared, I went off the pill. I'm late this month. So, if I find out that I'm pregnant, I'll know you were there, now won't I?"

ABOUT THE AUTHORS

A few years ago PATRICIA MATTHEWS was just another housewife and working mother. An office manager, she lived in a middle class home with her husband and two children. Like thousands of other women around the country she was writing in her spare time. However, unlike many other writers, Patricia Matthews' own true life story has proven to have a Cinderella ending. Today she is "America's leading lady of historical romance" with eleven consecutive bestselling novels to her credit and millions of fans all over the world.

For CLAYTON MATTHEWS, author of more than 100 books, 50 short stories and innumerable magazine articles, writing is not only his profession but his hobby. Born in Waurika, Oklahoma in 1918, Matt (as he is known to his friends) worked as a surveyor, overland truck driver, gandy dancer, and taxi driver. In 1960 he became a full-time author with the publication of *Rage of Desire*. More recent books by Clayton Matthews include his highly successful book *The Power Seekers* (winner of the WEST COAST REVIEW OF BOOKS Bronze Medal for Best Novel in 1978), *The Harvesters* and *The Birthright*, the first book of a trilogy. Books two and three, *The Disinherited* and *The Redeemers*, are slated for future Bantam publication.

The Matthews, who say they have a "paperback perfect" marriage, live in Los Angeles. Their first collaboration was *Midnight Whispers*.

Dear Readers:

January 1983 will be a red-letter month for the two of us, as we will both have new books coming out from Bantam Books at that time.

Matt's book, *The Disinherited*, begins in Texas in 1875 and follows the lives and careers of the members of the Moraghan family. It focuses primarily on Debra Moraghan, a strong and willful young woman who is determined to lead her life the way she wants to, but who finds herself caught in a web of hate and revenge woven by the generation that came before. She becomes the victim of Tod Danker, the son of her father's bitter and degenerate enemy, and her life is irrevocably changed.

Patricia's book, the thirteenth of her historical novels, is titled *Flames of Glory* and will be published in a beautiful large-format paperback.

The story begins in Tampa, Florida, in the year 1898 where thousands of people, including many famous persons, gathered prior to sailing to the Spanish-American War in Cuba.

This is a time of great excitement and confusion, the scene centering around the elaborate Tampa Bay Hotel. *Flames of Glory* features two heroines, one a young Cuban woman, Maria Mendes, the other, Jessica Manning, the daughter of a local banker. The two find the threads of their lives intertwining as they attempt to cope with changes that are occurring for both of them—the influx of young soldiers, the romantic choices they must make, and the complications caused by an opportunistic confidence man, Brill Kroger.

The last portion of the novel follows the main characters to the ancient city of Chichén Itzá, in the Yucatan, where the last hand, initiated by Brill Kroger, is played out.

On the following pages, you can sample an excerpt from both *The Disinherited* and *Flames of Glory*.

We both hope that all of you will read our books, and that you will obtain pleasure from the reading—for that's what it is all about, isn't it?

Wishing you all good things,

Patricia Matthews and
Clayton Matthews

An excerpt from
FLAMES OF GLORY
by Patricia Matthews

It was, at last, eight o'clock, and Jessica Manning was sitting beside her mother and father in the carriage. Her body was rigid with suppressed excitement and the desire not to wrinkle her new gown. It was a beautiful dress, and the wonder of it, the wonder of the whole evening ahead, loomed large in Jessica's mind.

The fact that she, Jessica, just fourteen years old that day, was being allowed to attend the grand opening ball of the new Tampa Bay Hotel, was the fulfillment of her greatest dream; and she felt that she could literally not bear it if even the least thing went awry.

She sat decorously, ankles crossed, feet in white kid slippers, one hand holding her small, white lace fan, the other touching one of the tiny, white silk rosebuds that gathered and adorned the full skirt of her gown. She hoped that she presented a picture of grace and poise, but inside she bubbled and tingled with delight and anticipation.

Her mother, sitting on her left, was splendidly beautiful in rose silk, the waist of her corset drawn in so tightly that Jessica wondered how she could even breathe; the corset made her waist so small that Jessica's father could span it easily with both his hands. Her father, sitting on Jessica's right, looked dignified and rather formidable, she thought, in his dress suit and the long tails, even though his face, beneath the tall, shiny top hat, was smiling.

There was a regular parade of vehicles of every sort upon the road. Mr. Henry B. Plant, the builder of the Tampa Bay Hotel, had invited everyone who was anyone in the whole of the United States, or so her father had told

Jessica. It was going to be the largest social event in the history of Florida, on this night of February 5, 1891.

The stream of vehicles winding toward the hotel was so thick that occasionally one carriage crowded another, sometimes colliding, but even the rudeness of a few could not disturb the good mood of the party-goers on this night, for they all knew that they were special. If they were not, they would not have received invitations to this lavish and prestigious ball.

As the Manning carriage approached the hotel, Jessica could see hundreds of electric lights, like stationary fireflies, outlining the towers; and as they moved nearer still, she drew in her breath with awe at the sight of the verandas and gardens hung with thousands of Chinese lanterns and fairy lights in shades of green, opal, topaz, and ruby.

Jessica had watched the hotel being built, and so she was familiar with the sight of the huge building, but to see it now, with its thirteen silver minarets ablaze with light, was like seeing a fairy-tale palace come to life, right before her eyes.

She must have sighed aloud, for Anne Manning turned to her, smiled, and patted her hand. "It is beautiful, isn't it, dear? The original cannot be more so, I'm sure."

Jessica nodded, not trusting herself to speak. She, like most residents of Tampa, knew the story behind the construction of the new hotel.

Mr. Plant, a wealthy businessman, had brought the railroad to Tampa in 1884; only seven hundred people lived in the white-sand city at the time.

Plant was an ambitious and competitive man; and when he heard that Henry M. Flagler, the multimillionaire railroad man, had finished his Hotel Ponce de Léon in St. Augustine and then built the Spanish/Moorish Alcazar, Henry Plant was goaded into announcing that he would construct "the greatest hotel in the world" in Tampa, using the Moorish/Turkish Alhambra, in Granada, Spain, as his model.

And Plant was as good as his word. He bought sixty acres of land from Jesse Hayden, who had purchased the acreage twenty years earlier by swapping a white horse and a wagon for it. Plant talked the city and county into building a bridge across the river at Lafayette Street, at the cost of eighteen thousand dollars, and extracted a promise from the local officials that his taxes would not exceed two hundred dollars a year.

This done, he began construction of his grand hotel. It cost over two million to build and about five hundred thousand to furnish, and those who had seen it inside and out declared it at least the eighth wonder of the world. The building was approximately twelve hundred feet long, and people said that a walk around the exterior equaled nearly a mile. The citizens of Tampa—now numbering six thousand—were justly proud of the beautiful edifice and looked forward to the fact that the hotel was certain to lure flocks of tourists and visitors to their city.

Now the Manning carriage was turning into the hotel's west entrance, and then they were pulling up in front of the steps, and Jackson, their driver, was helping Jessica's mother down from the carriage. Jessica could hardly breathe, such was her excitement.

Wyngate Manning escorted his wife and daughter through the throng of arriving guests to the wide front doors, and Jessica stepped into fairyland. Inside, all was one white blaze of light. Jessica's head swiveled constantly as she attempted to see everything at once, an impossibility that would leave her neck stiff for days after the ball.

She saw potted palms rustling in the winds moving through the great lobby that rose two stories high through balustraded open floors to the roof. Great masses of flowers were banked everywhere, and music seemed to come from all directions.

Jessica gaped in speechless awe as a handsome young page trotted past pulling a strange, high, two-wheeled vehicle. Riding in the vehicle was a regal young woman, dressed in pale blue, with diamonds flashing at her throat, wrists, and ears.

Jessica tugged at her mother's arm. "What was that, Mother? That strange cart?"

Her mother laughed and leaned down toward her so that her voice could be heard above the babble. "It's a jinrickisha, darling. They use them in the Orient. Mr. Plant imported them so his guests would not tire themselves walking down these long corridors."

Jessica wanted to ask if they might ride in one; but at that moment she was bumped by a large lady in red velvet and had to concentrate on clinging to her mother's hand and then on following in her parents' wake as they made their way through the crowd, toward one of the long corridors.

As they progressed, Jessica caught glimpses of the much talked about furnishings. She had heard that Mr. Plant had furnished the hotel with priceless antiques from Europe, but she was not prepared for the splendor that met her gaze.

Beneath their feet was the most beautiful carpet she had ever seen, a glowing red color with blue dragons woven into it. Along the walls and up the stairways were magnificent marble statues; and the rooms and hallways were filled with satin and brocaded sofas, inlaid and gilt chairs, onyx and marble tables decorated with gold leaf, hundreds of gilt-framed ornamental mirrors, and glowing bronze and porcelain lamps.

Never had she beheld such richness and beauty, and it seemed that she was not alone in her awe and wonder, for the adults, too, were exclaiming and sighing over the priceless items, the likes of which were not usually seen on this coast of simple, even primitive, board houses.

Jessica, following her parents down the seemingly endless corridor toward the dining rotunda, thought that this was easily the most wonderful and happiest day of her life. She knew that she would never forget it as long as she lived; and some day, when she was a woman grown, she would stay in this hotel, in one of the beautiful rooms she had heard so much about; for in her experience, this was absolutely the most beautiful and perfect place in the whole world!

It was hot behind the heavy drapery, but by moving her head to the left, Maria Mendes had an excellent view of the lobby and the arriving guests.

There was a large palm tree directly in front of the drapes, which concealed her presence, and through its green, gently moving fronds, she watched in awe as the richest and most famous people in the country streamed in.

How beautiful and elegant they looked in their silks, satins, and jewels! The wasp-waisted women, in their long gowns, with their hair elaborately coiffed; the men looking very tall and very elegant in their black dress suits. The lobby itself, with its statues, mirrors, palms, and flowers, looked like something from a dream of another world, a world that Maria did not yet fully understand.

She knew that there was a vast chasm between her people and these others, these North Americans in their expensive clothes and jewels, but she did not question this. It was simply a fact. She felt no jealousy, she merely watched, in awe and amazement, as they paraded past, laughing and chatting, nodding and smiling, like gods out of the old tales.

Her black eyes bright with excitement, Maria leaned farther to the left to get a better look at three people just entering the lobby—a tall, handsome man; a slender, beautiful blond woman in a rose gown; and a lovely blond girl, about Maria's own age.

The presence of the girl aroused Maria's curiosity. She was the first person that Maria, just fourteen, had seen at the ball who looked as young as herself. The girl was very pretty, dressed all in white, her long skirt caught in gathers and covered with white silk roses. She had a lovely silk shawl on as well, for which Maria felt a pang of envy; long, white gloves, and little, white kid slippers. Maria wondered who she was. She must be the daughter of someone very important to have been invited to the ball.

As the trio moved out of her view, Maria shifted her weight on the small stool upon which she sat. She was beginning to get hungry, but she did not want to leave her vantage point just yet. There was so much to see!

Down below, in the kitchen, she knew that her father and the other chefs were scurrying to and fro, stirring pots, making salads and sauces. As daughter of the head sauce chef, she could enter into that inner sanctum with impunity—so long as she had her father's permission—and be certain of being well fed. In that respect at least, they were better off than many Cubans in the area; most of them had to struggle to get enough to survive.

Another group of people passed, and two men stopped,

right in front of her hiding place, and began to talk as they lit up cigars. Maria knew that it was impolite to listen to other people's conversations, yet she could not escape without being observed. She drew back from the opening in the drapes.

"Well, old Henry has done himself proud, hasn't he?" said a deep voice.

"I should say so," the second man replied. "The furnishings alone must have cost a small fortune, and everybody in the whole world is here tonight. I heard that fifteen thousand invitations were sent out."

"And they must all be here. By the way, did you hear the story about Henry Flagler?"

The other man laughed. "*Which* story? There are dozens going around."

"Well, the way I heard it, Plant sent Flagler an invitation to the ball tonight, and Flagler wired back: 'Where is Tampa?' "

Both men laughed.

"But that's not the end of it. I understand that Plant wired back to Flagler: 'Just follow the crowd, Henry!' "

The men laughed again and began to move away, and Maria gave a sigh of relief. She did not know who Mr. Flagler was, and she did not care, although she knew he must be somebody rich and famous. She felt a glow of pride that none of these beautiful people, rich and famous though they might be, knew the hotel as she did.

Maria had watched it being built, watched as the silver towers were made to reach into the sky. And when it was finished and her father had been hired as the sauce chef, she had persuaded him to bring her with him to the hotel, and once there, she had made herself intimately familiar with its whole majestic length and breadth—the endless corridors; the huge lobby with its wonderful bronze statue of the lady and the goat; the beautiful, beautiful furnishings; the subterranean rooms under the lobby, which included rooms for billiards and shuffleboard, as well as mineral water baths, massage rooms, and café facilities, and even a hotel casino.

The room she liked best was the Grand Salon, with its priceless art objects and antique furniture. Her father had told her that the cabinets she so much admired had once belonged to Queen Isabella and King Ferdinand of Spain, and Mary, Queen of Scots. Maria thought the room looked like a great museum.

She also particularly liked the statues on the main stairway of the hotel—two African girls, who had beautiful, shiny black skin that gleamed in the light.

Maria felt privileged and rather smug in her private knowledge of the place. She loved the huge building and felt at home there, much more so than in her family's small cottage on the outskirts of Ybor City. Her father knew of her love for the hotel, and since she was his only daughter, he indulged her in letting her come with him to his work now and again. It was he who had arranged for her to be present on this wonderful night, despite her mother's strong objections, and Maria was grateful to him.

She smoothed the skirt of her blue cotton dress and pushed aside one long, shiny, black braid of hair that had fallen forward over one shoulder. She might not have wonderful clothes, like the beautiful people out there, but she had something else just as good—she *knew* the hotel intimately. They did not.

Maria smiled softly to herself, vowing that she would always remember this night of nights.

An excerpt from

THE DISINHERITED
by Clayton Matthews

Debra Moraghan stood on the veranda—packed earth for a floor, a thatched roof, a pole for a railing—and waited for her mother to come out of the adobe house behind her. Her father had just returned from his weekly trip into town for the mail pouch. In the pouch was a letter from her grandmother, Nora Moraghan, residing on the family plantation outside of Nacogdoches, in East Texas. Her mother had gone inside to read it.

Hands clenched around the railing until the knuckles shone white, Debra stared unseeingly into the distance.

Not that there was much to see in Brownsville, Texas—flat, arid land, dotted with mesquites, cactuses, and palms. The first time Debra had seen a palm tree she had thought of a shy girl standing on one leg, desperately trying to pull her skirt down to hide her nakedness. It was an image that had caused her to laugh then, and still brought a smile to her lips when she thought of it.

That had been nine years ago. Now, eight months short of her twenty-first birthday, Debra had more than fulfilled the promise of great beauty that Grandmother Nora had glimpsed in her long ago. Even in the long, faded gingham dress, the fullness of her figure was evident in the fine, full thrust of her breasts. She had brown eyes that could blaze with quick anger or sparkle with unexpected humor, and long auburn hair flowing to the sweet curve of hip. Her complexion was the color of bone china. She never browned, but instead burned a fiery red when too long exposed to the sun, and she had an infuriating tendency to freckle after the burn faded.

Debra had been afflicted by twin curses at approximately

the same time—the female curse and the propensity to burn under the sun's blaze. She blamed the second on the semitropic sun in Brownsville. Back home—she always thought of East Texas as home, always would—she could play in the sun and not burn. It was only after coming here that her skin became so sensitive. One more black mark against this cursed country.

A warm wind had come up as Debra stood on the veranda, and it picked up fine sand from the ground, which became a brown cloud. The minute particles stung her exposed skin like a thousand insects.

Dear God, was there ever such a dry, godforsaken place! she thought. Water, her father said; water was the answer. With water the thirsty earth would turn rich and fertile. But the only sources of water were the rare rains, the Rio Grande—a brown trickle just out of sight to the south—and artesian wells. Deep, deep down in the bowels of the earth was an inexhaustible reservoir of sweet, sparkling water. It was the source of their drinking water, but it was too expensive, too laborious a process, to bring to the surface in a quantity large enough to provide life to plants.

Her poor father! He had planted cotton but had yet to raise a decent crop—the rainfall was not sufficient. He had tried growing fruits and vegetables and had raised a profitable crop about one year in four. Their meager existence was due primarily to the sale of dates and figs—trees that could produce fruit with little water.

Poor father indeed! It was his fault that they were here, in this place of heat and drought and hungry bellies. True, he worked, worked harder than it seemed possible, from dawn until dusk, and then often, after a meager supper, he labored long hours by lantern light, endlessly scheming ways to bring water to the thirsty land.

But none of this was necessary, Debra reflected. But for his stupid pride, he could still be in East Texas, directing that prodigious energy and sharp mind—she did not deny his intelligence—toward attaining what was their rightful heritage. Grandmother Nora had offered them the use of her house, the only thing left to her in Sean Moraghan's will. Not only had she offered, she had begged her youngest son to stay.

Kevin Moraghan would have none of it, and here they were!

Debra gave an exasperated sigh, then turned her head and called, "Mother! You must have read that letter through a half-dozen times by now!"

"Coming, dear," her mother said in an unruffled voice.

In a moment Kate came out onto the veranda, the letter folded in her hand. Kate was still a great beauty; age had yet to mark her. The climate had not parched her skin, wrinkling it like a dried date, as it did most Anglo women. Her skin was without a blemish, her figure still firm, her eyes clear and usually laughing, despite the hardships of their life the past nine years.

Maybe, Debra thought with a flash of ribald humor, that's how come she had a third child four years back; she still heats Daddy's blood on occasion!

Kate said mildly, "The letter, Debra Lee, *was* addressed to your father, I do believe."

"Mother! How many times do I have to tell you that it's Debra, not Debra Lee!"

"Heavens above! May the good Lord forgive me that I should ever forget that my daughter reserves the privilege of choosing her own name."

"You know I hate two first names. Half the simpering girls in the South have two names. Betty Sue. Mary Louise. Boys, too, for that matter. It's disgusting."

"Disgusting it may be to you, young lady, but it's your birth name, and as long as you're in my household, it's what you'll answer to. Now, as to this letter"—Kate snapped it against the railing—"you wrote to Nora, didn't you?"

"Of course I did. Is that a crime? She *is* my grandmother."

"Writing to her isn't, no. But you asked her if you'd be welcome to visit."

"What's wrong with that? Every time she writes to us, she inquires as to when we're coming."

"Several things are wrong with that, my darling daughter. It's bad manners to ask. We can't afford the money for the fare. You're too young, and most important of all, you know how your father feels. So long as—"

"So long as Uncle Brian's on Moraghan, not one of us will ever set foot there. I should know, I've heard it often enough. What does Grandmother say in the letter?" She reached out a hand. "Let me see."

"Oh, no, young lady!" Kate stepped quickly to one side. "This letter is to your father."

"Then why did you read it, Mother?"

"You would make a good attorney, that you would." Kate's smile was edged with grudging admiration. "I read it, Debra Lee, because your father gave it to me to read."

Debra half turned away, then said casually, "Speaking of attorneys, did Grandmother mention Stony . . . Mr. Lieberman, in the letter?"

Kate stared. "Stonewall Lieberman? No reason she should, is there? You didn't ask about him in your letter, did you?"

Silence.

Kate sighed in exasperation. "Honest to God, Debra Lee, you can be a trial . . . no, worse. A pain in the ass."

Debra said stiffly, "I see no reason to be vulgar, Mother."

"Well, I do! Are you still mooning over that man? It's been nine years, and you saw him . . . what? Twice? At Sean's funeral and at the reading of the will. A total of an hour at the most." She laughed. "You may think you're mature enough to pick and choose your own name, but you've got a lot to learn about men, young lady. He's probably married, with a passel of kids by now. If someone mentioned your name to him, it likely wouldn't even register. Do you *really* think that he remembers you?"

Debra gave a toss of her head. "I don't see why you're carrying on so, Mother. I was just curious, is all."

"Sure, you were just curious. But to satisfy your curiosity . . . no, Nora didn't mention Stonewall Lieberman."

"But how about my visit to Moraghan? You said she—"

"Of course you're welcome, more than welcome! Nora has been after us, all of us, to come back since the day we left. But you're not going, Debra Lee. I've already gone into some of the reasons. If that's not good enough for you, I'll talk of this to Kevin tonight, and I'm sure he'll have a word or two to say on the subject."

Kevin Moraghan had more than a word or two to say, and they were said forcibly. "You are not going to East

Texas, Debra Lee, and that's final! From your willful ways, I know that what I say usually has little effect on you. But you are still under my roof, and you're not yet twenty-one. So long as both of these things hold true, you will do as *I* say."

Less than a year short of twenty-one, Debra thought, and that won't stop me anyway. For once, probably for the first time in her young life, she chose caution and didn't voice her thoughts.

Kevin was going on, "Furthermore, I forbid you to write to your grandmother again. It can only upset her."

"Yes, Daddy," she said submissively.

He peered at her suspiciously. "Headstrong as you are, I imagine my words are like hailstones bouncing off a tin roof, but one thing will stop you. It costs a great deal of money to get to East Texas from here, and I'm not giving you a cent toward it!"

Debra hugged a secret to herself—over the past few years she had been squirreling money away, a few coins at a time, and she had a respectable amount, at least enough to pay stagecoach fare to Corpus Christi. From there she would walk to Nacogdoches, if need be.

She said softly, "Yes, Daddy."

Her surprising meekness blunted the edge of Kevin's anger, and he had to grope for something to say. "Very well, just so you understand," he finally said lamely, and glanced at Kate, to find her staring at their daughter thoughtfully.

"If you will excuse me now, I think I'll go to my room," Debra said. As if nothing untoward had happened, she sailed across the room to Kevin and embraced him. "Good night, Daddy." She turned to kiss Kate. "Good night, Mother."

"Good night, dear," Kate said to her already retreating back.

There was a lengthy silence after she left the room.

Finally Kevin sighed and said, "What do you think, Kate? Did I get through to her at all? I've never seen her so . . . so agreeable. Do you think she's finally beginning to grow up?"

"Oh, she's grown up, right enough. She's a woman, is our Debra Lee." A pensive smile played about Kate's mouth. "Or hadn't you noticed?"

"Damnit, Kate, that's not what I meant!" Kevin said, exasperated. "You know she usually goes her own way, no matter what we say. I'm surprised she hasn't gotten into trouble long before this."

"Stubborn, willful, opinionated . . . all those things she is, but she's also bright as a new coin. She can handle herself well. In most situations, anyway."

"But she *is* headstrong, and liable to take it into her mind to do as she goddamn well pleases. Do you agree?"

"I agree, Kevin, and that troubles me, too." Without thinking, she added, "She comes by it naturally, I suppose. . . ." Oh, dear God, of all the things to say, Kate thought. She was afraid to look at her husband.

"Speaking of that—do you think she knows? Or even suspects?"

Kate forced herself to look at him. His worn face was calm, and she was uncertain as to his feelings.

Mentally she squared off, then said, "You mean, of course, does she know about Brian?"

His gaze didn't waver. "That's what I mean, yes."

"I'm sure not. There's no way she could know."

"We may have made a mistake in not telling her. If she ever finds out, it could destroy her, you realize that."

Read both FLAMES OF GLORY and THE DISINHERITED, on sale December 15, 1982, wherever Bantam paperbacks are sold.

PATRICIA MATTHEWS

Now You Can Read
All These Books
By One Of America's
Queens Of Historical Romance

☐ 22577 **EMPIRE** $3.50

☐ 13389 **MIDNIGHT WHISPERS** $3.50

☐ 22809 **TIDES OF LOVE** $3.50

☐ 01368 **EMBERS OF DAWN** $6.95
(A Large Format Book)

☐ 01328 **TIDES OF LOVE** $5.95
(A Large Format Book)

THE LATEST BOOKS IN THE BANTAM BESTSELLING TRADITION

☐	22577	**EMPIRE** Patricia Matthews w/Clayton Matthews	$3.50
☐	22687	**THE TRUE BRIDE** Thomas Altman	$2.95
☐	22686	**THE PATRIOTS** Robert E. Wall	$3.50
☐	22582	**A BOOK OF RUTH** Syrell Rogovin Leahy	$2.95
☐	22704	**THE SISTERHOOD** Michael Palmer	$3.50
☐	20901	**TRADE WIND** M. M. Kaye	$3.95
☐	20833	**A WOMAN OF TWO CONTINENTS** Pixie Burger	$3.50
☐	01368	**EMBERS OF DAWN** Patricia Matthews (A Large Format book)	$6.95
☐	20921	**TANAMERA** Noel Baker	$3.95
☐	20029	**CIRCLE OF LOVE** Syrell Leahy	$2.50
☐	20559	**TOMAHAWK** Donald Clayton Porter	$3.50
☐	22613	**ELIZABETH TAYLOR: Her Life, Her Loves, Her Future** Ruth Waterbury w/Gene Arceri	$3.50
☐	20026	**COME POUR THE WINE** Cynthia Freeman	$3.95
☐	22775	**THE CLAN OF THE CAVE BEAR** Jean M. Auel	$3.95
☐	20664	**THE GLITTERING HARVEST** Maisie Mosco	$3.50
☐	05006	**ZEMINDAR** Valerie Fitzgerald (Hardcover)	$19.95
☐	14142	**A WOMAN'S AGE** Rachel Billington	$3.50
☐	22719	**FROM THE BITTERLAND** Maisie Mosco	$3.50
☐	20106	**SCATTERED SEED** Maisie Mosco	$2.95

Buy them at your local bookstore or use this handy coupon:

Bantam Books, Inc., Dept. FBS, 414 East Golf Road, Des Plaines, Ill. 60016

Please send me the books I have checked below. I am enclosing $_____
(please add $1.25 to cover postage and handling). Send check or money order
—no cash or C.O.D.'s please.

Mr/Mrs/Miss_____

Address_____

City_____ State/Zip_____

FBS—10/82

Please allow four to six weeks for delivery. This offer expires 4/83.

BRING ROMANCE INTO YOUR LIFE

With these bestsellers from your favorite Bantam authors.

Barbara Cartland

☐	20746	VIBRATIONS OF LOVE	$1.95
☐	20747	LIES FOR LOVE	$1.95
☐	20505	SECRET HARBOR	$1.95
☐	20235	LOVE WINS	$1.95
☐	20234	SHAFT OF SUNLIGHT	$1.95
☐	14922	PORTRAIT OF LOVE	$1.95

Catherine Cookson

☐	12694	CINDER PATH	$2.95

Catherine Gaskin

☐	12956	I KNOW MY LOVE	$3.25
☐	14718	FAMILY AFFAIRS	$2.95
☐	14498	FIONA	$2.75

Emilie Loring

☐	20045	WE RIDE THE GALE	$1.95
☐	14292	I TAKE THIS MAN	$1.95
☐	14295	BEHIND THE CLOUD	$1.95
☐	14294	LOOK TO THE STARS	$1.95

Eugenia Price

☐	22583	MARGARET'S STORY	$3.50
☐	11849	SHARE MY PLEASANT STONES	$2.95
☐	22798	BELOVED INVADER	$2.95
☐	20727	LIGHTHOUSE	$2.95
☐	20970	NEW MOON RISING	$2.95

Buy them at your local bookstore or use this handy coupon:

Bantam Books, Inc., Dept. RO, 414 East Golf Road, Des Plaines, Ill. 60016

Please send me the books I have checked above. I am enclosing $_____ (please add $1.25 to cover postage and handling). Send check or money order —no cash or C.O.D.'s please.

Mr / Mrs / Miss _____

Address _____

City _____ State / Zip _____

RO—10/82

Please allow four to six weeks for delivery. This offer expires 4/83.